ROMANTIC TIMES PRAISES CONNIE MASON, WINNER OF A CAREER ACHIEVEMENT AWARD FOR WESTERN HISTORICAL ROMANCE!

TEMPT THE DEVIL

"*Tempt the Devil* is a grand and glorious adventure romp....The pace never falters and the cast of characters, from pirates to noblemen, is quite a crew."

FLAME

"Connie Mason is an expert at western romance. Her characters are fully developed and engaging. *Flame* is a page turner for those who like plenty of action and adventure out west."

PURE TEMPTATION

"...a pure delight...This lively, action-filled tale bubbles over with memorable characters and delicious sensuality."

THE LION'S BRIDE

"This wondrous tale is a must-read for the medieval fan and Ms. Mason's legion of readers."

SIERRA

"*Sierra* is a fast-paced story with loads of frying-pan-into-the-fire adventure. Ms. Mason has written a definite winner!"

Tempt the Devil

CONNIE MASON

LEISURE BOOKS NEW YORK CITY

To my readers who have deluged me with fan mail.

*To newspaper editors Don Holmes and Ann Dupee
for putting me in their pages.*

*To Clermont Publix Manager
for always making room for several cases of my books.*

To all my family and friends for their support.

A LEISURE BOOK®

March 1998

Published by

Dorchester Publishing Co., Inc.
276 Fifth Avenue
New York, NY 10001

ISBN 0-8439-4366-1

The name "Leisure Books" and the stylized "L" with design are trademarks of Dorchester Publishing Co., Inc.

Printed in the United States of America.

Chapter One

London 1715

It was a terrible day to die—was there ever a good one? Swirling mist and dense fog blocked out the sun. Defiant and proud, he stood on the hastily erected scaffold, his lip curled in a sardonic smile as his silver gaze swept over the jostling crowd making merry at his expense. A heavy black beard concealed the deep dimple in his left cheek. If it hadn't, his dark, demonic features would have been transformed instantly. His roguish good looks were enough to bring many a young maid swooning at his feet.

He stood tall and imposing, almost regal, a noose around his neck, hands tied behind his back, prepared to pay the devil his due. There'd be no more bargaining—nay, he'd traded his soul long ago. Yet lust for life spurted hot and fierce through his veins. Was this how it would all end? He supposed it must, given the life he had led. There was little he regretted, though in his estimation his evil reputa-

tion far surpassed his deeds. Still—it was a terrible
day to die. . . .

The coach moved cautiously through the throngs
of people lining the waterfront on Tilbury Point.
Few paid heed to the crest emblazoned on the door
or the liveried footman trying to clear a path for
the lumbering vehicle. The grand spectacle soon to
take place drew people from all walks of life, and
amidst the teeming mobs dukes rubbed elbows
with bakers and earls with beggars, with nary
a complaint. It was a pickpocket's paradise,
more lucrative than a country fair or market
day.

Inside the coach the rotund Lord Harvey Chatham, Earl of Milford, stuck his head out the window for a better view as his coach neared the
waterfront. All around him ragged peasants jostled
for position with well-dressed shopkeepers, law-
yers, and doctors. Ladies waved scarves as their
serving maids scurried to keep up with their mis-
tresses.

Drummers had been ordered out for the occasion, and were pounding out a staccato rhythm.
Behind them a line of dragoons held the masses of
humanity in some semblance of order. More dragoons carrying muskets stood at attention. Suddenly flutists joined the drummers and their music
trilled through the fog-shrouded air. Though it was
nearly noon, the weather was dismal for mid-July.
A chill mist dampened the air but not the spirits of
the crowd. Shouts, catcalls, and raucous singing
emerged from the mob as well as from windows
above the street level packed with spectators. The
noise was deafening, the spectacle as colorful as a
circus, the hoopla splendid for such an awesome

occasion. At exactly high noon the Thames was between ebb and flow tide.

"Damn me, we're almost too late," muttered the earl, a frown drawing his pleasant features into a scowl. "'Tis the crowds, m'dear, damn annoying. Not even this foul weather has dampened spirits on this auspicious occasion. You'd think the man was a hero instead of a notorious pirate."

"I wish you hadn't made me come along, Father. It's . . . it's so . . . bizarre."

"You're not turning squeamish on me, are you, Devon? You look so bloody pale all of a sudden." Concern colored the earl's words as he searched his daughter's lovely features. "'Twas Winston who suggested I bring you today. Thought you might enjoy it."

Devon fixed her father with an austere look. "Enjoy seeing a man hanged? Really, Father, both you and Winnie know me better than that. I think the custom barbaric."

"You should hate the man as much as I do, m'dear," Lord Chatham opined. "Diablo has cost me hundreds of pounds in lost cargo. I've invested heavily in shipping only to have most of my vessels plundered by Diablo and his kind. Winston's father lost nearly his whole fortune." This wasn't entirely the truth, for Winston's father, the Duke of Grenville, was a notorious gambler who had squandered most of his inheritance, but Lord Chatham did not burden Devon with that knowledge for the man was on his deathbed.

"Diablo," Devon mused. "I wonder if the man is Spanish. The good Lord knows the Spanish have caused us enough grief in recent years."

"Pirates owe allegiance to no one but themselves, m'dear."

Devon remained thoughtful, regarding the jabbering crowd through the coach window. Suddenly the coach ground to a halt, and against her will Devon's wide blue eyes were jerked toward Tilbury Point and the scaffold standing stark and forbidding against the leaden sky.

"We can go no further, Your Grace," the driver called down to the earl. "The road ahead is all but impassable."

"Drat!" Lord Chatham said, exasperated. "Well, no help for it, m'dear, we'll have to go the rest of the way on foot. I mean to see the devil breathe his last."

"I'm not moving, Father," Devon demurred. "I've no stomach for such goings on. If I hadn't agreed to meet Winnie here I'd have stayed home."

"And miss the excitement?" Lord Chatham asked, piqued by his daughter's lack of enthusiasm. "Your fiancé is to accompany us to Lady Mary's musicale after the hanging. Do you see Winston anywhere?"

"In this crowd?" Devon scoffed, shaking her splendid mass of golden curls. Piled elegantly atop her well-shaped head, Devon's hair was the color of ripened wheat. Combed out, it reached below her waist in a riot of rippling waves and spirals.

"Well then, I'm off, m'dear," the earl said, waving gaily as he stepped down from the coach. "Peters and Hadley will remain here to see that no harm comes to you. A festive occasion like this deserves a proper viewing."

Devon watched as her father's stocky figure was swallowed up by the mass of humanity crowding Tilbury Point. The only child of Lord Chatham, Earl of Milford, nineteen-year-old Lady Devon was considered the catch of the season. Tall and slender, her body was curving and regal. Her waist was slim, her hips tapered into impossibly long legs. Numerous men courted her, as much for her seductive beauty and grace as for her generous dowry. But for some reason Devon had chosen to accept the proposal of Viscount Winston Linley, the son of the Duke of Grenville. His pretty speeches and outward devotion as well as his blond good looks had won her hand, and they were to be married in six months, after Winston's resignation from the navy.

Following in his father's footsteps—he had been a naval officer before the dukedom fell to him with the disappearance of the young heir to the title—Winston had purchased a commission in the Royal Navy and had recently taken command of the *Larkspur*. Devon cared little that Winston's father had squandered the family fortune—she had enough money for both of them. Though she felt no great stirrings over Winston, Devon knew that he was a man who would not try to control her. Accustomed to being her own woman, she could not tolerate the thought of a marriage bogged down by restrictions and rules demanded by most men of this day and age. Winston had been a compromise, for he presented no threat to her independence and his devotion could not be faulted.

A loud cheer forced Devon's attention to the scaffold where Diablo stood, flanked by two burly guards. Did they expect him to escape with his hands tied behind his back and a rope around his neck, she thought disgustedly. She could see him clearly as she leaned out the window, succumbing to some perverse need to view the devil known only as Diablo.

Diablo faced death with a steadfast courage that Devon couldn't help but admire. A slow smile curved his lips with ironic humor despite the jeering crowd waiting for his untimely end.

A riptide of emotion surged through Devon as she peered up at the black-bearded pirate. The sea breeze tousled his raven hair, blowing errant strands across his forehead. The deep tan of his face sharply opposed the gaping, dirty white shirt that strained across his massive chest. The tight breeches hugging his narrow hips and muscled thighs took her thoughts in a wantonly sensual direction, and a guilty tinge crept up her neck. Reluctantly moving her wide blue eyes back to his dark, brooding face, Devon could not tell the color of his eyes from where she sat but noted the touches of humor hovering around his generous mouth. She was amazed at his ability to find amusement in his desperate situation. But then, what could one expect from a man who found joy in killing, raping, and robbing?

Diablo fixed his smoldering silver gaze on no one in particular, roving over the hundreds of revelers gathered for his hanging like vultures waiting to pick his bones. He squared his broad shoulders and smiled, determined to meet his fate with the same raw courage with which he had conducted his life. Diablo was aware of the stir he created among the women in the crowd, and with the arrogance of one fully cognizant of his virile male appeal, winked roguishly at a comely maid standing nearby. Her delighted squeal gave him little joy.

Then he directed his gaze farther afield to the line of vehicles clogging the street, finally settling on one coach where a ravishing blonde leaned out the window. If he had to die, he reflected, he'd find nothing more pleasing to take to his grave than the image of the enticing blonde. She was sheer perfection, from the golden ringlets curled on her forehead to the tempting fullness of her red lips.

Over the heads of the rowdy, exuberant crowd, their eyes met, clung, and Devon felt the world fade away around her. Instinctively she knew Diablo's eyes would be a clear, piercing gray. She no longer saw the hordes of people, nothing stood between her and Diablo. He was stunningly virile, with a power that coiled within him, exuding total masculinity. He was dark, dangerous, and devastatingly handsome—beard and all. And unscrupulous, barbarous, and obviously without remorse for his heinous deeds. The devil was well named.

It was all Devon could do to drag her eyes from the commanding figure sentenced to die a horrendous death. After he was dead, his body was to be hanged a second time on a gibbet placed in the Thames for all entering and leaving London Harbor to see. His head would be encased in a metal harness and his body strapped in a cage to hold the bones together once the flesh began to decay. Turning away, Devon tried not to feel pity, but her tender heart defeated her.

Sighing regretfully, Diablo watched the beautiful woman in the coach turn aside, fully aware that his rather colorful life was about to be snuffed out at the age of twenty-eight. There were still so many things left to experience, he reflected sadly. He had never known true love, or the joy of seeing a child of his loins brought into the world. And he had not righted a grave injustice done to him when he was a child, one that had irrevocably changed his life.

Diablo watched warily as the hangman approached bearing the black hood. He shook his head, refusing to face death as a coward. He much preferred dying with his dignity intact. He had already faced hell and conquered it, so dying held no fear for him. The hangman shrugged and looked to the dragoon captain for the order to pull the lever controlling the trapdoor. Diablo tensed, bracing himself for the endless drop into eternity. Then, amazingly, he opened his mouth and his rich, ribald laughter rolled over the crowd, the sound a derisive mockery of death.

His laughter sent a shudder through Devon's slender frame. The man was mad. Did he respect nothing? If imminent death didn't frighten him, obviously nothing did. Vaguely she wondered what it would take to bring a man like Diablo to his knees, then promptly dismissed the thought. A man with no scruples, one who laughed in the face of death, would bend before neither man nor God.

The drums struck a sharp tattoo and the fifes began a mournful wail. At the same moment Devon's attention was diverted by a disturbance in the crowd. Women screamed, men swore, many joining in the melee. Within minutes people everywhere were either engaged in combat or scrambling to get out of the way. To Devon it looked as if the solid sea of humanity was in motion, the noise deafening and frightening. She thought of her father somewhere in the midst of all this madness, and fear seized her. Her first inclination was to find him herself, but she soon realized the folly of her thinking. Her meager strength would be of little help in the crush of bodies. Leaning out the window, she called to the coachman and footman, bringing them swiftly to her side.

"Perhaps we should leave, my lady," Peters advised, alarmed at the turn of events.

"Not without Father," Devon protested, shaking her head vigorously. "I'm safe enough here. Take Hadley and find Father. Hurry, please."

Reluctant to leave but realizing that their employer could be injured by the ugly mob, the two men did as they were bid, soon losing themselves in the crowd. Devon watched apprehensively as the dragoons left their posts and plunged into the midst of the fighting in a vain attempt to maintain order. Devon wondered what had happened to change the course of events from a celebration to an all-out riot. Unbidden, her eyes flew to the scaffold where fate had seen fit to grant Diablo a temporary reprieve.

A gasp left Devon's throat and she blinked in disbelief. Was she the only one out of hundreds who saw what was taking place? A giant of a man, wielding a wicked-looking cutlass, leaped to the deck of the scaffold in one lithe motion. Dressed in wide pantaloons and a vest that bared his massive chest, he dealt handily with the guards flanking Diablo. He moved so swiftly that Devon barely saw the downward slash of the cutlass as it severed the ropes binding Diablo and removed the noose encircling his neck. Devon watched in stunned disbelief as the two men dropped down into the midst of the mob and were soon lost in the teeming masses.

Devon waited with bated breath for the cry of discovery, troubled by the jolt of elation surging through her. Though the devil inspired fear in her, she could not help but admire his courage and daring.

Then suddenly Diablo appeared at the edge of the crowd, somehow arriving unscathed and undetected, his huge rescuer protecting his back. Almost at the same time four disreputable-looking ruffians appeared from different directions, all gravitating toward Diablo. And horror of all horrors, they were headed directly for her coach!

Just as Devon gathered her wits and prepared to flee, Diablo flung open the door and leaped inside, landing squarely atop Devon's slim form. The air left her lungs in a loud whoosh, and a terrible fear assailed her. She struggled in vain against the weight pressing her into the squabs, but just then the coach took off with a jerk and she felt the almost sensual massage of Diablo's hard body grating against her own softness.

Devon raised her eyes to find him watching her. His silver eyes—she knew they'd be silver—gleamed with appreciation and amusement as he gave her an audacious wink.

"Well met, my lady." His voice was velvet-edged and rich with an underlying warmth that Devon found oddly disconcerting. "How fortunate I am to find refuge in the bosom of a beautiful woman." Slowly and seductively his gaze slid over her face to rest on the swell of her heaving breasts.

Devon gasped in dismay, angered at the suggestive tone of Diablo's voice and puzzled by the ripple of excitement he created in her. "Get off me you . . . you devil!" she blasted, pounding ineffectually on his broad chest. "And stop this coach immediately. My father will have your head for this. He's the Earl of Milford!"

"I saw the crest on the door from my—er—lofty perch," Diablo returned lazily. "That's the reason I chose this coach. That and the stunning lady I saw leaning out the window." The teasing laughter was back in his eyes and a seductive huskiness lingered on his voice.

"You won't get away with this," Devon hissed, hating the way this pirate had captured her senses.

"I already have," Diablo chuckled, the sound a low rumble in his chest. "And you, my lady, will see that I escape with my hide intact."

"I'll do no such thing!" Devon disagreed strongly.

A hue and cry went up behind them, and Devon realized that Diablo's daring escape had finally been discovered. Diablo also heard and reluctantly levered himself off Devon to peer out the window.

"Bloody bastards," he muttered as a company of mounted dragoons thundered after the purloined coach.

Devon swiveled to lean out the other window and was heartened to see that both her father and Winston had somehow found mounts and were riding with the dragoons. She turned to Diablo, gloating. "My father and fiancé are hard on our heels, and when they catch you you'll wish the hangman had done his job."

"Bloodthirsty little minx, aren't you?" Diablo grinned cheekily. "But then, you wouldn't have been at my hanging if you weren't. Sorry to disappoint you, my lady, but I've grown quite fond of my neck and this worthless life."

"A vicious, despicable life," added Devon. "Your vile deeds are legend. Murder, robbery, rape, every crime attributable to mankind. You're a . . . a . . . devil!"

"Aye, they call me devil," Diablo admitted, his expression turning grim. The clear silver of his eyes changed to murky gray, his sensuous mouth hardened, and suddenly Devon knew real fear. "I freely admit to thievery, even murder, but I've yet to commit rape. Do not goad me, my lady, or I might be tempted."

Devon recoiled from the bearded apparition, wishing she could melt into the cushions. She should have realized she couldn't reason with the devil.

Diablo turned away to concentrate on the dragoons pounding behind the coach. He was fairly certain they wouldn't be fired on as long as he had the earl's daughter for a hostage. The lovely lady was his ticket to freedom. He slid a speculative glance in Devon's direction, finding himself oddly curious to learn her name. Just then the coach lurched and Devon flew across the seat, landing in Diablo's lap.

A mischievous smile turned Diablo's eyes to a predatory silver. Instinctively his arms tightened around Devon's soft womanly curves and a groan left his lips. Nothing had ever felt so good. "What is your name?" he asked.

Mesmerized by Diablo's compelling gaze and deep-timbred voice, Devon answered instantly. "Devon. Lady Devon Chatham."

"Devon," Diablo repeated slowly. His eyes roamed appreciatively over her face and hair. "Damn, but you're a tempting morsel!"

Then, before Devon had a chance to gather her wits, his mouth slanted across hers hungrily. The kiss was surprisingly gentle, sending a shockwave through her entire body. But as it deepened, Devon felt his tongue trace the soft contours of her lips, then plunge inside to explore the moist inner recesses.

Shock sent her senses whirling. No one, not even Winston, had kissed her like that. When Diablo's hand came up to cup her breast, Devon regained her wits. But before she had the opportunity to protest, there came a banging on the coach roof. Diablo jerked upright, setting Devon on the seat next to him just as a wiry little man lowered himself through the window. Devon gaped as two more men quickly followed, crowding into the cramped confines of the coach.

"Well done, lads," Diablo congratulated heartily. "Where's Dancy?"

"On the driver's bench with Akbar," one of the men replied. "You all right, cap'n?"

"I am now, Squint. You lads arrived in the nick of time. A few minutes more and I'd be fish bait."

"You can thank Kyle and Akbar for that." Squint grinned. "We only followed orders. 'Course we didn't know for sure it would work, but we couldn't let you hang." He stared at Devon. "Who's the wench?"

"The lady is our luck, lads. Meet Lady Devon. Her father, the Earl of Milford, will make certain the dragoons let us board our ship without mishap. Where is the *Devil Dancer* moored?"

"She's anchored in a little cove near the mouth of the Thames," another of the pirates piped up.

"Excellent, Fingers," Diablo grinned. "Mayhap tonight we'll have a party and you can play us a tune." Named for his ability to play the reed flute, Fingers was tall and thin, his mismatched clothes hanging loosely on his lanky frame. He carried his flute with him everywhere.

"What about her?" asked a third man sourly, pointing to Devon. He was as fierce-looking a man as Devon had ever laid eyes on, with heavy dark brows, a permanent scowl, and wild black hair sticking out from under his wool cap.

"Lady Devon will be released unharmed once she's served her purpose, Rooks," Diablo explained.

"The shore battery will fire on us before we leave the Thames," Squint predicted glumly. "'Twill take some fancy maneuverin' to escape their bloody cannon."

"They won't fire on us with Lady Devon aboard," Diablo said confidently.

Finally Devon found her tongue. "What? Surely you don't mean to take me aboard your pirate ship! I won't go."

"You have no choice, my lady," Diablo pointed out. "But I give you my word no harm will come to you."

"The word of a pirate? You're asking me to trust a man known for his ruthlessness?"

For some reason Diablo found Devon's fury amusing, and a grin overtook his features. "You'll do as I say, my lady."

"The dragoons are gainin', cap'n," Fingers called out, hanging out the window.

"How much farther?" Diablo asked sharply.

"Ten minutes," Squint estimated, "if we keep up this pace."

They were traveling so fast that Devon knew she'd be black and blue from banging against the side of the coach. Diablo was only partially successful in protecting her with his own muscular form.

Behind them the dragoons were indeed gaining on the speeding coach. Both Lord Chatham and Winston Linley had managed to keep up with the soldiers, so when the dragoon captain drew his pistol and prepared to give the order to fire, the earl screamed out in protest.

"Stop, you fool! My daughter is in that coach. I'll have your head if she's hurt."

Shaking his head in disgust, the captain stayed his order. No matter how badly he wanted Diablo, he hadn't the nerve to contradict the wishes of an influential earl. Besides, he knew Lady Devon personally and would hate to see her come to harm at his hands.

"We're nearly there, Diablo," Squint called out. "There's the longboat waitin' in the shoals."

When Lord Chatham saw the coach skid to a halt on a point of land overlooking the mouth of the Thames, his heart sank to his well-shod feet. Then he saw a longboat waiting a short distance off shore, and fear for his daughter's safety twisted his gut. He turned to Winston and barked, "Use whatever means necessary to keep the shore battery from firing." Winston nodded grimly and thundered off.

Before the dragoons reached the place where the coach had stopped, five men including the huge, bald pirate called Akbar, quickly scrambled down the bank and waded out into the water where the longboat bobbed in the surf. Only when the dragoons slid to a halt a short distance away did Diablo step from the coach, dragging Devon behind him.

"Don't shoot!" Lord Chatham warned.

He dismounted, advancing a short distance, hoping to reason with the vicious pirate. "Let my daughter go, Diablo," he called out as Diablo pulled Devon relentlessly toward the shore. "Name your price."

"I have no need of your gold, milord," Diablo

answered. "Nor will I harm your daughter. When I am safely away she will be set free and escorted safely home. More than that I cannot promise."

"Have you no compassion? Devon has caused you no harm. She is but an innocent victim."

"Aye, milord, and I'm sorry for it, but you have my word, I'll keep Lady Devon safe."

By now Diablo had reached the edge of the water. Bending, he scooped Devon up in his arms and dashed for the boat bobbing in the surf a short distance away. He placed her inside and scrambled after her while his men took up the oars and began rowing. Afraid to fire for fear of hitting the earl's daughter, the dragoons stood helplessly on the riverbank and watched the longboat round the point, hugging the shore as it made its way unerringly to where the *Devil Dancer* was moored.

"Father!" Devon screamed as the shore drew farther and farther away. "Father—" The word ended in a sob as she realized the futility of her plea.

But Devon was not one to give up so easily. She jumped to her feet and tried to leap into the water, certain she could make her way safely to shore. But Diablo was too quick for her. He seized her waist and forced her down beside him. Struggling for her very life, Devon flung herself out of Diablo's restraining arms, and hit her head against the side of the longboat. The last sound she heard as she slid into darkness was her name on Diablo's lips.

Chapter Two

"Her breathing is regular, Diablo, I doubt that she's badly hurt. A slight concussion, perhaps. Who is she?"

The man who spoke was tall, nearly as broad and imposing as Diablo, with flaming red hair and midnight blue eyes. He was dressed in pirate regalia of baggy pants and blouse with a wide red sash wound about his slim waist. His clothes were surprisingly clean for a pirate and his fingers gentle as he carefully probed the purpling bruise marring Devon's temple.

Diablo's silver gaze slid over the reclining form stretched out enticingly on his bed. "She's Lady Devon Chatham, daughter of the Earl of Milford."

"Saints preserve us," the redhead intoned, rolling his eyes heavenward. During times of stress his Irish brogue was more pronounced than usual. "You aim high, my friend. What are you going to do with her? The men won't be too pleased having a woman aboard the *Devil Dancer*."

"The lady serves a purpose, Kyle," Diablo informed his lieutenant and second in command.

Kyle O'Bannon was the only man who knew Diablo's secret. He acted as doctor and treated the sick and wounded on the *Devil Dancer* when the need arose. He had become a fugitive after aiding his fellow Irishmen in a conspiracy against the crown while in medical school. He fled school, became involved in smuggling on the Cornish coast, and joined Diablo's crew while helping unload contraband from the *Devil Dancer*. From the moment the two men met they became fast friends.

"But for Lady Devon we would not have made it back to the ship," Diablo continued. "The lady's father was instrumental in keeping the dragoons from firing on us. Her being at the hanging was a stroke of good fortune. Already we are past the shore patrol and out of danger. Your plan to create a diversion at the hanging was absolute genius, Kyle." Diablo grinned, clapping his friend on the back.

"The lass is a real beauty," Kyle said wistfully, "so young and innocent. You won't hurt her, will you? I won't allow it."

"Relax, Kyle, Lady Devon will be set ashore on the Cornish coast and our friend Cormac can see her safely home," Diablo assured him. "I promised her father she'd not be harmed and I mean to keep my word. You're sure she's all right? She seems to be sleeping deeply."

"Aye, she'll be fine," Kyle said, relief coloring his words. If Diablo meant the girl harm, he was prepared to do battle with his captain. Though

Diablo wielded more authority than most pirate captains, every man aboard had a say in ship rules and the disposal of booty. And the girl was definitely booty. "Let Lady Devon sleep, it's the best thing for her right now."

"Aye," Diablo agreed. "You go on, I've a few things to attend to here before I join you. Fix a course for Land's End. We'll go in at dark and row the lady ashore."

After Kyle left the captain's spacious quarters in the ship's stern, Diablo lingered behind, his eyes returning time and again to the golden-haired beauty lying in his bed. She was somewhat taller than the average woman; slender, willowy, with jutting breasts, fine hips, and shapely thighs. Her facial bones were delicately carved, her mouth full and temptingly red. Long, sooty lashes lay curled against the creamy texture of her cheeks like two butterfly wings. Diablo thought Devon the most ravishing creature he'd ever seen and would have given his soul to learn the secrets of her luscious body.

Was she a virgin? Diablo wondered, his hands itching to test the smoothness of her flesh. Or had Devon's fiancé already savored the pleasure she had to offer? A surge of hatred jolted through Diablo at the thought of Devon's nameless, faceless fiancé bedding the gorgeous wench. Diablo's eyes stripping off her Devon's slipper-clad feet. Both her stockings were sopping wet from being dragged through the surf. He bent to the task of stripping off her shoes and stockings before she caught her death of cold.

Diablo groaned aloud when he reached beneath Devon's skirt to untie the ribbons holding up the sheer white stockings on her long, slender thighs. The skin beneath his questing fingertips quivered slightly as he slowly rolled the wisp of silk down one shapely leg. Never had he felt anything so soft or temptingly exquisite. It took all his willpower to keep his hand from straying upward to the beckoning nest of warmth pulling at his senses.

Devon's eyes flew open as Diablo's hand lingered on the inside of one thigh. Though she was nearly paralyzed with fright, her temper flared when she awoke to find Diablo taking liberties with her body.

"What are you doing!"

Diablo chuckled, the smile in his silver eyes a sensuous flame that ignited something deep inside Devon. "Removing your shoes and stockings, my lady," he replied, his voice tinged with amusement as he bent to his pleasurable task. "They're wet and you'll rest more comfortably without them."

"Take your hands off me!" Devon spat, swatting his hands away. "I'm not so helpless that you can ravish me at will."

"Ravish you, my lady? While you are unable to enjoy what I do to you? Never! If and when I make love to you, you'll know it."

Devon paled. No one—absolutely no one—had be̶ talked to her like that. "Why, you . . . you I'll . . .n! Satan! If you lay a hand on me Diablo ⸝."

laughter. Devo̶ back his head and roared with with his jet black ̶ought he resembled the devil silver eyes. Yet there wa̶ ̶nd beard and those strange the man, a sensuousness rev̶led in the hard lines of his face and the depth of his ̶es. His muscular strength was awesome, his bold fea̶ures frightening. But what was most surprising to Devon was Diablo's humor. It was so out of character, contradicting all she'd ever heard about the man.

Beneath Diablo's thick black beard Devon could make out the fine bones of a face that might be called aristocratic if one didn't know what he was. It was a well-known fact that pirates in the year 1715 came from all walks of life. Could Diablo possibly be from a noble Spanish family fallen on hard times?

"If I wanted to bed you, Lady Devon, I would do so with or without your permission, regardless of what you think of me."

Devon pushed herself to the farthest corner of the bed, expecting Diablo to pounce on her at any moment. She tilted her chin defiantly, determined not to give in without a fierce fight. "Don't come near me!"

"Feisty wench, aren't you? Rest easy, Lady Devon, I'm too tired right now to do you justice. How's your head?"

Since the moment she opened her eyes to find Diablo fondling her leg, Devon was aware of her pounding head. She winced when she found the bruise on her temple. "It hurts, no thanks to you. Why didn't you leave me behind?"

"Had I been stupid enough to do that we'd have been blown out of the water by the shore cannon."

"What are you going to do with me?"

"As I said before, you'll be set ashore."

Devon searched Diablo's face, wanting to believe him but afraid to trust his word. No woman was safe with him, and she'd be a fool to drop her guard where Diablo was concerned.

Sensing Devon's misgivings, Diablo added,

"You're safe enough in my quarters. No one will harm you here."

"Does that include you?" Devon challenged boldly.

Diablo did not answer immediately, staring at Devon strangely, his silver eyes taking in every inch of her charmingly disheveled form. His admiring glance was blatantly sexual, freezing the breath in Devon's throat. When he finally spoke, his voice, deep and sensual, sent a ripple of awareness through her.

"I'd be lying if I said I didn't want you, Devon. You're a damn tempting morsel to a man who's accustomed to seizing what he wants."

Mesmerized, Devon could not move when Diablo pinned her to the bed, his mouth devouring hers hungrily. Vaguely she felt the roughness of his beard scraping across the tender skin of her face, the heady sensation sending the pit of her stomach into a swirl. She tried to throttle the dizzying current racing through her, but when Diablo deliberately outlined her lips with the tip of his tongue and then plunged inside, she jolted in response. As the kiss deepened, Devon felt her body ignite in a way she never thought possible. The male hardness of his virile form left an indelible print on her own softness, his desire for her a hot lance between them.

He was slowly and completely demoralizing her, eroding her will to resist. But she had more moral fiber than that blackguard gave her credit for, Devon reflected, marshaling her strength. When Diablo renewed the attack on her senses, she broke free.

"Nay, don't!"

"Are you afraid of me, Devon?"

"Aye, I admit it. I . . . I'm afraid of what you'll do to me."

"I won't hurt you."

"You already have hurt me by taking me away from my father."

"And your fiancé?" Diablo prompted. "Have you forgotten him?"

"Of course not," Devon refuted, her eyes stormy with anger. "He's probably worried sick. If you had any compassion at all you'd turn around and take me back."

"Compassion? I am the devil, and devils have little compassion. I could easily ravish you here and now and no one would say me nay. But I won't." Diablo sighed regretfully. "I promised your father you'd be returned unharmed."

"A devil with a conscience, how refreshing," Devon bit out sarcastically. "However, I am grateful for not having to suffer your despicable attentions."

"I admire your courage, my lady." Diablo smiled, his eyes as keen as silver daggers. "Most men fear me."

"I am not a man."

"I've noticed." He raked her slim form appraisingly. "I only allow beautiful women in my bed. But alas, I fear I must forego the pleasure right now. But if you insist, I will find time later," he grinned, finding amusement in Devon's gasp of outrage.

"Get out of here!"

Diablo levered himself to his feet, his tall, lean form looming above her. "I'll be back," he drawled lazily. "Don't try to leave if you value your hide." Devon watched warily as the handsome rogue sauntered from the room with the rolling gait of one accustomed to balancing on the deck of a tossing ship.

Devon thought he looked every bit as evil as his reputation, except for his eyes. How could those silver mirrors portray such teasing humor when everyone knew the acts of depravity he was capable of? Were there two men lurking inside that attractive body?

The thought that Diablo intended to return galvanized Devon into action. When he entered the cabin again, she intended to be armed with more than words. There had to be some sort of weapon in the room. Diablo wouldn't have an easy time subduing her, if that was his purpose. No indeed, Devon smiled deviously, that miserable blackguard wouldn't find her meekly awaiting his pleasure.

Diablo grinned all the way to the quarterdeck. The spirited wench occupying his bed was a tasty morsel he'd give his right arm to possess. But even a fool could tell she meant trouble. For her own sake as well as his, he had to get her off the ship as soon as possible. Already his men were casting lustful glances in the direction of his cabin. His crew were loyal only up to a point, and some couldn't be trusted out of his sight. Normally pirates elected their captain from among their own. That's how he had come to possess the *Devil Dancer*. Over the years he had hand-picked his crew until he felt reasonably certain his orders would be strictly adhered to. But Diablo was no fool. Lady Devon was too beautiful, too enticing, to be exposed to his crew for any length of time. Besides, women on board were considered bad luck and he had no intention of flaunting tradition.

"The course is set, Kit, we should reach our destination day after tomorrow."

Diablo's brow furrowed. "How many times have I told you not to call me Kit within hearing distance of the crew, Kyle?"

"No one's around, Diablo," Kyle gestured. "Besides, your name means nothing to them. You've been Diablo too long now to make any difference."

"I suppose you're right," Diablo allowed, wondering if there was anyone on earth who really cared who or what he was. "Just the same, except in the privacy of my cabin, I prefer you call me Diablo."

"What about the lass?" Kyle asked, adroitly changing the subject.

"She's fine. She woke up shortly before I left the cabin."

"I hope you didn't scare the lass too badly—or hurt her," Kyle added sharply. "The poor thing has probably led a sheltered life and is unprepared to deal with the likes of you. Your ugly, bearded face would frighten even the hardiest soul."

Diablo tilted his head back and laughed richly. "The *poor* lass was upbraiding me furiously when I left the cabin. She displayed neither fear nor awe of my ferocious features. Believe it or not, Kyle, I didn't touch the girl, though it took considerable willpower to keep from ravishing her. Who knows, she might have enjoyed it." He shrugged eloquently; his silver eyes held a hint of longing Kyle did not miss.

Just then Akbar approached on silent feet, his incredible bulk surprisingly nimble. A wide smile split his fierce features as his black eyes raked Diablo from head to toe. Crossing his arms across his massive chest and wagging his bushy eyebrows, he said, "You look no worse for your stay in Newgate. Mayhap the beard is a trifle more unruly than normal."

"I'm rather fond of the beard," Diablo replied, stroking the luxurious growth with long, supple fingers. "It suits me."

"Wear it in good health, my friend," Akbar boomed, "and thank Allah you've still a neck to support it."

"I've you and Kyle to thank for that," Diablo replied, turning serious. "I must admit I was becoming rather nervous standing on the gibbet with a rope around my neck."

"We provided the distraction, but you're the one who got us all away safely," Akbar reminded him. "Some of the men are wondering about the girl. They think you should share her."

"The girl stays with me," Diablo said, his features hardening. "She'll be set ashore at Land's End. Spread the word that I'll defend my right to keep her for myself."

Akbar nodded but said nothing. He was astute enough to realize Diablo would not back down on this.

"A mite possessive of the lass, aren't you, Diablo?" Kyle questioned, looking somewhat puzzled. "What's so special about her?"

"Dammit, Kyle, you know I've never willingly turned over women captives to the crew unless they were whores to begin with and willing. Nor have I ever resorted to rape."

"What about all those lasses who shared your bed before they were set free or ransomed?"

Flashing a roguish grin, Diablo said, "I've forgotten nothing. I have a reputation to maintain, and the women were willing. But Lady Devon is—I don't know—perhaps she reminds me of another life."

"It's still not too late to return to that life."

"There's a hefty price on Diablo's head. No country in the world would welcome me, including England."

Akbar stood silently by, listening. His massive bulk towered over Kyle and Diablo, both large, powerfully built men. With his bald head covered with a colorful scarf and a gold hoop dangling from one ear, Akbar looked every bit the fierce, unprincipled pirate he was. He waited for the conversation to lag before speaking.

"We're in for a blow, Diablo," he warned, eying the lowering sky with misgiving. The day that had begun dismal and rainy now looked threatening as the rising wind whistled through the sails.

"So much the better," Diablo returned, pleased with the way things were working out. "The English navy won't be so anxious to give chase with a storm in the offing. It will provide ample time to put Lady Devon ashore. Cormac, our contact in Cornwall, will see that she reaches London safely.

"Warn the crew, Kyle, and see that the ship is prepared to ride out the storm. I'll be in my cabin if you need me."

The two men watched as Diablo turned and retraced his steps to his quarters. "Diablo appears anxious to return to the woman," Akbar said with a knowing grin.

"Aye," Kyle agreed, not quite as amused as Akbar. "He seems fair taken with the lass, and I don't like it. She's trouble, my friend, big trouble. She's the daughter of the Earl of Milford. Need I say more?"

"Allah help us," Akbar muttered. "Diablo aims

high. Does he intend to bed the woman before he puts her ashore?"

"He wants to, but whether he does remains to be seen."

"A quid says Diablo has her before he sets her ashore," Akbar wagered.

"I'm betting on the lass," Kyle countered, "and expect to be a quid richer for it."

Methodically Devon searched Diablo's cabin, carefully examining the contents of every drawer in the map-strewn desk. Finding no hidden weapon, she turned to the sundry articles of clothing hanging on hooks from the bulkhead, but to no avail. The only thing she found that remotely resembled a weapon was a dull letter opener, and that certainly wouldn't scare a man like Diablo. Then her eyes fell on the sea chest across the room. Scrambling to her knees, she began rummaging through its contents, finding an assortment of clothes, papers, and keepsakes. She was on the verge of giving up in despair when her fingers found what they were looking for lying at the very bottom. Her hand closed around cold steel as she drew a small-caliber pistol from the chest.

Devon noted that the pistol wasn't loaded and returned to the chest to look for ammunition. To her delight she found bullets along with all the paraphernalia needed to load and prime the weapon. Carefully following the process taught her by her father, Devon prepared the pistol for firing. Then she closed the lid of the chest, slipped the pistol into her pocket, and sat down on the bed to wait.

A smile lingered on Diablo's lips as he paused outside his cabin, thinking about the girl inside. She was keen-witted, feisty, had a tongue as sharp as a knife, and was far too great a temptation. Just looking at her set his blood to boiling. Most women would be quailing in fear, but he was sure that Devon was pacing the cabin and cursing him. He'd sell his soul to the devil to have her in his bed, willingly, for one glorious night. The thought produced a jolt to his loins as he slowly turned the handle and entered the cabin.

Devon sat on the bed, her eyes watchful as Diablo approached. "I've ordered some food," he said, his eyes roaming freely over her trim form. "It won't be what you're accustomed to, but nourishing nevertheless."

"I'm not hungry," Devon responded warily.

"Then you can watch me eat, I'm famished. Prison fare leaves much to be desired." He lowered himself into the only chair in the room, stretching his long-muscled legs out before him. A tense silence ensued.

Devon grew restive under Diablo's avid scrutiny and wished he would say something—anything. She felt more secure with verbal fencing than being the object of his lustful admiration. She squirmed like a mouse caught in a trap and felt in her pocket for the comfortable weight of the pistol. The tray of food that arrived a short time later was a welcome relief, and Devon relaxed somewhat as Diablo turned his attention from her to his dinner.

"Are you sure you won't join me?" Diablo asked, popping a slice of salted beef in his mouth.

"Nay," Devon sniffed haughtily, turning up her nose.

"Suit yourself. But I'd think you'd want to fortify yourself for—later."

"Later?" squeaked Devon in dismay. "Wha—

what do you mean? You said I wouldn't be harmed."

"I have no intention of harming you," Diablo grinned, his eyes flashing with silver lights.

Diablo knew he shouldn't bait Devon so relentlessly, but she was so charmingly innocent he couldn't resist. Was it an act or was she truly untouched? he wondered, finishing the meal. He shoved the tray aside and sat back, replete, thoroughly enjoying himself. It wasn't often he found the opportunity to associate with women of the upper class. Not that he lacked female companionship. On the contrary, women came easily to him. Women like Scarlett flocked around him like bees to honey. He could have her and those like her whenever he wanted. But Devon was different, and it pleased him to toy with her.

"You—still intend to let me go, don't you?" Devon asked, her bravado slowly disintegrating. Only the solid weight of the pistol against her thigh kept her from panic.

Diablo nodded slowly, a lazy smile hanging on the corner of his mouth. "A friend in Cornwall will see you safely to London. But that still leaves us with two long nights in which to become better acquainted," he said with sly innuendo. "I'd like to know every inch of you intimately."

"I know everything about you that I care to know," Devon responded, his erotic words creating a strange, uncomfortable emotion in her. She could feel the magnetic charge emanating from him and wondered if he still meant to ravish her.

Undeniably Diablo was a handsome devil, beard and all. He was dark as a Spaniard; his powerful, well-muscled body moved with easy grace. He looked tough, lean and sinewy. A humorous mouth set in a rugged, severe, albeit attractive face was strangely at odds with his profession. Devon doubted there was another man to compare with him and wished she was anywhere but in his intimidating company. The urge to be held by him unnerved and frightened her.

Diablo uncoiled his lean length from the chair and approached Devon with lazy grace. His body ached with the need to make love to her, but he wouldn't do it unless she invited him to, and that appeared unlikely. He sat down beside her, and she immediately leaped off the bed, pressing herself against the wall.

"Don't touch me!"

"You're beautiful, my lady."

"And you're a devil."

"Aye, a devil who'd trade his soul to attain heaven in your arms."

"You're mad!" Devon blasted, the determined look in Diablo's eyes fueling her fear. She had hoped to be spared the need to defend her honor, but Diablo was pressing her too assiduously. She was left with no recourse.

Diablo's silver eyes sparkled mischievously. He couldn't remember when he'd taken such delight in a woman. He knew he was treading in dangerous waters but couldn't resist. He admired Devon's spirit and thought her remarkably brave for one unaccustomed to the cruelties of life. He thought to steal a kiss, or two, to merely sample her sweetness, but Devon failed to recognize his teasing manner. He was brought up short by the sudden appearance of a pistol in Devon's shaking hand, pointed at his heart.

"I told you not to come near me." Her voice was slightly breathless despite her best efforts to be calm.

"I seriously doubt you could kill a man, Devon," Diablo challenged, advancing slowly. "Besides, the gun isn't loaded. I recognize it as one I keep stored in my sea chest."

"I loaded it," Devon gloated. "Do you think me stupid?"

"Nay, far from stupid, my lady. Now give over the gun before you hurt yourself. You have my word you won't be harmed. You'll be set ashore just as I promised, in the same condition in which you arrived."

Devon eyed Diablo dubiously. "I don't trust you."

"Give me the gun, Devon," Diablo said, "before someone gets hurt." He stretched out his hand, palm up.

"Nay." Devon's chin tilted at a stubborn angle, warning Diablo that his words had fallen on deaf ears.

Then Diablo made a move that nearly proved fatal. He lunged forward to seize the weapon from Devon's shaking hand. His strong fingers clamped around her frail wrist, causing an involuntary reaction in the finger poised against the trigger. Whether Devon would have pulled the trigger of her own accord was moot as the gun exploded in her hand. Diablo's eyes widened in shock and pain as he staggered backward, stumbled, then fell heavily, slamming his head against the corner of the marble-topped desk. Devon stared in stunned fascination at the red stain blossoming against Diablo's white shirt. He lay so still and white at her feet that she feared she had killed him.

The door to the cabin flung open, admitting Akbar, followed closely by Kyle. Devon recognized the huge Turk as the man who had cut Diablo from the gallows but did not recall Kyle, who had remained with the ship. Kyle paled, stunned by the sight of Diablo lying still as death with Devon standing over him holding the smoking pistol.

"Sweet mother Mary," Kyle whispered, shock rendering him motionless. "You've killed Diablo!"

A howl of rage exploded from Akbar's throat as he shouldered past Kyle to kneel at Diablo's side. His face was a mask of outrage and hatred as he swiveled to glare at Devon.

"I—I didn't mean . . ." Devon swallowed painfully, her sentence trailing off when she realized that nothing she could say would make any difference to Diablo's faithful crew. If he were dead, she fully expected to follow soon.

"Kyle, Diablo needs you," Akbar growled, jerking Kyle from his frozen stance.

Kyle hesitated but a moment, asking, "What about the lass?"

"Leave her to me," Akbar returned, fixing Devon with a baleful look.

"Don't—" Kyle's words were left unsaid as his attention was captured by Diablo, who picked that moment to groan. Kyle dropped to his knees, Devon all but forgotten.

But she was not forgotten by Akbar, who seized her roughly and dragged her from the room, thrusting her into the arms of two burly pirates. "Throw her into the hold," Akbar ordered curtly. "If Diablo lives he can decide what's to be done with her. If he dies . . ."

There was no need for him to continue. Devon held no illusions about her fate should Diablo die.

Chapter Three

Sometime during the night the threatening storm struck with all its fury. Deep in the bowels of the ship Devon huddled in a miserable heap. Cold, hungry, wretched, she curled up on a damp bale, terrified of the furry creatures that brushed against her legs. Her greatest fear was of dying under such deplorable circumstances far from her loved ones. Hours had passed since she was thrown into the hold, abandoned and utterly alone and forgotten in a world totally foreign to her. Did Diablo still live? she wondered dismally. Dear God, she hoped so. She never meant to kill him, just protect her honor in the only way she knew how. Truth to tell, she wasn't certain she could have pulled the trigger of her own accord. But Diablo had taken that choice from her.

Suddenly the ship tilted dangerously and Devon slid off the bale, landing with a splash in the ankle-deep water seeping into the hold. For a timeless interval she thought the beleaguered ship wasn't going to right itself, certain she would be consigned to the deep forever. It was a terrifying thought, and she recited every prayer she'd ever learned. Then slowly the ship began an upward sweep, only to heel over in the opposite direction. And so it continued throughout the long night and next day as the wind and rain wreaked havoc on the *Devil Dancer*.

"How is Diablo?" The door to the captain's cabin opened and Akbar was literally blown inside, dressed in raingear and dripping wet.

"The wound isn't serious," Kyle replied. "The bullet passed through his side cleanly, without damaging anything vital. He was damn lucky, the bleeding was minimal."

Akbar scowled, his fierce features becoming even more forbidding. "Why is he still unconscious? It's been nearly twenty-four hours."

"'Tis his head," Kyle explained. "A concussion, is my guess. He'll come around in good time." For his own safety during the storm Diablo had been lashed to the bunk.

Akbar grunted, his mind somewhat eased. He and Diablo had been friends since Black Bart captured the Turkish brigantine on which Akbar served. Because of his extraordinary size and strength, Akbar had been pressed into Black Bart's service. Though Diablo had been a lad at the time, he had saved Akbar's life during a storm when high seas threatened to wash his unconscious body overboard. Akbar had been struck by a falling timber and would have been swept over the side but for Diablo's quick thinking; he had lashed them both to the broken mast. An unlikely friendship had existed since then between the two men. When Diablo led a mutiny against Black Bart and seized the *Devil Dancer*, Akbar was at his side.

"Tend Diablo well," Akbar grunted as he turned to leave.

"How goes it topside, Akbar?" Kyle asked.

"We're riding it out well enough. The *Devil Dancer* is as trim and fit as any ship afloat."

"Aye, she is that. What about the lass? Where—"

The sentence died in his throat as the ship shuddered, followed by a loud crash.

"Allah help us," Akbar intoned, preparing to rush back out into the raging elements. When Kyle made to follow, Akbar shook his head. "See to Diablo, my friend." Then he was pushing through the door, his head bent against the howling wind and pelting rain.

"What's happening?"

Kyle whirled to find Diablo's eyes open, though he was still somewhat confused. "You're awake!"

"Obviously. Why am I tied to the bunk?"

"The storm. It's for your own protection."

Just then the ship lurched to the starboard, then righted itself, tossing like a cork on the towering waves. "Release me, Kyle, I'm needed topside."

"You're staying right where you are, Kit. Your wound is healing and obviously your concussion is mending, but you're still too weak to battle the elements. Akbar has things well in hand."

Diablo's brows furrowed. "I . . . what happened? What wound?"

"Don't you remember?"

"Nay . . . well . . . not everything. Was I shot?"

"Aye, I was hoping you could tell me how it

happened. Do you recall Lady Devon?"

A slow smile transformed Diablo's face. "Who could forget that little wildcat?" His eyes made a quick survey of the room. "Where is she?"

"She shot you, you know."

"Not purposely, Kyle. I'm certain she wouldn't have pulled the trigger if I hadn't goaded her. True, she threatened me with the pistol, but I more or less deserved it." A horrible thought suddenly came to him. "What have you done with her?"

Kyle looked decidedly uncomfortable. "I . . . I'm certain the lass is fine, Diablo."

"You're . . . certain? God's bones, Kyle, don't you know?"

"I was occupied with seeing to your injuries and thought little about her at the time. Akbar handled it, but I've not had the opportunity to question him for the storm struck shortly afterwards."

"How long have I been out?"

"Twenty-four hours."

Diablo cursed violently, working his arms free and attacking the knots that held him captive. The activity earned him a stab of pain followed by a wave of dizziness. Defeated, he fell back against the pillow, too weak to continue. "Damn you, Kyle, and damn Akbar if he hurt the girl."

Kyle thought his captain far too distressed for his own good and abruptly whirled, busying himself at the water pitcher. "Here, drink this," Kyle offered, ignoring Diablo's threats as he turned and held a cup to his captain's lips.

"What is it?" Diablo asked, his eyes narrowed suspiciously.

"Just water," Kyle said, his eyes not quite meeting Diablo's.

Grunting, Diablo drank deeply, then sputtered, slapping the cup from Kyle's hands. "God's bones! Laudanum! I thought I could trust you."

"You can. Now quit blustering and rest. I promise to check on the lass the first chance I get."

"Tell . . . Akbar . . . I'll have . . . his head if . . . she's been harmed," Diablo said, finding it difficult to concentrate.

"I will, my friend," Kyle vowed. I only hope it's not too late, he thought.

As luck would have it, Kyle found no opportunity to speak with Akbar until the next morning. The storm finally blew itself out with the coming of dawn, and the huge Turk immediately set the crew to repairing the mainmast and damaged rudder. A reading showed they had been blown far off course and were now floundering somewhere in the Atlantic. Until another sighting was made no one knew exactly where they were.

Before Diablo awoke, Kyle had released him from his bonds, then went to fetch a hot meal for himself and his captain, their first in two days. While he was gone, Diablo stirred, tested his limbs, and staggered somewhat unsteadily to his feet. He found himself able to stand despite the jolt of pain in the vicinity of his wound and could move about freely if he ignored the dull ache in his head. Setting his teeth against the stab in his side, Diablo proceeded to bathe and dress in clean clothes. Except for his grumbling stomach and worry over Devon, he felt remarkably able to cope with his duties.

Damn that Akbar, he silently upbraided. The man was far too zealous in wanting to protect him. He didn't think Akbar would take it upon himself to punish Devon, but one never knew about the fierce Turk. Diablo decided it was time he took over his own ship and proved to his crew he was fit to command.

Just then the object of his angry ruminations entered the cabin without knocking, coming up short at the sight of Diablo standing on his own two feet and looking none the worse for wear.

"Allah be praised. Twenty-four hours ago I thought you at death's door."

"And before that I was close to having my neck stretched," Diablo grumbled. "Mayhap I should change my name to El Gatto, the cat, for surely I have been blessed with nine lives." Then his lips turned downward into a fierce scowl. "Where is she, Akbar?"

At first Akbar looked puzzled, then comprehension dawned. "The girl! I've been too involved with the storm and saving the ship to give a thought to her."

"You forgot? You haven't harmed her, have you?" Diablo flared, his silver eyes kindling with anger. "Exactly where is Lady Devon?"

"Confined in the hold," Akbar said somewhat sheepishly. "In all the excitement I completely forgot about her."

"God's bones, man, that was two days ago!" Diablo thundered. "Has no one checked on her? Has she been given food and water?"

"I told you, the storm—"

"I want her out of there—now!"

"Aye," Akbar grumbled, turning to do his captain's bidding. "I'll see to it." He went out muttering dire predictions about women aboard pirate ships and trouble.

Deep in the belly of the ship, Devon was unaware that the storm had ended. Nearly comatose, she lolled in sodden misery atop the bale in which she had ridden out the storm. Covered with filth, her golden tresses a snarled nest, she had been sick many times during the past two days and was now dangerously dehydrated from lack of water. She felt herself near death—wished for it, actually. So when the hatch opened, allowing in the first light Devon had seen in two days, it proved too much for her. The terrifying figure looming like a huge ogre above her seemed like something out of her worst nightmare, sending her spinning into a deep, dark void.

Diablo raged furiously when Akbar entered his cabin carrying an incredibly dirty and unconscious Devon. He leaped to his feet, sending a plate of food flying. "Put her down on the bed," he barked, "and send Kyle in here."

Diablo wrinkled his nose, all too aware of the stench of vomit combined with dampness and mold clinging to Devon's clothing, and he spit out a string of curses. Devon's pale little face filled him with fear, as did the white line around her pinched lips. Without a moment's hesitation he stripped the reeking rags from her body and tossed them out the door. Then he drew a sheet over her and left hurriedly to fetch hot water. He returned shortly, and using clean linens from his sea chest, set himself to thoroughly cleansing Devon's body of accumulated filth. Only when he finished did he allow his eyes to feast upon the arrestingly beautiful charms of her perfect body.

Lightly he trailed his fingertips from her collarbone to the tip of one breast, mesmerized when the nipple hardened beneath his touch. The breath exploded from his chest in a painful jolt. Never had he felt anything so velvet soft, so exciting or tempting as Devon's white skin. Cresting the symmetrical mounds of her breasts, which were full yet not overly large, were coral tips puckered into tight buds. They seemed to be pouting for the touch of his mouth, and Diablo forced his wayward thoughts elsewhere as his gaze continued downward.

Diablo's loins swelled and his silver eyes widened appreciatively as they came to rest on the golden nest of tangled hair between Devon's smooth thighs. Beads of sweat popped out on his forehead and he knew a moment of panic. Some sixth sense that never failed him told him that this woman had the power to change his life. Even as he scoffed at the ridiculous thought that this woman—any woman—could mean more to him than brief sexual satisfaction, Diablo's eyes continued their sensual journey, devouring Devon's long, slim legs, shapely thighs, and trim ankles. Even her feet were narrow and dainty. In fact, everything about Devon pleased him. But she wasn't for him—he knew it and accepted it.

Whores, doxies, and widows of easy virtue were what he was accustomed to, not a lady bred and born. They belonged behind manor walls producing children for their aristocratic husbands. Once Diablo might have belonged to that world, but now it was too late. He had been cruelly thrust into a pirate's life and later freely embraced the profession, choosing to live and operate outside the law in the tradition of piracy.

Diablo and men like him were considered enemies of mankind. They owed allegiance to no one, claimed no country. Ships from any country could seize a pirate ship, bring it to port, try all the crew regardless of nationality, and hang them. Like his brothers, Diablo sailed the Pirate Round—a route stretching from North America around the tip of Africa—to pillage the eastern seas and return home —in this case Nassau—with their holds filled with booty.

Pirates were a barbarous lot, yet among themselves they passionately advocated a rude sort of democracy, with a high regard for justice and the rights of individuals and distaste for tyranny and abuse of power. They could be generous toward those they liked and trusted, often bestowing rich gifts. Shipmates losing eyes or limbs were allowed to remain aboard and earn a half-share of the booty.

Though a strict disciplinarian, Diablo was a fair man who treated women captives better than most pirates did. He recalled those days long ago, had fate been kinder to him, when his life might have taken a different course. And as he gazed longingly at Devon, he knew he couldn't take her cruelly no matter how he yearned to invade that tempting body. Were he offered the opportunity he'd not ravish her but would make leisurely love, bringing her gently to womanhood. With a sigh of regret, Diablo pulled the sheet over Devon's nude form, feeling strangely like a traitor to his profession. Not one of his acquaintances, save for Kyle perhaps, would deny himself a woman he wanted as badly as he wanted Devon.

"I'm sorry, Kit, I thought the lass was confined to a cabin," Kyle apologized as he stepped into the cabin. "I'd never knowingly allow her to be placed in the hold. How is she?"

"I hoped you could tell me, Kyle. And damn it, man, call me Diablo."

"Sorry, Diablo," Kyle muttered. "Move aside so I can have a look."

Diablo obeyed, watching closely as Kyle examined her. "She's dehydrated as well as exhausted," he pronounced at length. "Force liquids down her and let her rest and she'll be fine. You're aware, of course, that we've blown off course and there's no possibility now of putting the lass ashore at Land's End."

Diablo nodded grimly. "I suspected as much. Have you taken a reading yet?"

"Aye, we're roughly five hundred miles due west of France. It would be too dangerous now to return to English waters."

"What about damage?"

"The rudder was damaged and we've taken on water, but Akbar has the men working on the problem. Men are also mending the sails and fashioning a new mast. We'll be under way sometime tomorrow. What course should I set?"

Diablo was silent a long time, his eyes straying to Devon, who remained blissfully unaware of his dilemma. A man of his word, he had promised Devon he would set her ashore, but fate had intervened and willed otherwise. Deep down, Diablo felt relieved that the choice had been taken from him, for his instinct was to keep Devon with him until she came to his bed willingly.

"We sail for Nassau," he said, reluctantly tearing his eyes from Devon's still form. "There's booty in the hold and the lads need time ashore. Besides, the ship could use a good careen and it wouldn't hurt to remain invisible for a spell."

"What about the lass?"

"Needless to say, she'll remain under my protection for the time being."

"What?" Devon had been awake for several

minutes, listening. Now, hearing Diablo's words, she reared up in angry indignation, unaware she was nude beneath the sheet.

Both men turned as one, Kyle's loud gasp echoing Diablo's groan. Two pairs of eyes fastened on Devon's heaving breasts. Only then did Devon realize what was happening. Glancing down at herself, she shrieked in outrage, yanking the sheet up under her chin.

"Sons of Satan! Murderers! Rapists! Both of you. Where are my clothes? Why am I nude? Who are you?" This last question was directed to Kyle.

"Lady Devon, may I present Kyle O'Bannon, my lieutenant and right-hand man," Diablo said with a flourish. "We've done you no harm, my lady. Your clothes were wet and filthy. I couldn't in good conscience leave you in them."

"I thought I killed you," Devon said sourly, unwilling to reveal her relief at seeing him alive.

"Are you disappointed? I was lucky, the bullet passed through my side. 'Tis bloody uncomfortable but far from life threatening. I've suffered worse."

"Too bad," Devon muttered, clutching the sheet tightly. "I demand you give me my clothes and put me ashore as you promised."

"Your clothes were ruined and I had them thrown overboard, but you'll be provided with others," Diablo replied, smiling guilelessly. "As for the other . . ." He shrugged expansively. "I fear I'm forced to break my promise. You'll remain with me for the time being."

"I should have known you'd not keep your word, you lying blackguard."

"Look, Devon—"

"I'll leave you two alone," Kyle interrupted, swallowing a knowing grin. "I've work to do. I'm glad you're feeling better, my lady." Then he was gone, thinking he wouldn't trade places with Diablo for a captain's share of the booty. The lass had a tongue sharp enough to slice a man to pieces and obviously wasn't afraid to use it.

Kyle chuckled all the way to the quarterdeck. Diablo had his hands full with the lass, and Kyle didn't envy him. Once the crew learned that Devon was to remain aboard, trouble was sure to follow. It had been some time since the lads had been ashore, and Devon was too great a temptation for men starved for female companionship. Kyle hoped they'd reach Nassau before all hell broke loose.

Alone with Diablo, Devon fumed in impotent rage. Raking long fingers through his raven locks and looking decidedly disgruntled, Diablo said, "I'd strongly advise, my lady, that you act with caution where I'm concerned. You're in no position to make demands. Insulting me or my men will gain you damn little. You've already tasted a sample of Akbar's justice and should thank God that I survived your attack."

"Akbar! Is that the name of the barbarian who threw me in the hold? I expect no less from bloodthirsty scavengers," Devon flung out. "You should know that both my father and my fiancé will follow you to the ends of the earth. No one will rejoice more than me when you're finally swinging from the gallows."

"Ah, my lady, you wound me grievously," Diablo taunted, clutching his heart in mock pain. "And as enjoyable as sparring with you is, I have a ship to run. I'll see that food, water, and clothes are brought to you, but I wouldn't leave this cabin if I were you. My men are a rough lot who haven't had a woman in some time."

After delivering that thinly veiled threat, he sketched a rather clumsy bow due to the painful throbbing of his head, smiled beguilingly, and left the cabin.

Staring at the closed door, Devon was puzzled by the strange attraction that existed between her and the pirate. Deep in her heart she sensed that he wouldn't harm her and knew it was in her best interest to remain inside the cabin. Devon hadn't the slightest doubt that Diablo could be as ruthless and cunning as his name implied. Nonetheless, she experienced an odd lack of fear.

What would happen to her? Devon wondered dismally. Would she ever see her father or Winston again? She knew her father would move heaven and earth to find her and assumed Winston felt the same. Even now they could be aboard the *Larkspur* searching the ocean for her. That thought brought a measure of comfort to her.

A short time later a grizzled pirate limped into the cabin on a crudely carved wooden leg carrying a tray of food and drink. Famished, Devon ate and drank ravenously of the dismal fare as if it were the finest feast. She had just downed the last morsel when a trunk arrived filled with expensively fashioned women's clothing, and Devon spent considerable time sorting through the attractive array of garments. Vaguely she wondered what had become of the lady who owned the clothes, but the thought was so distressing she quickly put it from her mind.

Finally making her selection, Devon donned a modest gray daygown, the plainest of the lot. She had no wish to incite the lust of Diablo or his crew in any way. She wanted to be a little gray mouse unworthy of attention. She failed miserably. The fine silk gown molded her young curves to perfection. The high neck served to emphasize the bold thrust of her breasts, define the slim turn of waist, and outline gently swelling hips. White silk stockings, ruffled garters, and low-heeled slippers completed the demure outfit.

Next Devon attacked the tangle of golden curls swirling about her waist with a brush she found in the chest. She brushed until the heavy mass flowed down her shoulders and back in brilliant, silken waves. Then she explored the cabin, discovering, much to her relief, a chamberpot, and little else. Then she sat down to wait, pondering her fate and attempting to analyze the man known as Diablo.

After a time Devon grew bored and gingerly approached the door. Testing the knob, she found that it opened easily beneath her hand. Her first instinct was to rush headlong from the cabin, but Diablo's warning came back to haunt her. Yet the urge to examine her surroundings and learn exactly what she was pitted against was too great a force within her. Gingerly she eased open the door, noting that the stern cabin opened directly onto the main deck. She stood poised uncertainly in the doorway for several long minutes, blinking in the bright sunlight.

From all quarters Devon noted signs of vigorous activity. One group of men worked on the mainmast, which had been snapped in two, while others sewed on the huge sail laid out on deck. Still more men scurried back and forth engaged in various duties of repairing their ship. Neither Kyle nor Akbar were anywhere in sight, but Devon soon located Diablo standing on the bridge overseeing the progress. His hands braced on the rail, he bent to call something to one of his crew, and Devon's eyes roamed appreciatively over the muscles bunched beneath his white, open-necked shirt.

Why would a man like Diablo turn to piracy? Devon wondered, her eyes lingering on his face fringed with thick black hair. He looked quite ferocious with the luxurious growth, and Devon couldn't help thinking that he would be outrageously handsome without the beard, though with it he was still devilishly attractive. Bold, strong, stubborn, arrogant. Each of those words could be used to describe Diablo's unique features. Add to those, ruthless, demanding, and cruel.

Intuitively Devon realized it would be folly to venture forth among these rapacious pirates—men who respected nothing and no one. Greed ruled them and lust drove them. Devon silently turned to make a hasty retreat, but fate intervened.

"Ho, lads, 'tis Diablo's whore!"

Suddenly one of the pirates loomed before Devon, blocking her path. "Old Pegleg weren't lyin' when he said she be a beauty."

The man was short, stocky, and incredibly dirty. He wore an eyepatch over his left eye, and what was left of his hair clung to his neck in dirty limp strands. He grinned at Devon as if he could eat her up in one gobble as he reached out to fondle a blonde curl.

"Don't touch me, you cur!" Devon spat, wishing she had listened to Diablo and remained safely hidden.

"Yer too ugly fer the likes o' that fancy piece, Patch," one of the bystanders taunted crudely. "She's the cap'n's private whore."

"Ain't we always shared alike on the *Devil Dancer,* Davy?" Patch replied, impaling Devon with his good eye. "How can the cap'n object if we vote to pass the wench around?"

All work stopped as dozens of pairs of eyes swiveled to where Devon stood quivering like a cornered doe. She squealed in protest when Patch seized her around the waist and dragged her into full view. Her pounding fists had little effect on Patch's massive chest, her feeble protests earning her a cuff to the head that sent her reeling. Several of the men looked nervously toward Diablo, who had yet to notice the commotion for he had left the bridge to inspect the work being done on the rudder.

"Me first," Patch said, claiming Devon and swinging her high in his arms as he carried her to where the sail lay spread out on the deck. Suddenly Devon found herself flat on her back with Patch crouching above her.

Finding courage in the intensity of her anger, Devon scrambled to her knees while Patch paused to unfasten his clothing. From the corner of her eye she saw Diablo turn around, finally aware of the ruckus, and she knew instinctively that her salvation lay with him. He was a pirate, true, but she sensed no threat in him as she did in these other desperate men who would cruelly rape her. She watched expectantly as Diablo approached the circle of men surrounding her, at the same time keeping a wary eye on Patch who at that moment lunged for her.

Rising to her feet, Devon reacted instinctively, aiming a well-placed kick at Patch's privates. The man reared back, howling in pain, and Devon took to her heels, scrambling through the stunned crowd while screaming Diablo's name at the top of her lungs. Patch was still bending over clutching his groin when Devon reached the safety of Diablo's open arms. As his arms closed protectively around her, she was amazed at her sudden lack of fear.

"What are you doing out here?" Diablo asked, jerking Devon around to face him. "You foolish child! Didn't I warn you what would happen if you showed yourself on deck?"

"I . . . I thought . . ." Devon stammered, quailing beneath Diablo's hard glare.

Giving her a little shake, Diablo placed Devon behind him, then turned to confront Patch, who hadn't yet recovered from Devon's vicious blow. "What do you mean by this, Patch? Didn't you hear me claim the lady for myself?"

"I heard, Diablo, but it ain't fair," Patch complained bitterly. Several of the crewmen nodded in agreement. "Ain't none of us had a woman since them two French whores we took off that French sloop near Barbados. Why're ya bein' so damn selfish when ya never cared before?"

"I don't need to explain myself," Diablo bit out. "You signed the articles. You know the rules. The crew get their share of the booty after the captain and officers take their cut."

"Women ain't included," grumbled Patch sourly, appealing to his mates for support. "What say you, Davy, Leech, Snake? How about it, lads?"

The men named shifted nervously from foot to foot. Though they wanted to agree with Patch, they feared Diablo and his ferocious Turk too much to side publicly with him.

"It looks like this is between you and me, Patch," Diablo said with quiet menace. "The woman is mine. Do you want to challenge me for her? I've already offered to split my share of the booty with the crew to compensate for the loss of the wench, but I'm ready and willing to defend my exclusive right to her."

Patch seemed to have second thoughts about confronting Diablo. The captain was a powerful and cunning man, a fierce fighter and superb leader, fair and protective of his men. Yet he could be a harsh disciplinarian when the need arose. Under his able command they had taken many prizes and shared equally in the booty. Patch knew when he should back off and prudently decided to bide his time. Diablo couldn't be with the wench every minute of the day and night, and he'd find her alone sooner or later. It didn't bother Patch in the slightest that once he'd finished with Devon he would be forced to kill her in order to keep her from talking.

"Keep the wench, Diablo, and use her in good health," Patch said at length. "Your share of the booty will buy me more wenches in Nassau than I can handle." Abruptly he turned and swaggered away. The rest of the crew drifted back to their duties, the flurry of excitement ended before it really began.

Only Kyle and Akbar remained at Diablo's side, each positioning himself to reinforce their captain during the brief encounter. Had they been needed they would have fought staunchly beside Diablo.

"I knew the woman meant trouble," Akbar muttered, eying Devon balefully. It was apparent that the huge Turk had little use for women, finding them all unworthy of Diablo, whom he considered superior to any man alive.

"I should have locked her in," Diablo observed sourly. "I won't make that mistake again. Escort the lady to my cabin, Kyle, and lock the door." His silver gaze pierced Devon like twin blades of flashing steel.

Kyle nodded, grasped Devon's arm firmly, and half-led, half-carried her into Diablo's cabin. "You did a foolish thing, lass," he said, scowling. "You should have listened to Diablo. Locking you in is for your own protection."

Devon searched Kyle's attractive features carefully. Of all the men aboard the *Devil Dancer* he looked the least like a pirate. Tall and broad, red-haired and clean-shaven, he appeared more trustworthy than any of them, including Diablo. Surely such a man had some redeeming qualities, Devon reflected. The thought occured to her to appeal to him for help.

"Protection!" Devon scoffed derisively. "What kind of protection could I expect from a bloodthirsty scavenger?"

"You'd be surprised." Kyle smiled thinly. "You haven't been harmed yet despite the fact that you nearly killed Diablo. That alone should speak well for Diablo's intentions."

"Where am I being taken? Diablo promised to set me ashore."

"The storm blew us too far out to sea to make that possible, lass. You'll have to seek answers from Diablo." He turned to leave.

"Kyle—that is your name, isn't it?" Kyle halted, turned back to Devon, and nodded guardedly.

"Aye."

Devon licked her suddenly dry lips, hoping she hadn't misjudged Kyle's character. "Please, won't you help me? You know Diablo kidnapped me. Ask him to set me ashore anywhere and I can make my way back home. I'll see that you're handsomely compensated for your trouble."

"Ah, lass, I can't be bribed," Kyle said regretfully.

Devon looked so appealing he wished he could help her. But he'd not go against Diablo for anything. Though Diablo was a notorious pirate and could be ruthless and even cruel at times, few knew of the gentle side to the man. Kyle felt reasonably certain Devon would not be harmed.

"Then I'm wasting my time," Devon snapped waspishly. Deliberately she presented her delectable backside to Kyle. Grinning in obvious appreciation, Kyle left the cabin, locking the door according to Diablo's instructions.

Devon paced the cabin, venting her famous temper. Somehow she'd get out of this, she predicted, and when she did, Diablo would rue the day he set eyes on her. No matter where he took her, Winnie and her father would follow. When they caught up with that miserable blackguard, he would finally meet his destiny.

Chapter Four

An unappetizing meal was provided Devon later that day. Pegleg brought it in to her, then promptly left without uttering a word, locking the door behind him. When it grew dark, Devon lit a lamp and awaited Diablo's next move. She had no way of knowing he had decided to share Kyle's cabin, for he was still too angry with Devon to be in the same room with her. She had sorely tried his explosive temper, and he feared he would wring her pretty neck once they were alone. Finally Devon fell into an uneasy slumber, curled up fully dressed in the oversized bunk.

Immersed in a world of dreams, Devon did not hear the scrape of the lock or squeal of hinges as the cabin door was carefully inched open. The lamp Devon had lit earlier still burned, and Patch grinned evilly as his one good eye easily found her.

It had taken some doing to get the key to the

cabin, but Patch considered himself smarter than most of his fellow pirates. It just so happened he'd been standing nearby when Diablo entrusted the key to his cabin to Pegleg so that the one-legged sailor might bring food to Devon. Because Pegleg was an old man, Diablo trusted him not to molest his property. Patch couldn't believe his ears when he heard Diablo tell Pegleg he was sharing Kyle's quarters tonight. That evening, Patch had only to invite Pegleg to share a bottle of rum he had stashed away and purloin the key when the old sailor was too drunk to notice.

Patch waited until everyone was sleeping. He was more than a little contemptuous of Diablo's sleeping arrangements. Perhaps his captain's wound prevented him from enjoying the woman as fully as he might wish, Patch theorized, and he preferred to wait to bed her.

Patch eased inside the cabin, silently closing the door behind him as he drew the dirty scarf from around his neck. He planned to stuff it in Devon's mouth to keep her from crying out. His steps carried him to the bunk, where he paused to admire the entrancing sight.

Devon stirred uneasily. Something disturbed her slumber. Something menacing. Had Diablo finally returned to punish her for disobeying him? she wondered groggily. Slowly she opened her eyes and caught sight of the filthy one-eyed man looming above her. She opened her mouth to scream.

Diablo awakened with a start. He tried to rise, clutched his wounded side, then fell back against the pillow. Several agonizing minutes passed before he gathered the strength to lever himself to his feet. A ray of errant moonlight fell on Kyle's sleeping form. Nothing amiss here, Diablo mused, wondering what had roused him from a deep sleep. Then he remembered. Somewhere from inside his head came a silent plea for help. Devon! Was he so attuned to the little wildcat that he knew the moment danger stalked her?

Arming himself with cutlass and pistol, Diablo stealthily made his way along the moon-drenched deck to the stern, speaking briefly to the watch, who assured him all was well. He thought to return to his rest when he stumbled upon Pegleg lolling in a drunken stupor. At first he thought nothing of it. Then a terrible premonition seized him. With the agility of a jungle cat, Diablo whirled, moving lightly on the balls of his feet toward his cabin. His heart thumped wildly inside his chest and every instinct screamed of danger.

Diablo opened the door, then roared in outrage when he saw Patch reaching down toward Devon. Her eyes were wide and staring, her mouth gaping open in a silent scream.

"Touch her and you're dead," Diablo said with quiet menace, brandishing his cutlass in a widening arc. "It seems I arrived in the nick of time."

Patch spit out a stream of obscenities, cursing the fates that brought Diablo to Devon's rescue. He thought the man well named, for something more than luck had brought him here at this moment. Had Diablo indeed sold his soul to the devil as everyone claimed? Sliding Devon a look of intense longing, Patch stepped away from the bunk, ruing the day he ever sailed on the *Devil Dancer*. This wasn't the first time he'd clashed with Diablo nor would it be the last. Only the next time he'd win.

"I weren't gonna hurt her none, Diablo," Patch

whined obsequiously. "You shoulda shared the wench like always."

"You know the rules, Patch, and the punishment. Akbar!" he called out, knowing the huge Turk would be nearby, waiting for his call. Little happened on the ship without Akbar's knowledge.

Sure enough, within minutes Akbar stepped inside the cabin, a cutlass dangling from his fingertips. "I am here, Diablo." Not a muscle in Akbar's stern face revealed his thoughts as he stared forbiddingly at Patch, then shifted his disapproving gaze to Devon.

"Throw this scum in the hold. The first order of business tomorrow morning will be to administer punishment. Twenty lashes should suffice."

"Aye," Akbar agreed, herding Patch toward the door. When Patch hung back, a prick of Akbar's cutlass sped him onward.

Seventy curious men milled about on deck when Patch and Akbar appeared. Though those closest strained their necks to see inside the cabin, they found the door slammed firmly in their faces. But it soon became apparent what had happened and news spread through their ranks like wildfire. Patch had violated the rules and had earned himself a flogging.

"Did he hurt you?" Diablo asked Devon, his face set in grim lines. Though his stern visage did not relax, he approached the bunk slowly, fearful lest he frighten Devon more. But he needn't have worried, for Devon was made of sterner stuff than her fragile appearance suggested. She was more angry than frightened.

"That repulsive toad did me no harm." The shiver that swept over her slim frame belied her brave words.

Diablo swallowed a grin. He had to admit the feisty wench had courage—more courage than sense. Actually, he admired everything about her, and obviously so did his crew. In the future he would have to take precautions, even if it meant sleeping beside Devon each night, if only to protect her, torture though it might be.

"I think it's time I explained your position aboard the *Devil Dancer*, Lady Devon," Diablo began, stifling a chuckle as he imagined her response to his words.

"My—position?"

"Aye, so that there'll be no question in the future in the minds of my crew, or any misunderstanding between us concerning your place here. I made a mistake by leaving you alone tonight, but I won't do so again."

"Just what is my position, Diablo? You're aware, of course, that my father will pay handsomely for my safe return. Turn around and take me back home," Devon pleaded earnestly.

"There's my crew to think of, my lady. Seventy lives depend on how well we evade the English navy, as well as eluding other ships bent on our destruction. I was stupid enough to get caught once, but it won't happen again. I promise you'll be sent home when I find a way to do so without endangering our own lives. In the meantime you'll serve as my mistress."

Suddenly the need to touch Devon was so intense that Diablo couldn't resist the urge to reach out and lightly brush his fingertips across the high ridge of one cheek. Devon sucked in her breath, his caress tender yet erotically provocative. The look in his eyes told her he was aroused by her, and she fought against the sizzling attraction that quivered to life between them.

"You're crazy if you think I'll be your mistress," Devon snorted derisively. Her blue eyes blazed with defiance, and Diablo thought she never looked more adorable. Unconsciously she sent forth a heady blend of innocence and simmering passion, a volatile combination Diablo longed to savor.

"You have no choice in the matter, my lady." His voice was slow and lazy and subtly sensual.

Devon stared dumbly, fully aware that she should not succumb to the handsome rogue.

"I'll fight you every step of the way," she warned, her voice taut with a new kind of fear. Would he give her to his crew to enjoy if she defied him?

"We'll discuss it tomorrow, Devon," Diablo said wearily, surprising her. "Go to sleep, I'll not bother you tonight. My side aches abominably and I'm exhausted."

"Where will you sleep?" Panic colored her words.

"Right here beside you." Then he treated Devon to that beguiling smile that had the power to render her witless.

"I'll sleep on the floor," Devon demurred. She leaped off the bunk and began pulling the blanket from the bunk.

Diablo stayed her hand, drawing her roughly up against him. "You'll sleep in the bunk, beside me, even if I have to tie you down."

"You—wouldn't!"

"Try me, my lady. You've succeeded in wearing my patience thin. You know what I'm capable of, so I strongly suggest you leave off goading me."

Diablo meant only to frighten Devon, but she felt so damn good in his arms he yearned to kiss her, to taste the sweetness of her mouth, partake freely of everything she had to offer. A muffled protest died in her throat when his lips captured hers. The kiss was slow and lazy, and amazingly innocent. Something Diablo intended to remedy immediately.

"Open your mouth," he whispered against her lips.

Then his lips brushed over hers softly and he lifted her chin to deepen contact. She trembled, and some perverse imp inside her made her open her lips. His tongue slipped inside, touched hers. She quaked in his arms as they tightened about her, feeling the entire length of him molded to her softness. Something huge and hard pressed relentlessly against her belly.

Devon froze. Never had anyone kissed her in such a suggestive manner. Winnie would never presume to insult her in so demeaning a manner, but she expected no less from this son of Satan whose viselike embrace was squeezing the breath from her. Yet she could not deny her body's need to respond to his kiss with an answering heat. Then abruptly she found herself gently set aside. Stepping back, Diablo stared at her strangely, his thick black brows quirked quizzically.

"That was an amazing kiss for an innocent."

"You forced me!"

"If I were a gentleman, I'd agree. Unfortunately . . ." He shrugged with exaggerated eloquence, leaving Devon to draw her own conclusions. Then he calmly stretched out on the bunk, making room for her with overstated courtesy. Deliberately he closed his eyes, but Devon knew from the tenseness of his body that he was alert and waiting.

Gingerly she perched on the edge of the bunk,

eying Diablo warily. When he made no threatening move, she lay down, as close to the edge as she dared. Her body was as taut as a bow string, but gradually, when she realized Diablo offered no immediate threat, she relaxed, and at last drifted off to sleep. Diablo was not so lucky.

Lying beside Devon was sheer torture. Diablo had only to reach out and—no—not that way, he cautioned himself. One day soon he'd have Devon, but it wouldn't be rape. He wanted her—God, how he wanted her—willing and responsive. He figured he had plenty of time to wear down her resistance. On his island, in his home, there'd be no one for her to turn to but him.

Diablo realized that returning Devon to England at this time would be pure folly, for he assumed that by now her father and fiancé had the entire British navy combing the seas for her. And he damn well wasn't going to be caught again, or operate with the fleet breathing down his neck. Besides, the men had been at sea a long time and could use a spell in port, and the ship needed careening. There was plenty of booty to divide, so Diablo was reasonably certain the crew wouldn't grumble about being set ashore for a time.

Diablo groaned aloud when Devon turned in her sleep, seeking his warmth as she pressed full length against him. No matter how hard he tried, he couldn't prevent himself from slipping an arm under her head and drawing her into the curve of his body. With a will of its own his hand sought the soft rise of her breast. When she didn't awaken or protest, Diablo sighed, intensely grateful for that one small concession, and closed his eyes, finding surprising comfort in touching her.

* * *

Devon awoke with a start. Bright sunlight streamed through the two long windows and she blinked repeatedly. Her heart pounded with trepidation as she half-turned, expecting to find Diablo's lean length stretched out beside her. But to her immense relief he was gone. Nothing remained but the indentation where his head had lain on the pillow beside her.

Rising, Devon found water in the pitcher and washed thoroughly, keeping a wary eye on the door. She had just finished brushing her long blonde hair when Diablo returned bearing a tray. He looked freshly bathed and shaved and even more attractive than she remembered. His white shirt, festooned with yards of lace on the cuffs and down the front, was open at the neck and spotlessly clean. Tight black pants hugged muscular thighs, and left Devon no doubt concerning his masculinity. Curiously, he wasn't smiling that maddening smile she had become accustomed to.

"Eat, Devon, it's nearly time." He placed the tray on the desk and motioned her forward. Devon eyed the food with cool disdain, then turned her nose up at the unappetizing mess.

"Time? Time for what?"

"Have you forgotten so soon? The flogging, what else? Everyone aboard the *Devil Dancer* is required to be present at Patch's punishment."

"Flogging?" Devon repeated stupidly. "The custom is barbaric. Surely you don't expect me to watch."

"You're the reason the man is being flogged," Diablo reminded her. "The crew will expect you to be there. Besides, I fully intend to flaunt you as my mistress so in the future no one will doubt that you're mine."

"But I'm *not* yours!" Devon protested vigorously. "Nor will I ever be a man's possession."

"Oh, you will be mine, Devon." Diablo smiled ruthlessly. "Sooner than you think. Hurry, now, the crew is already gathering on deck."

Glaring at him murderously, Devon wolfed down her food without tasting it, then rose reluctantly to her feet. "I'm ready, but I'm not going to enjoy this."

As Devon moved toward the door, Diablo's critical silver gaze swept the entire length of her from head to toe. "Where did you find that drab dress?" Before she could form a reply, he ordered curtly, "Change it."

"Change it? But why? All the others are far more revealing."

"Just change it. I'll be back in five minutes." He stomped out the door without the courtesy of an explanation.

Fuming in impotent rage, Devon was grateful at least that Diablo allowed her to change in privacy. Rummaging through the chest of clothes put at her disposal, she chose an attractive gown fashioned of turquoise silk that shimmered with iridescent silver threads. The narrow waist pushed her breasts up until they threatened to spill out of the gown. Under different circumstances Devon would think nothing of wearing such a daring creation, but aboard this devil ship it seemed far from appropriate. Idly she wondered why Diablo insisted on such an ostentatious display. At the last minute she placed a lace scarf over her shoulders and felt somewhat reassured.

"That's much better," Diablo commented dryly when he reappeared moments later. His mouth quirked in amusement when he noted the concealing scarf, but he said nothing, allowing her that small concession.

Within minutes Devon found herself standing beside Diablo on the main deck of the *Devil Dancer*. Patch was already lashed to the whipping post, his back bared to receive the promised twenty lashes from the tarred rawhide whip nearly an inch thick. The crowd opened ranks, allowing Diablo and Devon to approach the condemned man. Evidently Akbar was to mete out the punishment for, naked to the waist, he stood over Patch, the rawhide whip held loosely in one huge hand.

"Oh, God," Devon gasped, pulling back. But Diablo was relentless.

"You started this, my lady, and you will see it to the finish. Begin, Akbar."

Flexing his enormous muscles, the giant Turk brought the first stroke whistling down on Patch's exposed back. The howl of agony that followed sent a chill down Devon's spine. The next strokes fell in quick succession, with no mercy, no respite allowed the screaming pirate. Patch made no visible effort to stifle his cries, and Devon's hands flew up to shield her ears. After ten strokes she could take no more.

"Stop! Please stop! You're killing him."

"He'll live, my lady," Diablo said tightly. "He'll live to think twice about flaunting my authority. Discipline is everything aboard a ship. If I relent now, my crew would no longer respect me and I'd find myself quickly replaced. Believe me, Devon, this is the only way. Continue, Akbar," he commanded, ignoring Devon's distress.

Patch's back looked like raw meat, and Devon felt herself grow weak with revulsion. Her knees buckled, and she was grateful for Diablo's support as he placed a strong arm around her, pulling her close. Otherwise she would have disgraced herself dreadfully by falling flat on her face.

"Steady, my lady," Diablo whispered as the whip rose and fell with relentless regularity. "'Tis nearly over."

Then it truly was over. Someone doused Patch's back with a bucket of salt water and he was half-carried, half-dragged to a place where Kyle could tend his wounds. Silently the crew melted away, leaving no man doubting that the lady belonged solely to Diablo and the devil would demand his dues from any unfortunate soul who coveted what Diablo considered his private property. It was exactly the response Diablo had hoped for.

Sickened by what she had witnessed, Devon did not object when Diablo turned her in the direction of his cabin. Only when the door was firmly closed behind them did she speak.

"That was the most heinous act I've ever seen!"

"Maintaining discipline is vital on my ship. You have no idea what these men are like or what they're capable of. Pirates are a breed apart. Some are deserters from the British navy; some were taken from crews of captured merchantmen and forced to join us, though a married man is never forced to join the brotherhood. They can be cruel, sadistic, and ruthless beyond your wildest imaginings.

"If I relented with Patch I would eventually lose control of my crew. I've worked too hard for my position to relinquish it at the whim of a woman."

"You say pirates are a breed apart," Devon challenged. "Where do you fit in? Are you a deserter? Were you captured and forced? From what country are you?"

"A long time ago I was forced," Diablo said, a faraway look in his eyes. "But later I embraced the profession freely and willingly. Does that answer your questions?"

"All accept for your nationality."

"I am from the sea." It was a stock answer given by pirates when asked where they were from.

"You're not uneducated and you speak well," Devon mused thoughtfully. "I suspect there's much you're not telling me. Why the mystery, Diablo? Your name is Spanish—have you been banished from your homeland or disinherited by your family?"

"Inquisitive little imp, aren't you?" Diablo chuckled. "Suffice it to say I do what I do because I enjoy the adventure—and the rewards." There was no mistaking his meaning, for his silver eyes sparkled with appreciation as they roamed freely over Devon's entrancing face and figure.

His look was so blatantly sensual, so charged with sexual innuendo that even an innocent like Devon reacted instinctively to the power of his personality. And she feared her reaction. Self-preservation forced her steps backward, only to have Diablo follow relentlessly.

"Don't touch me."

"You're my mistress, I can do as I please."

"I'm not your mistress. I have a fiancé. I'm to be married in a few weeks."

"Who is he, some aging earl willing to squander his fortune on you?"

"Not that it's any of your business, but he's young and a viscount. I don't need his money, I've plenty of my own."

"Only a viscount?" Diablo taunted, wagging a

shapely black brow. "Perhaps he's marrying you for *your* money."

"He loves me," Devon defended stoutly.

"Has he bedded you?"

Devon looked so startled that Diablo felt reasonably certain no man had ever touched her, including the virtuous fiancé.

"Does he kiss you?"

"Why—why, of course," sputtered Devon, by now totally confused. "Why are you asking me all these crude questions?" Devon definitely didn't like the way things were going. In fact, she hated the way her body responded to Diablo and his special magnetism.

"Does he kiss you like this?" Diablo took her in his arms, pressing tiny, teasing kisses on her mouth, eyes, and cheeks. Then he concentrated solely on her lips, his hand cupping the back of her head, tilting her face up to his mouth. He stopped long enough to whisper, "Or like this?"

This time his kiss was hard and deep and hungry. The fury of his kiss forced open her mouth and his tongue slipped inside, brazenly tasting her. Her eyes were closed, the trembling golden lashes poised upon her flushed cheeks like velvet butterfly wings. The shocking evidence of his arousal was like a rock between them, and panic seized Devon. Who did this odious pirate think she was? A woman of loose morals? She was Lady Devon Chatham, the daughter of an earl, educated, refined, and smart enough to know that she was on the brink of losing her precious virtue.

Suddenly she was free of those steel bands confining her, and her eyes blinked open. She was startled to find Diablo staring down at her with a smile that was arrestingly wicked. "You liked that, didn't you, Devon? I think you'll enjoy being my mistress. I know I will." His outrageous teasing sent her senses reeling, and she adroitly changed the subject.

"What about ransom? My father will pay you anything you ask for my safe return."

Breathlessly she awaited Diablo's answer, thinking that everything about the man was a contradiction. Not one blessed thing she'd ever heard about him made sense when one considered all that had happened since she'd had the misfortune to meet Diablo. Though she constantly provoked him, he hadn't harmed her. He could have easily brutalized her but had displayed amazing restraint. He might have done to her what men did to woman (she suspected what it might be but had no firsthand knowledge of it) yet had not ravished her except for a demanding kiss or two. He wanted her for his mistress yet appeared willing to give her time to adjust to his request.

"Nay, I want no ransom. I have riches enough."

"You promised to let me go," Devon reminded him, growing desperate.

"Aye, so I did." He smiled wolfishly. "Did you not know pirates were notorious liars? I've become quite taken with you, my lady. If I must spend time ashore I'd prefer to spend it with you. When I take to the sea again I'll see that you're returned to England."

"But not in the same condition in which you found me, I'll wager," Devon challenged.

His silver-gray eyes roamed her figure with wicked delight. "I'll do you no harm, if that's what you're worried about. But I mean to have your maidenhead, if it exists."

"You'd rape me?"

"I think not," he claimed with cool assurance.

Then he was kissing her again, his thick, wiry beard harsh against the tender skin of her face and neck. His lips moved restlessly over her eyes, cheeks, the end of her nose, before slanting hungrily over her mouth, the tip of his tongue probing along the line of her lips until they parted. He plundered ruthlessly the sweetness she sought to withhold, taking pleasure in the shudder passing through her slender form.

Traveling downward over Devon's tiny waist and generous hips, Diablo's big hands grasped the firm mounds of her buttocks, pulling her so close that hardly a breath remained between them. Desire was a hard knot inside him, and Diablo seriously doubted that he could withdraw without doing serious damage to his sanity. But he didn't want to rape Devon, or hurt her in any way no matter how badly he wanted her. He had all the time in the world to seduce her gently into his bed—she wasn't going anywhere but to Paradise, his very own island where his word was law. The thought of eventually having Devon warm, willing, and responsive beneath him was all the inducement needed to control his ardor.

"I have duties, my lady," he said, his breath rasping between his teeth. "You've won a reprieve for the time being. One day soon," he promised, his eyes turning to smoldering ash, "the devil will have his due."

Devon collapsed on the bunk the moment Diablo's virile form disappeared through the door. Evidently he still didn't trust her for she heard the scrape of the key turning in the lock. Or was it his mates he didn't trust? Either way, she was a prisoner on a devil's ship, the innocent pawn of a man who intended to use her well before discarding her. Never! Devon silently vowed.

Diablo was still smiling when he reached the quarterdeck, still aroused but glad he had decided against forcing the feisty little wench. Paradise was a beautiful island, highly conducive to seduction. Meanwhile, he'd work on Devon's senses, accustom her to his touch and slowly erode her fear and defiance.

"Don't you think you were a wee bit hard on the lass, Diablo?" Kyle asked. He had watched Diablo approach and did not miss the triumphant grin plastered across his face. "Forcing her to watch the flogging was cruel."

"The lady is tougher than you think, my friend," Diablo advised, eyes twinkling merrily. "Besides, it was necessary. You know as well as I how quickly the crew can turn against us. I can't afford to relax my guard. For the time being the men respect and trust me, and I want to keep it that way. Are the repairs completed?" he asked, changing the subject.

"Aye, Akbar is awaiting the order to raise the sails. I've set the course for the Bahamas."

"Nassau first, Kyle. We're to wait there for Le Vautour. When last we met he offered to sell our loot to the governor of New York in the American colonies. He and Le Vautour are great friends, and the Frenchman will get us a good price."

"Le Vautour—the vulture—can you trust that wily bird?" Kyle asked skeptically.

"As much as anyone in our profession," Diablo said with a shrug, though not really convinced. "I had hoped to visit the colonies myself to partake of their hospitality, but I think it unwise at this time, though it would be refreshing to visit a port and be welcomed with open arms."

"Aye," Kyle was quick to agree. "Boston and New York are renowned ports of call for pirates the world over. And when the brotherhood visits Philadelphia they act as if they own the place, and no one disputes their right. The American governors support us, give us provisions, crews, protection, and even hospitality."

"The colonies make a profit out of piracy, Kyle. They provide a market for our booty and sometimes give us fake sailing papers. For them, sheltering pirates is a blow against the British rule they abhor."

"The lass stays with you, I suppose," Kyle said dryly, once again bringing Devon into the conversation.

"I won't abandon her in a foreign land, if that's what you mean. I've decided to keep her as my mistress," Diablo revealed.

"Saints preserve us," Kyle muttered, shifting his eyes heavenward. "Are you daft, Kit? Isn't Scarlett enough for you? Why tempt the fates? There are beautiful women aplenty, both in Nassau and on Paradise."

"I've already decided, Kyle. No amount of argument will change my mind. Lady Devon intrigues me. I want her, dammit, and I'll have her! I've taken women captives to my bed often enough in the past, my friend, so why should one more bother you?"

"Tell me the lass is willing and I'll say no more."

Diablo had the grace to flush beneath his concealing beard. "She will be," he promised with male conceit.

Somehow Kyle doubted it. "What about Scarlett? You know how hot-tempered that she-devil can be."

"I'll handle Scarlett when the time comes. Say no

more. My mind is made up. For the time we're
ashore Lady Devon will be my mistress, and she'll
be willing." Suddenly a devilish gleam lit Diablo's
eyes. He always did enjoy a game. "I'll make you a
wager, my friend, seeing how interested you are in
the lady's fate. My share of the booty says the lady
will come to my bed willingly before we set foot on
Paradise. Either way, I promise she'll be sent home
unharmed when the *Devil Dancer* sails again."

"I accept," Kyle agreed, knowing the feisty lass
would lead Diablo a merry chase before she gave
in—if she gave in. "If I lose, my share is yours."

Chapter Five

Diablo returned to take supper with Devon that night. Lines of fatigue etched grooves around his mouth and he was definitely favoring his right side. A pang of remorse for the pain she had caused him sliced through Devon, but only for a moment. She considered it just punishment for the way he had ruthlessly kidnapped her.

Supper was a sorry affair, the food barely palatable. Diablo said little, staring at her in a disconcerting manner. Once he asked why her face appeared reddened and chafed, almost as if it had been bruised. She promptly replied that his wiry beard had damaged the tender skin, unaccustomed as it was to his rough use. At first Diablo seemed startled, then he turned thoughtful, occasionally fingering his luxurious growth as they ate.

Kyle arrived later to change Diablo's bandage. Devon busied herself with cleaning up the remains of their supper while Kyle worked over Diablo's torso. She wasn't certain she could trust herself to look objectively upon the smooth bronze skin stretched so tautly across the pirate's impressive frame. He was too tempting, entirely too virile and imposing to suit her.

Once his wound was dressed, Diablo left the cabin, and during the interval Devon hastily prepared for bed. She was about to crawl into the bunk fully dressed when Diablo returned. He took one look at her and said, "There are plenty of nightclothes in the chest I sent you."

"I—I'd rather not."

"I insist. You can't be comfortable like that." His silver eyes took on a predatory gleam as he opened the chest, lifting out a voluminous white garment made of linen and hardly conducive to seduction. "I'll help you."

"N—no! I can manage," Devon cried, snatching the gown from his fingers. "Turn around."

"I've seen you before and I must admit it only whet my appetite."

"Diablo, don't do this."

"Do what, my lady? Surely you must agree that I've been remarkably patient with you. I'd be laughed out of the brotherhood if it got out that I've yet to bed you."

"I won't tell anyone," she promised hopefully.

Diablo tilted his head back and laughed heartily. "Well said, my lady. Now get undressed so we can both get some sleep."

Surprisingly, he turned away, went to his own sea chest, and began assembling various paraphernalia. Hurriedly Devon pulled the gown over her head and stripped away the clothes underneath. When she finished she stood there uncertainly, still refusing to move to the bed.

"Get in bed," Diablo ordered tersely, aware of her every move though his back remained turned.

"I intend to put up a fight," Devon advised, lifting her chin defiantly. "I'll resist you every step of the way. Rape is the only way you'll have me."

Diablo sighed tiredly. "Get in bed, Devon, you're safe tonight."

Standing rigidly, Devon perched on the horns of a dilemma. If she wasn't so frightened of this handsome devil she would find humor in the situation. No, she corrected, she wasn't exactly frightened, merely intimidated by the aura of power surrounding him, and threatened by his virility.

Coming to a decision, Devon moved woodenly to the bed, sank down on its comfortable surface, and scooted as far to the opposite side as she dare. Diablo said nothing, just continued with what he was doing. Devon eyed him narrowly as he placed several pieces of equipment on the wash stand, turned up the lamp, and set to work. Dismay widened Devon's blue eyes when she realized what he was about.

"You're shaving!"

"Aye."

Totally absorbed, Devon watched in rapt fascination as more and more of Diablo's handsome face was revealed with each stroke of the razor. Firm, square jaw, full, sensual lips; his features spoke of power and ageless strength. What Devon thought most amazing was the way his mouth curled on the edge of laughter. But what really entranced her was the deep dimple hovering at the corner of that wide, mobile mouth. No wonder he wore a beard, was Devon's initial reaction, for without it no one would have believed that such a classically handsome face lurked beneath the beard of this fierce pirate whose very name inspired fear in the hearts of the bravest of men.

Only one word came to mind. "Why?"

"Because it pleases me," came his cryptic reply. "And I hope it pleases you as well. I'd not have your tender skin damaged on my account."

"Me? It matters little to me how you look, for it doesn't change what you are. Too bad you didn't slit your throat while you were at it."

Diablo shook his head, then burst out laughing. "You're priceless, Devon, truly priceless. I look forward to the day when I will know all the secrets your body possesses."

Before he snuffed out the light, Devon was treated to a fleeting glimpse of that devastating dimple in his cheek. Then she heard the rustle of clothes, and the bed sagged to accept his weight. When his warmth settled beside her, she started in spontaneous reaction.

"Lie still, Devon, and go to sleep."

Sleep! How could she sleep with Diablo's hard frame pressed so intimately against her? When he turned and pulled her into the curve of his body, she gulped convulsively and held her breath, preparing to do battle. But to her relief—or disappointment—he did no more than stroke the outer curve of her breast. Still, it was more than she was willing to allow.

"Don't touch me!" Inadvertently her elbow jabbed into his wounded side.

"Umph! Blast it, Devon, do I have to tie you down? That hurt."

"Good. Keep your hands to yourself."

"Hellion," he muttered, turning over. After making that stupid promise to Kyle, he hoped to slowly accustom Devon to his touch until she came to accept him naturally and willingly. He had hoped to create a need in her, one only he could assuage. But if tonight was any example, it looked as if he'd soon be parted from his share of the loot.

Devon sighed contentedly, serene and warm in her cozy nest. She felt safe, protected, and oh so comfortable. Something soft nuzzled her neck. Then a teasing, bristly sensation irritated the tender skin of her face. She frowned in her sleep but did not waken. Her breasts tingled, her long legs shifted restlessly beneath a caressing warmth she could not identify.

"Sweet, so sweet." The words, whispered in her ear, brought Devon fully awake.

Diablo was bending over her, covering her face and neck with teasing, nipping kisses. His hands, those large, rough hands, were under her nightrail, exploring the smooth texture of her flesh . . . her belly, her legs, tracing a hipbone with one calloused finger, tenderly fondling her swelling breasts. Then she felt a rush of air as her gown was raised and Diablo bent his dark head to touch his tongue to her aching nipples. He groaned once, then took the pouting bud into his mouth and began suckling with ever increasing vigor.

Devon's body jolted with the shock of it. "Stop it!"

"Ah, you're a ripe piece, sweetheart. See how your body responds to me? Let me make love to you. Let me teach you to enjoy all I can do for you."

"I want nothing to do with you or your kind," Devon resisted. The urge to lie back and let Diablo impose his will on her was so great she had to bite her lip to keep her sanity intact. "I'll never submit to you willingly."

"And I'll have you no other way," Diablo muttered beneath his breath, levering himself from the bunk. "It's growing late and I've a ship to run. I'll return later to take you for a stroll on deck." He flashed her a grin before rising in all his naked glory, unashamedly displaying the need she created in him.

Before she turned away from the entrancing sight, Devon caught a glimpse of long-muscled legs, firm-fleshed buttocks, slim waist, and impossibly wide shoulders. A flush crept up her neck when she tried to concentrate on anything but the virile length of that part of him she tried so hard to ignore.

It amazed Devon that she hadn't thought of Winston or their marriage in days. Not since Diablo came into her life like a swirling whirlwind to scatter her wits. What was the matter with her? she chided herself.

"Come along, my lady, the sun will do you good."

Diablo grasped Devon's waist firmly and guided her out the door onto the sun-drenched deck. It was a glorious day, and the crew scurried about their chores stripped to the waist, their bronzed torsos glistening with sweat. A few followed the slow progress of Diablo and Devon along the deck, but most, recalling Patch's fate, kept their gaze carefully averted, at least while Diablo guarded his mistress so zealously.

"You look radiant today, my lady," Diablo complimented as he eyed her choice of apparel.

Devon had chosen an attractive blue day dress, its deep oval neckline and sleeves lavishly embellished with lace. It hugged her supple curves to perfection, bringing attention to her tall, lissome form. She chose to ignore his compliment, pretending fascination in the ship.

Noting her keen interest, Diablo said, "She's a sloop, Devon. See her rapierlike bowsprit? She's fore and aft rigged, swift and nimble," he pointed out proudly. "She weighs one hundred tons and can do eleven knots under favorable winds. She carries a crew of seventy-five, fourteen cannon, and four swivel guns. Her shallow draft—less than eight feet—allows her to navigate shoal waters and hide in remote coves when necessary. Damn handy when being pursued. She also maneuvers well in channels and sounds."

Though Devon knew little about ships, she found herself listening raptly to Diablo's description, captivated by the deep timbre of his voice. "Have you always been her captain?" she dared to ask, intrigued by the man and the life he had chosen.

"Nay," he answered quickly enough. "She belonged to Black Bart and was called the *Marauder*, but I renamed her when I took over."

"What happened to Black Bart?"

"A mutiny, my lady. Needless to say, he no longer has need of his ship."

Wisely, Devon did not pursue the subject. Instead, she asked, "How did you come to be captured by the English, away from your ship and crew?"

"Curious, aren't you? But I see no harm in telling you. I was betrayed." His eyes turned murky, causing a shudder to ripple through Devon's body.

"Betrayed? By whom? Why?" It seemed highly unlikely that anyone would dare betray him.

Diablo stared out across the sparkling blue water,

his eyes shuttered. "If it takes the rest of my life I'll learn the man's name, and his reason. He'll never find me so careless again.

"We were hidden in a cove at a remote spot along the Cornish coast. Our hold was filled with French brandy and I was to meet our contact, a man I would trust with my life. I took but six men ashore with me in a longboat, and we had no sooner stepped on dry land than we were set upon by a company of dragoons. It was a trap. Kyle saw what was happening from the bridge of the *Devil Dancer* and immediately took her out to sea. He was following my standing orders in such a situation, to retreat with the loot and ship intact. Thus only a few men and I were carted back to London and tried for piracy. I later learned my message to Cormac had been intercepted and he knew nothing about our meeting. Luckily I used a code name and the authorities never learned who serves as our contact in the area."

"Whoever betrayed you must hate you," Devon observed.

"A pirate makes countless enemies, for reasons that need no explanations. Come along, sweetheart, it's time to take you back."

But Devon was reluctant to return to her dreary prison. "What made you turn to piracy?"

Abruptly Diablo's good humor vanished. "That, my lady, is none of your business. Shall we go?" He tightened his hand on her arm, unaware he was causing her pain until she cried out in distress. Only then did his expression lighten and his grip relax. "God's bones, sweetheart, my background would bore you."

Somehow Devon doubted it. The man was an enigma. A dark, unfathomable mystery that defied logic. Devil or man? Gentleman or rogue? Killer? Devon sensed that the answer lay in his dim past. Who was Diablo really? What terrible event in his shrouded background had turned him to piracy?

The days passed with surprising regularity. Though Devon felt in no way threatened by Diablo's absolute authority, she feared the erotic power he held over her senses. Each night he undressed and climbed into bed with her as if it were the most natural thing in the world. He still continued to caress, fondle, and kiss her, but made no further assault upon her virginity. She held on to the hope that she might still go to the altar as Winston's virgin bride. If she had overheard the conversation between Diablo and Kyle after Diablo had shaved his beard she would have revised her thinking.

"Dear Blessed Mother!" Kyle exclaimed, dismay coloring his words. "What happened? Did the lass snatch your chin bald?"

"I shaved," shrugged Diablo. "'Tis time."

"You *are* smitten with the lass, aren't you?"

"Nay," the devil denied. "'Tis only that I'm not overly anxious to part with my share of the booty." His eyes sparkled wickedly, belying his rather simple explanation.

"Have you won then, Kit? Do I lose my share?"

"Nay, your booty is safe—for the time being. But soon, lad, soon."

"The game has just begun, Diablo, I'm still wagering on the lass."

"The prize will be mine," Diablo predicted arrogantly.

* * *

Devon was standing on deck with Diablo when the first of the Bahamas came into view. The islands were like a bracelet of shining jewels set in a background of dazzling turquoise. Devon was enchanted with their clear sparkling water, coral reefs swarming with hundreds of varieties of fish, and white sand beaches.

"A brigand community thrives in Nassau on New Providence Island. Over a thousand pirates dwell there now," Diablo informed her.

"Are there no settlers?" Devon asked.

"No more than four to five hundred families, and they give us no trouble. The snug harbor is perfect for our needs. Too shallow for large men-of-war, but deep enough for the shallow draft craft favored by buccaneers. And the high coral hills afford a hawk's-eye view of approaching enemy or potential prizes."

He told her that the reefs abounded with conch, fish, and lobster. Fruit and vegetables grew in abundance, and fresh-water springs were plentiful. There were also wild pigs and pigeons to feast upon. The Bahamas provided a refuge perfect in every way.

"What about the governor?" Devon asked dubiously. "What does *he* think of the Bahamas being a pirate's haven?"

"All the governors have welcomed us," laughed Diablo, "and shared in the booty. We'll stay in Nassau but a short time before continuing on to Paradise."

"Paradise?"

"Aye, a small, secluded island where I built a house and live when not prowling the seas. Few know of it in this maze of islands and keys, but I have everything there I need. Some of the men keep women on the island, and there are even a few children."

Devon wondered if any of the children belonged to Diablo but thought it better not to ask. Shortly afterwards she was escorted back to the cabin and had to content herself with watching the proceedings from the long stern windows of Diablo's quarters. It was late afternoon when Diablo entered the cabin and advised Devon to pack a bag. At dusk they were rowed ashore.

"Where are we going?"

"I'm meeting someone in Nassau. We'll stay at the Wheel of Fortune Inn until he arrives."

Devon grew excited. An inn meant people, and perhaps someone willing to help her escape this devil's lair. Soon the longboat bumped against the shore, and Diablo lifted Devon out with a flourish, setting her on her feet at the water's edge. Devon surveyed her surroundings, and was shocked by what she saw.

A steamy tent town festered the white sand beach and coral outcroppings near the harbor. Hardly a permanent building existed anywhere, except for taverns where pirates drank and fought. As she and Diablo picked their way through the tent city, Devon saw men lolling inside with prostitutes, some coupling openly on the ground. Others gathered outside the tattered sail tents gambling away fortunes. Devon had no way of knowing, but Nassau supported the greatest concentration of pirates in the New World. Besides the thousand living on the island, at least another thousand lived aboard ships scattered throughout the harbor. It was a pirate's paradise, with no laws except that of fist and cutlass.

"Not a pretty sight," Diablo admitted, gesturing

at the shantytown and the lawless men inhabiting it. "Perhaps I should have left you aboard the *Devil Dancer*, but I wanted you where I can keep an eye on you. Once it's known you're my woman you won't be bothered. Even pirates have a code of honor they respect."

"I'm not your woman!" Devon denied hotly. "Nor will I ever be."

"The subject is debatable," Diablo said and grinned, flashing the dimple previously hidden by his beard. "For your own sake I suggest you act like my mistress. We'll work out the details later."

Devon was forming a scathing reply when Diablo halted before a rambling wooden structure a short distance from the harbor. A wooden sign hanging askew proclaimed it to be the Wheel of Fortune Inn.

"We're here," Diablo said, guiding Devon inside.

Devon halted abruptly just inside the door, certain she had stepped through the gates of hell. Only Diablo's arm about her waist kept her from turning and fleeing.

The huge common room exploded with people—mostly men. Men of all sizes, descriptions, and shapes. Tall, short, fat, thin, young, old. Most were ugly, grotesque even, but a few could be called pleasant looking. None were ordinary. They wore an odd assortment of clothes, mostly dirty and ragged, some colorful. They wore enough weapons collectively to outfit an army.

"Ho, look yonder, lads," a man brandishing a tankard of ale called out. "See what the wind blew in. If me old eyes ain't deceivin' me, 'tis the devil himself."

"Aye, and the devil's lady," added another. "Who's the wench, Diablo? Last we heard ye was waitin' ta git yer neck stretched. Thought we seen the last o' ya. Ye look a mite naked without yer beard."

"Greetings, lads!" hailed Diablo. "As you can see, death holds no fear for the devil. He'll not meet destiny till he's good and ready." At that remark cheers erupted in the crowded room. "As for the beard, I'm prettier without it, don't you agree?" His words brought forth a ripple of laughter.

"The wench, Diablo! Who's the wench?"

"I'll tell you this much, lads, she's mine and none's to touch her or they'll have me to deal with."

"To the devil's lady," toasted one of the pirates, raising his tankard in salute.

"Aye," echoed the combined assemblage. "To the devil's lady! May she melt the devil's heart!"

There wasn't one among the motley group of the most despised men in the world that didn't envy Diablo his beautiful prize. Nor was there a prostitute in the room who didn't envy the lady, for not a man on the island could compare with Diablo.

Devon was in a virtual state of shock. The multitude of armed, vicious-looking men and painted, gaudily dressed women assaulted much more than her senses. How in the world was she to find someone to help her escape in this assortment of scum? They were the dregs of humanity, men and women unfit to mingle with polite society. A wail of despair left Devon's trembling lips.

Alerted by her cry, Diablo tightened his arm around Devon's quaking shoulders. "Don't fret, my lady, no one will harm you while you're with me. Besides, we'll only be here until Le Vautour shows up."

"Those men, they're looking at me as if—as if—" Her words faltered, unable to describe the way the pirates' lustful, hungry eyes made her feel.

"Can you blame them? You're a damn beautiful woman."

While Devon stood frozen by her surroundings, Diablo had bespoken a room and was now guiding her up the stairs. The room assigned them was pleasant enough with large windows affording a magnificent view of the harbor. The furnishings were spartan but sufficient; the curtains and counterpane covering the bed somewhat ragged but reasonably clean. Devon supposed pirates weren't overly fussy, and she wondered what the bed linens looked like.

"I'll leave you now, Devon," Diablo said, interrupting her silent inspection of their quarters. "We'll have supper when I return. I think you're smart enough to know now not to leave the room, but for your own safety, lock the door behind me. I'll have a bath sent up."

Devon thoroughly enjoyed the bath, donning a lightweight linen frock suitable for the hot weather, which she found oppressive compared to England's cool, damp climate. She vigorously brushed her long blonde tresses until they glistened like silk, then tied it all back with a ribbon at her nape, opting for coolness instead of style. Then she sat down to wait for Diablo.

He returned shortly, followed by a pair of servants who carried in a tub of bath water and removed her dirty water. The moment they left, Devon realized that Diablo meant to bathe while she was in the room.

"Surely you don't mean for us to share this room," she said with cool disdain.

"Did you see anyone downstairs you'd prefer to share it with, my lady?" Diablo mocked, quirking a dark brow. With a deft motion he peeled off his white silk shirt. Flashing Devon an infuriating grin, he moved his fingers to the fastenings on his trousers.

"Wait! I—it's not decent."

"We've shared the same room for weeks, Devon, so why the sudden burst of shyness now? Soon we'll be as close as two people of the opposite sex can be." There was no mistaking his meaning.

"Why waste time on someone who doesn't want you?" Devon challenged. "Surely there are women in Nassau more willing than I to bed you."

"Undoubtedly," Diablo agreed amiably as he sat to remove his boots. "But a blue-eyed blonde has captured my fancy and none other will do." First one boot and then the other hit the floor. Then he stood to strip the final piece of clothing from his splendid form. "You can scrub my back, sweetheart."

"When hell freezes over!"

Deliberately Devon turned her back on Diablo's blatant display of pure masculine virility. His deep chuckle brought a flush of anger to her cheeks. She suffered through the humiliating experience of Diablo's bath with as much aplomb as she could muster, staring out the window while her mind tried to block out thoughts of his nude body.

"You can turn around now, sweetheart, I'm dressed." His voice held a hint of laughter. "I'm starving. This place isn't much, but the food is excellent."

Devon couldn't help but admire Diablo's figure resplendent in tight black pants and ruffled white shirt. Wide-top black boots and red sash added dash to the outfit. A black coat and a cutlass at the waist made him the most imposing man Devon had ever had the misfortune to meet. With his beard gone, he didn't look quite so ferocious, and she was struck anew by the mystery surrounding him.

He led her downstairs to a small table in the common room where the dinner he had ordered was being served. Just as Diablo predicted, the food was delicious, many of the dishes containing unrecognizable ingredients. The array of fruits stunned Devon, and she wasn't satisfied until she sampled them all, much to Diablo's delight.

The Wheel of Fortune Inn was even more crowded and boisterous than earlier in the day when she arrived, and Devon hated the way the drinking, carousing men stared at her. She wondered how Diablo, a man of obvious refinement, could tolerate living amongst men who behaved like animals. She watched warily as two more pirates staggered through the door, dressed in an odd assortment of clothes and armed to the teeth. One of them spotted Diablo and nudged the other. Then both headed directly for their table. Devon nearly choked on a large bite of fish when they halted before them.

"I knew they wouldn't hang ye with that big Turk lookin' out for ye," the shorter of the two said in greeting. "Ye surely are a sight for sore eyes, Diablo. What happened to yer hair?" One dirty finger pointed at Diablo's smooth chin. "Ye always were a handsome devil, but now ye're even prettier."

"Annie! Where in the hell did you blow in from? Is Calico Jack here, too?"

Annie! Surely she misunderstood, Devon thought. The pirate couldn't be a woman! But amazingly, it was true. A closer inspection revealed the outline of breasts beneath the wrinkled shirt, and rounded feminine hips nearly concealed by baggy pants.

"Aye," Annie said with a grin, "Jack be here. We arrived just today after sellin' our booty in the American colonies. Did ye know Mary is sailin' with us now?" Annie eyed Devon with interest but said nothing.

"Good to see you again, Mary," Diablo greeted the second pirate.

Though she tried, Devon couldn't disguise the look of amazement crossing her features. Two women pirates! And Diablo treated them as if lady pirates were a common occurrence instead of a rarity.

"I hardly recognized ye, Diablo," Mary smiled, revealing a mouthful of yellowed teeth. "Who's the wench? Is she the reason ye shaved yer beard?"

"Methinks my lady prefers me clean-shaven." His glance slid to Devon, who looked on the verge of apoplexy. "Sweetheart, meet Anne Bonny and Mary Reed, they sail with Calico Jack. Ladies, this is Lady Devon Chatham, my—er—companion." Devon merely nodded in acknowledgment, too stunned to speak.

"Lady, ha!" snorted Anne, a notorious pirate with a price on her head. "What would a lady be doin' with the likes o' you?"

Mary Reed apparently found that remark hilarious, for she burst into raucous laughter. "Aye," she heartily agreed, "yer doxy might look like a lady and have a fancy name, but she still earns her keep on her back. She's a rare beauty, though. I'll wager plenty have offered to take her off yer hands when ye tire of her."

By now Devon was over her shock, and the women's crude remarks left her seething with anger. "Doxy!" she sputtered, ready to explode. "I'll have you know I'm—"

"There's Calico Jack," Anne said, rudely interrupting Devon and waving her hands wildly at the flamboyantly dressed pirate who had just entered the inn. "Take care o' yerself, Diablo, ye're far too vital to swing from a gibbet." She turned to leave.

"Aye," chimed in Mary, nodding at Devon as she joined her friend. Soon they were lost in the crowd.

Devon frowned, staring at their departing backs with growing dismay.

"What do you think of my friends," Diablo asked teasingly.

"They're crude, vulgar, and in no way resemble ladies," Devon answered without hesitation. "Whatever would possess a woman to take up piracy?"

"Who knows?" Diablo shrugged. "I strongly suspect they do it for much the same reason a man embraces the brotherhood: adventure, money, greed."

"Is that why you turned to piracy?"

Diablo grew silent, his face inscrutable. During his pensive introspection, disappointment, bitterness, and soul-wrenching loneliness fleetingly crossed his face. The expressions spoke eloquently of anguish he had endured and burdens he bore. Devon seriously doubted she would ever know what was in Diablo's heart, for he guarded it too zealously. Obviously he had no intention of answering her question, for he rose abruptly, bringing their meal to an end.

"I'll see you to your room, Devon. I'm needed

aboard the *Devil Dancer* this evening, but tomorrow I'll take you on a tour of the island."

Profound relief surged through Devon, elated that Diablo didn't intend to force himself on her tonight. True to his word, he left her at the door, admonishing her to keep it locked until he returned later tonight. Needless to say, Devon had no intention of venturing alone anywhere in Nassau. She seriously doubted that any of these lawless creatures would help her escape. She would be jumping from the frying pan into the fire by taking her chances with this disreputable lot.

It was very late when Diablo returned and awoke her to unlock the door. He did no more than undress and slide into bed beside her, rolling her into the curve of his body and falling immediately asleep. The next morning he was gone before she awoke.

Later that day he appeared to take Devon on a tour of the island. If one overlooked the shantytown on the beach and the hulls of rotting wrecks littering the harbor, the island was a beautiful, sun-drenched land with regal palms and brilliant flowers bowing gracefully beneath cooling sea breezes.

"How long will we stay here?" Devon asked absently.

"Until Le Vautour arrives. Shouldn't be too many days."

"Then what?"

"Then we sail to Paradise. Some of the crew will remain in Nassau, but those with women on Paradise will join me."

"Where is your island?" Devon dared to ask.

"Not far from here on one of the unnamed keys. The natural harbor is too shallow for men-of-war, and a coral reef surrounds it and protects us from unwanted visitors. Only those who know the way in can enter."

"Diablo, I'm begging you again, please let me go. You know I'll never willingly consent to become your mistress." While he was in a mellow mood, Devon had to try one more time to reach his conscience.

The deep dimple flashed in Diablo's cheek, warming her all over. She hated the way this man made her feel, despised the responsive chord that thrummed to life when he smiled at her so beguilingly. She had to get away before his persistence eroded her willpower to the point where she would agree to anything he suggested—even to becoming his mistress. And that must not happen. She belonged to Winston. No man had the right to take what rightfully belonged to her fiancé.

"Sweetheart," Diablo said, his voice low and strident, "I haven't forced you, nor harmed you in any way. But that's not to say I won't. You know what I am, what I'm capable of." He reached out to caress her cheek, his touch oddly tender in the light of what he had just threatened. "I've been remarkably patient, but I can't say how long I will continue to indulge you. Damn the bet, willing or not, I intend to bed you!"

"Bet? What bet?"

"It's not important, sweetheart." They had arrived back at the inn and Diablo saw her to their room. "We'll discuss this later tonight."

Devon primped before the mirror. She wore a becoming dress of shimmering blue-green silk that daringly bared her shoulders and the tops of her breasts. She'd brought only three dresses from the ship and this one hadn't been worn yet. Servants had just carried out her dirty bath water, and Devon turned to lock the door as Diablo had instructed, but before she could turn the key the door burst open with a resounding bang.

"Who in the hell are you?"

The woman who spoke had hair the color of living flame, long trouser-clad legs, and a face so breathtakingly beautiful that Devon could only stare in wonder. "Where's Diablo?" the woman asked, sweeping the room with eyes that resembled brilliant emeralds. They were hard and cold and utterly ruthless.

"He's not here," Devon replied warily.

"I was told this is Diablo's room," the redhead claimed, eying Devon with cool disdain. "Who are you and what are you doing here?"

"I—this is my room."

Suddenly comprehension dawned. "You're his whore! How dare Diablo bring a fancy woman here with him. That blackhearted devil! Next time he'll think twice before flaunting his new mistress before me. A bit of fluff like you can't possibly satisfy him. He needs a real woman like Scarlett Defoe."

"I assure you, Miss Defoe, I'm not Diablo's mistress."

"What are you doing in his room?"

Devon bit her lower lip in consternation. It did indeed look damning. "I had no choice. I'm Diablo's prisoner."

"His prisoner! Ha! Likely story," Scarlett snorted derisively. "The door was unlocked when I came in, and Diablo would hardly be that careless were you a prisoner. Who are you?"

"Lady Devon Chatham."

"English?"

"Aye."

"Well, my lady," she mocked, "I'm Diablo's woman. And I don't share my men. Pack your things and get out of here."

"But—"

"Now." With slow deliberation Scarlett drew the cutlass strapped to her slim waist, brandishing it in Devon's face.

"Believe me, Miss Defoe, you are more than welcome to Diablo. I want nothing to do with that devil."

"You're lying," Scarlett scoffed. "Women are always panting after Diablo. Why should you be any different?"

"Not this woman. I wish only to return home."

"Then do so, and hurry it up. Find yourself another protector. I'll wager you'll have little difficulty doing so. Leave Diablo to me."

Devon would have liked nothing better than to leave, but not this way. Not throw herself on the mercy of cutthroats and brigands. At least she knew what to expect with Diablo.

Not one to be intimidated, Devon ordered, "Get out of my room, Miss Defoe. I'll leave when I'm good and ready and not before."

Scarlett's full red lips turned down sourly and her green eyes flared with sudden anger. She stalked menacingly toward Devon, sleek hips and long shapely legs moving with feline grace. Tight black pants hugged her curves like a second skin, her green silk shirt gaping at the neck and showing the tops of full unfettered breasts. Angered, she was magnificent, and Devon was surprised that Diablo could even consider another woman with Scarlett willing—nay, eager—to bed him. As Scarlett advanced, Devon suddenly realized her danger. The woman was armed, vicious, and apparently intent on murder.

Scarlett Defoe was a product of the Paris slums who had clawed her way out of degradation and into the position of being considered one of those fearless breed of women pirates as ferocious as any man. She had started her career as a sailor's doxy, then was heartlessly sold to a smuggler. The smuggler's ship was attacked by pirates and Scarlett was claimed by the captain. During a later battle the pirate captain was killed, and Scarlett, supported by a group of followers, took over the ship, which she renamed the *Red Witch*. Soon the crew came to respect her courage and daring, and none disputed her right to become their captain.

When Scarlett met Diablo she experienced her first stirrings of love, aware that it was all one-sided but willing to take what little of himself he offered. They became lovers, meeting mostly on Nassau and less frequently on Paradise. Until now Scarlett had managed to maintain her tenuous hold on Diablo's affections by banishing the competition, employing whatever method necessary.

Seeing Devon standing before her cloaked in youthful innocence and beauty made Scarlett realize that her undisputed position as Diablo's woman was reaching its conclusion. Devon was everything Scarlett wanted to be but was not. Devon was young, lovely, and appeared to be a lady. Perhaps the biggest insult to Scarlett's senses was Devon's obvious innocence. She advanced on Devon with deadly deliberation, the tip of her cutlass pressed menacingly into the soft skin of Devon's white neck. A drop of blood appeared at the site of the tiny wound.

Too late Devon realized the danger Scarlett presented, and regretted so many things. Her life was about to end without her ever having experienced love and fulfillment.

Suddenly a tall figure loomed in the doorway, and Devon's mouth formed the silent word with a joy that shocked her. "Diablo."

Chapter Six

"What in the hell is going on here?"

Scarlett's green eyes narrowed, but the blade pressing against Devon's throat did not waver. "I'm going to dispose of your doxy."

"God's bones, Scarlett, are you daft? Release Devon at once!"

"Nay, Diablo, you can't bully me. I know why you've brought the wench here and I won't have it."

"You've nothing to say about it, Scarlett, we made no promises to one another," Diablo said with quiet emphasis. He knew well Scarlett's volatile temper and genuinely feared for Devon's life unless he was able to defuse the situation. If Scarlett harmed Devon in any way he'd kill the brazen bitch on the spot.

Undaunted, Scarlett flicked the blade tip to draw yet another drop of blood, bringing a gasp of pain to Devon's lips. That tiny red droplet drove Diablo to fury as he drew his own cutlass, slashing it upward until it came to rest at Scarlett's breast.

"Lay down your weapon, Scarlett, you'll not hurt Devon." There was a hard edge to his voice, a deceptive calm that often preceded violence, and Scarlett was astute enough to recognize it instantly. It was that very quality that inspired fear in the hearts of his enemies. She knew if she angered him excessively Diablo would skewer her without a moment's regret.

Scarlett decided that killing Devon wasn't worth dying over. Reluctantly she lowered her cutlass, her face a mask of rage.

"Who is the wench, Diablo, and what's she to you?"

"The lady's name is Devon Chatham. Her father is the Earl of Milford."

"She claims she's your prisoner, though we both know why you brought her here," Scarlett hinted slyly.

"Aye, I suppose you could say that."

Scarlett's fierce scowl eased somewhat. She could understand holding an heiress for ransom—she'd done it herself a time or two. "Have you bedded her?"

"That's none of your business. I've never asked who you've bedded. You could have slept with your entire crew for all I cared. Now get out of here before I forget the friendship that existed between us."

Scarlett whirled, eyes blazing green fire as they raked Devon insolently from head to toe. "Have joy of her then, Diablo, until her ransom arrives. But I seriously doubt the pale little thing will satisfy you for long. What we shared was more than mere friendship. You know where to find me when you have need of a real woman."

With deceptive calm she jammed her cutlass inside her sash, aimed a seductive smile at Diablo, and strolled from the room, hips swaying with tantalizing grace. Diablo slammed the door behind her, then turned to Devon, a frown worrying his wide brow.

"Sweetheart, are you all right? I'm sorry about Scarlett. I didn't know she was in Nassau."

With more gentleness than she thought possible, Diablo drew Devon's quaking form into his arms. Taking a spotless white handkerchief from his pocket, he dabbed tenderly at the drops of blood surrounding the small puncture on her throat caused by the prick of Scarlett's blade. Then, to Devon's shock, he gently laved the wound with the moist tip of his tongue. Devon drew her breath in sharply, his gesture highly erotic and totally unexpected.

Somehow finding her voice, she said, "Scarlett is your mistress." Why did it have to sound like an accusation rather than a question, Devon reflected, exasperated with herself for caring.

"Nay, sweetheart," Diablo denied. "She was merely someone to help fill my lonely hours ashore. We are two of a kind and understood one another."

Against her will Devon melted into Diablo's embrace, welcoming his comfort, accepting his protection. But when his tongue touched the sensitive skin of her throat it ignited a fire that burned its way into every part of her body. His lips naturally gravitated from that vulnerable spot upward to her mouth, slightly parted with dismay. Diablo accepted the invitation, slipping his tongue into the moist opening, tasting, exploring to his heart's content.

Emotionally drained, Devon swayed dangerously, and Diablo's arms tightened around her supple curves, his hands roaming with seductive slowness from waist to buttocks to breasts where he paused to savor those delightfully full mounds. Devon sighed, knowing she should resist, but with his touch too tantalized to care. Winston's tepid kisses and tame caresses were nothing compared to this man's touch.

"I want you, sweetheart." His raspy breath tickled her ear, sending a ripple of awareness through her tense body. "I've wanted you from the moment I laid eyes on you, so prim and proper, yet more beautiful than words can describe. If it wasn't for that damn bet . . ."

"Bet?" murmured Devon, the word reaching deep into her subconscious to snatch her back to reality. "What bet?"

"It's nothing, sweetheart, nothing to concern yourself over. Just concentrate on what I'm doing, how beautifully your body is responding to my touch." Deliberately his thumb drew circles through the cloth of her dress around her nipples, and when the buds tautened, he pulled gently at them with the tips of his fingers. The effect was devastating to both of them. "God's bones, Devon, let me love you. I want to be the man to lead you into womanhood."

Nothing in Devon's previous knowledge prepared her to deal with a man like Diablo whose wide experience made him irresistible to women. She directed a look filled with panic into his passion-glazed face, caught in the tingling enchantment of his passion. Though every nerve ending screamed for surrender, she resisted the need to give herself to Diablo. The man was a pirate, a thief, and a despoiler of women, no matter how handsome or desirable, and Devon could not forgive him for snatching her from her loved ones. By now her poor father must be distraught, not to mention Winston's anguish over her abduction.

"Nay, don't, Diablo. I know nothing of what you're talking about."

The smile in his eyes contained a sensual flame that sent a jolt of fire sizzling through her veins. "Let me teach you and I swear you'll enjoy it."

His monumental conceit succeeded only in destroying the euphoria she had experienced from the moment Diablo's lips and hands had claimed her. Shrugging free of his arms, she hissed, "I want nothing to do with you or your loving. Because of you I was nearly killed by that red-haired witch. Don't expect me to fall into your arms like all those loose women you're accustomed to."

"I knew from the moment I laid eyes on you that you were like no other woman I've ever known, sweetheart."

It was true, Diablo reflected soberly. She had fire and mettle and refinement and beauty. She was an arresting mixture of hoyden and lady, without the simpering dullness of so many well-bred young women. Throughout her ordeal she had defied him at every turn, well aware that he had absolute power over her. He sighed and plowed distracted fingers through his hair. No matter how courageous or defiant, he still wanted her. Unaccustomed to self-denial, Diablo felt that he was losing the tenuous hold on his senses. He would have to seduce her soon or lose his mind.

All restraint fled as Diablo reached for her,

dragging her back into his arms. Passion was thick and molten within him. His eyes slid over her lazily, his voice seductively sensual. "I want you, sweetheart. I promise I won't do anything you don't want me to do."

Devon stared at him with a desperate mixture of hope and disbelief. She knew she could not stop him if he decided to take her without her permission, but his words promised a chance, albeit a slim one, to prevent him from having his way.

"You mean it? You'll stop when I ask? You won't—hurt me?"

"Hurt you?" His voice assumed the same wickedness as his smile. "The last thing I want to do is hurt you. True, I want to hear you cry out—but in pleasure, not pain."

Then Devon felt his hands on the bodice of her dress, unfastening each tiny button with great expertise. When he brushed the material aside and tugged the ribbon holding together her chemise, a shudder, not entirely of fear, passed through her. Diablo sucked in his breath, awestruck. Her breasts, pale as alabaster, were crowned with impudent pink nipples, taut and wetly tempting to a man who had been starved for so long.

Reverently he touched one fleshy bud, smiling when it puckered delightfully. He responded by playing with it, first pulling and squeezing lightly, then rolling it between his fingers and thumb, teasing it mercilessly with his feather-light touch. The thick pebbly texture fascinated and aroused him, producing a clamor deep in his loins.

While his fingers were busy with one nipple he bent and ran the tip of his tongue around the other. First he dragged the tip of his tongue across the bud, then lashed it with light, teasing strokes, finally pulling it into the wet cave of his mouth. He suckled gently as his tongue continued its fiery dance.

Devon reeled drunkenly, dismayed at the magnitude of the response he evoked in her. Blood pounded in her brain, leapt from her heart, and made her knees tremble. How could a vile pirate affect her like this when a decent man like Winston failed to inspire her with little more than indulgent fondness? Then all thought fled as Devon felt the rest of her clothing leave her body, and she stood gloriously nude before Diablo's hot, probing eyes.

"God's blood, Devon, you're like a beautiful masterpiece, fragile yet flesh-and-blood real. Every other woman pales in comparison. I think—I think if any other man tried to touch you I'd kill him."

Sweeping her into his arms, he placed her on the bed, bending to strip her of shoes and stockings. Then he stretched out beside her, fully clothed. Intuitively he sensed the awakening embers he roused within her and rejoiced, wanting to fan them into hot flame to match his own. Gently his hand outlined the circle of her breast, then slid across her silken belly. His touch was light and teasing, and to her dismay, Devon found herself welcoming the sweet agony of full arousal.

"Do you want me to stop?" Diablo asked. "I always keep my word." His tongue trailed a path of liquid fire down her ribs to her stomach while his hands searched out all her pleasure points.

Devon moaned softly, lost in a sensual fog where nothing mattered but the way Diablo made her feel, all warm and melting inside.

"Tell me, sweetheart," Diablo prodded relentlessly, "should I stop?"

A tiny puff of air lodged in Devon's throat as his bold caresses took him to the soft burning core of her, that forbidden place that ached for his touch. Another breath caught on a gasp as his fingers found her moistness and became more insistent, his watchful eyes never leaving her face.

Devon wanted to resist, tried desperately to voice a protest that would stop this exquisite torture, but having Diablo desist now would be tantamount to plunging off the face of the earth into darkness. Against her better judgment she was succumbing to Diablo's masterful seduction and his will was becoming hers.

"I understand, sweetheart," Diablo murmured, flashing his dimple. "You don't have to say anything, just relax and let me love you."

He left her for a moment, and when he returned Devon felt the hairy roughness of his chest rasp against her sensitive nipples. He buried his face in the fragrant silk of her hair, thinking how small and fragile her body felt in his arms, yet her breasts were womanly and full against him. All his senses were intoxicated with the taste and smell of her, and he fought against the overwhelming urge to take her swiftly and love her voraciously until his enormous hunger was appeased.

Suddenly Diablo was desperate to remove his restrictive trousers and he shifted, sliding them down over muscled thighs and legs. Then he kicked off his boots, his undergarments quickly following. His manhood, now thick and throbbing, surged against her. Before Devon squeezed her eyes tightly shut she caught a glimpse of that huge male part of him. She thought him magnificent; just looking at him made her mouth go dry.

"Open your legs, sweetheart," he urged, his voice

quivering with excitement. He felt like a lad with his first woman.

Looming above her, his leg insinuated itself between her thighs and he guided himself into the moist cleft. His warm sex nudged the opening and Devon tried to jerk away, shocked out of her sensual haze. Surely she was too small for him.

"Diablo, no! You can't! It's not possible."

He brought her back hard and thrust forward while his arm wrapped around her waist so there was no escaping him. "Trust me, sweetheart, it's not only possible but thoroughly enjoyable. You'll see, just relax, I don't want to hurt you."

She resisted fiercely for a moment, then, seeing no hope, relaxed as he suggested, not once considering asking him to stop. He had brought her too far for that. His initial thrust brought a cry of pain as she felt herself fill and stretch with his hugeness. Her whimpers served only to inflame him as he pressed harder, deeper, into that virgin passage. Then he felt the membrane give beneath his relentless prodding, and thrusting forcefully, entered her fully, delighting in the moist heat that contracted around him to hold him snugly.

"It's done, sweetheart, I won't hurt you again," Diablo said gently, remaining motionless to allow her time to adjust to his size. "God's bones, you're so tight and warm it's all I can do to keep from exploding."

Devon felt as if she were being torn apart. She had expected some pain, if girlish gossip could be believed, but nothing like this. Just when she felt certain she would die, the pain began to recede, replaced by an unfamiliar sensation that began at the place of their joining. It grew with each passing moment, causing her to move her hips experimentally. Yes, the pain was definitely gone, and she looked at Diablo questioningly, as if to ask, what now?

Diablo groaned, his control slowly disintegrating. "Now—comes the—pleasure," he gasped disjointedly, sensing her question.

He rocked her gently at first, teaching her the rhythm. She gloved him so tightly with her moist heat that every thrust brought a friction so exquisite it bordered on pain. "You're wonderful," he mouthed in her ear. "It's as if I've waited all my life for you." Deliberately he quickened his pace, rejoicing in the wonder visible in her sky-blue eyes.

"Diablo!" she cried, unprepared for the floodtide of sensations bombarding her with lightninglike ·jolts of pure rapture. Not knowing what to expect next frightened her.

"Kit, call me Kit," he urged, desperate to hear his name on her lips.

"Kit! I feel so—I don't know what's happening and it scares me."

"Let me come, sweetheart, don't rush it. Ride with the storm, flow with it, you'll know when the time is right. I can't believe you're so wonderfully responsive. Don't think, just feel."

Right? Right for what? Devon wondered, urgency driving her toward the center of the storm Diablo described.

Suddenly Diablo's thrusts became frenzied, and instinctively Devon rose up to meet him, abruptly aware that he was the storm and she was riding it to some distant pinnacle of discovery. His body was covered with a fine sheen of sweat, his breath harsh and panting. He hated leaving her behind but could hold back no longer.

He needn't have worried, for Devon was with

him every step of the way. "Kit! Kit! I think—oh, God!" Waves of ecstasy shuddered through her, her pleasure pure and explosive. That which she struggled to reach came to her in a rush of sweet agony.

Diablo knew by the fluttering contractions that enveloped and stroked his manhood the very moment when rapture seized her and sent her soaring. Only then did he allow his own passion to gallop to a thundering climax. Then he collapsed, taking care to rest the bulk of his weight on his elbows. His eyes were silver pools of wonder and delight.

"You're amazing," he said smiling, his voice a breathless shudder. "I kidnapped a lady and discovered a wildcat."

Still awed by what had happened, Devon struggled to control her own breathing. "I—didn't know," she whispered wonderingly.

"How could you?" Diablo replied, finally finding the energy to flip to his side. "I was the first."

A slow flush crept up Devon's neck and she attempted to cover herself.

"Nay, I want to look at you. Your skin is so soft and white, like the purest alabaster. Your breasts just fit my hands and your nipples—ah, sweetheart, your little pink nipples were made for my mouth." As if to prove his words he bent over and took one pouting bud into his mouth, suckling gently.

The action seemed to release Devon's frozen senses, and she stared at Diablo with something akin to horror. What had she done? How could she give up so easily that which rightfully belonged to another man? "Don't touch me!" she gasped, pushing him away.

Stunned, Diablo scoffed, "A little late for that, isn't it?" His thick eyebrows angled upward, lending him a devilish look.

"You—you raped me! You took advantage of my innocence despite your promise."

"I heard no protests," Diablo refuted. "I made love to you, sweetheart, and you enjoyed it. It will be even better next time for there'll be no more pain."

"Next time! There will be no next time," Devon denied hotly.

She closed her eyes, vividly recalling those magic moments when nothing existed but the ecstasy they shared. It must never happen again. For Winston's sake and their future together she must resist the pirate's considerable charm and seductive prowess. Diablo was a contradiction of every rule. Bold, ruthless, blackhearted. Tender, charming, loving. Which was he?

Suddenly a vague memory stored away in a chamber of her brain prickled her conscience. "Who is Kit?" Her question brought a scowl to Diablo's face.

"I know no one named Kit!"

"You asked me to call you Kit. Did you think me too addled to remember? Is Kit your real name?"

A strangled sigh escaped Diablo's lips and he rolled to his back, placing his forearm over his eyes in an oddly vulnerable gesture. "Only Kyle knows me as Kit, but he's forbidden to use the name. If I revealed the name to you it was in a moment of weakness. I must ask you not to use it—except in the privacy of our bedroom," he added wickedly.

"Then I shall never use it," Devon pledged. "Now, please, let me up. Are you not satisfied at having your way with me? What more can you want?"

"Do you really need to ask?"

With agile grace he slid his weight atop her, fully aroused again. It truly stunned Diablo to think a mere woman could produce such conflicting emotions and swift arousal in him.

"Nay, Diablo, not again," Devon resisted, pushing against his chest. "I told you I—"

"*Mon ami*, are you in there?"

The heavily accented voice accompanied by a pounding on the door did exactly what Devon's protests failed to do to Diablo's ardor. "God's bones," he groaned as if in pain, "why now?"

"Open the door, Diablo, tis Le Vautour. We've business to conduct."

"Aye, I'm coming," Diablo answered crossly, none too pleased at the untimely interruption. "Cover yourself," he growled at Devon as he shrugged into his pants.

Scooting downward, she pulled the sheet under her chin, her eyes wide and questioning. "Who is it?"

"The man I've been waiting for," came his terse reply. Then conversation ceased as Diablo padded barefoot to the door.

"It's about time, *mon ami*," the visitor boomed in a commanding voice the moment the door opened to him.

Before Diablo could protest, the man pushed his way inside. "Don't tell me you're abed at this early hour," the Frenchman guffawed, staring deliberately at Diablo's bare feet and equally bare chest. His eyes sparkled with mirth until he spied Devon curled up in bed, her tousled blonde curls poking out from under the sheet. The entrancing sight sobered him immediately.

"Ah, *mon ami*, I have intruded upon your amusement, no? Introduce me to your *chère amie*. An enticing piece, from what little I can see of her. Perhaps I can persuade you to share her."

An enraged yelp left Devon's lips as she flung the sheet over her head.

"Wait for me downstairs, Le Vautour," Diablo said tightly. "The lady belongs to me, I'll share her with no one."

"Ah, so that's how the wind blows," Le Vautour remarked, casting covetous glances at Devon's delectable form outlined beneath the sheet. "It does my heart good to see you tied in knots over a bit of fluff." He laughed heartily, slapping his well-muscled thigh.

Le Vautour, the vulture, an apt nickname for a man who looked every bit the bird of prey he was named after. He was tall and thin, his beaked nose a perfect fit for his long, not unhandsome features. Somewhat of a dandy, he dressed exceptionally well for a pirate, carefully choosing fashionable clothing made in France, his native country. Sly and crafty by nature, Le Vautour instilled trust in few of his comrades. He was known to be cruel and heartless in his dealings with captives and peers alike. His eyes, jet-black, fathomless pits, were hooded like those of a hawk, making it impossible to know what he was thinking.

"Get out of here, Le Vautour," Diablo repeated, herding him toward the door. "I'll be down in fifteen minutes."

"I insist that you and your *chère amie* join me for supper," Le Vautour invited eagerly. "I'd like to meet her under—um—more appropriate circumstances."

Silver lightning flashed in Diablo's eyes as he slammed the door behind Le Vautour. Damn! he seethed impotently, why should Le Vautour seeing Devon anger him so? He was acting like a jealous husband. Husband! God forbid! He threw up his hands in disgust, turning toward Devon who was peeking over the edge of the sheet.

"Le Vautour has arrived. Hurry and dress, Devon." Just thinking about Le Vautour's disparaging remarks about Devon made his voice harsher than he intended. "We've been invited to supper."

Devon gasped in dismay. "Surely you don't mean for me to join you!"

"I'm afraid so, sweetheart," Diablo said, his voice gentling. "The man won't be appeased until his curiosity is satisfied. I don't trust him, but circumstances force me to deal with him. It's best if I don't anger him or give him cause to back out of our agreement."

The common room of the Wheel of Fortune Inn buzzed with activity. Pirates of all description laughed, talked, fought, and consorted with prostitutes everywhere Devon's gaze took her in the crowded room. She toyed distractedly with her food while Diablo and Le Vautour talked business. But Devon was not fooled. Though Le Vautour appeared engrossed in planning the joint venture with Diablo, his black gaze swept over her again and again. His look was lazily suggestive, and Devon tried hard to ignore it. Besides, she knew by his stiffening shoulders and clenched jaw that Diablo saw it, too, and liked it as little as she did.

When Diablo was momentarily distracted by a friend who called to him from across the room, Le Vautour seized the opportunity to wink provocatively at Devon. Flushing, she lowered her head, concentrating on the congealing mess in her plate.

Then Scarlett swaggered through the door and a hush descended over the room. Everyone present knew how it was between Diablo and Scarlett and wondered what the she-devil would do now that Diablo was openly courting another woman. It was obvious a rousing row was eagerly anticipated, and all eyes turned to watch Scarlett's slow, sensual progress across the room. Unerringly her steps took her to where Diablo sat with Devon and Le Vautour.

Hoping to avoid another nasty confrontation and spare Devon further shame, Diablo rose abruptly, excused himself, and hurried to head off the flame-haired virago.

"At last," Le Vautour sighed, impaling Devon with his piercing black eyes. "I thought we'd never be alone, *ma petite*. You do not seem too happy about your arrangement with Diablo. Now that I've seen more than the top of your head I find myself yearning to know you intimately. I can offer you much more than Diablo, and I'm a better lover. What do you say, *ma chère*, will you be my mistress? I'll arrange everything."

Devon's mouth flopped open. It rankled to know that everyone thought her the kind of woman who could be easily bought and sold. She hated Diablo for bringing her so low. She'd do anything to escape him—anything. Perhaps she could even use Le Vautour to help her escape this hellhole. Not that she would ever agree to become his mistress. But perhaps he was greedy enough to accept the promise of money to carry her away from Diablo and the strange power he had over her. Never would she forgive him for seducing her so thoroughly and making her enjoy it. It was something that couldn't—wouldn't—happen again.

Diablo breathed a heartfelt sigh of relief when he managed to prevent Scarlett from creating a scene. Only when he promised to come to her aboard the *Red Witch* so they might talk in private did Scarlett agree not to vent her displeasure at Devon in public. After tossing a venomous glance in Devon's direction, the leggy redhead joined a group of friends seated around a table relating lusty tales of daring deeds and misdeeds.

Diablo's silver eyes glinted with dangerous lights when he saw Le Vautour leaning intimately toward Devon, speaking earnestly. So engrossed were the two they failed to hear Diablo approaching. But Diablo's hearing was keen. He distinctly heard Le Vautour ask Devon to be his mistress. And by the thoughtful look on Devon's face it appeared she was actually considering the offer.

"Devon isn't free to accept or decline your offer, Le Vautour," he informed the Frenchman curtly.

Startled, Le Vautour looked up, a bland smile appearing on his dark, intense features. "Ah, *mon ami*, you cannot fault a man for trying. Mademoiselle Devon is an enchanting creature, but so is Scarlett. Even a fool could see that Scarlett is none too happy about being replaced and I merely offered Mademoiselle Devon my protection should she desire it. Why should you have a monopoly on beautiful women?"

"As I said before, Devon cannot possibly accept your insulting offer."

Le Vautour searched Devon's face with slow perusal. "Let the lady speak for herself. I meant no insult."

"Devon's not free to make a decision," Diablo repeated tightly. "I'm holding her for ransom."

"You mean she's your prisoner as well as your

mistress?" Le Vautour asked, astounded.

Suddenly Devon came alive, her eyes ablaze with angry fire. "I'm no man's mistress! When I'm returned to my father, he'll see that you and your kind are wiped off the face of the earth."

Leaping to her feet, she pushed her way through the crowd and up the stairs to the privacy of her room, collecting her dignity around her like a regal mantle.

Chapter Seven

Devon longed to lock the door behind her but Diablo had the key. Being forced to associate with men like Diablo and Le Vautour sent her into a frenzy of wrathful indignation. But she'd show them, she silently vowed. She was a match for any man. Using cunning and guile she'd escape Diablo somehow and one day marry Winston, if he'd still have her.

Her thoughts were scattered when the object of her rage burst into the room. "I love the way you look when you're angry," Diablo drawled lazily. "You please me so well, sweetheart, I may never let you go."

"You wouldn't dare keep me against my will! Father will search the world over until he finds me."

"And your fiancé? Will he join in the search?"

"Of course. He loves me."

"They'll not find you, sweetheart, until I'm ready for them to find you," Diablo assured her confidently. "And after what we shared together in this room, that might never happen. It was exciting, Devon. *You* were exciting. I could—"

"Stop it!" Devon shouted, covering her ears. "I won't listen to this. You forced me! It will never happen again."

"It will if I say it will." He reached for her but she deftly evaded him. "You've created a hunger in me that needs constant feeding."

"Go find Scarlett and gorge yourself on her."

Diablo laughed with wry amusement. He found her wit and spunk highly entertaining, and her body wildly sensual and responsive. She could protest all she wanted, but he knew she wasn't immune to him. He had brought rapture to her virginal body once and longed to do so again. But given her state of mind Diablo decided not to press her further tonight. Besides, he promised Scarlett he'd meet her aboard the *Red Witch* and it was time he left. He only hoped he could convince the red-haired vixen that their association had run its course and it was time to move on.

"Perhaps I *will* find Scarlett," he taunted, turning to leave. "For your own safety I'm locking you in. I won't be back till morning. Be prepared to leave when I arrive."

"Leave? Where are you taking me?"

"To Paradise." Then he was gone, leaving Devon with a new worry. How would her father and Winston ever hope to find her on a hidden island protected by a natural barrier that kept out unwanted visitors?

"I'm surprised you were able to tear yourself away from your doxy," Scarlett flung out disparagingly. "She's not your type, Diablo. You'd do well to stick with your own kind."

"The only reason I'm here is to settle this between us. I've made you no promises about our future. We simply enjoyed one another when we chanced to meet. And in between times I've not been celibate, nor do I imagine have you."

"True," Scarlett agreed, "but this is the first time you've brought a woman to Nassau. Do you intend to take her to Paradise? To my knowledge, I'm the only woman you've ever brought there to share your bed. What is this woman to you besides a hostage? I don't like sharing my men."

"And I don't like bossy, possessive women," Diablo countered, his temper flaring. "I told you before I'm holding Devon for ransom. I'll take her wherever I damn please."

"Does that include your bed?" Scarlett asked with a derisive toss of her fiery head. "She doesn't look the type to enjoy it, not like I do. I need you, Diablo. Stay aboard the *Red Witch* with me tonight and I'll show you how much. Remember how good we were together?"

Scarlett didn't begrudge Diablo an occasional woman, for she was no saint herself. What she didn't like, wouldn't stand for, was another woman coming to mean something more to him than a warm body or a moment's solace. And astutely Scarlett sensed that Lady Devon Chatham was a woman who could easily replace her permanently in Diablo's affections. Not only would Scarlett miss his expert loving, she would earn the contempt of her peers for losing Diablo to another woman.

Her hips swaying provocatively, Scarlett approached Diablo, running the back of one hand over a clean-shaven cheek. "I miss the beard," she purred. "It chafed me most erotically in delicious places. But I suppose I can grow accustomed to seeing your handsome face exposed."

Grasping him behind the neck, she pulled his face down to hers until their mouths touched. Greedily she seized his lips, kissing him with all the passion and longing that mere words failed to convey. Her fingers went to his shirt and eagerly began working the buttons through the buttonholes. Diablo groaned, his body reacting spontaneously to Scarlett's kiss and to her body molding his from thigh to breast. The sudden rise of his flesh brought a delighted grin to Scarlett's red lips.

"You want me, Diablo. By damn, I know you do!"

"You're an enticing wench, Scarlett, and as you well know I'm not made of stone."

Thrilled by his response, Scarlett pressed closer, certain that once Diablo was in her bed he'd have no further need for another woman. She was confident of her ability to make him desire no one but her. But Diablo had other ideas. Though his body might have reacted spontaneously to Scarlett's seduction, his mind rejected her utterly. Having tasted Devon's sweetness mere hours ago and been gloriously sated, he refused to soil the unique experience by bedding Scarlett. He had enjoyed Scarlett thoroughly while it lasted, but it was over.

Deliberately removing her busy fingers from his shirt front, Diablo set Scarlett aside and stepped back. "Behave, Scarlett. Don't debase yourself by begging. You're a beautiful woman and can have any man you want."

"I want *you*," Scarlett said with bitter emphasis.

"What happens after you ransom the little slut? If you reject me now, don't expect to be welcomed back with open arms once she's gone. My pride won't allow it. If you leave me tonight, my devilish love, I'll never forgive you. You'll find I make a better lover than enemy."

Diablo searched Scarlett's face, his eyes narrowed to slits. He held no illusions about Scarlett, she would indeed make a formidable foe, but he felt certain he could handle any threat she presented. The simple truth, one that surprised him utterly, was that he no longer desired Scarlett sexually. Since he had met Devon, all women paled in comparison, and if he couldn't have Scarlett as a friend he didn't want her at all.

"So be it," he intoned, his smile fading. "I had hoped we could remain friends even though I no longer want to be your lover."

"Go then!" Scarlett spat. "Get out of my sight. Just remember what they say about a woman scorned."

Overjoyed to be allowed on deck, Devon watched the islands and cays that made up the Bahamas slip by. She had been escorted aboard the *Devil Dancer* early that morning by Diablo, who hadn't returned until dawn to the room they shared.

Some islands looked like bright jewels set in brilliant aqua circled by snow white. Others were mere rocky formations surrounded by barrier reefs separated from land by a wide lagoon. On one island, which Diablo said was Andros, the vivid pink of hundreds of flamingos captured her attention. The water was so clear and blue she could see thousands of tropical fish beneath its surface.

Devon could easily understand why the Bahamas were a pirate's fiefdom and the Caribbean a pirate's lake. There were many nooks, crannies, creeks, shallows, rocks, and reefs for a ship to hide in. And from what she gathered from bits of overheard conversation, the appointed governors were ineffectual in routing pirates from their shores. In fact, pirates like Charles Vane, John Thurber, Blackbeard, Stede Bonnet, and Calico Jack found the Bahamas a virtual paradise. No wonder Diablo chose to make his home in these hospitable islands.

Thinking of the devil must have conjured him up, for Diablo appeared as if by magic at Devon's side. They had had little opportunity to speak privately since he had escorted her aboard.

"Beautiful," he said softly. Though he spoke of the passing scenery, his eyes never left Devon's face.

"Are the islands inhabited?"

"There are a handful of settlers on one or two of the larger islands, but for the most part they remain uninhabited."

"What about Paradise? Do you own it?" Devon questioned.

Diablo laughed, pleased by her interest. "Believe it or not, I do own Paradise. It was granted to my family years ago, and I doubt that any of my living relatives even remember it."

"Your family? Tell me about them."

Diablo's eyes became hooded and a remote sadness settled over his handsome features. "I have no family," he refuted. "Look to the starboard!" Adroitly he turned her attention away from his personal history.

Devon looked to where Diablo pointed, seeing a

large land mass lush with vegetation, a wide lagoon with pure white sand forming a beach, and high coral hills at its center. No sign of life was visible, and Devon assumed it to be another uninhabited island.

"Welcome to Paradise." From all of Diablo's glowing descriptions, Devon had expected something extraordinary. But Paradise looked much like any of the other lovely islands and cays surrounding it.

Sensing her disappointment, Diablo smiled a mysterious smile. "Look below the waterline and you can see the coral reef I spoke of. It completely surrounds the island, making it impossible to approach if one does not know where to find the hidden break in the reef. Only ships with drafts five to eight feet can safely negotiate the treacherous shallows."

Devon turned her attention to the sparkling water below. She gasped when she saw the jagged coral that had the power to rip a ship's hull apart.

"It's time I took the wheel," Diablo said. "Few of my men are capable of navigating through the narrow gap in the reef without doing damage to the hull. If Kyle were here he could do it, but I sent him with Le Vautour to protect our interests."

"I don't trust that Frenchman. I never know what is going on in his devious mind and I refuse to tell him the secret of my island. I've made arrangements to meet Le Vautour and Kyle in Nassau after our booty is sold to collect the profits. Afterwards I'll return to Paradise with Kyle."

Devon's avid gaze followed Diablo as he sprinted across the deck, secretly admiring the play of muscles across his back and the flexing of his taut buttocks. With each step he took, the ripple of corded sinews reminded her of the unleashed strength of his whip-cord lean body. Though she tried not to remember, nothing could make her forget how tenderly, how passionately he had made love to her. He made her feel adored and protected. How could it be possible for a pirate to make her feel cherished? she wondered distractedly. How could a man of his calling bring her the kind of happiness she had never known existed? Was it likely that Winston could fulfill her in the same way? Somehow she doubted it.

Devon's musings came to an abrupt halt when she realized the ship had turned toward shore and was riding in on a brisk breeze. She held her breath, listening for the scrape of coral against the hull. But Diablo handled the trim craft as masterfully as he did women, clearing the reef with only inches to spare. The air left her lungs in a whoosh, only to be drawn in again when she realized they were still traveling full speed with no order given to trim the sails. At their speed they would soon slam into the surf and become beached in the soft white sand.

Bracing herself for the crash, Devon aimed a desperate glance at Diablo. To her utter amazement he seemed completely at ease, as if wrecking a ship were something he did every day. The shore loomed ahead with alarming speed and Devon closed her eyes, gripping the railing with all her meager strength. When the expected impact did not come, she opened her eyes tentatively.

She was amazed to find that they were entering a hidden river just wide enough to accommodate the *Devil Dancer*. Lush vegetation at the shoreline obscured the mouth from all who were not aware of it. Unless the exact location was known, one would never know it existed. They sailed slowly up the channel for some distance until they entered a wide lagoon rimmed with a crescent of white sand. She could hardly believe her eyes. Not only had a dock been built in the lagoon, but neat rows of huts and warehouses basked lazily beneath the hot afternoon sun. She could see people rushing out of their houses and crowding the beach to greet them. Most were women and old men, but a few children could be seen scampering beside their mothers.

Devon looked at Diablo, who was squinting into the sun to check the trim of the sails. "Too much canvas," he called out to Akbar, who relayed his orders to the men on deck and aloft. "Shorten the main topsail. Sails fast to yards. Larboard bank! Anchor at ready." With practiced ease Diablo maneuvered the *Devil Dancer* to her berth beside the wharf.

Devon heard the anchor cable rattle over the side, then the splash as the big iron hook crashed into the deep lagoon. Diablo strolled to where Devon stood by the rail.

"You could have warned me," she accused. "I thought sure we'd crash into the shore."

"Do you trust me so little?" Diablo teased. His dimple flashed and Devon deliberately turned her eyes away from the entrancing sight.

"I don't trust you at all," she argued. "I should have known you'd make your home someplace that's totally inaccessible. Does anyone know your secret?"

"Damn few," Diablo allowed. "Only those I completely trust."

"*I* know," Devon whispered shakily. Her eyes

grew round as saucers when she realized what that meant. Either Diablo trusted her with his secret or he never meant to let her go. It could also mean he would kill her when she was of no further use to him.

A frown knitted Diablo's dark brow. As Devon had so aptly pointed out, he had failed to consider the fact that bringing her to Paradise was foolhardy, placing scores of lives at her mercy, mostly innocent women and children. He was exposing more than his own vulnerability, and he hoped he'd not live to regret it.

Soon the gangplank was in place and Diablo guided a reluctant Devon onto the dock and through the jostling, happy crowd waiting to greet their men. Only those men who kept women on Paradise had come on the *Devil Dancer*, except for Akbar who rarely left Diablo's side. Those free of responsibilities or entanglements had remained in Nassau to drink and wench until the ship was careened and the wood infected with teredo worms replaced. Then she'd return to Nassau to collect the crew and return once again to piracy.

Curious eyes followed Devon's progress along the beach. Some called out greetings to their chief, welcoming him home after his sojourn in an English prison. Others, nudging one another in delight, made lewd speculations about Devon and her relationship to the handsome pirate. By the time they left the crowd behind, Devon's cheeks were burning. What truly rankled was being referred to time and again as "the devil's lady."

Studying her surroundings carefully and storing the information for later use, Devon noted that Diablo was leading her down a dusty track past warehouses and crude huts that comprised the village, then up a slight rise. By the time she reached the top she was breathless and perspiring. She had no bonnet to shade her from the sun, and her golden hair clung damply to her neck and cheeks. The charming sight made it difficult for Diablo to concentrate.

God's bones, he wanted her! Once had but whet his appetite for the gorgeous wildcat. The way he felt now, a hundred times wouldn't be enough. What in the hell had possessed him, he wondered, to bring Devon to Paradise. The consequences could be far-reaching and devastating. Though he hated to admit it, the little vixen had entranced him from the beginning. He knew he should have released her as he had promised, but when the storm conspired against his plans, taking Devon to his island seemed the natural thing to do. There was only one way to flush her out of his system and that was to sate himself with her sweet flesh.

At the top of the rise, Devon came to an abrupt halt. Hidden from the beach by a copse of tall trees that provided shade from the relentless sun stood an imposing house. Devon hardly expected to find a magnificent dwelling after seeing the crude buildings in the village on the beach.

Built entirely of wood, the rambling two-story dwelling was surrounded by a wide veranda, its numerous windows opened to admit gentle sea breezes. Tall, graceful columns supported the upper-floor veranda that stretched across the front of the house. The exterior had mellowed to a pale tan, and though not so grand as the stately Chatham House, its clean lines and simplicity charmed Devon.

"I know it's nothing like you're accustomed to," Diablo said anxiously. For some reason he wanted Devon to love his home as much as he did. "But you'll find it comfortable and well staffed. You'll want for nothing while you're my guest."

"It—it's more than I expected," Devon admitted shyly. "Actually, it's quite grand. Do—do you keep slaves?" Her nose wrinkled in distaste, for she had little use for slavery. "It must take many people to maintain the island. Do you grow a crop? Or keep animals?"

"I raise sugar cane," Diablo said and smiled, pleased by her interest. "But I hire Arawak Indians from neighboring islands to work the fields and staff the house. I keep no slaves. I find the Arawaks quite dependable, and the arrangement works well. Rum is distilled on the island and sold to the American colonies."

Once again Diablo's answer surprised Devon. She would have thought him the type to keep slaves to do his bidding, picturing him as a cruel taskmaker. Must he destroy every preconceived idea she had of him, forcing her to view him as a humane being rather than a ruthless despoiler of people and property?

"Come along, sweetheart, I'm sure Tara has a cool drink waiting us."

"Tara?" Devon asked curiously. Who was Tara? Another of Diablo's women? There must be scores of them roaming the face of the earth.

As if on cue a tall, slim woman stepped through the front door. A wide, welcoming smile tilted the corners of her full lips. Smooth tan skin stretched tautly across high cheekbones beneath huge sloping eyes as black as midnight. Delicately sloped brows lent her a fragile beauty that Devon found fascinating. Her hair was long and black as ebony, worn simply behind her ears and held in place by a spray of fresh flowers. A colorful sarong skimmed her lithe, willowy figure without being blatantly suggestive, leaving bare tan calves and slender ankles. Devon thought her quite lovely though somewhat past the first bloom of youth. She appeared to be in her late twenties. Somehow the thought that this beautiful woman was Diablo's mistress aroused an anger in Devon, one she was unprepared to deal with.

"There's Tara now." Diablo quickly closed the gap between himself and the native woman, sweeping her into his embrace, much to Devon's consternation. Her laughter, a lovely tinkling sound, set Devon's teeth on edge.

Tara wriggled free of Diablo's arms, slapping at him playfully. "Welcome home," she said, smiling enchantingly. "I feared we would never see you again when I heard you were in prison, though in my heart I knew you were resourceful enough to escape the hangman."

"Then you knew more than I did, my lovely Tara. I truly thought I was being dispatched to hell to meet the devil. But at the last minute a beautiful lady saved my life." One long arm reached out to draw Devon to this side.

Tara's delicate brows arched quizzically above slanting black eyes as she stared at Devon.

"Devon, Tara is my housekeeper." Then to Tara. "This is Lady Devon Chatham, your new mistress. You are to obey her every whim while she is here as my guest. She is to be denied nothing—except the right to leave until I allow it."

Devon impaled him with a murky stare, barely suppressing her anger. How dare Diablo dictate her life! Then, remembering her manners, she nodded politely to Tara, wondering about the woman and her relationship to the handsome pirate.

Seeing Devon with Diablo shocked Tara. She had been employed by Diablo for several years, being somewhat older than Devon gave her credit for, and in all that time he had never installed a woman in his home as mistress, though Tara knew that many women, Scarlett included, would kill for that honor. Now, out of the blue, he brings home a mistress. Granted, Devon was a raving beauty, and clearly an aristocrat, but what use did Diablo have for such a woman? Sensing that Diablo was waiting for her approval of Devon, Tara made the only response available to her.

"Welcome, my lady. Please come inside. I'm sure you'd like to freshen up while I prepare something cool to drink. If everything isn't to your liking you've only to tell me."

Pleased by Tara's words, Diablo took Devon's hand and led her inside, pride in his home written all over his expressive features. And the moment she entered the house Devon knew why. The rooms were large, light, and airy. A gentle breeze wafted through the open windows, setting the lacy curtains in motion. The furnishings were exquisite, and Devon wondered how many ships Diablo had plundered to obtain them. Mostly they were of French design, with several good English pieces strategically placed for effect. A staircase rose majestically from one side of the central hall.

"Show Devon to the front guest room," Diablo said, "and order a tub for both of us. Her trunks are being brought up by cart."

"Of course." Tara nodded agreeably. "Follow me, my lady."

Devon hesitated, unwilling to place herself in the hands of Diablo's mistress. "Go on, sweetheart," Diablo urged, giving her a gentle push. "Tara will take good care of you."

Before Devon turned to follow Tara, she said, "Your home is lovely, Diablo."

"I want you to be happy here, Devon. This setting was created solely to enhance your beauty."

Embarrassed that Tara should be privy to Diablo's flowery words, Devon returned curtly, "I don't expect to be here long enough to fully appreciate your island." Whirling, she followed a somewhat shocked Tara up the stairs.

The room assigned Devon contained everything she could possibly want or need. What truly surprised her was that it was obviously decorated with a lady's taste in mind. A canopy bed hung with pale blue curtains dominated the large, airy room filled with delicate white and gold French furnishings. Lacy blue curtains blew lazily in the breeze, fluttering against walls hung with gold and blue wallpaper. A thick Turkish carpet beneath her feet cushioned her steps. Devon noted that two doors led from the room and wondered if both were dressing rooms.

"Does it suit you, my lady?" Tara asked in a lilting voice.

"It's lovely," Devon allowed.

"Diablo will be pleased."

"I don't care if Diablo is pleased or not."

"I—don't understand," Tara said, puzzled. Diablo's woman didn't appear overly enthusiastic about being on Paradise. Didn't she know it was an honor to be chosen by Diablo?

"Nay, I don't suppose you do. Are you Diablo's mistress?" Devon asked bluntly, her curiosity too great for verbal sparring.

The heavy black lashes that shadowed Tara's cheeks flew up as she was caught off guard by Devon's rude assumption. "Is that what Diablo told you?"

"Diablo told me you were his housekeeper, but I'm neither blind nor stupid."

Consternation marred Tara's lovely brow. "You have nothing to fear from me, my lady." Had Diablo hinted that they were lovers? Tara wondered. Until she found out just what Diablo wanted Devon to know, she decided to divulge nothing. At least not until she had spoken with her enigmatic employer.

"Perhaps Diablo can best answer your question," Tara said cryptically. "I'll see to your bath."

The bath felt wonderfully refreshing, the scented water deliciously wicked as it slid over Devon's satiny skin. She sighed contentedly and closed her eyes, resting her head against the rim of the tub. The trunk containing her clothes had arrived shortly before the bath, and Tara worked efficiently at putting them away while Devon lolled in the tub. Suddenly Tara glanced toward one of the doors that Devon had yet to explore, nodded, and quietly left the room.

"Hand me the bathsheet, Tara," Devon said, holding out her hand but too lazy to open her eyes. When the soft material touched her fingertips she reluctantly cranked her eyes open and rose gracefully to her feet. She sensed his presence long before he spoke.

"It's a damn shame to cover all that radiant beauty."

A gasp left Devon's throat. "Diablo! What are you doing here? Where's Tara?"

"Gone. I dismissed her."

"What must she think? How dare you invade my privacy."

"It matters little what Tara thinks," Diablo confided. "I pay her well to follow my orders and she's completely loyal to me. This is my home and no doors are locked against me. I go where I want, when I want."

Devon shook with impotent rage, holding the bathsheet against her breasts as a shield. Diablo's grin widened as he snatched the sheet from her fingers and held it outstretched. "Step out, sweetheart," he urged. "Cook has a light lunch waiting for us."

"I'm perfectly capable of drying myself," Devon sniffed haughtily. Her attempts to snatch the sheet from his hands proved futile.

"You're compelling me to use force," Diablo sighed with mock regret, seizing Devon around the waist and lifting her from the tub with ease.

Setting her on her feet, he spent several leisurely minutes carefully perusing her nude form while she slowly burned with embarrassment. "Everything about you is perfect," he proclaimed with slow relish.

Tiny drops of glistening water clung to the creamy surface of her skin, dripping off the coral tips of her breasts. The thick thatch of golden hair between her legs curled in tight ringlets, hiding the treasure beneath that Diablo longed to explore. Heaving a tremulous sigh, he stepped forward and slowly began drying her with the soft bathsheet. Not an inch of flesh was left unattended as Diablo lavished loving attention on her quivering form.

The simple chore was nearly too much for him, and he closed his eyes against the wealth of feelings assailing him. The sweet, tantalizing fragrance of her rose up to taunt him. His heart thundered in wild acceleration, and his hands shook with the effort.

To her chagrin, Devon was not entirely immune to Diablo's slow perusal or the warmth of his hands on her body. A soft melting pervaded the core of her, turning her bones to liquid. He was freshly bathed and shaved, and the scent of him tantalized her senses. The tangy odor of spice and tobacco combined with his own natural masculine aroma to draw her further into his web of seduction. Mesmerized, Devon offered no resistance when Diablo lowered his mouth to hers. His lips were hard and searching, his thrusting tongue seeking her sweetness. Crushing her to him, he showered tiny nipping kisses around her lips and along her jaw. A low moan left Devon's throat as she melted inside, ready and willing to do his bidding.

"God's bones, Devon, I can't seem to get enough of you," Diablo breathed raggedly. "Since that night at the Wheel of Fortune I've thought of nothing but loving you again. I want you, sweetheart, and your response tells me you want me just as badly." His words had the effect of dashing cold water in her face.

"No, don't touch me!" Instead of clinging, her arms shoved ineffectually against his massive chest. "I don't want you. I'll never let you do *that* to me again. Only my husband has the right."

"How will you stop me?" Diablo's lips stretched upward in a predatory grin. "I made you want me once, I can do so again. Forget that fiancé of yours and concentrate on pleasing me."

"You'll find me not so willing next time," Devon asserted firmly. "I'm not the innocent I was, easily seduced by smooth words."

Diablo's answer was to swoop Devon off her feet, carry her to the bed, and toss her down onto the soft surface. Kneeling above her, he pinned her to the bed with his considerable weight. "Give over, sweetheart," he urged raggedly. "I'll have you no matter what you want."

"Then go ahead," Devon challenged, going limp beneath him. "Get it over with."

Diablo went still. No, he wouldn't take her that way, not by force. He'd make her want him, prove to her she needed him as badly as he needed her. He pulled her legs apart and knelt between them. His hands slid hot and sure up her slim calves, over the resisting softness of her thighs. He stroked her breasts, her belly and back down her thighs. Devon caught her breath, commanding her body not to respond and failing miserably.

He devoted loving attention on her breasts, rubbing his thumbs over her nipples, then kneading the soft fleshy mounds before using his mouth to draw on the taut nubs. Kneeling between her parted thighs, Diablo's face hardened with determination, his eyes a haunting shade of gray, cold as steel and just as merciless. Suddenly Diablo was a man Devon didn't recognize, a frightening man who stirred something primitive and foreign in her.

"Kit, no . . ." Devon did not realize she had used that forbidden name. She tried desperately to close her legs against him, but he was holding them open, gently stroking her soft warm center.

"Shh—I won't hurt you," he said gently, finally finding the response he sought. But he wanted more—much more than mere response.

Devon jerked violently when he dipped his head and kissed her between her legs, the heat and wet pressure of his mouth against her creating a fiery need she never knew existed until now. "Nay—you musn't!"

Shock at what he was doing sent her to the edge of sanity. His mouth was a brand, his intimate caress a torment, and she was a living flame, but still she fought against his erotic invasion.

Grasping her hips, Diablo brought her closer still, holding her firmly while his tongue continued its gentle massage. Sensing Devon's reluctance and fear, Diablo urged, "Don't be afraid, sweetheart. Give to me." Then he continued his tender torture, his tongue parting, seeking, laving the moist center of her being with practiced thoroughness.

"Kit—!" His name left her in a breathless gasp as ecstasy overwhelmed her and carried her beyond herself to a shuddering release. She regained her senses to find Diablo stripped of his clothes and poised above her, his shaft a hard lance demanding entry.

"Devon, you little witch, what have you done to me? I'm obsessed with you. If I didn't know better I'd think myself in—" His words faltered and an astounded look contorted his features. What he had nearly admitted needed time and serious thought and was better left unsaid.

Then his mind went blank as he probed deep and long within her body. Her moist warmth surrounded him as his loving torment turned frantic, shuddering his tribute, thrusting wildly, his rasping voice calling her name as he took them both to heaven.

Chapter Eight

"Sweetheart, did I hurt you?" Devon's soft sobbing intruded on Diablo's euphoria, injecting a discordant note in an otherwise blissful moment.

"I hate you!" she exclaimed. "I never wanted this to happen again. I promised myself it wouldn't."

"If it makes you feel any better, sweetheart, you never had a chance against me. The devil always wins. He devours innocents like you."

"What must your mistress think?"

"My mistress? To whom are you referring?" A hint of amusement turned Diablo's eyes into sparkling diamonds.

"Do you think I'm stupid?" Devon exploded. "I saw how Tara looked at you. How could you be so callous, so—so—unfeeling?"

Shock followed disbelief across Diablo's face. "You think Tara is my mistress?"

"Isn't she?" Devon challenged.

"Nay. She is my housekeeper, no more. Are you

jealous, sweetheart?" The thought of Devon being jealous of other women pleased Diablo immensely.

"But—I thought—"

"There's no woman in my life but you, sweetheart," Diablo said, his voice ripe with emotion and strangely subdued. "With you in my bed I neither need nor want another."

A tremor passed through Devon's slender body. She saw the heart-rending tenderness in his gaze, and her own heart turned over in response. She fought an overwhelming need to remain close to Diablo, to be everything he wanted. Despite his despicable profession, his maddening arrogance, he had released an emotion long held locked within her heart. Why couldn't it be Winston who unleased her passion? The answer was simple. Her fiancé's tepid charm couldn't compare with Diablo's devastating appeal. The very air around him crackled with electrifying magnetism.

Yet deep in her heart Devon knew she would continue to seek her release despite her unholy attraction for the pirate. Her future lay with Winston, one of her own kind, not with a man wanted for committing every crime known to man. It was as inevitable as breathing that Diablo would hang one day, and Devon prayed she'd not be forced to witness it.

"Are you cold, sweetheart?" Diablo asked solicitously. He noted her tremor and hoped it meant he affected her in the same way she affected him. Before Devon could form an answer he fitted her snugly into the curve of his body, his arms protective. "I love the way you feel." His hands began a leisurely journey over the hills and valleys of her soft flesh. "You inspire me with the strength and stamina to make love endlessly. I never seem to tire when you're in my arms."

"Not again!" Devon squawked, dismayed. "You can't!"

"Just watch," Diablo smiled wolfishly. "Nothing you do or say will keep me from you. Nothing!" The fierceness of his words brought a shiver of fear to Devon's breast. It was a promise she was to remember many times in the future.

Desperation drove Devon as the days passed one after another with no mention of her release. Each night Diablo joined her in her bed, making love to her so tenderly it often brought tears to her eyes. The longer she was exposed to his special brand of loving, the more she feared she could never leave him with her heart intact. He was bold, arrogant, fearless, tender—and totally corrupt. Each time he took her, Devon continued to resist, to withhold a vital part of herself. She discovered it was the only way to retain her sanity. Repeatedly she begged to be allowed to return to her father, but Diablo would hear none of it nor promise her anything.

Much of Diablo's time was consumed with duties pertaining to his ship and men. When he was absent he was careful to assign one of his trusted men—usually Akbar—to guard Devon. Yet to all intents and purposes, Devon was mistress of his house, her orders strictly adhered to by all the servants. Tara made certain she consulted daily with Devon about menu choices and mundane housekeeping matters.

Diablo's housekeeper treated Devon with grudging respect after Diablo explained to her Devon's role in his life. Astute as well as beautiful, Tara soon realized that Devon had become more than a mere mistress to Diablo. Never had she known her employer to be so obsessed with a woman. Yet it was obvious to Tara that Devon did not appreciate her exalted position, that she eagerly awaited the day when Diablo would return her to England. But Tara seriously doubted that day would ever arrive, and thought it would prove quite interesting to watch the outcome of the little drama unfolding on Paradise.

Meanwhile, Tara seemed pleased to have the fierce Akbar nearby. She'd always been fascinated by the huge Turk, though he rarely seemed to notice her. Perhaps now she'd learn what made the man so unresponsive to women and attempt to remedy it.

Nearly a month after her arrival Diablo informed Devon that all repairs had been completed on the *Devil Dancer* and it was time to meet Le Vautour in Nassau and return Kyle to Paradise. He had allowed them sufficient time to sell their booty in the American colonies and return.

"Try to miss me, sweetheart," Diablo said wistfully. "I know I'll miss you. The next two days will seem like an eternity."

Surprisingly, Devon did miss the roguish devil who had captured her senses. Her heart was pounding excitedly when he returned to Paradise two days later. He greeted her exuberantly, pleased with the results of his business dealings with Le Vautour, which netted him and his crew a small fortune. He informed Devon that Kyle would be joining them for supper that night.

Wanting to please Diablo, Devon took extra care on her appearance. Exactly why she wanted to look her best escaped her, but two days without Diablo seemed like an eon.

One of the gowns Diablo had presented to her was a lovely turquoise silk that Devon hadn't yet worn. At first she thought it too fancy, but then changed her mind, deeming it perfect for the occasion. Tiny cap sleeves set low on her bared shoulders, a snug bodice, and a wide ruffle along the hem displayed her figure to perfection. With Tara's help her blonde tresses were dressed in a most becoming style. When she walked into the dining room that evening, Diablo was entranced. And so was Kyle.

The meal was a happy and congenial affair, but it was obvious that Diablo had eyes for no one but Devon. His silver gaze devoured her with hot longing, wishing they were alone so he could show her how much he wanted her. Almost regretfully, he asked Kyle to entertain Devon while he saw to a few details involving the dividing of the profits from the booty Le Vautour had sold for them. Then he disappeared into his office, promising to hurry.

"How have you fared, lass?" Kyle asked. His midnight blue eyes seemed to probe into her very soul.

"Well enough," came her terse reply, leaving much unsaid.

"Are you happy here on Paradise?"

"As happy as one can be in prison."

"You look radiant. Obviously Diablo has done you no harm. Has he not mentioned your ransom? Repairs on the *Devil Dancer* are nearly completed and he'll soon return to sea. The crew have had their fill of land and are anxious to ply their trade once again."

"Diablo has said nothing to me about leaving Paradise," Devon revealed, her anger flaring. "How long does he expect to keep me prisoner? What will happen to me once he leaves? I want to go home, Kyle! Why doesn't he release me? Or demand ransom? I don't want to be his whore!"

Unbeknownst to Kyle or Devon, Le Vautour stood just outside the open window, eavesdropping. After Diablo and Kyle left Nassau, he had run into Scarlett at the Wheel of Fortune Inn and was forced to listen to her vindictive rantings over Diablo's infatuation with his lovely captive and how he had ruthlessly abandoned Scarlett. The longer he listened, the more convinced he became that with Scarlett as an accomplice he could take Devon away from Diablo and pay him back for killing Black Bart. A devious plan hatched in his mind, and Scarlett eagerly agreed to help.

It didn't take much persuasion on Le Vautour's part to wrest the secret of Paradise Island from Scarlett, or enlist her help in ridding Diablo of his beautiful captive. Le Vautour had hoped, after their joint venture in disposing of the booty, that Diablo would invite him to Paradise. But he knew now that Diablo was far too cautious to divulge his secret to someone he didn't trust. Therefore he'd have to rely on his cunning to defeat the wily Diablo.

Le Vautour sailed from Nassau mere hours after Diablo. Following Scarlett's explicit directions, he found the break in the reef and sailed through with no more than a scrape or two. But instead of steering the *Victory* up the river to the hidden lagoon, he anchored at the mouth and under cover of darkness rowed a small boat to Diablo's village. Concealing the craft in the rich vegetation farther down the beach, Le Vautour used the dark shadows to advantage as he made his way to Diablo's house, again following Scarlett's directions. That's how he came to be eavesdropping at Diablo's window. If his plan worked, he would soon have Devon, leaving Scarlett to Diablo. He didn't divulge the best part of his scheme to Scarlett, for if she knew it would result in Diablo's death she would never have agreed to help him.

Le Vautour heard everything Devon said, and it proved enlightening as well as astounding. He had assumed that Devon was with Diablo willingly, despite Diablo's claim that he was holding the lady for ransom. In fact, Le Vautour seriously doubted that Diablo had ever requested ransom from Devon's wealthy family.

Devon's outburst and damning words proclaiming herself Diablo's whore left Kyle speechless. He had no idea what to say to ease her conscience or alleviate her shame over what Diablo had done to her. He should have known better than to wager his share of the booty on Diablo's ability to seduce Devon, for his hot-blooded friend had proven more than once that women found him irresistible.

He was saved from either condoning or condemning Diablo's behavior when Devon, choking on a sob, turned and fled from the room and out the door into the darkness. Kyle did not follow, remaining inside to confront Diablo with Devon's plight. If Diablo intended to return to sea, it was no more than right that he send Devon back to her family.

From the dark shadows outside the window, Le Vautour watched with gleeful anticipation as Devon fled from the house. It was just the opportunity he had been hoping for. He had heard Diablo take his leave earlier and had seen him enter his study, assuming that Kyle would follow shortly. Le

Vautour chortled with glee when Kyle did indeed leave, storming into Diablo's study to confront his chief about his intentions toward Devon.

Devon did not stop when she reached the veranda. Glancing over her shoulder, she was relieved to see that Kyle hadn't followed, and she continued on until she came to the path leading down the hill into the village. Not brave enough to venture further on her own, she came to a halt, breathing heavily from her exertions. Would she never be allowed to leave this place? Did her father think her dead? Or was he searching for her, worrying over her fate instead of taking care of himself? He was no longer a young man, and Devon wondered what her abduction would do to his health.

Devon gazed wistfully at the two ships bobbing at anchor in the bay, bathed in brilliant moonlight. If she ever left here alive, the tranquil beauty of the island was something she'd remember to the end of her days. Entranced by the dancing moonbeams above sparkling water and the swaying palm trees, she failed to hear the soft patter of footsteps behind her.

"An impressive sight, isn't it, *ma chère*?"

Devon started violently. "Le Vautour! My God! How did you get here? Does Diablo know you're on the island? I thought—"

"Forget Diablo. Are you so frightened of him, *ma chère*? I would never treat you so shabbily if you were mine. In fact, you're the reason I'm here."

"I'm not frightened of Diablo at all," Devon contended, recalling how tenderly he had made love to her the night before. If she didn't know better, she'd think he actually cared for her. He made her feel so protected, so cherished, she knew that if she didn't leave soon the tiny bud she harbored in her heart would soon blossom into love and demand recognition. And Devon was determined that would not happen. "What do you mean you're on Paradise because of me?"

"I know you wish to leave Diablo," Le Vautour said boldly.

Devon's mouth flew open in astonishment.

"If you're wondering how I know," Le Vautour said, smiling blandly, "I heard you and Kyle talking a few minutes ago."

"You eavesdropped!" Devon accused.

"Of course," Le Vautour admitted dryly.

"I don't suppose it's exactly a secret that I'm a prisoner here," Devon complained bitterly. "If Diablo means to ransom me, I've heard nothing of it."

"Were you my prisoner I'd keep you tied to my bed forever."

Though handsome enough, this pirate was nothing like Diablo. Devon sensed in Le Vautour a cruelty that was missing in Diablo, a flaw in his character that far surpassed all Diablo's bad traits. Blushing furiously, she turned away from his probing gaze, recalling that this was the man who had found her in Diablo's bed at the Wheel of Fortune Inn but a few short weeks ago.

"Please leave me alone."

"Let me help you, *ma chère*," Le Vautour urged, his voice a husky whisper. "Trust me and I'll take you back to England, if that's what you truly desire."

"Trust you? I hardly know you, so why should I trust you?"

"You want to leave here, don't you?"

"I—yes, of course I do."

"My ship is at your disposal, ready to whisk you away from here. Come with me and I'll see that you reach England safely." Darkness obscured the predatory gleam in his obsidian eyes.

"Leave with you? I couldn't possibly . . ." Her words faltered as she paused to consider Le Vautour's offer.

At first it seemed ludicrous that she leave with the infamous pirate. She would be changing one captor for another. On the other hand, she desperately needed to escape Diablo and his devastating effect upon her before she was lost forever. Though Le Vautour was hardly one to inspire confidence, Devon decided it couldn't hurt to listen to his proposal and learn exactly what he had in mind.

"Why would you help me? What do you stand to gain?"

"Ah, *ma chère*, a great deal if your father is suitably grateful for your safe return. I understand he is quite wealthy."

Devon nodded astutely. "As you well know, my father is the Earl of Milford and I can guarantee he will be extremely generous to the person who sees me safely back to England, unharmed and untouched," she emphasized.

"Why would I harm so beautiful a lady?" Le Vautour refuted breezily. "Especially one who will make me rich."

"And you promise to make no other demands on me?" Devon wanted to know.

"Demands, *ma chère*? I would have you know I am a Frenchman and a gentleman." Highly affronted, he straightened to his full six-feet-three.

Devon seriously doubted that the pirate knew the

meaning of the word. "When would we leave?" She glanced toward the beach and saw only the *Devil Dancer* outlined against the moonlit sky. Where was Le Vautour's ship? How had he found Paradise?

"Soon, very soon. Rumor has it that three Spanish galleons recently left Florida, their holds loaded with gold and silver." Only a part of that statement was true. "I mentioned it to Diablo when we met in Nassau, and he expressed a strong desire to claim the treasure for himself. His ship is in top shape and his crew eager to return to sea, while my *Victory* is in no condition to battle the Spanish."

Devon slowly digested Le Vautour's words, wondering how far she could trust him. She knew he thought her attractive, but did his greed exceed his lust? Thus far he had done nothing to cause her concern, merely offering her a way off the island in exchange for money. If he harmed her in any way, she'd make certain her father learned of it and would refuse to reward him for his trouble. Still . . .

"Wipe the uncertainty from your mind, *ma chère*," Le Vautour advised, reading her mind. "I promise to bring you no harm."

"Where is your ship? Do you know another entrance to Paradise?" Her mind whirled in confusion.

"Leave the details to me," Le Vautour advised. "I will be here when the time is right."

"But, how . . ."

"Devon, are you out there?"

"Diablo!" Devon hissed in warning. "You know he'll never willingly let me go."

"Leave everything to me. I must go now, it's best I'm not seen. If you are serious about leaving

Diablo, don't mention my being here." With the stealth of a fox Le Vautour melted into the shadows. "I'll be in touch, *ma chère*, be prepared."

"What are you doing out here by yourself, sweetheart?" Diablo asked suspiciously when he came upon Devon standing alone at the crest of the hill. "You *are* alone, aren't you?"

"Of course, unless you count the moon and stars."

"It is a beautiful night, I can't blame you for lingering out here." Sidling closer, he embraced her from behind, resting his chin on her bright head.

"Were your dealings with Le Vautour profitable?" Devon asked idly.

"Better than I had hoped. Of course Kyle was along to see that Le Vautour held up his end of the bargain. Our booty brought a good price, and even after Le Vautour's cut the men will be pleased with their shares."

He did not mention that his share would be enriched by Kyle's cut even though he didn't intend to take all his friend's earnings despite their bet. Kyle had berated him thoroughly for using Devon for his own pleasure without a thought for her tender feelings. Kyle had urged him to return Devon to her father, and that was when Diablo had broken down and admitted that he loved Devon, that he could no more let her go than he could stop eating or breathing.

"Then you found Le Vautour to be trustworthy?" Devon probed, jerking Diablo from his musings. She hoped his answer would ease her misgivings about the French pirate.

"Only so far as it pleases him to give his trust." Diablo frowned, annoyed by Devon's interest in the buccaneer. "Why are you so curious about Le Vautour? I admit he cuts a handsome figure in his fancy clothes."

Realizing her mistake, Devon quickly said, "I don't care a fig about the man. I was merely making conversation."

"With you in my arms, conversation is the last thing on my mind," Diablo said, nuzzling her neck. "Come inside, sweetheart. Kyle is gone and I've thought of nothing but undressing you all evening. Admittedly that gown looks outrageously lovely on you, but my greatest pleasure comes with removing it, as well as all the other fripperies underneath that conceal your beauty."

Devon sucked her breath in sharply. His voice was low and strident, the most sensual she'd ever heard. Time and again she'd vowed to resist his devastating appeal, but her resolutions faded beneath the assault of ragged, spontaneous emotions. When he was near, nothing mattered but the need to touch and be touched. Nothing counted but being loved by this vital man who possessed her with wild abandon and loved her to distraction. Finding herself responding to Diablo's loving with the same wild abandon was reason enough for Devon to leave him. Soon she would be beyond redemption and bound to him forever.

But forever had no meaning where Diablo was concerned. The hangman stalked him wherever he roamed. Involvement with him was too uncertain, too dangerous. It would mean pain and separation and certain death. Not knowing when or where death awaited him was too painful for Devon to contemplate, and so, for her own peace of mind, she must leave him. Still, until she left she could see no earthly reason not to enjoy his loving. One day soon nothing but a vague memory would remain of the man she could easily love.

"Do you know what I'd like, Diablo?" Devon suggested impulsively.

"If it's within my power, it's yours," he promised rashly. "Just don't ask that I let you go. I—can't."

"I'd like for us to make love out here, beneath the moon and the stars, with the cool grass for a bed."

Her soft evocative words turned him instantly hard. When he finally spoke, his voice was spiked with jagged edges. "Just hearing you ask me to love you is more than I ever hoped for." He turned her in his arms, and his mouth covered hers with a scorching passion that singed all her nerve endings.

Anxious to test the texture of his skin, Devon slid her hands under his shirt, delighting in the tempered strength beneath her stroking fingers. The firm flesh and rippling muscles that shifted beneath her touch felt like steel sheathed in velvet, and Diablo groaned in frustration.

Savoring the honeyed sweetness of her kiss, he slowly bore her to the ground, at the same time shrugging out of his shirt to allow her better access. Devon lost all knowledge of time and place as she nuzzled his chest, her lips locating the tiny nubs on his flat male breast. She nipped and sucked with delicious abandon as Diablo jerked in response.

"God's bones, sweetheart, I wish I knew what triggered this burst of unbridled passion. I'd like to think it's due to my great appeal, but something tells me there's more to it than that."

"Don't question my motives, Diablo," Devon purred seductively. "Just enjoy this night."

"And all the nights to come," he added, flashing a devilish grin that exposed the dimple lurking at the corner of his mouth. "I adore you, sweetheart."

Devon knew that his words, spoken in the heat of passion, meant little, but they contributed to the magic of the moment. A moment that might never be recaptured. With efficient haste Diablo disrobed her, her nude body glowing like mellow alabaster in the moonlight. Then a terrible urgency seized him and he could wait no longer. There was no time to remove his trousers, no time for tender words or kisses, only the need to possess her now, here, forever. With shaking fingers he unfastened his trousers, freeing his rigid manhood to seek the ultimate prize.

"Sweetheart, I'm sorry," he gasped raggedly. "I can't wait."

His pulsing staff surged proudly into view as he loomed above her, kneeling between her legs on the soft grass, kissing her flat velvety stomach and then each breast in turn. With practiced ease his hard male body slid into the sweet melting warmth of hers. He buried himself deep—so deep—inside her welcoming heat, eliciting a groan from somewhere in the depths of her soul. She was as ready and receptive as he was eager.

Mindless in his hunger, dauntless in his quest, he thrust, withdrew, then thrust again, his passionate rhythm shared by Devon's fragile, trembling form as she raised herself to meet him. Deliberately pacing himself, he strove to bring her the greatest pleasure possible. Some terrible need inside him drove him, some tiny hidden voice told him that soon this must all end. It was too good to last, his love too one-sided to provide lasting happiness, his life too uncertain. Devon was not his to love.

Then all thought was abandoned when Devon stiffened and cried out. Only when the last tremor left her body did Diablo unleash his own stampeding passions. Afterwards Devon lay contentedly in his arms, England and Winston nothing but a passing thought.

Stroking her soft flesh, his heart pounding in his ears, Diablo gasped, "I never thought I'd find a woman I could love, sweetheart—and then you came into my life. If only . . ."

"If only what?" Devon asked with breathless anticipation. If he told her he was in love with her, she'd never find the courage to leave him.

"Never mind, it's too late anyway. Years too late. Besides, I need to make love to you again, more leisurely this time, in bed." Scooping her up in his arms, he walked slowly back to the house.

"Diablo, wait, our clothes! What will Tara think?"

"She'll think nothing. She's not even here. She's spending the night in the village with her widowed mother."

Finding comfort in his words, Devon relaxed in Diablo's strong arms, unaware of the pair of avid, lust-filled eyes following their progress.

Unbeknownst to them, Le Vautour had remained to witness their rapture. While they made wild love he burned with the need to possess the stunning blonde. Though she had known passion in the arms of Diablo, Le Vautour recognized an innocence about her that fired his desire. He had no doubt that Diablo had taken her maidenhead and no other man had used her sexually. Devon was so refreshingly youthful and untainted that Le Vautour would promise her anything to have her in his bed.

Besides, all indications to the contrary, Le Vautour hated Diablo. He had been waiting years to get close enough to that devil to do him some grave mischief. He had deliberately ingratiated himself with Diablo in order to pay him back for a past injustice done to a man who was more than a friend to Le Vautour. Years ago Diablo had led a mutiny that resulted in Black Bart's death, a man more like a father to Le Vautour than his own. Moreover, Diablo had seized Black Bart's ship, claimed it for his own, and renamed it *Devil Dancer*. Now, at long last, Diablo would learn the true meaning of betrayal. Lady Devon might not know it, but she would be the instrument of her lover's downfall.

Le Vautour chuckled beneath his breath. He knew that the Earl of Milford would pay dearly for his daughter's safe delivery no matter how many men had shared her favors. Once on his ship, Devon would be his despite his promises to the contrary. He'd have it all, Devon's tempting body and her father's money. Lying to suit his own purposes bothered Le Vautour not at all. Men like him—and that included Diablo—were accustomed to using trickery to gain their own ends. What made revenge all the sweeter was the knowledge that Diablo seemed genuinely fond of the lovely Lady Devon. Will he still feel that way when the lady betrayed him?

"Devon, what ails you?" Diablo asked, looking up from his dinner and frowning. "You've hardly touched a bite of food in the past two days. Are you ill?"

Devon jumped at the sound of his voice. "What! Sorry," she apologized sheepishly. "Nay, I'm not sick, just—distracted, I guess."

Actually, she was more than distracted. It had

been two days since she'd spoken with Le Vautour about leaving, and the strain of waiting was fraying her nerves. Each day she remained with Diablo, every time he made tender love to her, drove a spike into her heart, aware that she would soon leave him forever. It was as inevitable as life and death that they part; they didn't belong together, no matter what her heart told her. Love is a capricious emotion, it creeps up on you when you least expect it and leaves you devastated when you realize it can never be, Devon reflected.

"I know what will raise your spirits," Diablo hinted, grinning wolfishly. "I don't think I'll ever tire of . . ." His words faltered as loud voices interrupted their intimate meal. Tara rushed into the room.

"What is it, Tara?" Diablo scowled, annoyed by the ruckus. Domestic disputes were best left to the housekeeper, he hated to be disturbed by the staff's bickering.

"It's—"

"Ho, Diablo, is that any way to greet a friend?" Stepping into the room, Scarlett coolly surveyed the intimate setting.

"Scarlett, what in the hell are you doing here?" Diablo jumped to his feet, a scowl darkening his broad brow. "If I recall, we parted on less than friendly terms in Nassau."

"I don't believe in holding grudges," Scarlett returned saucily. "Besides, petty arguments have no place in business dealings."

"True," Diablo allowed, wondering what Scarlett was up to. It wasn't like her to take their split lightly. Knowing Scarlett like he did, Diablo strongly suspected she had some trick up her sleeve, and she wasn't on Paradise to renew old friendships. "All right, Scarlett, tell me, what brings you to Paradise?"

"Not in front of your doxy," Scarlett said spitefully, nodding at Devon.

"If you're speaking of Lady Devon, I suggest you watch your tongue," Diablo warned. "Come into my study, we'll not be disturbed there." To Devon, he said, "Sorry, sweetheart, I'll be back as soon as I find out what Scarlett is up to."

"Don't wait up, my lady," Scarlett taunted after Diablo left the room. "My business will no doubt take some time." Her husky voice hinted that more than business would be conducted behind the closed door.

"Take as long as you like, Scarlett, I'm not Diablo's keeper," Devon returned haughtily.

Devon fumed as Scarlett strutted off after Diablo, her tall figure superb in tight pants, full-sleeved shirt, and colorful vest. From the moment she entered the room Devon realized she was the "friend" Le Vautour had mentioned. Did Scarlett's abrupt arrival have anything to do with Le Vautour and his plan to take her off the island? she wondered.

Admitting to herself that she had grown to love Diablo was the most difficult thing Devon had ever done. But no matter how hard she tried she could no longer deny her feelings for the pirate rogue. Aye, Devon decided resolutely, love him or not, she'd still leave when Le Vautour came for her. She knew that Diablo would only break her heart, while Winston was the kind of man she could depend upon. She didn't need the heartache the pirate would bring to her. Telling herself it didn't matter if

Scarlett succeeded in seducing him, Devon retired to her room to contemplate her bleak future with a man she could never love while the hangman's noose awaited the one she did love.

"I'm waiting, Scarlett," Diablo said, thrumming his fingers impatiently on the top of his desk. "Tell me what brings you to Paradise."

With exaggerated slowness, Scarlett took a seat opposite Diablo, crossed her incredibly long legs, and fixed him with the full seductive power of her green eyes. "I have some information that might interest you."

"What kind of information?" Diablo asked shrewdly.

"Did you know there's a substantial reward out for Lady Devon? The earl is quite anxious to recover his daughter, judging from the size of the reward. Stede Bonnet's ship was captured three weeks ago by a navy frigate and instead of being destroyed it was allowed to proceed on its way in order to relay the message to Nassau.

Diablo had already heard the rumor in Nassau when he had gone to meet Le Vautour and Kyle. News traveled fast in the Caribbean. The system worked better than a newspaper as word traveled from ship to ship around the Caribbean and pirates' ports of call.

"Aye, I heard."

"What are you going to do about it? The woman belongs with her own kind. She'll bring nothing but trouble to you if you insist on keeping her. Can't you see she's not for the likes of you? But you and me, we're alike, my friend. Neither of us demands more of each other than we're willing to give. You're a handsome rogue, Diablo, and the best damn lover I've ever had."

An amused smile hung on the corners of Diablo's lips. "I'm hardly in a position to take Devon back to England."

"The *Red Witch* is at your disposal, Diablo. I'll be happy to take the lady back to her daddy and collect the reward. I'm not as notorious as you, and the price on my head not so great. I can easily get in and out of England to do your bidding."

"Most accommodating of you, but I'm not sending Devon back. Not now, maybe not ever, and certainly not with you."

A red haze obscured Scarlett's vision. Before she fell in with Le Vautour's plan she wanted to give Diablo every opportunity to rid himself willingly of his new mistress. By Devon's own admission she was a reluctant prisoner and anxious to leave Diablo's protection. But what truly dismayed Scarlett was the fact that Diablo appeared smitten with the lady and reluctant to part with her, leaving Scarlett with no alternative. For Diablo's own good she was forced to join Le Vautour in his endeavor.

"Is that all you wanted, Scarlett? It's getting late and—"

"She'll keep," Scarlett bit out, her voice tinged with disgust. "I'm sorry I missed you in Nassau a few days ago, but Le Vautour told me your venture proved quite profitable. Are your men ready to sail?"

"The *Devil Dancer* is ready to go to sea the moment I give the command."

"But you can't tear yourself away from your little whore."

Diablo's eyes turned murky as he regarded

Scarlett coldly. "That's enough, Scarlett! Don't judge all women by your own standards. Devon is a lady, an innocent virgin until I stole that from her."

His words served only to intensify her hatred for Devon. She'd do anything to save Diablo from himself, certain that one day Devon would lead him to the gallows. But he was too damn infatuated to see it.

"What if I told you that three Spanish galleons, their holds loaded with gold and silver, were within striking distance?"

Diablo regarded Scarlett warily. "How do you know that?"

"I saw them with my own eyes not two days ago. I followed them from Florida waters and know exactly where to find them. I'd take them on alone, but they are armed and I don't dare risk my ship and men without help. I'm telling you because I need your aid. Join me and we'll split the booty equally."

Diablo's attention sharpened at the thought of attacking the despised Spanish. Already he could smell the tangy odor of the ocean and taste spindrift on his lips. Spanish galleons! God's bones, he'd give anything to relieve them of their precious cargo. Even after splitting the booty he'd have enough to retire for life. Maybe enough to offer Devon—no, he chided himself. Devon belonged to a different world and one day must be returned to her own kind. Not even his great love for her could leap across the abyss to unite them.

When he first heard rumors in Nassau, Diablo thought it merely gossip, since no one seemed to know for certain or had seen the elusive fleet, but he knew that Scarlett had no reason to lie. Still, something inside Diablo prodded him to caution, despite the fact that buccaneers lived by a code of honor. "Who else have you told about this?"

"No one, do you think me stupid? When I failed to find you in Nassau I came directly to Paradise. You're the only one I'd trust to help me."

"Le Vautour probably knows but his *Victory* is in no shape to give chase. He intends to drydock her for a month in Nassau to make necessary repairs."

"Are you with me then?"

Several tense minutes passed as Diablo gave careful consideration to Scarlett's proposal. It wasn't the first time she had enlisted his help in similar ventures, so why should he refuse now? They had dealt well together before and could do so again. They may have parted in anger in Nassau, but evidently Scarlett regretted her hasty words and approached him now as a way to mend their friendship. His primary objection was leaving Devon on Paradise unattended. He smiled inwardly as a solution came to him. Though Kyle would protest vigorously, he would be left behind to protect Diablo's prized possession.

"When do we leave?"

A wide grin split Scarlett's beautiful features. "The sooner the better, if we want to intercept the galleons before someone else finds them."

"Some of my crew are in Nassau," Diablo replied. "If I sail with the morning tide I can pick them up and rendezvous with the *Red Witch* on the west side of New Providence Island."

"I'll be there," acknowledged Scarlett eagerly. "Don't bother to show me out, I know the way."

Diablo had already buried his head in a ledger when Scarlett slipped from the room. But instead of letting herself out the front door, she sidled up the stairs, keeping carefully to the shadows. Her prior knowledge of the house led her directly to the room assigned to Devon. Not bothering to knock, she turned the knob and stepped inside.

Chapter Nine

Clad in a diaphanous bedgown that Diablo had given her, Devon stood before the windows gazing wistfully into the star-studded night. Light from a single candle outlined her figure beneath the gauzy material, painting it gold to match the bright strands of hair brushing her waist. The click of the latch brought her instantly alert and she whirled, expecting to see Diablo. The welcome died on her lips.

"You! What are you doing in my room? Where is Diablo?"

Scarlett eyed Devon malevolently, aware that this lovely vision awaited Diablo and would soon be decorating his bed, the sole recipient of his ardor. Her hands clenched in barely suppressed anger, and she would have flown at Devon if Diablo wasn't nearby to come to her defense.

"I have something to say to you," Scarlett bit out.

"How did you find your way to Paradise?" Devon

asked, moving away from the window.

"I'm no stranger to Diablo's island," Scarlett smirked. "He trusts me."

"Say what you will, then leave," Devon returned shortly.

"Be prepared to leave tomorrow. Diablo sails on the morning's tide, and Le Vautour says to tell you to expect him."

Devon blanched. Evidently Scarlett was privy to her plans to leave Diablo and had been enlisted by Le Vautour to help. What had Scarlett said to Diablo to make him leave so suddenly? Devon trusted Scarlett even less than she did Le Vautour. "I'll be ready."

"I must go before I'm discovered." With the stealth of a sleek cat Scarlett edged toward the door, reached for the knob, then paused. "Why?" she asked curiously. "Why do you want to leave Diablo? Few men are as handsome. I've never known a better lover, and he seems genuinely fond of you. Perhaps you think yourself superior to him."

"You wouldn't understand," Devon said dismissively. Scarlett was not one to invite intimacy, nor did Devon wish to divulge how deeply it would hurt to leave Diablo. That bit of knowledge must necessarily remain buried deep within the chambers of her heart.

With a snort of disgust, Scarlett slowly pivoted and left the room as quietly as she had entered.

Diablo rubbed the back of his neck to ease his tired muscles and looked longingly toward the stairs. After Scarlett left he sent one of the servants to the village with a message for Kyle. A short time later Kyle arrived and Diablo imparted all the information provided by Scarlett about the Spanish galleons. Grumbling crossly, Kyle left to round up the crew and ready the ship for immediate sailing, none too happy about Diablo's request that he remain behind. Though Kyle had protested vigorously, Diablo was adamant, trusting no other man to look after Devon in his absence.

Nothing remained now but for Diablo to join Devon in her bed and make slow, passionate love to her till morning. Taking the stairs two at a time, he entered her bedroom on silent feet. She was not asleep as he expected but was sitting in a chair gazing forlornly out into the black velvet curtain of night.

"Might I hope that wistful look is because you miss me?" Diablo teased.

"Diablo!" Leaping to her feet, Devon went eagerly into his waiting arms. "It's so late. I've been waiting for you."

"Come to bed, sweetheart. The night is nearly spent and I can't leave without loving you."

"Leave?" The right note of surprise and regret entered her voice. "Am I going with you?"

"Not this time, love. This is—business. Kyle will remain behind to keep you amused."

"I don't need to be amused," she replied, dismayed. How could she leave the island with Kyle dogging her steps? "I don't need a watchdog, either. Besides, knowing Kyle as I do, he'll want to be with you."

"Nevertheless, he stays. He'll receive his share of the booty just like the others."

Before Devon could voice another protest, Diablo scooped her into his arms and placed her on the bed. She watched avidly as he shed his clothes, the dim light illuminating the bulging muscles of his magnificent torso. His powerful frame moved with

easy grace as he stood before her proud and una-
shamed. Devon stared in fascination at his tempting physique, acutely conscience of the male aura of
sexuality he exuded. That male part of him that
gave her so much pleasure sprang forth boldly from
the dark forest between his thighs, and Devon
reached out boldly to stroke the velvet staff into
throbbing life.

Diablo seized her hand. "Nay, sweetheart, I don't
want the night to end before it begins. Lie back and
let me love you."

Knowing this was the last time she would be with
Diablo like this, Devon's own driving need became
a living flame within her. She wanted to put her
brand on this man so that she'd remain in his
memory beyond time and space. "It's my turn,
Kit," she said with bold innuendo. "Let me love
you."

Before he could protest she pulled him down
beside her on the bed, shrugging out of her bedgown
while he watched in breathless anticipation. "I'm
all yours, sweetheart," he managed to gasp as she
slid her body full length atop him.

Putting her hands, lips, and mouth to good use,
Devon used everything Diablo had taught her to
bring him the greatest pleasure he had ever known.
When she straddled his slim hips and took him
deep into her moist sheath, he was driven out of his
mind with need. She set the rhythm and Diablo
eagerly followed until the blood pounded through
his veins and desperation seized him. Then he
grasped her hips, holding her captive, his impatience growing to explosive proportions as he thrust
wildly—deeply.

Devon groaned in sweet agony as the turbulence
of his passion swirled around her. She was a glow-

ing image of fire, passion—and love. Then she soared to awesome, shuddering ecstasy. "Kit!"

Diablo did not stop, but continued his loving torment until he reignited the dying flame of her passion into blazing splendor. Never had he felt so strong, so virile, wishing it never had to end. But eventually his body took over and he poured himself into her.

"Are you awake, sweetheart?"

"Aye. Must you leave already?"

"Not yet, there's still time for us to love again, but first there's something I need to say."

Devon tensed. Did she really want to hear Diablo's words? Intuitively she sensed what he wanted to say and thought it better left unsaid. She wanted their parting accomplished without tender sentiments, without either of them revealing personal feelings that could never become reality. "Kit, won't it keep? This is hardly the time for—"

"There's no better time, sweetheart. I love you, Devon. I never thought I'd say that to any woman, but you're different from any woman I've ever known. I want to spend the rest of my life with you. I want children from your body. I want—God's bones, sweetheart, I want us to be together forever. No matter what it takes, I'll find a way."

"Kit, nay, you don't know what you're saying." Diablo's words thrilled Devon whether he meant them or not. Her own heart was filled with so much love for him she had to bite her tongue to keep from crying out her feelings.

"I know exactly what I'm saying. You don't know how much I love the sound of my name on your lips. My real name. I'd almost forgotten I had a name other than Diablo."

"Kit, listen to me!" Devon pleaded. "I must leave. This attraction between us is doomed. There's more than love involved here, there are other people to consider. There's my father and—and my fiancé. You and I are from different worlds. It would never work. How could I stay with you, knowing that one day word would come telling me you'd been caught and hanged?"

"What I feel for you goes beyond mere attraction," Diablo confided. "If we were from the same culture, contemporaries, so to speak, would it make a difference?"

"Possibly," Devon admitted slowly. "But what good is conjecture when we both know what you are and how your life will end?"

"When I return, sweetheart, there's a story I want to tell you. One that will shock you, but one I think will make a difference in what you feel for me."

"I seriously doubt there's anything you could say that will change things."

"I've bared my soul to you, Devon. Me, Diablo, a man notorious for his secrets and proud of his female conquests. Who would have thought I'd be brought to my knees by a woman half my size, one who makes love like an angel? God's bones, Devon, why can't you love me as much as I love you?"

Devon flushed, biting her tongue to cry out her own love but knowing it would only cause them more grief. "If it helps, I do care for you, Kit. More than I care to admit. But it's senseless to talk about something that was doomed from the beginning."

"I agree," Diablo grinned wolfishly. "Especially when I want desperately to make love to you again. Just think about what I've said while I'm gone. When I return, perhaps my explanation will persuade you otherwise."

"Devil you might be, but when you make love to me you take me to heaven," Devon sighed, melting into the warmth of his body. "Take me to heaven, Kit."

"Gladly, sweetheart, if you take me along with you."

Diablo was gone. She'd never see his captivating smile again. Tears of remorse watered Devon's eyes as she recalled their passionate parting just before dawn colored the sky. She knew that Diablo hadn't the slightest inkling she'd be gone before he returned. His parting words reaffirming the love he bore her were nearly her undoing. Choking on a sob, Devon could only wish him God's speed, too distraught to speak. If she so much as opened her mouth she'd blurt out that she loved him, that she'd never forget him, and that Winston would never take his place in her heart. But she remained mute. How could she stay with Diablo knowing that one day they'd be torn apart and she'd likely be forced to watch him hang from the gallows? Better to part now before children came along to complicate their lives. How would she tell their offspring their father was a notorious pirate responsible for countless deaths?

Though Devon's appetite was virtually nonexistent, she appeared in the dining room for breakfast, not wishing to arouse undue suspicion. Tara was extremely perceptive and might take it upon herself to alert Kyle should Devon act other than normal.

Devon had just spooned the last mouthful of food in her mouth when Kyle joined her, looking decidedly unhappy. Devon knew immediately what bothered him and understood his disappointment. Being left behind to guard over a woman certainly was no task for a man accustomed to adventure on the high seas.

"I'm sorry to be so much trouble, Kyle," she said sincerely. "I know how much you want to be with Diablo. If it were up to me you'd be aboard the *Devil Dancer*."

"Aye," Kyle agreed glumly. "But Diablo wouldn't have left me here with you if he didn't care for you."

Devon flushed, unable to meet Kyle's eyes. What would he say if he knew she meant to leave Diablo before the day was out? Then suddenly a disturbing thought entered her mind. What would Le Vautour do when he found Kyle attending her? Surely the pirate wouldn't hurt Kyle, would he?

Excusing herself, Devon went upstairs to pack clothes necessary for her journey. Kyle watched her slow progress up the stairs, puzzled by her odd behavior. He had hoped she'd remain for some stimulating conversation, but it was not to be. Unaccustomed to the vagaries of women, Kyle shrugged and left the house to see to the onerous duties concerning the plantation that Diablo had dumped in his lap.

Hidden in a shallow cove on a neighboring island, Le Vautour watched with unconcealed glee as both the *Red Witch* and *Devil Dancer* cleared the shoals and sailed away from Paradise. Scarlett had played her role admirably in leading Diablo from his roost. Le Vautour waited until the ships were out of sight before navigating the reef and finding his way to Diablo's hidden cove. When the *Victory* was anchored in the bay, Le Vautour's men swarmed ashore, finding little difficulty subduing the women and children left behind. With no one to stop him, Le Vautour walked boldly up to the devil's lair.

When he reached the house he became more cautious, deciding to conceal himself until he scouted the lay of the land and learned if Diablo had left someone behind to guard his prize. His caution proved prudent, for he had just scuttled for cover when Kyle walked out the door.

Hiding behind a dense thicket of bougainvillea beside the house, Le Vautour watched as Kyle walked toward the rear of the house. Le Vautour assumed he was going to the cane fields, and waited until he was out of sight before exposing himself. Making certain no one was in sight, Le Vautour sidled through the front door.

Luckily Tara was working in the kitchen connected to the house by a dogwalk, and the other servants were engaged in duties elsewhere. Having been told by Scarlett which room belonged to Devon, Le Vautour climbed the stairs and entered her room unannounced.

Devon had just placed the last of her belongings in a bag when she whirled to find Le Vautour standing at her elbow. "You could have knocked," she bit out, more angry than frightened.

"I didn't want to alert the servants. Are you ready?"

"Diablo left Kyle behind."

"I know," Le Vautour replied anxiously. "He just left the house, so we must hurry. My men are prepared to raise anchor the moment we're safely aboard." He grasped her arm to hurry her along.

"Wait! My bag. I've packed a few necessities."

Le Vautour spied the bag, scooped it up, and urged her down the stairs. Devon had intended to leave Diablo the locket she wore around her neck as a small memento, but at the last minute decided she couldn't part with it for it bore the likeness of her mother. He would just have to make do with his memory of their time together.

Le Vautour's hand was on the doorknob when Kyle walked unexpectedly into the hall from the back of the house. So great was his shock he had no time to react or even to defend himself as Le Vautour dropped Devon's bag and drew his cutlass. Though the Frenchman aimed for Kyle's heart, the big Irishman had the presence of mind to turn aside at the last minute so that the blade sliced through his arm and into his side.

Devon screamed as Kyle started a slow spiral to the floor. "You've killed him! You heartless brute, you've killed Kyle."

"Non, *ma chère*," Le Vautour denied, nettled by Devon's outburst and anxious to be away. "He'll survive. I strongly advise you stop that screeching before you alert the whole island. I thought you wanted to leave."

"I—do, but I didn't want anyone hurt. Are you certain he'll be all right?"

"What's this all about, lass?" Kyle found the voice to ask. "Are you leaving Diablo? How did Le Vautour find Paradise?"

"Forgive me, Kyle," Devon sobbed, heartbroken over how things were turning out. "I didn't mean for this to happen. I wanted to leave here quietly with no one the wiser. Le Vautour is taking me back to England where I belong."

"You can't trust him, lass," Kyle warned, growing weak from loss of blood. "Mark my words, Diablo won't let you go so easily. And you, Le

Vautour, make the most of your time for your days are numbered."

Le Vautour laughed nastily. "I fear neither man nor devil." Then he picked up Devon's bag, gripped her arm, and dragged her out the door.

"Devon, don't go, you don't know what you're doing," Kyle pleaded, depleting the last of his strength.

"I can't leave him like this," Devon balked, straining back toward Kyle.

But Le Vautour was not to be denied. He wanted Devon nearly as much as he wanted the reward for returning her to her father. He pulled, prodded, and pushed her all the way to the village, her meager strength no match for him.

The *Victory* was the only ship riding at anchor in the protected bay, and Devon could see men scurrying about the deck in preparation for sailing. When they reached the beach, the helpless villagers stood by as Le Vautour wrestled the devil's lady into a waiting longboat. Within minutes they were rowed to the ship and Devon was unceremoniously dumped aboard. Soon the *Victory* slipped its moorings and Le Vautour was negotiating the narrow river and gliding through the treacherous reef protecting the island.

Once they were in open water, Le Vautour turned the wheel over to his lieutenant and rejoined Devon where she stood at the rail watching forlornly as Paradise disappeared over the horizon. For a short space of time the island had truly become her paradise.

"Don't fret, *ma chère*," he soothed. "In two or three weeks, depending on the winds, you'll be with your family and I'll be all the richer for it. 'Twill be my pleasure to make your journey a pleasant one. Come along, I'll see you to your cabin."

Le Vautour's leering grin set Devon's teeth on edge, but she was determined to ignore his sly innuendos. In the two weeks or so it would take to reach England she vowed never to be alone with the devious pirate or to place herself in a compromising position.

To her chagrin, Devon felt reasonably certain the cabin to which she was assigned was the captain's domain. It was richly decorated and completely masculine, and none but Le Vautour would possess so many fine things. When he returned to the bridge to set the course and issue orders pertaining to their journey, Devon carefully examined her surroundings.

Innocently naive, she believed that Le Vautour intended to occupy other quarters, that collecting ransom for her safe return was uppermost in his mind, and she would be safe from his lust for that reason. So far he had done nothing to disabuse her of that notion, and she clung desperately to that hope.

Devon retired early after supping alone, and finding no lock on the door was determined to ask to have one installed the next day. Before she fell asleep, she uttered a prayer for Kyle's swift recovery and thought wistfully of Diablo, the man she loved more than her own life but could never have.

Le Vautour stood before Devon's door for a long interval, his loins throbbing with the need to possess the beautiful blonde goddess occupying his bed. Considering himself too wise to be ruled by his lust, he finally turned away. Time was on his side. First he'd attempt to seduce Devon, and failing that, resort to more forceful methods. After watching her and Diablo couple on the ground like two animals, Le Vautour was determined to have her as hot and eager for him as she obviously was for her devil lover.

The following days passed pleasantly enough despite the despondency Devon suffered. The knowledge that she would never see Diablo again had sent her spirits plummeting. Lately she had come to think of him as Kit, not Diablo, for the name suited him better. He was hardly the devil people made him out to be. Once Kyle had confided that Kit had never deliberately killed anyone. He attacked mostly merchantmen, frightening them into submission by putting a shot across their bows and waiting patiently for surrender. Often a ship was captured without striking a blow. Only when the *Devil Dancer* was challenged by navy vessels did a fight ensue and men were injured or killed. Moreover, Kit's prisoners were never treated harshly. Some were ransomed, but usually passengers were left on the ships to make their way back minus their cargos.

The name "Kit" gave Devon little clue as to Diablo's origins. She had originally thought him Spanish, but detected no sign of an accent. He spoke flawless English—not the low street dialect but with perfect diction. The man was not only a mystery but a contradiction. Kind, tender, gentle, loving. Arrogant, overbearing; a pirate notorious for unscrupulous deeds, most of them embellished lavishly as they passed from mouth to mouth and country to country. Who was he really? She was destined never to know, for their paths would never again cross.

The fourth day out Devon awoke to overcast skies and brisk winds. "Looks like a storm brewing," she remarked when Le Vautour joined her on the deck.

"I doubt it," he said, sniffing the air. "A bit of a blow, mayhap, but nothing serious. "'Twill be naught but a brief summer storm."

Le Vautour truly believed the coming tempest would be of short duration, and he chose tonight to seduce Devon. Each passing day sorely tested his patience, until he had to have her or explode. He thought himself amazingly forebearing given his Gallic temperament, and could wait no longer to enjoy the wench.

Devon remained skeptical despite Le Vautour's assurance that a major storm wasn't in the offing. "I'll take your word, Le Vautour," she said doubtfully. "About the lock on the door, it still hasn't been installed." So far the Frenchman had ignored her frequent requests for a lock, promising vaguely to have it done as soon as time permitted.

"*Ma chère*," Le Vautour replied, feigning concern, "have you been disturbed since setting foot on my ship? Have any of my men accosted you?"

Grudgingly Devon admitted that Le Vautour ruled his ship and men with an iron fist. She knew he dealt swift and cruel punishment, for many times in the past days she heard the whistle of the whip followed by grunts, moans, and screams of agony. So far she had managed to hold her tongue about Le Vautour's handling of his men.

"Nay, I've not been molested."

"And you won't be," he stated arrogantly. "My crew knows I demand strict obedience. But enough of that, I've ordered cook to prepare a special feast for us tonight. A small offering to celebrate our alliance."

"Hardly an alliance," contradicted Devon.

"What else would you call it, *ma chère*? I would say it is mutually beneficial. You get your freedom and I get—what I want," Le Vautour said cryptically. "So, about supper . . ."

She could hardly refuse, Devon considered thoughtfully. Angering Le Vautour was the last thing she wanted. She had willingly placed herself in a vulnerable position and already regretted it. She had never meant for anyone to be hurt and fervently prayed Kyle was recovering from his wound. Of Diablo, she tried not to think. When she did the pain was unbearable.

"Of course I'll sup with you," Devon allowed with grudging acceptance. "I'm grateful to you even though I deeply regret your rash actions concerning Kyle. It was a senseless act and could have resulted in his death."

"But a necessary one if we were to leave without interference. I assure you the man will live. So, *ma chère*, until tonight." With a gallant gesture totally at odds with his calling, Le Vautour brought Devon's hand to his lips. Then he spun on his heel and strode off with a jaunty bounce.

Distraught, Devon paced the confines of the cabin, fully aware of the grave mistake she had committed by placing herself at Le Vautour's disposal. Though he'd not touched her, his black eyes all but devoured her each time they met, and she despised the way his probing gaze rested far too often on her bosom. Kyle was right, the man did not inspire trust. At least she knew what to expect, she reasoned, and was prepared to deal with it.

A short time later Le Vautour arrived accompanied by two crewmen bearing assorted dishes from which the tempting aroma of food wafted. The pirate had dressed himself like a dandy, sporting a blue velvet frockcoat and a white shirt dripping with yards of lace. Prancing about the cabin, he saw to the placement of food and drink and then dismissed the men with a lazy wave of his hand.

"You look ravishing, *ma chère*," he purred once they were alone.

Actually, Devon had done nothing to enhance her natural beauty, merely wearing one of the dresses she brought along with her.

"Shall we eat?" she suggested. "The food smells delicious and I'm famished."

"Excellent idea," Le Vautour agreed. His hawk-like features sharpened and he ogled Devon as if he'd prefer to taste *her* rather than the food. Though he was not unhandsome, his sly regard of her set her nerves on edge.

While they supped, pelting rain lashed at the windows and the howling wind made eating difficult. Their meal was interrupted when several dishes slid from the table to the deck.

"It's all right," Devon assured a disgruntled Le Vautour. "I was finished anyway."

"This is not how I planned the evening, *ma chère*," he apologized, rising. Bracing his feet on the swaying deck, he helped Devon to her feet and over to the bunk. "You'll be safer here until the storm abates." But instead of leaving as Devon expected, he settled down beside her.

"Aren't you needed on deck?" she asked, her voice strangled with rising panic.

"Peck is quite capable at navigating through the

tempest. As I said before, the storm will be of short duration. Perhaps we can create a storm of our own inside this cabin," he hinted slyly.

"I prefer that you leave," Devon insisted indignantly. "I wouldn't want to keep you from your duties."

"You're no innocent, *ma chère*, you know what I want." Le Vautour's narrow face assumed a predatory gleam as he reached for her. "You knew what to expect when you sailed with me." Grasping her waist, he dragged her into his arms.

"You promised!" Devon cried, pounding her fists against his chest. "You said you'd deliver me to my father unharmed.

"Harming you is furthest from my mind," Le Vautour said smoothly. "I know Diablo has enjoyed you and I merely wish the same privilege."

"Let me go! You're nothing like Diablo. What happened between us has nothing to do with you. Besides, one word from me and my father will send you packing without a cent."

"Your father will pay—and pay well," Le Vautour laughed. "As long as I hold you hostage I can name my price. Besides, you'll not see your father until the reward is in my hand. By then I'll be long gone and it will be too late to cry foul. I want you, *ma chère*—now."

Driven beyond restraint, Le Vautour seized Devon's lips in a kiss so forceful it pressed the breath from her lungs. Suddenly his hands were everywhere, on her thighs, her breasts, her hips, squeezing her buttocks until she cried out in pain. Drawing renewed strength from somewhere within her slender body, Devon fought back furiously, the turbulence of the storm matching the turbulence of her struggles. Forced down into the surface of the bunk, she felt the weight of Le Vautour's considerable bulk smothering her.

"You brute!" she gasped as he fought to subdue her.

"I didn't want it to be like this, *ma chère*," he wheezed breathlessly. "I had hoped you'd submit willingly, but if not I'm prepared to use force. Which will it be?"

"Damn you, Le Vautour! Now I know why neither Diablo nor Kyle trusts you. You're crazy if you think I'll submit to a bastard like you."

"I'm a better lover than Diablo. Scarlett can vouch for that."

Hearing Diablo and Scarlett linked together in that manner served only to reinforce Devon's rage and she renewed her struggles. But she soon became aware that her efforts were futile in the face of Le Vautour's lust for her. She felt the pull and heard the sound of cloth being torn as her bodice split and slid away from her body. Le Vautour's black eyes gleamed with salacious intent as he stared at Devon's pale breasts laid bare by his heavy hand.

"*Mon Dieu!* You're magnificent, *ma chère*. Once I put my brand on you you'll want no other man."

"You arrogant, conceited pig!"

Le Vautour's face hardened and he began tearing at Devon's clothes, her careless words stripping away the veneer to reveal the cruel streak in his flawed character. "You little bitch," he sneered menacingly. "Am I not good enough for you? What does Diablo have that I lack?"

"A heart!" spat Devon, condemnation ripe on her tongue. "Leave now and I'll say nothing to my father."

Le Vautour was far too aroused to worry about the earl hundreds of miles away in England. Shifting, he began tearing at his own constrictive garments.

When Devon realized how close she was to being ravished, she opened her mouth to scream, but the sound was lost to the wailing wind. Instead of subsiding, if anything the violence of the storm had intensified, but Le Vautour was aware of nothing but his overwhelming lust. Then suddenly fate intervened to save Devon from his vile intentions.

The ship keeled sickeningly, balanced precariously for what seemed like hours, then righted itself . . . only to lurch in the opposite direction before once again leaping upright. The two struggling bodies rolled to the edge of the bunk, then slid off to land with a thud on the deck.

"*Mon Dieu!*" exclaimed Le Vautour, scrambling to his feet. He had his hand on the door when a loud crash signaled more danger. He turned to shout at Devon over the din of the raging elements, "I'm not finished with you!" Then he was gone, prying the door open against the onslaught of lashing rain and whipping wind.

A small sob left Devon's throat as she crawled onto the bunk and slipped beneath the covers, hanging on to the sides to keep from being thrown off. God had heard her plea and granted her a reprieve, but what would happen when Le Vautour returned? she asked herself despondently. Would she have to go through this again?

The storm continued to unleash its fury and Devon began to wonder if she'd survive the terrible tempest. The sea was a cruel mistress who destroyed indiscriminately and jealously kept what she claimed. Devon was convinced she would die an ignoble death, never to be heard or seen again.

Would she be missed? She wondered glumly. By her father, surely, and perhaps Winston, and maybe Diablo, for a short time. Until he found someone to take her place.

Diablo—Kit— What would he think when he returned and found her gone and Kyle wounded because of her? Would he hate her? Perhaps it was best if he did. Whatever it was that had lured him away from Paradise could have only been some trick cooked up by Scarlett and Le Vautour, Devon reasoned, and Diablo was bound to be furious when he discovered the hoax. Did he care enough to come after her? For his own good she certainly hoped not. Returning to England would be tantamount to writing his own death warrant.

A terrible crash brought Devon's thoughts skidding to a halt. The sound of shouts and cries rising above the roaring wind cleared her mind of all but the necessity for haste as she leaped from the bunk and threw a cloak over the tattered remnants of her clothing, certain the ship was in danger of sinking and determined to leave the confines of the cabin.

Her hand was on the door latch when the panel burst open, forcing her backwards. Several men, soaking wet and looking half-drowned, pushed into the cabin bearing the body of a man. Devon recognized Le Vautour immediately. She made way as they carried him to the bunk. Only then did she notice the piece of jagged wood about a foot long protruding from his thigh and the peculiar angle of his right arm.

"What happened?"

"The mainmast snapped and the cap'n couldn't get out of the way fast enough," growled Peck, Le Vautour's lieutenant.

"Will he live?"

"Who's to say?"

"Where's the doctor?"

"Dead. Crushed by the mast. He wasn't as fast as Le Vautour."

The man's callous reply shocked Devon. "Who's to treat him if the doctor's dead?"

Suddenly another crash rent the air and Peck said hurriedly, "Do what you can. I'll leave one man to help, but the rest are needed on deck." Then he was gone, followed by all but a small, grizzled pirate obviously too old to be of any use on deck.

Devon stared at Le Vautour with something akin to horror. That he was badly wounded was obvious. For what he intended to do to her she felt she had every right to let him die. But she couldn't. He was a human being, albeit a miserable one, and she was humanitarian enough to help. Not that she was all that versed in the art of healing. Far from it.

"What ye gonna do, lady?" the ancient pirate asked, staring uncertainly at his bleeding captain.

"What's your name?"

"They call me Gabby 'cause I like to spin yarns."

"Well, Gabby, what do you suggest? I'm willing to do what I can, but I've not done this sort of thing before."

"I've helped the doc some, lady, but I ain't particularly knowledgeable. I'd say that splinter gotta come out," Gabby advised, "and the bleedin' stopped. Then we can set that right arm."

Gritting her teeth against a sudden rise of nausea, Devon helped Gabby remove the large splinter from Le Vautour's leg. Then they cleansed the gaping wound by dousing it copiously with rum, and managed to stop the bleeding to a trickle while the captain remained blissfully unconscious. Luckily no bones were broken in the thigh. After binding the wound with clean cloths, they set to work on the broken arm.

Devon sent Gabby in search of a board to serve as a splint. While he was gone, Devon determined the break was in the lower arm between elbow and wrist. When Gabby returned, they pulled the bone into place and taped the arm to the board. Then they administered a liberal dose of laudanum found in the doctor's bag retrieved by Gabby.

Afterwards, Devon collapsed in a chair and closed her eyes while the grizzled pirate cleaned up Le Vautour and put him into a nightshirt. Only then did she realize that the storm had abated and the ship had somehow ridden out the tempest. She was amazed to find she was still alive and unharmed, though the damage to the *Victory* had to be heavy.

During the following days the pirate crew was much too busy to bother with Devon as they worked tirelessly to repair their ship. Not wanting to appear conspicuous, she remained safely inside the cabin. Too hurt to be moved, Le Vautour remained in the cabin, forcing Devon to sleep on a pallet. Gabby came in and out freely, bearing meals and performing more personal duties for his wounded captain. Peck appeared daily to check on Le Vautour's progress, as well as to receive orders once the captain had regained his senses. It spoke well for Le Vautour's leadership that his men were willing to continue under his rule rather than elect a new captain.

By some miracle, or perhaps the generous rum bath, Le Vautour's wound did not fester and was healing slowly but surely. A week later he was able to hobble to another cabin, supported between two burly pirates. He was vain enough not to want Devon to see him in diminished health. It was obvious, though, that his right arm would never regain its previous dexterity. Still, he had much to be grateful for. But being the kind of man he was, he was more bitter than grateful. On the verge of possessing Devon, fate had conspired against him and deprived him of the very thing he had spent considerable time planning and plotting for. Now, due to his injuries, it looked as if he'd have to forego the pleasure of her body and settle for the earl's reward, for he was in no condition to pursue his former objective and unlikely to be so for some time to come.

No one was more thankful for Le Vautour's disability than Devon. Unable to continue with his plan of seduction, but still desirous of receiving full payment from her father, he kept his crew from molesting her. When he was finally able to hobble around under his own steam, he visited Devon in her cabin.

"So, *ma chère*, the trip didn't go exactly as I had planned," he began breezily. "I'd hoped by now we'd know one another intimately."

"I'd not wish you unnecessary pain, but I'm not sorry. You'd have raped me if you hadn't been injured," Devon maintained.

Le Vautour's lips thinned sourly. "Rape is a harsh word. You had only to cooperate."

"What do you want, Le Vautour?" Devon asked, adroitly changing the subject.

"If I were able I'd show you what I want. But as things stand we'll reach England before I'm strong enough to do you justice," he complained bitterly.

"Four or five days should bring us to the mouth of the Thames."

Home, Devon thought with a rush of emotion. Would she be able to move effortlessly into her former life after knowing and loving Diablo? Facing Winston after willingly sharing Diablo's bed would be no easy task. More difficult still, she thought glumly, would be marrying her fiancé—if he still wanted her. Seeing her father again promised to be the one bright spot in her bleak future. She'd just have to learn to live without the handsome pirate she had come to love. Suddenly a disturbing thought entered her head.

"How can you just sail into London harbor? Aren't you taking a big risk? Won't you be arrested?"

"The British flag will fly from our mast," Le Vautour grinned slyly. "It should work if we do nothing to incur suspicion. I plan to be in and out of London before the authorities realize I've even been there. Where will I find your father?"

"Probably at our London townhouse," Devon replied thoughtfully. "Father doesn't much care for the country since mother died."

"Excellent, *ma chère*," Le Vautour gloated.

The *Victory* encountered no difficulty sailing up the Thames into London harbor. To her chagrin, Devon learned she was not to go ashore immediately but must wait until Le Vautour contacted her father and collected his reward. She could do no more than pace the cabin while the pirate made his way ashore. Before he left he posted a guard at her door to prevent an ill-advised escape.

The one thing Devon regretted was having to part

with the locket she always wore around her neck bearing her mother's photograph. But she knew her father would never believe Le Vautour without proof. When he had asked her for something her father would readily recognize, it was the only thing she had to offer.

Chapter Ten

"Are you telling me my daughter is aboard your ship, safe and unharmed?" demanded the Earl of Milford?

"*Mai oui*," Le Vautour replied smoothly. "Lady Devon will tell you herself how I risked life and limb to rescue her from the devil's lair."

"God's blood, man, where is she? Why isn't she with you? Or is this all a hoax?" His face grew beet red and a fierce scowl distorted his features. "I've suffered untold anguish over my daughter's abduction. Who are you?"

"Lady Devon is aboard my ship, monsieur, unharmed and in good health." Le Vautour was unperturbed by Lord Harvey's rage. "I am called Le Vautour."

"Le Vautour!" spat Lord Harvey, recognizing the name instantly. "A bloody pirate! No doubt you and Diablo are in cohoots to bilk me out of my money. It won't work, Le Vautour. Get out of here before I summon the authorities. There's a price on your head."

"Tsk, tsk, *mon ami*, you misjudge me."

"I am not your friend, Le Vautour. I think you're lying through your teeth. Devon's fiancé and I have not been idle these past weeks; not even the Royal Navy could find a trace of that scoundrel, Diablo, and we despaired of ever seeing her again. That blackguard's promise to return my daughter was nothing but empty words."

"Do you recognize this?" Le Vautour dangled the locket belonging to Devon by its slender gold chain before Lord Harvey's nose.

"Where did you get that?"

Snatching the locket from Le Vautour's hand, Lord Harvey examined it thoroughly before releasing the catch. The moment he saw the picture of his dead wife he knew the pirate spoke the truth. Devon would never willingly part with her treasured keepsake except under unusual circumstances.

"Now do you believe me?" Le Vautour taunted. "I have caused your daughter no harm and intend to deliver her safely into your hands."

"How much, Le Vautour?" Lord Harvey was prepared to pay and pay dearly for his beloved daughter.

"You are astute as well as wise," Le Vautour replied. "I will not haggle with you, monsieur. I want three thousand pounds. In gold. I went through great hardship to bring your daughter to you and incurred much expense." He was thinking of Scarlett who demanded a full third, as well as his crew who would also share in the windfall.

The earl's mouth flew open. "My God, man, that's robbery! I don't keep that much cash on hand."

"But you can get it with little difficulty," Le Vautour advised smoothly. "I will allow you sufficient time to procure the necessary funds. Give me half now and the rest when your daughter is delivered to you. If you value her life you will tell no one about me or alert the authorities of my presence in England until I am well away from these hostile shores."

A man of power and the brains to go with it, the earl was not a man prone toward rash judgments. Yet his daughter was dearer to him than his own life. His answer came swiftly, the only one available to him under the circumstances.

"You'll have your money, Le Vautour. Half now and half when Devon is released. Furthermore, you have my solemn word the authorities will know nothing of this until you are safely gone."

Le Vautour was no fool. He recognized the earl's caution and applauded it. "Agreed," he said.

He looked on greedily while the earl opened his safe and counted out fifteen hundred pounds, noting that the man had spoken the truth. That sum had nearly depleted the amount kept in the safe. "There's one condition, Le Vautour," the earl said, holding the sack of gold coins well out of the pirate's reach.

Shifting his gaze from the bag of gold, the Frenchman narrowed his eyes suspiciously. "No tricks, monsieur," he warned ominously, "or your daughter will suffer."

"I'm in no position to offer tricks," Lord Harvey snapped. "I value my daughter's life too much. I'm only requesting that you tell me where to find Diablo. I aim to see him brought to justice and hanged for what he did to my daughter. The spies I dispatched to Nassau returned with very little information. All they learned was that Diablo had his own hideaway somewhere in the Bahamas. But either no one knew its location or they feared Diablo too much to talk. Yet it is common knowledge that Devon was in Nassau for a short time."

"It's true Diablo inspires fear in many, and few would betray him," Le Vautour muttered sourly. "Diablo's island is well protected and virtually impregnable unless one knows the secret." The Frenchman was ever resentful of the awe and respect shown Diablo by his peers. His name ranked in importance with Blackbeard, Calico Jack, and Stede Bonnet.

"But you know how and where to find him, don't you, Le Vautour?" the earl said shrewdly. "Will you share your knowledge? For a price?"

The pirate needed little prodding. Betraying Diablo was exactly what he had planned from the beginning. "Add another five hundred pounds and the information is yours," he said slyly. "I've just come from Diablo's Paradise and know the route. But even after you find the island, getting to Diablo is difficult. He's only on Paradise for short periods of time, and the island is surrounded by a barrier reef that protects it from intruders. None but shallow draft ships may enter, and then only if one knows exactly where the break in the reef is located and how to find the secret entrance to the lagoon."

"Will you help me, Le Vautour? I want to see Diablo captured and punished. I want that devil hanged for his crimes."

Le Vautour had nothing to lose by divulging Diablo's secret, and much to gain. Disposing of Diablo would fulfill a promise of long standing, one he had made when Diablo brought about the death of Black Bart and stole his friend's ship. The debt of honor had been outstanding far too long, and it was time Diablo was made to pay for leading the mutiny that took the life of Black Bart. But in the unlikely event that Lord Harvey's plan failed, Le Vautour wanted no one to know who had betrayed Diablo. If it got back to that devil, his retribution would likely be swift and lethal.

At length, Le Vautour said, "Diablo is no friend of mine. I will tell you his secret only if you promise not to divulge a word of this conversation to anyone, including your daughter, who saved my life when I was injured during a storm at sea. I certainly wouldn't want her to think badly of me."

Lord Harvey couldn't imagine Devon coming to the aid of a thoroughly despicable man like Le Vautour, until he recalled his daughter's gentle and caring compassion for all human life. "You have my word, I will not tell Devon. But I make no such promise concerning her fiancé, who wants Diablo brought to justice as badly as I do."

Le Vautour considered the earl's words for the space of a moment. "You are a man of honor, and therefore I agree with your terms. Listen closely while I tell you how to reach Paradise. Or better yet, bring pen and paper and I'll draw a map.

A quarter of an hour later Le Vautour left to return to his ship while Lord Harvey hurried to his bank to withdraw the outstanding amount due the pirate. Arrangements had been made to meet at the wharf in London harbor where the *Victory* was moored.

As she stood at the rail of the *Victory*, Devon's heart beat with trepidation as a closed carriage bearing the Chatham coat of arms drew to a shuddering halt beside the quay. The door opened and her father's beloved face searched the deck until he found her. Eagerly she ran to the gangplank but was stopped by Peck, who looked to Le Vautour for orders.

"Not yet, *ma chère*," Le Vautour cautioned. "Your father and I have business to conduct before you are free to join him."

The pirate had returned just an hour ago and informed Devon she was to leave shortly, as soon as her father arrived and the ransom was delivered. Devon assumed that an agreement had been reached and she couldn't wait to leave this vile ship. She was ecstatic when Le Vautour allowed her on deck where she could be readily seen by the earl. Now, seeing his dear face, which had aged dramatically these past weeks, she knew her decision to leave Diablo had been the right one, though it had left her heart permanently damaged. She watched warily as Le Vautour limped down the gangplank, favoring his injured leg. His right arm was still in a sling, but all his injuries were healing well.

Lord Harvey stepped from the carriage before his footman could aid him, his anxious eyes riveted on Devon's slim form.

"You have the gold?" Le Vautour asked when he faced the rotund earl.

"Aye, all of it. Release Devon."

Nodding, the pirate turned and signaled Peck, who sent Devon on her way down the gangplank. She took off at a run, throwing herself into her father's protective arms. Only then did the earl place the bag of gold into Le Vautour's hands. Moving with utmost haste, he lifted Devon into the carriage where she collapsed in a sea of tears against his ample chest. Abruptly the carriage jerked forward, leaving Le Vautour standing on the quay, happily counting his money.

"There, there, sweetheart," the earl soothed clumsily. "It's all over. You're safe now."

Lord Harvey had no way of knowing that his endearment succeeded only in bringing on a fresh torrent of tears, for it brought to mind all those times Diablo had called her sweetheart. Sometimes teasingly, sometimes coaxingly—but always with love.

"Was it so terrible, m'dear?" the earl asked when Devon's tears showed no signs of abating.

"Nay, Father, not really. I'm sorry if—if I gave you that impression. Diablo didn't harm me. He was quite gentle, in fact, though he had ample cause to treat me harshly. I—I shot him the day he brought me aboard his ship. It wasn't a dangerous wound, merely disabling him for a time."

Lord Harvey's florid face went blank with shock. "Good God, girl! You shot Diablo and lived to tell of it? The man is a cold-blooded killer, it's a miracle he didn't order your immediate death."

"Diablo—he's not what people think," Devon said lamely, trying to explain the man she had come to love.

Lord Harvey regarded Devon through narrowed eyes. "Has the scoundrel bewitched you, daughter? He's taken dozens of lives, stolen thousands of pounds worth of goods, and sunk countless ships. Only the devil knows how many women he's ravished. The man is devoid of all honor. He promised to set you free, but proved by his failure to do so that his code of honor consists solely of lies and deceit."

"Diablo *was* going to set me free, Father, but a

storm blew us off course. He was also quite ill from his wound at the time and unable to order my release. He—"

"Cease, Devon, I've heard enough of that man's virtues! I didn't want to dredge up painful memories, but under the circumstances I feel I must. Did Diablo do anything to—harm you while he held you captive?"

Devon's eyes became shuttered. She knew exactly what her father referred to. It was no more than any parent would ask, yet a simple answer was impossible. In the end she spoke the truth—or as near the truth as she could come without hurting either Diablo or her father.

"If you're asking if Diablo raped me, the answer is no. I told you I wasn't harmed." Her flushed cheeks revealed more than her cautious words.

What Devon failed to reveal was that what had begun as her seduction had ended with their mutual pleasure . . . that in a shockingly short time she had gone to Diablo willingly, welcomed his intimacies, craved his love, responded to him with wanton abandon. She could tell none of these things to her father.

Devon's words did little to ease Lord Harvey's suffering. He found it difficult to believe she had escaped Diablo's clutches unscathed. It was widespread knowledge that the devil devoured beautiful young girls like Devon. But for his own sanity as well as hers, he chose to accept her words.

"Thank God. I was so afraid he—ahem—well, never mind, m'dear. All is well now, and you'll never have to think about your ordeal again. I promise that blackhearted devil will soon hang for his crimes."

Horrified by the thought, Devon fell silent, content for the moment to bask in her father's love. She was astute enough to realize that her welfare came first with him and he would go to any lengths to protect her from harm. Their silence continued until the carriage ground to a halt before Chatham House. Lord Harvey alit first and helped Devon descend, then he guided her to the door, his arm curled solicitously around her slim shoulders. But before they reached the entrance, another carriage came careening around the corner, skidding to an abrupt halt behind the Chatham rig. Both Devon and her father turned to watch as a slim man of medium height with brownish hair and a thin mustache bounded out.

"Devon, thank God you're safe!"

"Winnie, how did you—"

"I sent a message, m'dear," Lord Harvey explained hurriedly. "'Tis no more than right, Winston *is* your intended husband. Your abduction has been hard on both of us. The poor boy's been distraught."

"It's all right, Father," Devon allowed, though all she truly wanted was to go to her room and collapse on her bed.

"Come inside, Winston," invited the earl. "The street is no place to air family discussions."

Seated in the familiar comfort of her father's study, Devon studied Winston from beneath lowered lids while the earl told him of Le Vautour's visit and Devon's safe return. Had she ever really looked at the foppishly dressed man she had agreed to marry? she asked herself distractedly. He was handsome enough in a classic, effeminate way, she allowed, but compared to Diablo's virile face and form, he appeared soft and weak. His muddy brown hair hung lank on his forehead and his eyes were a pale shade of blue. His skin lacked the dark, healthy glow of a man accustomed to long periods of time in the open. He was adorned like a dandy in peacock-hued satin that did little for his pasty complexion.

Yet something must have attracted her to Winston, Devon realized. Perhaps it was his devotion to her. Or his pretty manners, which had once seemed an admirable trait but now struck her as being sissified. It certainly wasn't his ardor for her that drew her, for Winston was totally lacking in that department. She might once have thought such reticence desirable in a man, but after experiencing Diablo's exuberant loving it had lost all appeal. Suddenly she became aware that the men had stopped talking and were staring at her curiously.

"Is something amiss, m'dear?" Lord Harvey asked anxiously. He had noticed Devon's distraction and worried about her state of mind. He knew of few women who could survive what she had just gone through and took great pride in Devon's courage and fortitude.

"'Tis nothing, Father," Devon assured him sweetly. "I suppose the shock of being home when I never expected to see you again has left me quite fatigued. I'd like to be excused."

"Can you spare another moment, dear?" Winston asked solicitously.

"Of course, Winston," Devon agreed, thinking she owed him that much for betraying his trust.

"I want us to be married immediately, and your father agrees."

"Immediately? Why such a rush?"

"He's right, m'dear," concurred the earl. "Neither of us want you hurt by gossip mongers. They'll have a field day once they learn you're back."

"That's correct, Devon," Winston added. "The only way to save your reputation is by marrying immediately."

"Hang my reputation!" Devon snapped. "I've done nothing wrong. I didn't ask to be abducted."

"We know, dear," explained Winston patiently, "but the first thing everyone will think is that your virtue has been compromised."

"What if it has been? Would it matter to you?" Devon questioned bluntly.

"Well, ahem, of course not, dear. Nothing matters as long as you're restored to us safe and sound."

Devon was appalled by the thought that society would condemn her even if she hadn't been a willing participant in her abduction. It was to Winston's credit that he was still willing and eager to marry her. But an immediate marriage held no appeal for her. Besides, so much had happened in the past weeks that she needed time to sort through her feelings and consider her future.

"I hardly think a hasty marriage will solve anything, Winnie. I need time to think. I've just gotten home, let me recover before rushing into anything."

Winston's smooth brow wrinkled into a frown, his displeasure obvious. "Our marriage is scheduled to take place in a few weeks. What I'm suggesting is not unreasonable."

What neither Devon nor her father knew was that Winston was close to financial ruin and in desperate need of Devon's generous dowry to satisfy his creditors. He would have married Devon no matter what Diablo had done to her. He strongly suspected she was no longer a virgin, but that was the least of his worries. It merely saved him the distasteful task of deflowering her himself.

Recognizing Devon's obstinacy, Lord Harvey

came to the rescue. "My daughter has been through a harrowing experience and is exhausted. Let the subject rest for tonight. Perhaps Devon will change her mind once she's had time to think about this."

"Of course. How callous of me to force the issue when Devon is obviously distraught and needs rest. Good night, dear," Winston said, bending to place a chaste kiss on her forehead. His lips were cool and dry, and Devon gave an involuntary shudder.

She nodded in reply, glad to see him leave. When had her feelings changed so drastically? she wondered dully. At one time she considered Winston everything she wanted in a man. Before Diablo cast his spell on her.

"I'll see you out, Winston," Lord Harvey offered.

"I'll be in my room, Father," Devon called as she rose to follow them out of the room. Both men watched as she disappeared up the stairs.

"I won't have Devon badgered," the earl warned Winston when they were alone. "I'm sure she'll come to see the advantage of wedding without delay once she's had time to consider the consequences. Right now there's something of more importance to discuss. I know how and where Diablo can be found."

"Devon told you where that bastard is hiding?"

"Nay, but the pirate Le Vautour did. He seemed none too reluctant to part with the information, for a price. The man is totally lacking in scruples. He even drew a map to aid us."

"Let me go after him," Winston said, his eyes bright with dreams of glory. "Think what destroying that menace to society will do for my reputation. Even the king will have to sit up and take notice. I'll have no difficulty obtaining three men-of-war from the navy to join my own *Larkspur*."

"No warships, m'boy. Le Vautour told me Diablo's stronghold is guarded by a coral reef preventing all but shallow draft vessels from entering the sheltered harbor through the narrow passage. The map shows where the break in the reef occurs and pinpoints the entrance."

"Shallow draft vessels. Hmmm," mused Winston thoughtfully. "A little more difficult to obtain, but not impossible."

"How long will it take to find and prepare such ships? I want the bastard brought to justice."

"I shall be knocking at Diablo's door within a month; six weeks and I'll be back in London," boasted Winston.

"Splendid, splendid," beamed the earl. "We'll plan a wedding six weeks from today."

"What if Devon isn't willing?"

"She will be," promised the earl.

Diablo paced the bridge as the *Devil Dancer* plowed smoothly through the blue-green water. He was bored, restless, and angry. The *Devil Dancer* and the *Red Witch* had crisscrossed the Atlantic for weeks looking for the elusive Spanish galleons. He strongly suspected there never was a Spanish fleet laden with riches. But what did Scarlett have to gain by lying? He intended to find out tonight. He'd signaled the *Red Witch* earlier inviting Scarlett to sup with him aboard the *Devil Dancer*. Both ships would seek shelter that night in a secluded inlet on the coast of Puerto Rico.

The moon reflected thousands of tiny diamonds on the sparkling water when Scarlett stepped aboard the *Devil Dancer* and was shown directly to Diablo's cabin. She looked fetching in tight breeches, flowing white shirt, and high boots that molded the long length of her legs. But Diablo, dressed in unrelieved black, saw neither her beauty nor the seductive pose she struck for his benefit. Unaccustomed to being ignored, Scarlett stomped over to the chair Diablo held out for her and sat down with an angry thud.

"Our meal will arrive shortly. Would you care for a drink while we're waiting?"

"Brandy, if you have it."

"Of course."

Scarlett regarded Diablo with riveting attention as he busied himself with their drinks. She loved the way his muscles rippled beneath his shirt, the movement of his taut buttocks when he walked, the bold display of his manhood inside the tight confines of his trousers. But to Scarlett's dismay, all her efforts of seduction had failed since Devon had come into his life. She longed to tell him the witch was gone but wisely decided it was in her own best interests to let him discover that for himself.

Scarlett sipped her brandy with obvious relish while their supper was being served. "I'm afraid the fare is poor tonight," Diablo said. "That's one of the reasons I asked you here tonight. Our stores are severely depleted, and I assume yours are too."

"I thought you asked me because you like my company," Scarlett said coyly.

Diablo frowned. "I'm tired of this wild goose chase. We've tracked back and forth across the ocean with nothing to show for it but an empty hold and men grown edgy from lack of action. Not even a merchantman has crossed our path. Scarlett, I'm beginning to think you invented those Spanish galleons."

"Why would I do that?" Scarlett asked with feigned innocence.

"Aye, why?" Diablo repeated. "What will you gain from lying?"

"Nothing, I wasn't lying. Finish your meal, Diablo, 'tis a good supper considering supplies are short."

For several minutes Diablo devoted himself to his food, then shoved his plate aside and stood. "I'm setting our course for the Bahamas tomorrow. Do what you want, but don't count on me for help."

Scarlett pushed her own plate back and rose to her feet. Swaying seductively, she walked to within inches of him, the tips of her unfettered breasts brushing the incredible breadth of his chest.

"You're going back to *her*," she accused, her voice a sultry whisper. "You know I can give you everything she can, and more. What does a lady like Devon Chatham know about pleasing a man?" Her hands played teasingly over his chest, her fingers skillfully unbuttoning the buttons of his shirt. "I can offer you more, so much more. We're alike in so many ways."

Boldly Scarlett's hand dropped to the bulge straining against Diablo's tight trousers, and she chortled gleefully when his manhood jumped in response. "You want me, admit it!"

"I'm a man, Scarlett," Diablo ground out, grasping her wrists in a viselike grip. "My body may respond to manipulation, but my mind and heart reject you utterly. This may come as a surprise, but I love Devon. She moves me as no other."

"Love, bah! You're not capable of love. Forget about that witch and be my lover again."

"Nay, Scarlett, there's but one woman I want to make love to, and I'm going back to her tomorrow."

"You poor besotted fool! Wake up! The lady doesn't want you."

Diablo's silver eyes narrowed dangerously. "What do you mean?"

Sensing her danger, Scarlett immediately sought to placate him. "Nothing, I meant nothing. I'm only trying to convince you that women like Lady Devon have no place in your life."

"Get the hell out of here, Scarlett! I refuse to listen to anything you have to say about Devon."

Recognizing Diablo's rage and the tight control he was exerting to maintain his temper, Scarlett turned and fled the cabin, happy to escape unscathed. She had seen the results of Diablo's fury before and had no wish to experience it herself.

Diablo navigated the barrier reef with practiced ease, yet he couldn't shake the sense of foreboding that had plagued him since his conversation with Scarlett. As the *Devil Dancer* sailed into the snug little harbor, people gathered on the beach to welcome their returning men. By the time the ship docked beside the single pier and Diablo walked briskly down the gangplank, Kyle was there to greet him. The glum look on Kyle's face did nothing to ease Diablo's worry, nor did the sling holding Kyle's arm in place against his chest.

"The *Devil Dancer* is riding too high in the water for her hold to be filled with riches," Kyle said in sober greeting. "Did the Spanish fleet elude you?"

"Either that or there never were any galleons out there to begin with," Diablo grumbled crossly. "I'm beginning to believe the whole thing was a figment of Scarlett's imagination, though I've no idea what she hoped to gain from it. But enough of the elusive galleons, how is Devon? Why didn't she accompany you to the beach? I hope the little hellcat has missed me."

There was so much love in Diablo's eyes that Kyle cursed Devon and Le Vautour a thousand times over. "Sweet Jesus, Kit, I'm sorry. I—it happened so damn fast, there was nothing I could do." Kyle's disjointed reply sent fear lancing through Diablo's heart.

A string of oaths left his bloodless lips. "You're not making sense, Kyle. What happened? Has something happened to Devon?" Though Diablo felt it necessary to ask the question, his keen intuition had already supplied the answer.

"There's no easy way to tell you, Kit," Kyle explained contritely. "Devon is gone. I've failed you." Never had Kyle felt so woefully inadequate.

"Somehow I already knew it," Diablo replied grimly. "What happened? How did she get off the island? Was she taken by force? By God, I'll kill the bastard who took her!"

"No force was necessary," Kyle said regretfully. "She went with Le Vautour willingly enough."

"Le Vautour!" spat Diablo with fury. Suddenly his eyes fell to the sling cradling Kyle's arm. "Is that his handiwork?"

"Aye. I tried to stop him, but it happened so quickly he skewered me before I could draw my weapon. I swear, Kit, I'll never be caught unaware again."

"I can't believe Devon would stand idly by and watch Le Vautour wound you without interfering. He could have killed you. Doesn't she know the kind of man she's dealing with? Why in God's name would she go with Le Vautour when she could scarcely stand the man?"

"Don't misjudge her, Kit. She did not condone what Le Vautour did to me. If not for her he would have killed me. Le Vautour offered to take the lass home to England, and she struck a deal with him." His voice held a note of accusation as he added, "You should have returned her to her father as you promised."

"Don't lecture me, Kyle," Diablo warned, his eyes holding all the warmth of cold steel. "And don't make excuses for Devon. She planned this behind my back, scheming and plotting with a man who's totally lacking in scruples."

"I tried to tell her, Kit, but the lass has a mind of her own."

"So I've noticed," Diablo concurred dryly. "Are you well enough to assume your duties?"

"Aye, what are your orders?"

"How soon can you have the *Devil Dancer* replenished for a long voyage?"

"Surely you're not going after Devon?" Kyle asked, stunned.

"How soon, Kyle?"

"Barring misfortune, the lass is already in England. She's been gone over a month."

"How soon, Kyle?"

"Twenty-four hours."

"See to it. Consult with Akbar about repairs and replacement of crewmen."

"Why, Kit? Why are you so adamant about chasing after Devon when she obviously doesn't want you?"

"Have you forgotten that I'm responsible for scores of lives on Paradise?" Diablo asked tightly. "Devon knows too much about Paradise and its secrets."

"Surely you don't think . . ."

"I've not lived this long by placing my trust in chance. I'd like to think Devon won't tell her father or fiancé how or where to find us, but I'm far too realistic to take her silence for granted. I'm going up to the house to speak with Tara. Please see that my orders are carried out without delay."

Dismissing Kyle with a curt nod, Diablo whirled and walked briskly past the cluster of women and children who were joyously greeting their men.

Hiding behind his stoic expression and empty eyes, Diablo concealed the terrible hurt over the ease with which Devon had abandoned him. The world must never know how a fragile girl had nearly destroyed him. How she must have laughed when he bared his soul to her, declaring his feelings like a lovestruck adolescent. No wonder Devon had not shared her own feelings with him, for her heart had remained untouched while his own beat hot and strong with a passion born of perfect love.

Chapter Eleven

"Sail ho!"

Diablo came instantly alert. "Where away?"

"Astern to starboard."

Diablo swung to the starboard, his spyglass sweeping the horizon. "She flies no flag. Does she look familiar to you, Akbar?" He handed the glass to the huge Turk.

"She's still too distant to tell."

"May I look?" Kyle asked, reaching for the glass. "Hmm, her lines are familiar but I'm not certain. Do you suppose it's Le Vautour's *Victory*?"

"By God, I hope so," swore Diablo fervently.

"And if it is?" Akbar challenged. "What if the lady is still aboard?"

"'Tis my guess Devon is in London by now," Diablo returned, "unless she remained aboard the *Victory* to serve as Le Vautour's mistress."

"Oh come now, Diablo," Kyle scoffed. "The lass would never—"

"By the Prophet's beard, it *is* Le Vautour!" Akbar sang out gleefully. "I'd recognize the *Victory* anywhere." Kyle had returned the spyglass to the Turk, who avidly followed the course of the approaching ship. He passed the glass back to Diablo, who confirmed Akbar's suspicion.

"I think you're right, my friend." Diablo smiled with grim satisfaction. "Send the men to battle stations."

There was a wild scurry as men from every part of the ship, armed with cutlasses, daggers, pistols, and boarding axes, hurried to their stations at Akbar's command. When all was in readiness, Diablo stepped forward, his voice booming loud and clear above the din and excitement.

"Have you the stomach for a fight, lads?"

A resounding collective "Aye" was everything that Diablo hoped for.

"I'll tell you now 'tis one of our own and she's unlikely to be carrying booty," Diablo said.

"'Tis Le Vautour, I recognize her rigging," shouted Dancy.

"Aye, lads," Diablo concurred. "He's stolen my lady and launched a vicious attack upon my lieutenant. I've sworn vengeance. Are you with me, lads?"

"We're with ya!" shouted Rooks, naming himself spokesman.

"You'll not be sorry. I'll personally reward every man loyal to me out of my own pocket to make up for lack of booty. Good fortune, lads."

"Do we sink her?" Akbar asked, aware that Devon could very well be aboard the *Victory*.

"Nay, Akbar, not until I'm certain Devon isn't aboard. When we're close enough, put a shot across her bow and see what happens. Mayhap Le Vautour will surrender without a fight."

Le Vautour recognized the *Devil Dancer* immediately, and a string of oaths spewed from his lips. He should have known the devil would come searching for him. He had hoped the British navy would finish Diablo off, but he'd not back down from a confrontation now, nay, he welcomed it with eager anticipation. Already his men were occupying their battle stations, prepared to defend their ship. The sky was cloudless, the sun bright and warm, and Le Vautour decided it was a good day to avenge the death of Black Bart.

"Fire!" Akbar shouted, and the starboard guns belched a stream of gray smoke. The shot cleared the bow of the *Victory* according to Diablo's instructions. Immediately the *Devil Dancer* tacked sharply while its starboard guns were being reloaded. An answering volley from the *Victory* fell short of its mark.

"Le Vautour wants to fight," Akbar chortled gleefully. The two ships were evenly matched, but he knew the Frenchman could not match Diablo in skill and cunning.

"Aim the cannon into the rigging," Diablo ordered curtly. "I want to bring the bastard to his knees without harming Devon if she's aboard."

"I always said the woman would bring you trouble," Akbar grumbled beneath his breath. "She chose to go with Le Vautour, so I see no need to worry about her fate."

"You have your orders, Akbar, see to it." Diablo's tone demanded instant obedience, and Akbar called for another round, this to be aimed high in the rigging.

His efforts were amply rewarded when the shot sheared off the top of one of the *Victory*'s masts. Le Vautour's gunners had not yet found their mark as their answering shot soared over the *Devil Dancer*'s prow to fall harmlessly into the sea. Or perhaps it was Kyle's superb handling of the wheel. Whatever the reason, Diablo's gunners managed to disable a second mast. Then the *Devil Dancer* took a direct hit, but luckily the shot did no more damage than put a hole in the hull above the waterline. Fortunately it missed the cache of ammunition stored on deck, and the fire it started was quickly doused.

Diablo smiled with grim satisfaction as he noted the several small fires burning aboard the *Victory*. None looked serious enough to sink her, but so many men were involved in putting them out that most of their guns fell silent. Diablo used the lull to his advantage, maneuvering the *Devil Dancer* to within boarding distance of the floundering *Victory*.

"Run out the boarding planks!" he shouted above the din of battle and wild cheers of his crew. "Le Vautour is mine," he cried as everyone surged over the side.

Within minutes the crew were swarming aboard the *Victory*, dodging burning rubble and engaging in hand-to-hand combat. It had been far too long since they'd enjoyed a rousing fight, and each man was eager for blood.

Diablo spied Le Vautour standing on the quarterdeck, cutlass in hand, his mouth curved into a snarl. "Come ahead, you devil's spawn," the Frenchman challenged. "I've been waiting a long time for this. Ever since you killed Black Bart and stole his ship."

A puzzled frown furrowed Diablo's dark brow. "Black Bart brought about his own demise." Slowly he advanced up the ladder to the quarterdeck. "If not me, someone else would have led the mutiny. Bart was a cruel, perverted man, and the world is a better place without him. Why should it matter to you?"

"Black Bart was like a father to me. I've waited years to avenge his death." He aimed a vicious slash of the cutlass to Diablo's middle, forcing him to suck in his breath as the blade whizzed by with a fraction of an inch to spare.

"Where is Devon?" Diablo asked, easily deflecting Le Vautour's second thrust with the flat of his cutlass. "Is she aboard the *Victory*? Woe be to you if you've done her any harm."

Le Vautour laughed crazily, slicing again at Diablo's vulnerable midsection. "Your whore came with me willingly enough."

Filled with incredible fury, Diablo clenched his jaws as he danced sideways, parrying Le Vautour's thrust. "You bastard, is Devon aboard your ship or not?"

"You're too late, Diablo, the lady is in England. She's a delectable piece, I understand fully your reluctance to part with her. We became quite—intimate—during her stay aboard the *Victory*. It was part of the bargain we struck," he boasted, embellishing the lie with a sly grin.

"You lying, blackhearted braggart! Devon would never let you touch her."

Then all talk ceased as each man concentrated on killing the other, the larger battle raging around them with increasing vigor. Both crews were evenly matched, equally cunning and brave, but Diablo's men, driven by fierce loyalty, slowly began turning the tide in their favor. By now Diablo had received several minor cuts, but so had Le Vautour. Suddenly two of Le Vautour's men leaped up the ladder to the quarterdeck, brandishing cutlasses, followed closely by two crewmen from the *Devil Dancer*.

Inadvertently one of Diablo's men jostled him, and he fought for balance, dropping to one knee. Chortling gleefully, Le Vautour saw victory at hand, and lunged viciously at his fallen enemy. But Diablo, who had outfoxed many a wily foe in his numerous ventures, was too quick-witted for the sly pirate. He deliberately let down his guard when he stumbled, inviting Le Vautour's thrust to his vulnerable chest. Grinning evilly, the Frenchman plowed forward, and was stunned to find that Diablo had nimbly rolled aside and now raised his own cutlass up and under Le Vautour's guard, driving the blade into his gut. Le Vautour's eyes widened, then went blank as he fell, dead before he hit the deck.

The battle ended swiftly with Le Vautour's death. A thorough search of the ship turned up a cache of gold hidden in Le Vautour's cabin as well as other money and a rich store of valuable objects. Though the hold was indeed empty as Diablo suspected, the *Victory* yielded a surprising amount of booty for the crew of the *Devil Dancer*.

When offered a choice, Le Vautour's surviving men eagerly joined the ranks of Diablo's crew. Once all the wounded were transferred aboard the *Devil Dancer*, the *Victory* was torched. His face an inscrutable mask, Diablo watched stoically as the *Victory* upended and slid beneath the sea. He thought it a just end for the man who had brought him nothing but grief. With Devon now in England she was all but lost to him. Suddenly Diablo's life, once filled with excitement and adventure, held little meaning.

"What are your orders, Diablo?" Kyle asked, sensing his friend's dark mood. "Do we go to England after the lass?"

"Nay, Kyle, 'tis too late for that. Devon has made her choice." His eyes were bleak, his face as if carved from stone. "Let's go home."

"I wouldn't worry about Devon betraying the secret of Paradise," Kyle offered lamely. "She knows what would happen to the people living there."

Kyle wouldn't have spoken so confidently had he known what was taking place a few hundred miles south on the small island called Paradise.

Diablo sailed the *Devil Dancer* through the coral reef with an ease born of practice. But as the ship neared the sheltered harbor it became apparent that disaster had struck the tiny settlement. The buildings lining the beach had been reduced to splintered rubble, and the huts beyond were leveled to the ground. A pitifully few survivors stumbled from hastily erected shelters to greet Diablo as he sprinted down the gangplank. A slim woman rose from where she knelt offering comfort to the wounded and waited for Diablo, her back hunched wearily. By now Kyle and Akbar had caught up with their captain, all three too stunned to do more than gape at the wanton destruction and careless loss of life.

"It happened a few days ago," Tara said, her voice a dull parody of itself.

"God's bones, Tara, who did this?"

"The English. Three ships led by the *Larkspur* sailed into the cove and began shelling without warning. They gave no quarter, offered no mercy. It made little difference to them that only women, children, and old men occupied the island. They could see for themselves that no ships were anchored in the cove." She raised sad brown eyes imploringly to Diablo. "Why, Diablo? Why would they do such a thing? How did they find their way to Paradise?"

Diablo had no answers. In his anguish his face was terrible to behold, his sensual mouth a thin line, his silver eyes as cold and murky as death. Suddenly the answer came to him, driving the breath from his lungs with the force of a sledgehammer. "I'll kill the treacherous little slut!"

"Diablo, surely you don't think that Devon . . ." Kyle began.

"Have you some other explanation, Kyle?" Diablo ground out remorselessly. Kyle flushed, unwilling to admit that Devon had betrayed them but unable to draw any other conclusion. "I thought not." Diablo turned his attention to Tara. "Are these the only survivors?"

By now the crew had clamored down the gangplank and were frantically searching among the survivors for their loved ones.

"There are a few more people up at the house," Tara revealed. "And most of the Arawaks working the cane fields were spared."

"The house still stands?"

"It can't be seen from the beach, so that's probably why it wasn't destroyed. The English must have been angry to find you gone when they arrived, for they set about destroying everything in sight. Then they left. We've buried the dead, and most of the wounded have been treated."

"You've done well, Tara, I'm grateful. I hold

myself entirely responsible for this—this senseless massacre. If I hadn't foolishly brought Devon here, none of this would have happened."

Akbar muttered his wholehearted agreement, intense hatred burning from the depths of his black eyes.

Though Kyle prayed it wasn't so, he had to acknowledge the overwhelming evidence pointing directly to Devon. Who else could have betrayed them?

"We'll start rebuilding immediately," Diablo said.

"Why?" Kyle shrugged. "The English know the secret entrance and can find their way in here any time they please."

"This time we'll build across the cay on the opposite shore."

"What about the reef? It circles the entire island. How will we get in and out?"

"I've prepared for just such an eventuality," Diablo revealed. "If you recall, I've thoroughly explored the entire cay on those occasions when the *Devil Dancer* was being repaired and my presence was not needed. There's another navigable passage that I've told no one about. I've never attempted it, but I'm sure the *Devil Dancer* can slip through the gap. See that the survivors are loaded aboard the ship, Kyle. We'll leave immediately and begin rebuilding. We're fortunate to have Le Vautour's men to help."

"What about your house?" Tara asked.

"'Tis nearly the same distance from either shore and it suits me well enough. I'll continue to use it while on Paradise. Meanwhile, I've plans to make."

"Plans?" Kyle asked, fearful that Diablo was

thinking of doing something rash. "Surely you're not—"

"Aye, Kyle," Diablo nodded soberly. "When I'm finished with Lady Devon Chatham, the deceitful bitch will rue the day she was born."

"Where have you been, Winston?" Devon asked listlessly. "You've been gone ever so long."

"Did you miss me, dear?" Winston smiled feebly. He had assumed that Devon wouldn't even notice his absence while he was off on his expedition. "How are the plans progressing for our wedding?"

"Didn't Father tell you?"

"I haven't seen him yet." Remembering that he hadn't greeted Devon properly, he kissed her lightly on the forehead. "Is there some problem?"

Problem? Devon nearly laughed aloud at Winston's innocent question. What problem could there be besides loving a man totally wrong for her, a man wanted for committing vile crimes against mankind? No other man, Winston included, could take Diablo's place in her heart. Yet Devon knew exactly what kind of future awaited her if she chose to remain a spinster. She'd have the protection of her father's name while he lived, but if there were no male heirs the title and bulk of his estate would go to a distant relative. That's why the earl was anxious for Devon to marry and have a child. Not that he'd force her to marry someone she detested. But if she remained single she'd be dependent on a distant cousin for her livelihood.

"You haven't answered my question, Devon," Winston persisted.

"Well—er—there is somewhat of a problem,"

Devon stuttered. "We can't be married until October."

"But that's weeks away!" protested Winston. Would his creditors wait that long? he wondered.

"Only four weeks, Winnie. What's four weeks compared to a lifetime?" That terrifying thought brought a shudder to her slender frame.

"Four weeks *is* a lifetime," declared Winston gallantly. "Why the delay?"

"The dressmaker needs more time to complete my gown and those of my bridesmaids. A girl only marries once, you know."

Devon had only decided to marry Winston a week ago. Until then she had remained adamantly opposed to the match. An incident that had recurred with alarming frequency for several mornings had changed her mind. There was no longer a doubt in Devon's mind that she was carrying Diablo's child. She had yet to miss her second cycle, but every instinct told her she'd bear Diablo's baby. She had to marry Winston, for she'd not shame her father by bearing an illegitimate child.

Winston sighed, distressed by the delay. "October first, dear, no later," he stressed. "I've waited a long time to make you my bride."

"October first," Devon concurred. Abruptly she changed the subject. "Where have you been these past weeks? Father said you took the *Larkspur* on a mission. I thought you'd resigned your commission."

"'Twas a routine mission, dear," Winston lied smoothly. "But fear not, I plan on resigning once we're married and devote all my time to you."

"How is your father? You haven't mentioned him recently."

"Same as usual. He knows little of what's going on around him but defies us all by living." His callous words shocked Devon.

"I'm sorry," she muttered.

Just then Lord Harvey entered the room, his face lighting up when he spied Winston. "Welcome back, m'boy," he blustered. "When did you arrive?"

"Just hours ago."

"Devon, m'dear, there's a matter I would discuss with your fiancé. Will you excuse us?"

"Certainly, Father, I need to visit the dressmaker anyway." She paused at the door. "I'm glad you're back, Winston."

Her words so lacked enthusiasm that Lord Harvey frowned, wondering if he was doing the right thing by urging Devon to marry Winston. But at the moment more pressing matters occupied his mind.

"Well, m'boy, tell me quickly, was your mission successful?"

"Only partly," Winston returned sourly. "Diablo wasn't on his island, but we made damn certain he'd return to a pile of rubble."

"You shelled his settlement? Was that wise? I want Diablo, not the lives of innocent people."

The thought that lives had been lost made Lord Harvey decidedly uncomfortable. It also hinted at a serious flaw in the young man's character, one never before revealed.

"How can you call people who live in Diablo's stronghold, under his protection, innocent?" defended Winston. "They are all pirates and outlaws."

He deliberately failed to mention that no one but women, children, and old men had been seen in the village before the shelling. Some of his men had been appalled by the carnage left in their wake, especially since Diablo was not in residence, but Winston cared little about the lost lives.

"Perhaps, but I like it little," the earl said with a frown. "Have you and Devon settled on a wedding date? I must admit she waited until the last minute before agreeing to the marriage."

"October first."

Lord Harvey nodded. "I think marriage is just what Devon needs. This incident has changed her, and frankly I'm worried. She's no longer the same girl I knew before that devil carried her off."

"I hate to broach so delicate a subject, Your Grace, but do you think Diablo raped her? I know she denied it, but perhaps she is reluctant to talk about her ordeal."

"Devon wouldn't lie to me," the earl said huffily. "Are you having second thoughts about the wedding?"

"Of course not," Winston objected. "I'd marry Devon tomorrow if she'd agree. I feel fortunate she chose me from a long list of suitors." What he didn't say was that he needed money so badly he would have married Devon even if every pirate in the Caribbean had raped her.

"All right, m'boy, October first it is. I'm sure you'll make her happy."

Actually, Lord Harvey was beginning to harbor strong doubts about Winston's character. He loved Devon too much to give her to a man unworthy of her love and respect. The last few times he'd visited his club he heard bits of distressing gossip about Winston's unusual sexual preferences, but they were so outrageous he dismissed them out of hand.

Hearing about the indiscriminate shelling of innocent people today only added to the earl's uncertainty. But Lord Harvey considered himself a fair judge of character and he rarely listened to gossip. As long as Devon seemed happy with her choice, he would not interfere.

The rambling mansion on London's fashionable Grosvenor Square appeared in need of refurbishing, but was nonetheless impressive. The man poised at the front entrance was richly dressed in an elegant dove gray satin waistcoat and matching pants, fine hose of the purest silk, lemon satin brocade vest, and leather shoes sporting fashionably high heels and large silver buckles. He wore a fancy powdered wig and carried a sword of the finest Toledo steel strapped around his slim waist. Yards of Brussels lace dripped from his cuffs and shirt front. He would have cut a handsome figure even if his muscular body had not been a perfect example of masculine beauty.

Raising his large calloused hand, he lifted the brass knocker and rapped sharply. He wasn't exactly certain what had brought him to Linley Hall, but something deep inside him had guided his steps to the place still committed in his memory though it had been many years since he'd called it home. He fidgeted nervously while waiting for someone to answer his summons. He identified immediately the aged butler who answered the door, but the staid old man appeared not to recognize the elegantly dressed stranger.

"May I help you, sir?"

"I would like to speak to—the Duke of Grenville."

"I'm sorry, sir, but the duke lies near death in his home in the country and does not receive visitors. Perhaps the viscount could help you."

"The viscount?" He was startled to hear of the duke's illness, but his expression remained carefully blank.

"Aye, sir, the duke's son. Fortunately you've found him at home."

"By all means, then, let me speak with the duke's son."

"Whom shall I say is calling?"

"Just tell Winston that a—relative wishes to speak with him."

Reluctantly the butler stepped aside, allowing the man to enter. Peters had been with the Linleys for many years and knew of no living relatives. "Please wait here."

The visitor took interest in every facet of the entrance hall, lavishing attention on several portraits adorning the wall. Peters found him engrossed in the portrait of a former duchess when he returned a few minutes later. "Sir, the viscount will receive you in the study, but only briefly. He has another appointment within the hour."

Before Peters could point out the direction, the elegant visitor nodded, making his way directly to the study, which the old man thought rather odd.

Peering over a stack of unpaid bills, Winston regarded the imposing man standing before him with a certain misgiving. "Peters said you were a relative," he remarked without introduction. His blunt greeting was utterly lacking in social grace. "If you're looking for a handout you've come to the wrong place." Winston did not really think the steely-eyed stranger needed money, or anything else, but he saw no reason to mince words.

"I don't need your money, Winston. I could probably buy all you possess and still leave the bulk of my fortune intact. I'm sorry to hear about your father." He didn't sound sorry at all.

"A stroke," explained Winston. "He can't speak, walk, or communicate in any way. I don't know what keeps the old fool alive. If your business is with him you're too late. Who are you? I have no relatives that I know of."

"Look closely, Winston, and think back fifteen years. Are you certain you don't recognize me?"

Squinting myopically at the tall, lithe man whose rugged, sun-bronzed face bore no familiarity, Winston was about to order him from the house when something in those silver-gray eyes nudged his memory. Winston's brow furrowed in deep concentration, stripping the years from the fuzzy layers of his brain. Suddenly his face turned as white as death and he could not control the shaking of his hands.

"Nay! By God, it can't be! You're dead! They swore they killed you." Great heaving sobs conveyed Winston's shock, and his terrible fright was clear.

"So you finally recognize me."

Words began spilling from Winston's mouth. Damning words, words that laid bare secrets long buried in lies and deceit.

"I knew nothing about it, Kit, I swear it. It was all my father's doing. He's the one who hired the men. After your father died there was nothing standing between him and the Linley fortune but one small boy. He was greedy. He wanted it all, wealth, title—your entire inheritance."

"So he hired men to kill me and dump my body in the Thames," Kit accused coolly.

"I knew nothing about it until years later. I thought—everyone thought—that you'd met with an accident, or were the victim of foul play."

"I was. Treachery is the worst kind of foul play. Your father—my uncle—has had control of my money all these years."

"After seven years you were declared dead and the title and fortune passed down to Father. What happened? Why didn't you come back when you were able?"

"If you're implying that I should be dead, you're right. Fortunately, greed saved my life. The men your father hired to kill me saw a way to earn extra money. They sold me to a press gang, and for years I slaved aboard a ship under a harsh master and conditions I'd not wish on a dog. A twelve-year-old grows up fast when each day of his life consists of the worst kind of depravity and cruelty imaginable."

"My God, Kit, I had no idea. You've got to believe me. But—how did you become—er—wealthy? Surely you haven't been at sea all these years. Why haven't you contacted us sooner? Do you care nothing for your title or inheritance?"

"At one time I cared a great deal," Kit revealed bitterly. "I spent years planning my revenge. Then suddenly it no longer mattered. The only family I cared about was gone. I had new friends, and my life took an entirely different direction. Besides, from the looks of things," he added, staring pointedly at the stack of bills, "it appears there's little left to claim but an empty title."

Winston flushed guiltily. "Father made some unwise investments, with disastrous results. Then there was his gambling. He always was a terrible businessman. But if you saw him now you'd know

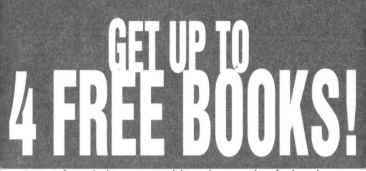

GET UP TO 4 FREE BOOKS!

You can have the best romance delivered to your door for less than what you'd pay in a bookstore or online. Sign up for one of our book clubs today, and we'll send you **FREE* BOOKS** just for trying it out...**with no obligation to buy, ever!**

HISTORICAL ROMANCE BOOK CLUB

Travel from the Scottish Highlands to the American West, the decadent ballrooms of Regency England to Viking ships. Your shipments will include authors such as CONNIE MASON, SANDRA HILL, CASSIE EDWARDS, JENNIFER ASHLEY, LEIGH GREENWOOD, and many, many more.

LOVE SPELL BOOK CLUB

Bring a little magic into your life with the romances of Love Spell—fun contemporaries, paranormals, time-travels, futuristics, and more. Your shipments will include authors such as LYNSAY SANDS, CJ BARRY, COLLEEN THOMPSON, NINA BANGS, MARJORIE LIU and more.

As a book club member you also receive the following special benefits:

- **30% OFF** all orders through our website & telecenter!
- **Exclusive access to** special discounts!
- **Convenient** home delivery **and 10 day examination period to return any books you don't want to keep.**

There is no minimum number of books to buy, and you may cancel membership at any time. See back to sign up!

*Please include $2.00 for shipping and handling.

YES! ☐

Sign me up for the **Historical Romance Book Club** and send my TWO FREE BOOKS! If I choose to stay in the club, I will pay only $8.50* each month, a savings of $5.48!

YES! ☐

Sign me up for the **Love Spell Book Club** and send my TWO FREE BOOKS! If I choose to stay in the club, I will pay only $8.50* each month, a savings of $5.48!

NAME: _____

ADDRESS: _____

_____

TELEPHONE: _____

E-MAIL: _____

☐ **I WANT TO PAY BY CREDIT CARD.**

☐ VISA   ☐ MasterCard   ☐ DISCOVER

ACCOUNT #: _____

EXPIRATION DATE: _____

SIGNATURE: _____

Send this card along with $2.00 shipping & handling for each club you wish to join, to:

**Romance Book Clubs
20 Academy Street
Norwalk, CT 06850-4032**

Or fax (must include credit card information!) to: 610.995.9274.
You can also sign up online at www.dorchesterpub.com.

*Plus $2.00 for shipping. Offer open to residents of the U.S. and Canada only.
Canadian residents please call 1.800.481.9191 for pricing information.
If under 18, a parent or guardian must sign. Terms, prices and conditions subject to change. Subscription subject
to acceptance. Dorchester Publishing reserves the right to reject any order or cancel any subscription.

JOIN NOW!

he's paying dearly for what he did to you. He's an empty shell, more dead than alive."

"'Tis no more than he deserves," Kit observed remorselessly.

"I'm doing my part to restore the family fortune," Winston added quickly. "I'm marrying an heiress on the morrow. Her father has arranged to finance a complete restoration of Linley Hall and our country estate."

A burst of raucous laughter erupted from Kit's throat. "You? Marry? Surely you jest. Does your bride to be know that you're—?"

"Kit, please! Few know my secret."

"Don't you think your bride deserves to know?"

"I'm perfectly capable of doing my duty where she's concerned, and begetting an heir should prove no hardship," Winston declared somewhat uncertainly. Actually he had no idea if he could pull it off but was willing to have a go at it.

"Funny," Kit mused, "I thought I was the only one able to provide a Linley heir."

"You're dead! I mean," Winston corrected, "everyone thinks you're dead. Why did you come back? Do you expect to right a wrong committed fifteen years ago? Is that why you're here? You're too late, Kit, Father is dying a slow, painful death."

"Curiosity brought me back," answered Kit truthfully. "I've thought about this house so often through the years I had to return. I was a twelve-year-old boy uprooted in the cruelest fashion. Ten of the past fifteen years have been pure hell."

"I swear I knew nothing about it," repeated Winston, sweating profusely. This man he barely recognized looked powerful enough to tear him limb from limb if he so desired. "What do you intend to do? I'm going to be married, Kit, you can't deprive me of all I've come to expect in life. Have pity!"

"Pity, bah. Don't grovel, Winston, it ill becomes you. Did anyone show me pity? I don't know if you're guilty of conspiring with your father or not, and evidently he's in no condition to tell, but I've not come to rob you of your ill-gotten gains. As I said, curiosity brought me here. But you needn't worry, I'll be leaving England soon enough."

Kit knew it was dangerous to remain in London, for there were some who could identify him. He had come to London for a purpose, and it wasn't to reclaim his lost title and possessions. Still, the urge to confront his uncle had been too great to resist. But all thought of revenge fled when he learned the man responsible for his terrible ordeal lay near death. And since Winston had been a lad of eighteen at the time, Kit couldn't be certain his cousin had had anything to do with the crime.

"Thank you, Kit," Winston breathed shakily.

Kit had no way of knowing that Winston was not nearly as innocent as he pretended. He had indeed known of his father's plan to do away with the heir to the Linley fortune, having overheard his father talking with the men hired to do the job. He could have warned Kit in plenty of time to foil the devious plot, but chose not to, for one day it would all pass down to him.

"Don't thank me, Winnie," Kit said tersely. "If you're guilty, your day of reckoning will come. In the meantime, I wish you joy of your—your—bride." Kit's statement was accompanied by a scarcely suppressed snicker. "And God pity the poor unsuspecting wretch. Don't bother to show me out, I know the way."

Pausing outside the mansion, Kit wondered what perverse desire had brought him to Linley Hall. Everything it stood for had been cruelly denied him fifteen years ago, and there was no turning back. Stepping smartly into his hired rig, he signaled to the driver and forced himself to relax, anticipating with great relish the mission that had brought him to London.

Tomorrow, Devon thought dully as she prepared for bed. Tomorrow she'd be climbing in bed with Winston, allowing him to use her body in the same way Diablo had. How could she bear it? How could she stand to have another man touch her when it was only Diablo she desired, only Diablo she loved? Yet Devon realized that her child's future depended on her wedding Winston. There'd be talk enough when her child came early, and sooner or later Winston would have to be told.

Sighing despondently, Devon still wasn't certain she could actually marry Winston. Perhaps she'd confess everything to her father in the morning and accept his condemnation.

Facing away from the partially open window, Devon found that her hopes of finding sleep were not to be realized. It was long past midnight and a chilling breeze blew through the narrow opening past the fluttering curtains, bringing a shiver to Devon's slight form. She did not see the figure dressed in unrelieved black who had just stepped through the opening and stood very still, blending into the shadows. A sudden chill swept through her, and Devon arose and walked toward the window, certain that the draft was preventing her from sleep. Just enough moonlight danced in the room to illuminate Devon's face. Diablo's silver eyes narrowed with hatred as he greedily devoured her entrancing face and form. Though he could barely stand the sight of the traitorous bitch, it didn't stop him from appreciating her beauty. His hands clenched tightly at his sides as he struggled to control his raging temper. He wanted Devon to know exactly why he was going to kill her. He was determined that she hear all the gruesome details of the unprovoked attack on innocent people before she died. Diablo wanted her to realize fully what terrible havoc she had wrought by betraying the secret of Paradise.

Devon reached the window and lowered it. But something had distracted her. She sensed she was not alone, and every nerve in her body screamed with awareness. How many times had she inhaled that spicy, musky odor while held so tenderly in those strong arms? She would recognize his scent anywhere, know the moment he walked into the room even if she were blindfolded.

"Diablo . . ." The name whispered across her lips like a summer breeze, soft and yearning—and oh so gentle.

Diablo stepped from the shadows, the light from the window falling across the stark planes of his face. Devon gasped, the hatred blazing from his silver eyes so fierce that she retreated in alarm. Like a stalking panther Diablo followed, grasping her shoulder and spinning her around to face him. Devon winced, his cruel grip confusing her. Never had he touched her with anything but tenderness. Had he changed so completely because she had left him? Or was it because she had left with Le Vautour?

"Diablo, please! You're hurting me."

"You traitorous bitch! The reason I didn't kill you immediately is because I wanted you to know what you're dying for." His face was hard, cruel, unforgiving, his voice remorseless.

Horrified, Devon did not recognize this cruel man. He was an avenging stranger, one bent on murder. "What have I done?"

Diablo's huge hands left Devon's quaking shoulders, rising to grasp the slim column of her neck. "It would be so easy," he drawled menacingly, "to snap that pretty, deceitful neck. A little pressure here," he applied just enough pressure to make her head spin dizzily and gasp for air, "and all the needless deaths you caused would be avenged." Abruptly the pressure eased, and a shuddering breath filled her aching lungs.

"Tell me, Diablo," Devon rasped painfully, "what did I do? If I must die at your hands I want to know the reason."

"I hope you're pleased with your handiwork. Because of you, dozens of innocent women and children lost their lives. But you knew that when you directed the British to Paradise," he accused. "You knew I'd be gone, leaving no one to protect the defenseless people in the village. Before I kill you I want to hear from your own lips why you did it. Did you hate me so much?"

Diablo's face was carved in stone, and Devon marveled at the fleeting memory of his gentle kisses, for surely this angry, ruthless stranger could never display such tenderness. But it was his words and false accusations that stunned her. She'd told no one, not even her father, how to penetrate Diablo's stronghold. In fact, she'd thought it strange that she was not questioned more thoroughly about the time she'd spent in the pirate's stronghold. Though her aching throat was dry and hoarse, she had to try to make Diablo understand she was guiltless. Not only her life but the life of her unborn child—Diablo's child—depended on it.

The pink tip of Devon's tongue flicked out to moisten her dry lips. "I didn't do it, Diablo. No matter what you believe, I told no one about Paradise. I'd never do that."

"You let Le Vautour skewer Kyle. How do I know how far you'd go to repay me for keeping you on Paradise against your will? God's bones, Devon, I loved you! How you must have laughed at my trite words. Why did you have to hurt innocent people to punish me?"

"I swear I had nothing to do with it!" protested Devon. "Couldn't the British have found the way on their own?"

"Impossible!" Diablo roared. "The island is impenetrable unless one knows the secret passage."

"Maybe one of your friends—" Devon suggested lamely.

"Believe it or not, pirates live by a code of honor. Only a selected few know my secret, and none would dare betray me. Nay, my lady," he sneered sarcastically, "'tis you who told and you who'll pay the price.

The pressure on her neck increased, and Devon closed her eyes, words no longer possible as Diablo's face twisted into a grimace.

Devon had no way of knowing that the terrible grimace on Diablo's face was caused by the excruciating pain in his heart. His hands shook with the effort to maintain his hold on the slim column of

Devon's neck, and the anguish visible on the pale oval of her face made his quest for revenge all but impossible.

He had loved her so dearly, trusted her so implicitly, that her fervent denials gave him pause. There was a possibility, albeit a remote one, that Devon hadn't betrayed him. She was so breathtakingly beautiful, so exquisitely formed, and felt so right in his arms that Diablo feared he could never destroy so perfect a creature, no matter what her crime. Though his love for her had died the moment he saw the destruction wrought by English guns, he had never before killed a woman. The remote possibility that Devon was innocent, combined with a force far stronger than his thirst for revenge, caused him to falter. Devon felt the pressure on her neck ease. Though the unholy light in Diablo's eyes continued to blaze with mistrust and doubt, the will to live flamed in Devon's heart. Instinctively she knew that the next moments would be crucial in determining whether she lived or died. It was that thought that compelled her to reveal her secret. She was responsible for a life other than her own, and it was time Diablo knew of it.

"Kill me, Diablo," she croaked hoarsely, "and your child dies with me."

Stunned disbelief met Devon's words. "What lies are you spouting now?"

"'Tis no lie, Diablo, I'm expecting your child. Go ahead and end my life if you care nothing for your child."

He swore, an outrageous stream of vile oaths. "If I find you're lying I'll derive great pleasure from your death."

Drawing herself up to her full five feet five, Devon

taunted calmly, "Do it now if you don't believe me."

A long silence ensued while Diablo stared pointedly at Devon's middle, his eyes hooded. "'Tis far too early to show," she said, sensing his unasked question.

Suddenly a horrible thought occurred to Diablo. "I'll not be duped into claiming Le Vautour's child."

Devon drew her breath in sharply, too stunned to do more than sputter angrily as she drew her hand back and slapped Diablo's face with resounding force. "You despicable cur! I'd never let that slimy creature touch me!"

Somehow Diablo believed her. But that hardly solved his dilemma. Though he might hate Devon, that hate did not extend to the child she carried—his child—if she did indeed carry a child. What in the hell was he going to do about it?

Ever astute, Devon perceived his problem and offered her own solution. "I'm going to be married tomorrow, Diablo. You need not worry about your child. I'll love it, of course, and Winston need never know it's not his."

Diablo froze as bells went off in his head. "Winston? Winston Linley? You're fiancé is Winston Linley?"

"Have I never mentioned his name? I'll become Winston's bride tomorrow. He's only a viscount now, but upon his father's death will become the Duke of Grenville."

"God's bones!" If Lord Harvey hadn't been hard of hearing he would certainly have been roused from his deep slumber by now. "Are you daft, Devon? Do you know what you're letting yourself in for? What must your father be thinking to allow you to marry a man like Winston?"

"You don't know what you're talking about. Winston is sweet and sensitive, and he loves me. He'll provide a good home for your—my child. If it's a boy, he'll become the future Duke of Grenville."

A fierce smile stretched Diablo's lips into a grimace. "Aye, he will, won't he. Too bad Winston will never get the opportunity to claim my child." The moment Devon uttered Winston's name Diablo knew exactly what he must do. "Get dressed," he commanded, "you're coming with me."

"I'm going nowhere with you," Devon resisted stubbornly. "You should be grateful to Winston. You don't need the responsibility of a child."

"Let me be the judge of what I need or don't need," Diablo retaliated sternly. "If you don't get dressed immediately I'll carry you out in your bedgown."

"I'll scream, and Father will come to investigate."

"If you value his life you'll remain quiet and do exactly as I say."

The cold, implacable expression on his harsh features told Devon he was perfectly capable of carrying out his threat, and she moved stiffly to the wardrobe, pulling out the first dress she touched. While she quickly dressed, Diablo lit a candle and began stuffing articles of clothing from drawers and wardrobe into a large pillowcase. He worked efficiently and quickly, knowing which things Devon would need until he could provide her with others. When he finished he pulled a warm cloak from a hook and threw it over her shoulders.

"Surely you don't expect me to go out the window!"

"And risk harming my child? If there is a child," he added skeptically. "Nay, sweetheart, we'll leave by the front door."

"Someone will hear us," she said hopefully.

"Not if we're very quiet. I'm certain you love your father and wish him no harm." His threat was perfectly understood. "Let's go."

"Wait! Let me write a note to Father. He's no longer a young man, the shock of losing me again could kill him. Please, Diablo, if you ever held any feelings for me, allow me this small favor."

Perhaps it was the huge tears rolling down her pale cheeks, or the pleading in her blue eyes. Whatever the reason, a small crack appeared on the hardened surface of Diablo's heart and he nodded reluctant agreement. "Make it brief."

Diablo had to turn away from Devon's blinding smile as she sat down at her desk and scrawled a hasty note. Suddenly he ripped the paper from her hand, wadded it up, and replaced it with another.

"Tell him you're leaving with me of your own accord and he's not to come after you," Diablo directed. "Also leave a message for Winston saying you had no intention of marrying him. You might suggest to your father that he investigate Winston's background more thoroughly."

"What!" Devon asked, pausing in midstroke.

"Just do as I say. One day you'll thank me for saving you from this marriage—if you live long enough," he added ominously.

Still numb with shock and consumed by grief over Diablo's unjust accusations and his threat to kill her, Devon finished the note and handed it to Diablo to read. He gave the contents a quick perusal, nodded his satisfaction, and set it where it was sure to be found. Then he blew out the candle, grasped Devon's hand, and led her out of the house into the blackness of the night. With a stab of regret, Devon realized it might be the last time she set foot in her beloved home.

Chapter Twelve

"By Allah's beard, Diablo, what are you thinking of?" hissed Akbar when he saw his captain leave the house by the front door dragging Devon behind him. "If you couldn't do the job yourself, why didn't you allow me the privilege of killing the woman? I'd not turn squeamish like you obviously did."

"Enough, Akbar. Let's get out of here before the whole town comes clamoring after our heads," Diablo grumbled. Deep in his heart he must have known he couldn't bring himself to hurt Devon.

Ignoring her protests, he lifted her into the hired coach and leaped in beside her. Closing the door with a bang, Akbar, muttering dire predictions, climbed into the driver's box and whipped the team through the darkened city.

"You'll not get away with this," Devon warned, glaring at Diablo angrily. "The authorities will catch you before you clear London harbor."

Diablo smiled with deceptive charm. "Do you think I'm stupid enough to sail into London harbor? I suggest you try to rest, Devon, for we've a long journey ahead of us."

Devon eyed the door, but Diablo was one step ahead of her. "You'll not do anything to harm my child, so forget about leaping from the coach. After my son or daughter is safely delivered, you can do whatever you want with your life."

"Surely you wouldn't be cruel enough to take my baby from me!" Devon gasped. "You loved me once."

"Aye, once I *did* love you," Diablo admitted softly. "That was before you dealt with Le Vautour behind my back and betrayed me. While I was falling in love, you were plotting revenge. Was I too far beneath your social standing to take seriously? An earl's daughter and a pirate, how you must have laughed at my simple love."

"I never laughed, Diablo, truly," whispered Devon with sadness. "Why can't you understand? I had to leave. A love between us was doomed from the start. The horrible thought of having to watch you hang from the gallows one day prevented me from following my heart."

"Lies, all lies!" Diablo responded with a disgusted sneer. "But you needn't worry, I'll not kill the mother of my child. If you really are pregnant, you'll be cared for until my child is born, then you'll be free to go—alone."

Shocked by his cruel words, Devon fell silent, the thought of abandoning a child of her flesh heartbreaking. Diablo retreated into a brooding silence, vivid memories tugging at his mind. Nothing had been sweeter than Devon's warm, willing body responding to him, eagerly accepting his caresses, returning them with ardor, taking him deep into the secret passages of her flesh, joyfully and without restraint. What a consummate actress she was to make him believe she was beginning to care for him.

Diablo's musings were interrupted when he felt a weight resting against his shoulder. Glancing down at Devon's sleeping form, he was startled to see her blonde head nestled trustingly against him. His hands clenched into tight fists in an effort to keep them at his sides instead of placing his arms around her slender shoulders and snuggling her against the curve of his body. Ultimately he did exactly what he fought against, holding her as one would a delicate flower. Until their child was born, her comfort and care lay solely with him. He had taken her from the safety of her comfortable home and was glaringly aware of his responsibility to see that nothing harmed her or their baby. With that thought in mind, Diablo tightened his arms around her supple form, the soothing motions of the coach lulling his troubled mind and body into restless slumber.

Three days later the coach entered a small town on the rugged Cornish coast. Thoroughly exhausted, Devon had begun to think the long journey would never end. Every bone in her body ached from the constant jostling on the rutted roads. Though they had made brief stops along the way to eat and refresh themselves, Devon was never allowed far from Diablo's sight, much to her embarrassment. Nor did they spend a night in one of those inviting inns. Instead, Diablo and Akbar took turns driving, pulling off to the side of the road only during the darkest hours of night to rest the horses, relying on lanterns during the twilight and early morning hours.

Very little conversation had been made between Devon and the two men. Akbar's dark, condemning looks were enough to render her mute, while Diablo retreated beneath a facade of cool disdain, making silence far preferable to his verbal abuse. The coach rattled through the town of Penzance, heading toward the sea. If she hadn't been so upset and exhausted, she would have thoroughly enjoyed the wild, bleak moors and unrivaled scenery passing before her eyes.

High on a windswept cliff overlooking a snug cove sat an ancient weathered castle whose crumbling walls attested to its antiquity, and somehow Devon wasn't surprised when the coach turned up the road leading to the imposing edifice. A lone man waited on the stone steps as Diablo leaped nimbly down from the coach to greet him and be welcomed in return.

"So, my friend, you're back. I trust your mission was successful."

The man spoke in a booming voice that commanded attention from friend and foe alike. He stood nearly as tall and broad as Akbar, sporting a full head of curly black hair and a generous ebony beard reaching nearly to his barrel chest. He appeared somewhat past thirty with intelligent blue eyes beneath shaggy brows and a wide mouth all but hidden by his beard. The bulging muscles in his thighs and arms spoke eloquently of the active life he led and the hard physical work he did.

"My mission was—enlightening, if not successful," Diablo said cryptically. "Be prepared for a surprise, Cormac." He turned back to the coach and literally dragged Devon through the open door. "Meet Lady Devon Chatham."

"You brought the wench here!" Cormac blasted, aghast. "Are you daft, man? I thought you intended to get rid of the girl, not bring her with you."

Devon clung to Diablo's arm, cringing beneath Cormac's obvious disapproval and ferocious countenance. Hardly aware of his protective gesture, Diablo placed a supportive arm around Devon's quaking shoulders.

"There's an explanation for this, Cormac," he informed the man. "You'll hear it later. But first things first. Is there a place Devon can rest? She's exhausted."

"Aye," Cormac replied, eying Devon with the practiced eye of a connoisseur of women and liking what he saw. "There's plenty of empty rooms in this pile of rocks."

Following Cormac inside, Diablo propelled Devon forward, Akbar following close behind with the bundle of clothes. The room assigned to Devon was on the second floor.

"I'll arrange for a bath and see you're brought a meal," Diablo said curtly. "Then I suggest you rest. I'll not have you endangering my child." Turning abruptly, he left the room. His mouth hanging open, Cormac followed close on his heels.

Now that she was alone at last, rage conquered Devon's exhaustion. How dare Diablo abduct her again and dictate her life, she fumed impotently. The man wanted to kill her, for God's sake! And still might, once her child was born. Escape, that's it, she thought, rushing to the door. Only to find it locked from the outside. The windows were out of the question, for the room looked over the sea with only jagged rocks below to break her fall.

Diablo himself unlocked the door later to admit a blank-faced maid and two rather disreputable-looking men with the tub and hot water for Devon's bath. Much to her relief, Diablo did not linger. Afterwards, a tray of food was brought by the same dour maid while Diablo stood nearby waiting to relock the door once the woman left. Though the food looked appealing enough, Devon had little appetite, and she wandered over to test the bed. Climbing between the musty sheets, she soon fell into a deep, troubled sleep.

"'Tis amazing how your life has become hopelessly complicated in so short a time," Cormac remarked, his lips twitching suspiciously. Truth to tell, this new development greatly amused him and he was sorry he would have to miss out on the fireworks that were sure to follow. "I don't envy you, Diablo. What are your plans concerning the wench?"

"I can't harm a woman carrying my child." Diablo frowned, his distress evidenced by his black scowl.

"The wench might be lying to save her hide," Cormac suggested slyly.

"My thoughts exactly," Akbar concurred sourly. "Diablo is far too trusting. It proved fatal once, and I thought he had learned his lesson. My advice is to—"

"I don't need your advice," Diablo interjected, "nor did I ask for it. I thought you said dinner was ready, Cormac, I'm starved."

Seated at the table and eating the hardy fare provided by their host, a friend of long standing who often fenced loot for Diablo, and a smuggler to boot, Diablo asked a question that took everyone by surprise. "Is there a minister in Penzance?"

His simple request brought a roar of protest from Akbar.

A night of uninterrupted sleep was just what Devon needed. These past days, so hectic and fraught with upheaval, had left her drained. In her heart she knew she had come close to death. Having nearly met her end at the hands of the man she loved had jolted her badly, leaving her shaken and unsure of her future.

Diablo quietly entered Devon's room and saw that she was still sleeping soundly despite the bright sunlight pouring through the arched windows. He intended to awaken her but instead paused beside the bed regarding her with a mixture of loathing tempered with the great love he once bore her. He tried desperately to maintain the impenetrable wall he had erected around his heart. She looked so sweetly innocent. He quickly discarded that notion when he considered the loss of lives she had been responsible for. Recalling the reason that had brought him to Devon's bedside, Diablo softly spoke her name.

Devon's eyes opened slowly, fear clouding her vision. "What is it?" The strange gleam in Diablo's silver eyes nudged her from sleep into the cold reality of his hate. Had he changed his mind about sparing her life?

"You must get up now," he said coolly. "The *Devil Dancer* will return for us today and there's still much to be done. Come downstairs when you're ready." Abruptly he turned and stalked from the room, as if he could barely stand the sight of her.

Daring to breathe again, Devon scrambled from bed, quickly washing and donning a clean dress from her bundle, which had been placed in her room the night before. The door had been left unlocked and she descended the stairs to where Diablo paced below, impatiently waiting for her.

"Come along, your breakfast is waiting."

"I'm not hungry," Devon replied sullenly.

"Your tray was untouched last night. You'll eat today if I have to force-feed you." He grasped her arm and propelled her into the dining room. Only one place was set. "We've already eaten," came his terse explanation.

The oatmeal stuck in her throat, but hot tea helped wash it down. When she had choked down enough to satisfy Diablo they left the crumbling mansion. The coach, with Akbar handling the horses from the driver's box, awaited them at the front entrance. With nary a word of explanation, Diablo boosted Devon inside, settling down beside her. She was surprised to see her bundle of clothes neatly tied and placed on the floor. Then Cormac joined them in the coach, looking fierce and frightening dressed in the rough clothing of a border lord, but nevertheless imposing. The door was barely closed before the coach jolted forward.

"Where are we going?" Devon asked sharply.

Cormac's shaggy brows flew upward. "Haven't you told the lass?"

"She'll do as I say," Diablo responded curtly, then fell silent.

"I'll do nothing of the sort," Devon balked. "I have a right to know where you're taking me."

More silence. Cormac merely shrugged and directed his attention out the window. Soon the coach entered the village at the foot of the cliff, continuing its furious pace until it clattered to a halt before a small weathered building at the far edge of town.

"What is this place?" Devon asked, a frisson of fear shivering down her spine.

"The town is called Penzance and this building serves as our church," Cormac saw fit to explain. Diablo said nothing, maintaining his brooding silence, while in the driver's box Akbar could be heard muttering Turkish obscenities.

"Church? I don't understand." Devon was truly puzzled and looked helplessly at Diablo for an explanation.

Realizing the time had come to reveal his plans, Diablo broke his long silence. "We're here to be married."

"Married! But I thought you hated me? Nay, I won't do it," she protested vigorously. "I had always hoped the man I married would love me."

"Like Winston?" Diablo mocked cruelly.

"Well, aye, like Winston," Devon freely admitted. "Why are you doing this?"

"It should be obvious even to you. I won't have my babe come into this world a bastard. Believe it or not, Winston isn't the paragon of virtue you think him."

"What makes you so certain?" Devon challenged. "You don't even know Winston."

Diablo's tightly clamped jaw told her he would say no more on the subject. Instead, he dragged her toward the small church. Cormac opened the door, and she soon found herself being forcefully led down the long aisle where a somberly dressed man awaited them.

"Ah, there you are," he said and smiled warmly. "I was beginning to think you changed your mind. What a beautiful bride," he complimented, beaming at Devon. "Shall we proceed?"

"Aye, pastor, begin," Diablo nodded curtly. "We sail within the hour and are anxious to be wed."

The pastor asked no questions, knowing Cormac as he did and aware of the other man's profession. Were it not for smuggling and piracy, half the families in Penzance would be starving and the other half destitute. His own little church couldn't survive without help from men like Cormac. Opening his prayer book and facing the young couple, Pastor Clement began reading the brief ceremony that joined Devon and Diablo in marriage.

Stunned, Devon opened her mouth to protest but was silenced by Diablo's harsh whisper. "Don't give me reason to carry out my original plan. I could still kill you."

Her world spinning crazily on its axis, Devon did not hear Pastor Clement address Diablo as Christopher, or Diablo's answer to the time-honored question. She wasn't even aware that it was time to speak her own vows until Diablo nudged her in the ribs. Inhaling deeply, Devon muttered, "I will," in a voice so soft the pastor asked her to repeat it.

Then it was over and Diablo was sliding a heavy gold band on the appropriate finger. She was married! Lord help her, she had just become the devil's bride! Diablo's kiss was cool and perfunctory and quickly over, but Cormac bussed her soundly on the cheek. From Akbar she received naught but a dark scowl.

In a self-induced trance, Devon signed the marriage paper, taking no notice when Diablo added his signature. If she had noticed, she would have

been astounded to see the name Christopher
Douglas Linley, Duke of Grenville, inscribed there-
in. Then she was outside the church, being hustled
into the coach. And so began her first day of
married life.

The coach left the town immediately, traveling
along a high, spectacularly beautiful and lonely
road closely following the sea. Several miles later
they ground to a halt on a bleak windswept stretch
overlooking a small, deep cove where the *Devil*
Dancer rode at anchor.

During the bumpy ride from Penzance, it had
appeared that Devon was all but forgotten as Diablo and Cormac discussed ships and cargos and
schedules. Had she dreamed her marriage to Diablo? Was this all a terrible nightmare from which
she'd wake up safe in her own bed? Nay, the heavy
gold band on her finger was too real, its weight more
like a tight noose than a token of love. Could she
ever hope to win back Diablo's love? she wondered
bleakly. Did she even want to?

Suddenly the conversation between Cormac and
Diablo came to a halt and Diablo stepped out of the
coach, lifting his hand to help Devon. "We must go
the rest of the way on foot," he informed her.
Cormac scrambled into the driver's box newly
vacated by Akbar.

"Fair winds and the devil's own luck to you,"
grinned the huge smuggler. "Come again when your
hold is bursting with French wine or Spanish spices
and oil and I'll guarantee the best prices. Luck to
you also, my lady," he said to Devon, certain she'd
need luck if she expected to live harmoniously with
her volatile husband.

"Farewell, my friend," said Diablo, "and thank

you for your hospitality as well as the loan of your coach." After Akbar retrieved Devon's bundle of clothes as well as those of Diablo and himself, the vehicle clattered off down the deserted road.

"Come along, Devon." Grasping her upper arm, Diablo propelled her toward the edge of the cliff.

At first Devon thought he intended to toss her into the sea, until she saw Akbar disappear down a well-trodden path leading to a narrow crescent of beach below. Though the path was steep it was not particularly arduous, and Devon negotiated it easily with Diablo's help. For the sake of his child and for no other reason, Devon suspected he would let nothing happen to her. Thank God it wasn't the vindictive Akbar who had been entrusted with her safety, else she doubted she would have reached the beach alive.

"Are you all right?" Diablo asked anxiously when they reached the bottom. Breathless, Devon nodded. "Here comes the longboat."

Within minutes the longboat sent from the *Devil Dancer* bumped into the shore. Two men leaped out to hold it in place in the rolling surf. Sweeping Devon into his arms, Diablo carried her through the knee-deep turquoise water and dumped her unceremoniously into the boat. She noted the look of stunned disapproval on the men's faces when they recognized her. Did Diablo's entire crew hate her for committing an act she knew nothing about?

Devon learned how much she was despised the moment her feet touched the deck of the *Devil Dancer*. An angry clamor raced from one end of the ship to the other until Diablo saw fit to put an end to it.

"What's that bitch doin' aboard, cap'n?" called

out Dancy. "Did ye bring her so's we all can watch her hang from the yardarm?" Dancy had lost a woman and child in the shelling of Paradise Island.

"Give her to us!" shouted another. Only once before in her life had Devon felt such overwhelming fear, and that when Diablo had had his fingers curled around her neck.

"Cease, lads!" Diablo commanded, thrusting his hand into the air to gain attention. Most complied, though many continued to grumble. "Lady Devon became my wife this day. We were legally married in Penzance by Pastor Clement not an hour ago."

A collective roar of protest and violent disapproval greeted his words.

"Traitor!" shouted one of the pirates.

"Why did you do it?" called out another.

"If the man who called me a traitor will step forward, I'll be happy to disabuse him of that notion." His dark scowl and forbidding features produced no challengers. "Lady Devon is my wife, and I'll allow no one to treat her with disrespect. Now, lads, we've a ship to sail." Grumbling among themselves, the men hopped to obey as Akbar barked orders that put the ship into motion. They were still in English waters and all too aware of their danger.

"Why didn't you tell them I wasn't guilty?" Devon demanded to know.

"How could I tell them something I don't know myself?" Diablo answered, glowering with fierce resentment.

Suddenly Kyle appeared at Diablo's elbow, and Devon smiled in genuine welcome, certain she had at least one friend aboard the *Devil Dancer*. But Kyle's condemning frown and cool words left

Devon little doubt that she could no longer count Kyle among her friends.

"I'm happy Diablo didn't kill you, lass," he remarked dryly, "but if I thought him capable of wringing your neck I'd never have let him return to England in the first place. What puzzles me is his reason for marrying you and bringing you here where you're hardly welcome. Whatever possessed you, Diablo?"

"Kyle, please believe me, I had nothing to do with the attack on Paradise," Devon pleaded.

Kyle seemed not to hear. "What did you hope to gain by talking Diablo into marrying you? Are you prepared to live with his hate?"

"I didn't talk him into it, he—"

Her explanation was lost to the wind when Diablo crudely announced, "Devon is carrying my child."

"Holy mother of God! Is that true, lass?"

Devon's face turned bright red. She had hoped to hide her shame for a while longer. "I—I believe it to be so," she admitted in a strained whisper.

Instantly Kyle's fierce scowl melted into a look of pity. He didn't envy Devon living with a man whose love had been turned into hate and mistrust by her deplorable act. Uneasily he wondered what Diablo's plans for his wife would be after their babe was born. Kyle knew that Diablo could be utterly ruthless at times and feared that his implacable resentment would force him into something he might later regret. He found no words in his heart to encourage Devon, using his silence to convey his feeling of inadequacy. If Devon had been guilty of divulging the secret of their cove, then she richly deserved whatever punishment Diablo provided.

Kyle's response to Diablo's astounding news was to repeat, "Holy mother of God."

Devon did not step outside Diablo's cabin for three days, not that she had any wish to. The profound animosity of the pirate crew drove from her mind all desire to walk among them. Her daily exercise consisted of pacing the narrow confines of the cabin and basking in fresh air and sunshine obtained by standing at the open windows overlooking the ship's stern.

She had not seen Diablo since he'd left her standing in the center of his cabin while he collected his personal items, which Devon assumed he had moved to wherever he was sleeping. She had more than sufficient time to dwell on the months and years to come, if she was allowed to live that long. After her babe was born would she be discarded like an old shoe, never to see her child again? Nay! she shook her head in vigorous denial, she'd not allow that to happen. Who would care for her child? Tara? Scarlett? The thought was more frightening than that of her own death.

As Devon paced the cabin, a nagging pain tugged at her gut. For two days the pain, sometimes sharp and unrelenting, other times vague and diffused, had made Devon all too aware of her vulnerability. Her very life depended on Diablo's good will. When the old pirate, Pegleg, who supplied her meals and saw to her comforts, carried in her supper, she refused it with a polite shake of her head, which was duly reported to Diablo.

That night Devon retired at her normal time, aware that something strange was happening inside her body, something she could not prevent. It was a long time before sleep claimed her, and nearly dawn when she awoke in excruciating pain. She knew immediately the cause of her agony. The sudden rush of blood told her that her monthly courses had resumed with a vengeance and she hadn't been pregnant after all! She strongly suspected that the upsets in her life these past months had stopped her monthlies. Wracked by pain, Devon crawled out of bed, cleaned herself up, and removed the soiled sheets from the bunk. Summoning the last of her depleted strength, she rolled up in a blanket and lay down on the bare mattress.

Then the tears came one after another, deep, soul-destroying sobs that spoke of her despair. She felt as if her insides were on fire, and the thought that she'd not have Diablo's babe to love only added to her pain. She normally experienced pain at the onset of menses but nothing like the crippling cramps that were tearing her apart now. Curled into a ball, Devon fell into a light sleep, her cheeks streaked with tears.

Pegleg cautiously entered the cabin after receiving no answer to his discreet knock. With pounding heart he stared at Devon's blanket-shrouded form curled up on the bunk. What little he could see of her face appeared white and drawn. Then his eyes fell on the bloody sheets wadded up and tossed in a corner. Abruptly he turned and fled as swiftly as his peg leg would allow.

Minutes later Diablo burst into the cabin, pulling Devon from the depths of a druglike sleep. She moaned groggily as he grasped her shoulders. "Devon, are you ill?" Her pale face and wide blue eyes blank with pain frightened him badly.

Finally Devon realized what he was asking. "Go

ahead and kill me, Diablo," she stunned him by saying. "But I wasn't lying, I truly believed I was pregnant."

"Have you lost my child?" Devon had assumed that his harsh voice and stony features conveyed rage while in truth he was feeling a far different emotion.

"Perhaps there never was a child," Devon admitted dully. Then a severe cramp spasmed her gut and her face screwed up into a grimace.

"Are you in pain?" Diablo's solicitous words contrasted oddly with his furious scowl. Devon merely nodded, unable to speak with her insides twisted in agony.

Diablo whirled and left the cabin, returning almost immediately with Kyle. Kyle knelt before Devon, smoothing the tangled hair from her damp brow. "Have you lost the babe, lass?" he asked anxiously. What little doctoring he performed hardly included treating female problems. Then his eyes fell on the soiled sheets. "When did it happen?"

"During the night," Devon said weakly, "but I'm not certain now there ever was a child. My life has been in a turmoil of late and . . ."

"Shh, no need to explain," Kyle soothed. "Has there been much pain?"

"Aye," Devon acknowledged, "but 'twill pass. It always does."

"Are you still bleeding?"

"A little, the worst is past."

Kyle said nothing, assuming that Devon knew her own body far better than anyone else. When she appeared to be dozing, he rose to face Diablo, who hovered anxiously at his elbow.

"Well, what do you make of it?" Diablo asked.

Kyle directed his gaze to the blood-stained sheets, then back to Devon's pale face. "She's lost a fair amount of blood," he opined with careful thought. "It's entirely possible Devon's monthly time resumed after an interruption due to stress. But," he pointed out, "it's more likely she miscarried. You've been far from gentle with her, and the shock and upheaval she's suffered is enough to make her lose the babe."

"What can we do?"

"Nothing. As long as she's not hemorrhaging, her young body will heal itself in time."

"Is there no way to tell if Devon was truly pregnant or merely lying to save her skin?"

"I'm no doctor," Kyle reminded him. "I know little about female ailments or cures. Setting broken bones and sewing wounds is as far as my knowledge stretches. But I do think a dose of laudanum would do more good than harm."

Diablo agreed.

"You won't hurt Devon now that she's no longer carrying your child, will you, Kit? I know what she did, or what *we think* she did, but killing her will solve nothing."

"You think I'd kill my own wife?" Diablo asked, glowering darkly.

"I happen to know why you married Devon. So do most of the crew. They're still angry at you for bringing her aboard the *Devil Dancer*."

"My plans for Devon's future are no one's concern," Diablo bit out. "And I'm perfectly capable of protecting what is mine. Sooner or later I'll find out if she betrayed us. Until then she'll not be harmed. See to your duties, Kyle, I'll see to my—Devon's—care."

* * *

During the following day and night Devon awoke frequently, always to find Diablo sitting beside her, offering water or food and wiping her brow. Though she refused the food with a shake of her head, she never failed to drink deeply. When she finally awoke to the light of day, her mind was clear, her pain greatly diminished, and Diablo gone. She was amazed to find herself lying on clean sheets, dressed in a fresh bedgown and her hair neatly brushed. When had Diablo turned ladies maid? she wondered, the thought bringing a wan smile to her lips. Somehow she couldn't picture him performing that duty. But if not Diablo, then who?

Feeling much better, Devon decided to get up and dress for the day. She was just sliding her long legs off the side of the bunk when Diablo entered the cabin bearing a tray. He stared at her legs, bared from the thighs down, with more interest than he'd shown her since he'd taken her from her home. She blushed profusely and made a futile attempt to tug down the hem of her bedgown.

"Pegleg was busy so I brought your breakfast," he said, raising his eyes reluctantly. "Are you feeling better?"

Eying him uncertainly, Devon nodded. "Aye, and hungry, too." His moods were so unpredictable she never knew how to proceed where he was concerned. Mostly he glowered at her with hate-filled eyes, his expression wavering between downright hostility and bare civility.

Devon noted that Diablo was letting his beard grow again, reminding her of the first time she had seen him, standing defiant and proud with a noose around his neck. Even then his virile masculinity had beckoned to her, and his charm eventually won her love. She wasn't certain when she first realized she loved the handsome rogue. Perhaps it was the very first moment she laid eyes on him. Diablo might be a pirate, but Devon intuitively knew that he was nothing like the crude men who sailed the seas in search of blood and booty. Something in his background suggested gentle breeding, for whenever he let his guard down he displayed the fine manners of a gentleman.

"Kyle thinks you should remain in bed another day or two," Diablo said, interrupting Devon's thoughts.

"I feel fine," Devon insisted.

"Nevertheless, it's best you follow orders." He set the tray on her lap, then perched gingerly on the edge of the bunk. "I want the truth, Devon, no more lies." Given his words, his voice was oddly gentle. "Did you tell me you were pregnant in order to save your skin?"

Devon shook her head, sending her tangled mass of blonde tresses flying. "You might as well kill me now if you think that, Diablo. I wouldn't lie about something as important as that. The only reason I agreed to marry Winnie was to give your child a name."

"Winnie," Diablo mocked. "An apt nickname. Has he given you no inkling about his—sexual preferences?"

"I—don't know what you mean." Devon was truly puzzled. She knew that Winston had none of the passion and fire she'd come to expect from Diablo, but she assumed he kept his under tight rein in deference to her innocence.

"I can excuse *you* for not recognizing the truth, but not your father. Your marriage to the man would have been a sham. Winston has no use for women. Now do you understand?"

Devon's delicate brows arched nearly to her hairline as she became vaguely aware of Diablo's meaning. In certain areas her education was woefully lacking.

Her puzzled expression brought a snort of disgust from Diablo's lips. "To put it bluntly, Winston is the type of man who prefers men in his bed."

Devon's face turned a brilliant red, then green, before settling into a ghostly white. "You mean— Oh, surely you're mistaken. Why would he wish to marry if he was—that kind of a man?"

"Surely you're smart enough to figure that out for yourself."

"I don't believe it. How would you know such a thing? Father would never agree to that kind of marriage."

Rather than mention things he wasn't ready to divulge, Diablo said, "Eat your breakfast, Devon, I've a ship to run. If you're feeling well enough tomorrow, you can get out of bed. Meanwhile, rest and regain your strength."

"Diablo, wait! Where are you taking me?"

He grinned, but the smile never reached his eyes. "To Paradise."

"Go to the devil!"

"I'm afraid he's already claimed me."

Then he was gone.

Chapter Thirteen

The sound of belching cannon brought Devon leaping to her feet. Three days had elapsed since her illness and she now felt well enough to dress each day. Her appetite had returned and her paleness was replaced by a rosy glow. Just as Kyle predicted, Devon's youthful exuberance quickly reasserted itself, returning her to good health. She was young, healthy, and Diablo's wife. No matter what he had threatened, she was still alive and suddenly eager to face her future. Diablo had loved her once and there was no reason he wouldn't do so again.

The guns boomed with deafening redundancy, and Devon flew to the door. She was far too curious to remain inside while her husband faced danger, or even death.

Diablo stood on the quarterdeck, feet spread apart, hands on slim hips, directing fire at the Portuguese merchantman doing its best to evade the *Devil Dancer.* "Fire another round across her

bow, lads," he shouted above the deafening roar.
"She's lightly armed and no match for us. She'll
surrender without a fight."

The cannon boomed again, and just as Diablo
predicted, a white flag replaced the Portuguese
banner flying from the mast. As often happened,
Diablo had subdued the captain and crew without
striking a blow. In a short time the *Devil Dancer*
had maneuvered alongside the merchantman, and
men were using grappling hooks to secure the two
ships together. When the Portuguese captain spotted Diablo pacing the bridge, he shouted across the
distance, "Who are you and from where do you
hail?"

"From the sea!" returned Diablo, giving the
traditional pirate reply. Then he leaped to the deck
below, grasped a line, and swung nimbly across the
narrow strip of sea separating the two ships. He
landed neatly at the captain's side. Throwing caution to the wind, Devon rushed to the rail, hoping
to hear something of what was being said.

The Portuguese captain trembled before Diablo,
who towered nearly a foot above him. He had heard
of this devil disguised as a man but had never had
the misfortune of encountering him. He wondered
if the pirate was truly a Spaniard as rumored and
addressed him in Spanish. "I am Diego Figuero,
captain of the *Louisa Esperez*."

In perfect Spanish, one of the three languages he
spoke, Diablo replied, "I am called Diablo. What
cargo do you carry?"

Captain Figuero licked his dry lips, looking decidedly uncomfortable. "We are carrying nothing
but passengers this trip." He deliberately neglected
to mention that he had been sent to England to

return the ship owner's beautiful daughter to Portugal in time for her wedding.

Diablo snorted in disgust. He had hoped to rid the *Louisa Esperez* of much riches. "Assemble the passengers on deck."

Devon silently observed the proceedings as a group of frightened men, women, and children spilled from the passageway onto the deck, prodded by Akbar. Last to appear were two women, both young and beautiful. But judging from their manner of dress—one richly garbed and adorned with jewels, the other more plainly attired—they appeared to be mistress and maid.

Diablo looked over the poor selection of hostages, fuming over the lack of booty and silently considering which, if any, were worth holding for ransom. Not that he took the captain's word that the *Louisa Esperez* carried no cargo. His crew were turning the ship upside down in search of booty, and if nothing of value was found he'd have to look to the passengers for a source of income in order to placate his men.

Diablo's narrowed gaze stopped abruptly before a stunning, richly dressed and bejeweled woman— no more than a girl, really—and regarded her with interest. She was a fiery wench, loudly protesting her rough handling, and a satisfied smile teased the corners of his lips. He was willing to bet the volatile senorita was the pampered daughter of a rich don, one willing to part with a fortune in ransom.

"What is the meaning of this?" the senorita spouted angrily as Akbar nudged her forward. "Do you know who my father is?"

"This one is more trouble than she's worth," the huge Turk grumbled crossly.

"Why no, senorita, who is your father?" Diablo asked, assuming a placating tone.

The girl's dark eyes grew large and luminous at the sight of Diablo's imposing figure and handsome features. She thought him the most dashingly attractive man she'd ever seen. Her huge orbs devoured him greedily and her sensuous lips curved in a smile meant to entice and beguile as she posed artfully before him, pushing her rounded breasts forward to full advantage.

"My father is Miguel Esperez, owner of this ship and many others like her. I am Carlotta Esperez and this is my maid, Marlena. We have been visiting relatives in London." She offered far more than Diablo had asked. "Who are you?"

"They call me Diablo. Your father must be a wealthy man, Senorita Carlotta," Diablo probed.

"Extremely wealthy," Carlotta concurred guilelessly. "And not without influence. If I am harmed, Father will be relentless in his pursuit of you."

"I do not harm beautiful women," Diablo denied, "but neither am I stupid enough to let you go without relieving your father of part of his fortune. If your father is as rich as you say, he'll agree to whatever ransom I demand."

"My father loves me and will pay anything," Carlotta replied confidently.

Privately she thought it would be a great adventure to spend time with the handsome pirate. He didn't appear at all cruel or threatening. Besides, once she returned to Portugal her strict parents would put an end to her wild ways and she would marry a man she despised. In London she had taken several lovers and seriously doubted she could settle down to any one man. Despite her young age, she had been introduced to sex early by a handsome footman in her father's service. Her marriage had been arranged years ago to an elderly friend of the family, and she dreaded the thought of returning to Portugal and the dull life of a married woman when she was still so young and vital. She viewed Diablo as a way to delay her return as well as experience an adventure of a lifetime, the handsome pirate a bonus thrown in.

"Senorita Carlotta, you must not give this devil so much information," Captain Figuero cautioned, dismayed by his charge's lack of propriety. "Your father entrusted me with your safety, and I fear I have let him down." He turned to Diablo. "The lady is gently born and reared. Her reputation will be severely damaged if you insist on holding her for ransom. Have mercy."

"Senorita Carlotta will not be harmed," Diablo contended, smiling beguilingly at the haughty girl. His roguish grin filled her with an excitement she found difficult to contain. "I will do nothing to compromise her virtue."

Then Diablo called his lieutenant and quartermaster, ordering the *Louisa Esperez* thoroughly searched and anything of value removed before returning with the crew to the *Devil Dancer*.

"Your crew and passengers are free to continue on your way, captain," Diablo informed Figuero. "I ask only that you relay a message to Senor Esperez concerning his daughter. Tell him neither Carlotta nor her maid will be harmed unless he fails to deliver the ransom in Nassau in two months' time. I will be there to receive it exactly sixty days from today. Once the ransom is in my hands the women will be released."

"What ransom do you demand?" Figuero asked.

"Five thousand pieces of eight."

"What! That's preposterous."

"Surely I am worth that much," Carlotta sniffed with a toss of her glossy black head.

"I wholeheartedly concur, the lady is worth at least that much," Diablo agreed, swallowing a chuckle. "You have my word the women will not be harmed."

"The word of a pirate? Bah!"

"Nevertheless, you have it. And now, senorita, allow me to escort you to my ship."

Carlotta trilled excitedly when Diablo swept her into his arms. "Hang on, senorita, I won't let you fall. My lieutenant will see to your maid."

Carlotta's slim arms circled Diablo's neck, the corded muscles rippling enticingly beneath her touch. "I'm not afraid," she replied, her heart beating in vigorous tumult. "You're so strong, I know you'd not let anything happen to me."

Easily supporting her slim form, Diablo grasped a dangling rope and swung gracefully across the chasm to the *Devil Dancer,* his wild flight not hindered in the least by Carlotta's meager weight.

A frown marring her smooth brow, Devon observed the proceedings aboard the *Louisa Esperez* with annoyed interest, caring little for the brazen way one of the women strutted before Diablo. Even from a distance she could tell the woman was young and radiantly beautiful in a dark, exotic way. When Diablo swept the woman into his arms, Devon nearly exploded with jealousy and rage. Did he intend to keep the lissome beauty for his own pleasure? Considering his voracious appetite, it was entirely possible, for it appeared he had little desire for his own wife. No matter what had persuaded him into marriage, Devon reflected, she was now his wife and shouldn't have to put up with his infidelity.

Diablo dropped lightly to his feet scant inches from where Devon stood, Carlotta still clinging to his neck. Amused and flattered by Carlotta's not so subtle attempts at seduction, he took his time untangling her arms and setting her on her feet. He noted Devon's fierce scowl and looped an arm around Carlotta's tiny waist, gaining perverse pleasure from provoking Devon's anger.

"What are you doing out here?" Diablo scolded, finally acknowledging Devon's presence.

Devon had no intention of admitting she had left the cabin because she feared for Diablo's safety. "I wanted to see what was happening."

"Now that you're here you may as well meet Senorita Carlotta Esperez. Senorita Carlotta, this is Lady Devon." The moment Carlotta saw Devon her smile turned sour. She viewed the lovely blonde as a serious contender for Diablo's affections.

Devon fumed with silent rage. She should have known Diablo wouldn't acknowledge her as his wife when he obviously expected to share Carlotta's bed.

"Who is this woman?" Carlotta asked in heavily accented English, surprising Diablo. He should have known the woman spoke the language, having just spent time in London. "Another hostage like myself or your—*puta?*"

Red dots of rage exploded behind Devon's eyes. She wanted to fly at the sly senorita and tear her eyes out. Realizing her intent, Diablo's placed a restraining hand on her arm.

"My relationship with Lady Devon is none of your concern, Carlotta." His censuring tone was like a dash of cold water in Carlotta's face.

Diablo's words did little to relieve Devon's hurt over his deliberate slight. She felt strongly that he should have introduced her as his wife. Then Kyle arrived with Marlena, Carlotta's maid. Though the girl looked frightened out of her wits, her beauty could not be denied. Smaller than her mistress, her shiny black tresses had come loose from her demure chignon and curled around her face in charming disarray. Devon thought the girl to be about her own age. From the way Kyle was devouring her voluptuous form and lovely features, it was obvious he thought her more than attractive.

"Are you all right, Carlotta?" Marlena asked, more concerned for her mistress than herself. Having served the haughty young woman since the age of twelve, Marlena felt familiar enough with Carlotta to address her informally.

"Of course, you goose, Diablo would not allow anything to happen to me." Carlotta directed a glowing smile at Diablo. "When we are in the company of others, Marlena, we will speak English. You understand and speak the language as well as I do."

"Sí, Carlotta," Marlena agreed. "What will happen to us now? I'm frightened."

"No need for fright," Diablo assured the tiny brunette. "No one will harm you. When Senor Esperez sends ransom you will both be freed."

"Truly?" she ventured, unable to believe his words after hearing of the despicable deeds visited on defenseless women by pirates.

"Truly," Diablo returned, thinking the girl quite fetching. Then he turned to Devon. "Pack your things, Devon. Carlotta and Marlena will occupy your quarters. 'Tis large and can easily accommodate both of them."

"Why, thank you, Diablo," simpered Carlotta coyly. "That's very thoughtful of you."

"Where will I sleep?" Devon demanded to know. It took all her considerable willpower to control her temper.

"You may have my cabin, Devon," Kyle offered generously. "'Tis no more than a cubbyhole but far better than sleeping on deck." He bent Diablo a censuring glare, unaware that he had spoken up before Diablo could suggest just such an arrangement himself.

"Come along, ladies, I'll show you to your quarters," Diablo said, returning Kyle's scowl. "Your trunks will be delivered shortly."

Flinging Devon a condescending look, Carlotta took Diablo's arm as he led her to the cabin that was to be her home for the next several days. Marlena followed meekly behind.

Though Kyle's small cabin offered none of the amenities she took for granted in Diablo's comfortable quarters, Devon was nonetheless grateful for a place to sleep. Did her husband hate her so much that he expected her to sleep on deck among men who despised her? she wondered, exasperated by the inconsiderate lout's neglect. It gave her a smidgeon of satisfaction that Diablo didn't plan on sharing Carlotta's bed, for if he did he'd hardly assign Marlena to the same cabin.

Kyle's cabin sported only one porthole, a far cry from Diablo's airy quarters with two full-length windows overlooking the ship's stern. Nothing was said about confining her to her cabin, and since

Devon had recovered completely, she spent most of the following days sitting in solitude on a pile of ropes on the ship's bow. When time permitted, Kyle stopped to speak with her, and so did Marlena, but the little maid was kept far too busy by her demanding mistress to allow for lengthy conversation.

Though Diablo mostly ignored her, he did ask after her health from time to time. What truly rankled was the way Carlotta seemed to dominate Diablo's free time, often joining him on the bridge or coaxing him into strolling the deck with her. It hurt Devon to think that Diablo paid the fiery Spanish beauty attentive court while all but ignoring his own wife. Yet more than once Devon caught Diablo regarding her through hooded eyes, his silver gaze fixed on her slim form with an unreadable expression that puzzled her. When she was brave enough to meet his stare, she'd find herself the object of his intense scrutiny. And today was no exception.

Their eyes collided across the expanse of rolling deck, reaching out toward one another yet unwilling or unable to breach the gap separating them. The silent message conveyed by the intensity of Diablo's gaze brought a flood of color to Devon's cheeks. Then the spell was broken when Carlotta deliberately strutted into Diablo's line of vision, smiling archly and batting her long dark lashes. Reluctantly Devon turned away, too proud to admit to her jealousy as Carlotta looped her arm through Diablo's and purposely led him in Devon's direction, pausing often to admire the view.

When they drifted past the spot where Devon sat, the wind flung bits of their animated conversation back to her. The dark Spanish beauty leaned intimately against Diablo, her words, those that Devon heard, sounding suspiciously like an outrageous invitation.

"Marlena will do exactly as I say. If you come to me tonight she will remain discretely on deck and not interfere."

Diablo's reply was lost to her, but Devon read eagerness in his laughter and approval in his eyes. She had no way of knowing that Diablo's laughter was due entirely to amusement. Not only did Carlotta's audacity and daring amuse him, but amazed him as well. Originally he thought her an innocent virgin, but as the days passed he seriously doubted he'd find her virginal should he accept her blatant invitation to share her bed. As for his smile, it was directed at himself for thinking her merely a young flirt testing her wings when her actions clearly labeled her a woman who had partaken freely of love's bounty with numerous lovers. And now Carlotta wanted to add him to her list.

Diablo thoroughly appreciated Carlotta's exotic beauty, but was aware that her shiny ebony locks were not the vivid gold of Devon's. Though her complexion had the look of creamy ivory, pale and glowing, he much preferred Devon's more vibrant coloring, reminding him of fine apricot brandy with a sprinkling of cinnamon freckles scattered across the bridge of her nose. And Devon's blue eyes were as stormy as the sea he loved so much, while Carlotta's flashing black orbs revealed nothing but her own feelings of self-worth. How different things could be between them if Devon hadn't betrayed him.

The thought of becoming a father thrilled Diablo. Especially with Devon as the child's mother. He knew of no other woman he'd want to bear his babe. If she'd had a miscarriage as Kyle suggested, he could not fault her, for he had put her through hell and treated her atrociously before bringing her aboard the *Devil Dancer*. But if she'd deliberately lied about being pregnant, he'd never be able to forgive her. Unfortunately, he'd never know for certain.

"Diablo, did you hear me?" Carlotta prodded, pouting prettily. "I've just invited you to share—the evening with me."

"Perhaps another time," Diablo hedged, wondering why in the hell he didn't jump at the invitation. Then he saw Devon staring at him as if he'd just plunged a dagger in her heart, and knew exactly why the thought of pleasuring himself with Carlotta gave him little joy.

"What exactly is Devon to you?" Carlotta asked, following the direction of Diablo's gaze. There was anger in her voice as well as jealousy. Accustomed to being doted upon by all her acquaintances, she did not enjoy Diablo's straying attention.

"Ask Devon," Diablo said cryptically. "Please excuse me, Carlotta, I've duties to perform." Shrugging off Carlotta's clinging arms, he turned and made his way back to the bridge.

From the corner of his eye he noted that Devon had joined Marlena and Kyle as they strolled by. When Carlotta approached them, Devon politely excused herself and left. With rapt attention Diablo observed the seductive sway of Devon's skirts, convinced he'd never seen a woman move with such sensual grace. He'd thought of nothing but making love to her since he brought her aboard the *Devil Dancer*. At first he was too damn angry to trust himself anywhere near her, then her illness had prevented him from consummating their marriage. Nothing stopped him now but his own stubborn pride. He didn't need a wife, wasn't certain he still wanted Devon, but he had to have her or go out of his mind.

The supper Pegleg brought lay untouched on the narrow table. Devon pushed it aside, having no stomach for food when Diablo was in another cabin making glorious love with Carlotta. Devon was haunted by the grim specter of the man he had been before he thought she betrayed him. Humorous, loving, passionate, tender, not this cold, brutal stranger who delighted in taunting and humiliating her. Stripping off her clothes, Devon lay down in her thin shift, deciding the night was too warm for the constricting bedgown. Since they had entered southern waters the weather had changed dramatically, making the small cabin hot and stifling. Devon knew they couldn't be far from the Bahama islands and wondered what fate awaited her in Diablo's home. Would he still pay assiduous court to Carlotta once they were on Paradise? Sprawled atop the narrow bunk, Devon fell into a fitful sleep. And then the dream began. The same dream that had plagued her constantly since she had left Diablo weeks ago.

In her dream Diablo was making love to her. Sweet, tender love in the gentle way she'd grown accustomed to. With a flick of the wrist he removed her gown, peeling off his own clothes and joining her in bed. Then he was pressing her down against the unyielding surface. Suddenly the usual course of the dream altered as Diablo became a sneering stranger, taking her with passionate violence instead of gentleness. Devon's eyes flew open, as she became aware that no dream could feel so real. And she was right. The flesh-and-blood Diablo crouched above her, nude to the waist and grinning like the devil he was named after.

"Diablo! What are you doing here?"

"You're my wife, Devon," Diablo reminded her.

"I'm sorry to hear you admit it," came Devon's scathing reply. "I'd so hoped it was all a bad dream. What about Carlotta?"

"Carlotta? What about her?"

"Have you finished with her already? I mean—I assumed you'd spend the night with her."

"I don't want Carlotta, though her offer quite dazzled me."

"I don't believe you."

"Then we're even, for I don't believe you. You're the only one who could have betrayed me. But that doesn't stop me from wanting you. Lord knows I've tried, but I have no pride where you're concerned. You're my wife and it's your duty to satisfy my needs."

Devon exploded in furious anger. "Duty! I owe you nothing. I became your enemy and bride at the same time. Twice you've abducted me, once on the eve of my wedding. And don't for a minute think I believe that drivel about Winston. I'd prefer your cruelty to our loveless coupling."

"Cruelty!" Diablo sneered. "You know nothing of cruelty. I could tell you, but I'd rather demonstrate."

His mouth slanted over hers brutally, hurting her, making her gasp out a protest. He paid no heed to her obvious distress, his arms encircling her like steel bands, holding her so tightly she could scarcely breath. The fury of his kiss forced her mouth open. Immediately his tongue penetrated deep inside with none of the tenderness she knew him capable of. He took her mouth and used it ruthlessly, forced it to his will, conquered it without mercy. The sudden unleashed violence badly frightened Devon and she feared she might faint.

His hand closed over her right breast, burning through the thin material of her shift to her skin. Against her will her nipple puckered against his palm, sending a shaft of pure fire straight to her loins. His kiss deepened savagely while his hand plundered the tender mound, caressing, kneading, searing her skin like a brand. His fingers thrust inside the shift and the fine muslin gave with a soft ripping sound. She lay trembling, helpless beneath his ravening desire. Then her shift left her body with a controlled savagery that made her heart shiver in her breast. Even if she wanted to protest, she could not have. Her blood surged hot and fierce in her veins, her legs trembled, and a fierce need erupted within her to equal the devouring hunger revealed in his face.

The silvery moonlight behind Diablo cast his head in dark silhouette, making it difficult for Devon to read his expression. His initial savagery startled her, but strangely she no longer felt threatened as he stared at her without moving for a long, breathless moment. She felt her breast beneath his fingers swell and tighten, bringing a jolt of both pain and pleasure. Instinctively she arched, offering him more of her tempting curves. A harsh, ragged growl left his throat. Then, in a movement so swift it startled her, he came down on top of her, his weight crushing her into the hard surface of the bunk.

"God's bones, sweetheart, I don't know who's suffering more, you or me. How can I hurt you when all I want is to love you? Your sweet body was fashioned expressly for mine. I touch you and you respond instantly. I want to be inside you so badly I hurt."

His arms wrapped around her slender body, crushing her to him, all thought of brutality long forgotten. His mouth closed over hers, and he kissed her with a fierceness that made her head spin. The wiry mat of hair on his chest was abrasive against her breasts, and she shivered in response to the stimulus. He must have felt her arousal, and it fired his own, stifling the impulse to take her swiftly to ease his terrible need. It had been so long—too damn long—and he'd had no other woman since Devon. As his lips moved to suckle the tender tips of her breasts, his fingertips slid down between her thighs, parting them as he sought to arouse her fully.

"God's bones, you're so hot and wet and oh so sweet I want to slowly savor every inch of you."

He lowered his head then, spreading light kisses over the triangle of golden curls nestled between her thighs before sending his tongue sliding along the tender cleft. He heard her call his name but ignored her breathless gasp to delve ever deeper into the warm moist cave welcoming his loving invasion with a rush of secret fluid. His tongue continued to caress her gently as he savored the sweet essence of her body. Devon was too pleased by the marvelous sensations he created within her to be shocked by the way he made love to her. Then the wonderful quickening inside her exploded, splintering into a whirlwind of light and colors and shapes.

Before Devon fully regained her senses, Diablo had discarded his trousers and thrust inside her, so deep she thought his hugeness would split her in two. She gasped, grinding her hips against his urgent, instinctive response as her passion began to slowly renew itself.

"Kit, oh God! When you're loving me like this I don't even know my own name."

Suddenly Diablo cried out, thrusting again and again, and then one final time to hurry Devon to her own reward. Her cry echoed his, quivering as Diablo wrapped his arms tightly around her, holding himself deep inside her until she was still.

For several long suspenseful minutes they lay motionless, entwined together, collecting their thoughts as well as their breath. Diablo's face was completely shadowed so that Devon could not decipher his expression. He shifted his weight to lay beside her, and Devon lifted one slender hand to touch and then slide down his hip. Her light caress set off a reaction in him that Devon hardly expected as he swore, the words harsh and shocking.

"You're a damn witch and I'm a bloody idiot." The words were no sooner out of his mouth than he was jerking her hard against him, his mouth assaulting hers with hot hungry kisses.

It rankled to know that no matter what Devon had done he continued to desire her. He was finally ready to admit to himself that he had married her to keep anyone else from having her. With Devon he had known the joy of love, the bitter anguish of betrayal, and an erotic pleasure he could not adequately describe in words. He despised his vulnerability where Devon was concerned, deplored his reaction to her pleading blue eyes and lying lips. Suddenly the thought of all the suffering and destruction that Devon had visited on Paradise brought Diablo's wild caresses to an abrupt halt. Expelling a snort of self-loathing, he leaped to his feet.

"Damn your bloody hide! You're like a drug in my blood. Your sweet kisses and siren's body have the ability to move a statue, and I'm not made of stone. Do you expect me to forget and forgive so easily?"

"You've nothing to forget, Kit, for I've done nothing that needs forgiving." The name slipped easily from Devon's lips, and since Diablo did not protest she repeated it. "Kit, please, why don't you trust me?"

"Trust a woman who ran off with a man like Le Vautour? Surely you jest."

"I'm certain Father can clear up this misunderstanding," Devon suggested. "The longer I think on it, the more convinced I am that Le Vautour betrayed your secret."

"Are you suggesting that your father is responsible for shelling a defenseless village and taking innocent lives?"

Pulling on his pants in angry motions, Diablo whirled, his hard features all but obscured by the darkness. Though she couldn't see them, she knew his eyes were as cold and colorless as ice, and a shudder passed through her body.

"No, oh no, Father would never do that." Suddenly a thought came to her. Perhaps it was wild speculation but it had enough merit to mention. "Do you know the names of the ships that attacked Paradise?"

Devon held her breath, waiting for his answer. She recalled that shortly after she returned to London Winston had left aboard the *Larkspur* on a mission lasting a month or more. Afterwards he resigned from the navy to prepare for their wedding. He had been very secretive about where he had been, and now all the pieces began falling into place. Le Vautour, hoping for a more generous reward and driven by his hatred for Diablo, must have told her father about Paradise Island. And of course Father had passed on the information to Winston. Her abduction by Diablo must have affected Winston greatly, prompting him to attack a village inhabited by defenseless women and children.

"Tara did mention the *Larkspur*," Diablo reflected. "Why, does the name mean anything to you?"

Devon sucked her breath in sharply. *Larkspur*! Winston's ship. Without her knowing it she was indirectly responsible for the shelling of Paradise. If not for her Le Vautour would not have ventured to England in the first place. "The—the *Larkspur*," she stuttered, "'tis—'tis Winston's ship. But I swear . . ."

"You bitch!"

". . . that I said nothing to him," Devon finished lamely. "It had to be Le Vautour. He hated you though he tried to hide his feelings. He waited a long time to avenge the death of Black Bart."

"'Tis logical," Diablo allowed grudgingly, "but can you deny you brought Le Vautour to England? Akbar was right, you've caused me nothing but trouble. I was too besotted to listen to him. God's bones, Devon, I fancied myself in love with you!"

"And now?" Devon prompted, sitting up and pulling the sheet to her chin.

"What I feel for you now is pure and simple lust," Diablo said, his voice laced with self-disgust.

"Then turn around and take me back to England. Since I'm not carrying your child, you owe me nothing. Forget I ever existed."

The mattress sagged under Diablo's weight as he

perched on the edge of the bunk and lit a lamp so he could look at Devon. "Forget you? I wish to God I could. Have you forgotten we're man and wife? What's mine I keep. Besides, after tonight you just might be carrying my child."

"How long will you keep me, Kit?" Devon challenged. "One day you'll be caught and hanged, or killed in a sea battle. What will become of me then?"

Seeing Diablo's stricken look, Devon pressed on. "Perhaps I'll be passed on to your men? Or do you propose the other pirate captains draw lots for me? What if there's a child? How will we survive?"

To his profound regret, Diablo could answer none of those poignant questions.

Chapter Fourteen

Sleep eluded Diablo after Devon posed her evocative questions. It rankled to know that everything she said was true. Should he meet an untimely end, Devon would be left completely at the mercy of unscrupulous men. He'd wish that fate on no woman. No matter how difficult it was to admit, he still cared too much for Devon to abandon her to pirates and scoundrels.

So exactly what were his options? he asked himself grimly. Until Devon challenged him he had thought himself invincible and piracy the only way of life. Every day was a rousing adventure filled with an excitement found in no other profession. He thrived on danger, welcomed the hazards involved in every venture. And the rewards were well worth the risks. Piracy had made him rich enough to provide for future heirs for generations to come. It was the thought of those potential heirs that gave Diablo pause.

Did he want his sons and daughters living on the edge of society, shunned and reviled the world over? The answer was a resounding no.

Perhaps, Diablo reasoned, it was time to change the course of his life and mend his wild ways. He could become a planter on Paradise, or settle in America. England and most of Europe were out of the question, for the possibility would always exist that he'd be recognized as the scourge of the sea.

Leaving the brotherhood was something Diablo had never before considered, but then he'd never had a wife, or the possibility of children. He meant what he said when he told Devon he kept what was his. The thought of returning her to England to marry a man like Winston was reprehensible. Giving up pirating was definitely something he should contemplate, Diablo decided as he rolled up in a blanket and tried to find a comfortable position on the hard deck. With three women aboard, there were no cabins to spare and he deliberately refrained from remaining with Devon in her bunk. He greatly feared the effect she had on him and needed a clear head to run his ship and control his crew.

Devon's hair flowed like thick honey down her back as she raised her face to the warm sunlight. In the distance the Bahamas sparkled like jewels tossed upon the shimmering surface of the water. The blue-green water sliced beneath *Devil Dancer*'s hull as wind filled her burgeoning sails. The swiftly approaching islands were an inspiring sight despite Devon's misgivings about her future on those sun-drenched, verdant shores. It had been two days since Diablo had come to her cabin and made love to her. Evidently their passionate coupling had

affected him as much as it had her, for since that
night she often caught him staring at her in pensive
contemplation. She knew that her provocative
probing made him delve deeply into his conscience
and wondered if he had reached a decision about
what to do with her.

"Are those distant islands our destination?"
Carlotta sidled up beside Devon, joining her at the
rail where she stood enjoying the balmy breezes.

"Aye," Devon replied, none too happy to have
her solitude interrupted by the fiery senorita.

"He's a handsome devil, isn't he?" Carlotta
sighed, shifting her gaze to where Diablo stood on
the bridge. "His eyes—they're like none other I've
ever seen. When he looks at me I forget I am a lady.
He has only to ask and I'd—"

"I'm sure you would," Devon interjected rudely,
wishing the woman would leave her in peace. She
didn't care how often Diablo bedded Carlotta. Or
so she tried to tell herself.

Carlotta's dark eyes blazed in sudden defiance.
"What is Diablo to you? I know you don't share his
bed so you can't be his mistress. And Kyle is paying
too much attention to Marlena for you to be his
whore. Perhaps one of Diablo's crew claims you,"
she suggested.

Devon's temper flared, her eyes shooting blue
flame at the smirking Carlotta. It was long past time
for the Spaniard to be told the truth. "I am Diablo's
wife."

"You lie!" Carlotta screeched, capturing the attention of everyone nearby. "You're nothing but a
puta! You might be Diablo's whore, but never his
wife."

"Ah, but Devon is indeed my wife, Carlotta,"
Diablo interjected with a smile. Caught completely

off guard by Diablo's sudden appearance, Carlotta could only stare at him, her eyes huge as saucers. "Devon would not lie about something as important as our marriage."

"Why wasn't I told this before?" Carlotta demanded to know.

"Because it didn't concern you. I rarely reveal details of my personal life to people I hold hostage. Or have you forgotten your position aboard the *Devil Dancer*?"

Devon's mouth flopped open and she gaped at Diablo with stunned fascination. His contempt was obvious for the fiery brunette who had made a game of practicing her seductive wiles on him. How many men, Devon wondered, had Carlotta lured into her sensual web?

"Married, bah!" Carlotta spat derisively. "Isn't it customary for husband and wife to share a bed?"

"Why, Carlotta," Diablo wagged his finger playfully, "have you been spying on me? Do you keep track of my movements every minute of the day and night?" He looked pointedly at Devon and winked, evoking memories of the teasing, captivating pirate who had landed in her lap at his own hanging. "I surely hope not, for I'm certain a chaste young woman like yourself would swoon with embarrassment if she spied on my activities."

"Oh!" Carlotta fumed, stomping her foot in frustration. "You're horrid! But what else might one expect from a pirate?" Wheeling, she flounced off, her skirts swirling in angry motion around her slim ankles.

Devon giggled delightedly. "I'm afraid you've made Carlotta angry."

"She's a spoiled young woman who cares for no one but herself. Besides, I already have a woman who more than satisfies my needs." A smirk appeared at the corners of his mouth, and when he looked at her there was a gleam in his eye, bringing a becoming blush to Devon's face. Diablo thought she looked adorable and found it exceedingly difficult to remember that Devon was a deceitful witch who had betrayed him.

From the corner of his eye Diablo caught a glimpse of Akbar's glowering features and knew that his Turkish friend was reminding him in his own way that women couldn't be trusted. Noting the direction of Diablo's gaze, Devon looked pointedly at the ferocious Turk.

"Akbar doesn't like me. He never has."

"Akbar has no use for women," Diablo revealed. "He was once a guard in the sultan's palace where he caught the eye of the sultan's favorite concubine. Normally Akbar wouldn't be allowed anywhere near the harem, but Tallah bribed the head eunuch and soon Akbar was visiting Tallah regularly. Another concubine, jealous of Tallah's position and popularity with the sultan, eventually betrayed them."

"How terrible," Devon murmured, seeing Akbar through new eyes. "No wonder he feels about women as he does. Did he love Tallah?"

"Who's to say? When Tallah was questioned she tried to save her skin by saying Akbar forced her. It didn't work. Tallah was placed in a sack and thrown in the sea. Because Akbar had distinguished himself in the sultan's service, he was spared death. Instead he was sold into slavery and ended up as a galley slave aboard a Spanish galleon. For many years he was chained to the oars, and his hatred of women became an obsession."

Devon shuddered. "How did he escape?"

"Black Bart attacked the galleon, and Akbar was freed. He joined the brotherhood and that's how and when I met him. Most of the galleon's slaves are still part of my crew. I saved Akbar's life once and he appointed himself my guardian. He's repaid me many times over by saving my skin more times than I can count. He feels strongly that women are a dangerous lot, good for only one purpose."

"I wish he'd realize I present no danger to either of you."

"That remains to be seen, doesn't it?"

Diablo insisted upon taking Devon to the old village first to view the destruction he believed her responsible for. Everything looked peaceful at first glimpse, but as they entered the cove through the hidden river, Devon saw the devastation of the once bustling little village.

She stared in horror at the pile of bleached, splintered wood littering the beach. "Fortunately the fields and house weren't torched, and the Arawak laborers fled into the woods to hide until the English marauders left."

"Your house is still standing?" Devon asked, amazed as well as pleased.

"Aye, the English didn't bother to come ashore, else I fear it would have been destroyed as well."

They didn't remain anchored long in the cove, and Diablo said little, still too upset over the sneak attack to discuss it without growing enraged. When he was certain that Devon had viewed every aspect of the senseless destruction, the *Devil Dancer* returned the way she had come.

"Must you blindfold me?" Devon asked crossly as Diablo tied a scarf over her eyes. He did the same with Carlotta and Marlena.

"I'm taking no chances. I trusted you once but no more."

"I'd never tell," purred Carlotta.

Diablo all but ignored her. "Kyle will keep you company while I take the ship through the reef," he told Devon.

Devon slumped against the rail. "He'll never trust me again, will he, Kyle?"

"Can you blame him? All those people killed in the shelling were his responsibility. Many of our crew lost women, and in some cases, children.

"I had nothing to do with it, Kyle, why won't you believe me?"

"I—perhaps you didn't," acknowledged Kyle reluctantly. "It could have been Le Vautour, just as you said. But for the present, Diablo is too angry to think sensibly. Give him time."

"What are you two talking about?" queried Carlotta curiously. The conversation told her nothing but the fact that Diablo was angry with Devon for some offense, and perhaps she could use it to her own advantage.

"It's none of your concern, Carlotta," Kyle scolded. He thought the young aristocrat spoiled and vain and disliked her callous treatment of her little maid.

"Humph!" huffed Carlotta, fingering her blindfold. "Can I remove this yet?"

"Aye," Kyle allowed, "we're inside the reef now and already sailing up the secret passage."

At first glance Devon thought it looked like the same place she had just left, until she noted the raw new wood of the huts lining the beach, so different from the weathered dwellings in the old village. There were even two new warehouses on the beach where a long pier jutted out into the deep water of the cove. To Devon's thinking, this side of Paradise was equally as beautiful as the other. She learned just how narrow the cay was when they walked to Diablo's house.

Sensing Devon's question, Diablo explained, "The cay is several miles long but less than two miles wide. The barrier reef circles the entire cay, and my explorations discovered only two places where it could be breached. The secret canal we entered on the opposite shore flows through the interior of the island and exits here. This cove is deeper than the other but much more difficult to locate."

"What's to stop the same people who shelled the old village from entering at the same place and sailing around the cay to where we are now?" Devon asked.

Diablo grinned, his teeth a white slash in his tanned face. "Sandbars. Too many to count. A ship attempting to circumnavigate the cay inside the reef would run aground the moment they left the deep water of the cove. 'Tis virtually impossible."

Tara was on hand to greet them, as beautiful and poised as Devon remembered. "Welcome home, Diablo." A wide smile split her exotic features.

"You've done well, Tara," Diablo complimented.

"The field hands and Le Vautour's crew did most of the work. I did no more than supervise their efforts," she said proudly.

"Le Vautour's crew!" Devon exclaimed. "Is that scoundrel here?"

"Le Vautour is where he'll cause no more trouble," Diablo said tightly. He turned away, but Devon was not about to drop the subject.

"What do you mean?"

"I sank the *Victory*. Le Vautour went down with his ship."

Devon's breath left her lungs in a loud gasp. "You killed him! Now we'll never know if he was the one who betrayed you."

"Devon, there's no longer a need to pretend. You're my wife now, and I'll not harm you for your deception."

"Are we to spend the rest of our lives at odds over my supposed betrayal? I'll convince you of my innocence if it takes a lifetime."

Wisely Diablo chose not to reply and they entered the house. He took Devon directly to the large, sunny room on the second floor she had previously occupied, while Carlotta and Marlena were shown to another part of the rambling structure by Tara.

"This will be our room," Diablo said, daring Devon to defy him. "You're my wife and there's no reason I should deny myself. I never denied I wanted you, and your body's response to my loving tells me you desire me just as fiercely. Living as a eunuch was never my intention."

Devon bit back a peppery retort. But in the end she decided not to protest. After experiencing Diablo's loving again aboard the *Devil Dancer*, she knew it was impossible to resist him; it was glorious being in his arms again, the sweet magic of his loving claiming her mind and body. Since they were now man and wife, she had no reason to withhold herself from him or act the outraged virgin. It was far too late for that. She was determined to make Diablo love her again, to trust her and accept her as his wife in every way.

The good Lord only knows why he had married her, except for the undeniable fact that her body gave him great pleasure. Call it lust, if you will, Devon smiled inwardly, but she'd have his love one day. And his trust.

Carlotta did everything in her power to complicate life for Devon while she remained on Paradise. And to make matters worse, Tara blamed her for the death and destruction wrought by the English. While waiting for Carlotta's ransom, Diablo chose to remain close to his home base. He also occupied Devon's bed every one of those nights. At times Devon thought him the same teasing rogue she had grown to love. Then suddenly she'd find him staring at her oddly, a scowl furrowing his brows, and he'd be instantly transformed into that steely-eyed, inscrutable stranger she no longer knew and often feared.

Somehow Devon sensed that her father could explain exactly how Diablo's secret had been discovered, but she also knew him to be incapable of ordering senseless killings. Too bad, she lamented, that Le Vautour had died before he could be questioned. If pressed, he might have cleared up this whole mess. How could she go through life with Diablo hating her? With everyone on the island hating her?

Devon thought often of her father and wondered how her going off with Diablo had affected him. Did he also hate her for deserting him? That unbearable thought brought tears to her eyes and a piercing pain in her heart. And what of Winston? Were Diablo's crude remarks about him true? More importantly, how did Diablo know such a thing? True or not, Devon realized now that she could never have married Winston while loving Diablo as she did.

From where he stood in the sheltered doorway, obscured by evening shadows, Diablo silently observed Devon. She looked sad sitting in a cane rocker on the veranda and staring forlornly into the distance, the gentle breeze ruffling her honey-colored tresses. She did not notice him, but it was still light enough for Diablo to see the sparkle of tears on her cheeks. They reminded him of tiny diamonds on pale satin. He realized that her life was far from happy here among people who despised her, and Carlotta's petty jealousy only added to her distress.

Thank God that haughty Spanish bitch would soon be gone, he thought sourly. With that prickly problem disposed of, he hoped his life with Devon would become less complicated. As long as he remained a hunted man it was unlikely they could live a normal life. Yet he could not bring himself to send her away. Though he hated to admit it, he loved her too much to part with her, even though their future promised no happiness for either of them.

He stepped out from the shadows. "Devon." The name was a caress on his lips.

"You startled me."

"You're crying."

"Crying? I'm not," she denied, a sniffle belying her words.

"Ah, sweetheart, let me dry those tears."

Dropping to one knee beside her, he curled his hand around her nape, drawing her face down to his. Then she felt the moist tip of his tongue gently flick the pearly drops from her cheeks, savoring the salty texture against his lips.

"Lord help me I've tried to hate you," Diablo whispered into the pink shell of her ear. "No matter what you've done, I still want you with a deep abiding longing. Come, sweetheart, I want to make love to you—now."

Mesmerized, Devon clasped his warm hand and allowed herself to be drawn deeply into the seductive web he wove around her senses.

"Disgusting!" Carlotta snapped acidly. "Look at them, they behave like animals. It's a wonder they don't couple right here on the ground."

She and Marlena had stepped out onto the veranda in time to observe an exceedingly intimate moment. Her cruel remark failed to produce the desired effect, for Diablo merely laughed, catching Devon up in his arms and bounding into the house and up the stairs with an urgency born of need.

"Animals!" Carlotta repeated, stomping her tiny foot in a jealous rage. It wasn't fair that Devon should have such a virile man as Diablo when she was destined to become an old don's bride.

"I think it's beautiful," sighed Marlena wistfully. "I wish—"

"Banish those thoughts from your mind," Carlotta snapped. "Your future does not include love and marriage. If you are fortunate, one day some man might bed you, but nothing will come of it. You'll soon bore him and find yourself discarded like an old shoe. Come along, a short walk before I retire might improve my humor."

Diablo set Devon on her feet, her lush body slowly sliding down his long length. When she lifted her head his eyes were turbulent with passion and she felt a surge of lazy heat spiral through her loins. His hands slid down the front of her body, over breasts and belly and the soft place between her legs. Slowly he began peeling away the layers of her clothes until she stood gloriously nude before him. Then he kissed her, his mouth warm and gentle and softly persuasive.

His hands cupped her bottom, his fingers lightly stroking the soft rounded flesh. "I thank God for your passion," he whispered, loving the spark of desire his touch had ignited. "I don't want to hurt you, only love you."

His words had the desired effect as Devon melted against him. She belonged to this special man, she always would, no matter what fate dealt them. Without breaking eye contact, Devon's nimble fingers worked furiously at the fastenings holding together Diablo's clothes. Laughing, he pushed her fingers aside and swiftly shed his offending garments. Standing proud and naked at last, he scooped Devon high in his arms and fell with her across the bed. He rolled with her so that she was sprawled on top of him.

Her eyes bright with passion, Devon gently stroked his furred belly, her fingers walking through the soft wedge of curly dark hair that stretched across his chest. The gulf between them was still enormous, but each time they loved a tiny portion of their differences melted away, and Devon sought to make the most of it. She wanted to put their troubles behind them, heal his mistrust, and make this moment a magical interlude out of reality.

Bending low to place small teasing kisses on Diablo's face, Devon was stunned when he deftly eluded her, his hands clutching her shoulders and pushing her upright. Obediently she sat up, his hands sliding down the front of her body, moving intimately over her breasts and belly and bright thatch of hair between her legs. Then he shoved her thighs apart so she could straddle him. Her eyes widened but she made no objections.

"I want to see all of you when we make love. Your breasts are so beautiful . . ." He reached up to touch them, then scraped his thumbs teasingly across her nipples. Shafts of pure fire shot through her. "Do you like that?"

"Yes, oh yes."

Smiling with wicked delight, Diablo abandoned her breasts to guide his hands over her ribcage, tiny waist, the delicate curve of her hips, the tautness of her belly. Heat melted her bones and she begged him to quench the fire he ignited inside her.

Devon gasped as the warm strength of his hands caressed her knees and slid up the silken length of her inner thighs to rest lightly on her soft mound. She froze as exploring fingers parted the curling nest of hair, stroked over it gently, finally discovering the secret wellspring of passion nestled there. When his fingers worked magically against her, Devon jerked, cried out, her head falling forward and her eyes closing at the sudden intensity of her passion. Her hands braced against his chest kept her from collapsing.

Finding her nipples so close to his lips, Diablo took first one ripe bud then the other into his mouth, sucking vigorously, licking, rolling the tiny nubs between his teeth until Devon's body began vibrating with compelling need. When his fingers delved deeply into the moist heat of her, she shrieked with joy. Watching her face with intense longing, Diablo continued his loving caress until the last tremor left her body.

"Now I want you to love me." His voice was a husky whisper against her ear.

Devon's head lifted and her eyes struggled open

as she tried to make sense out of his words. His meaning became clear when his hands moved to her hips, lifting her upward and lowering her carefully onto his steely length. She gasped as his fiery heat probed against her. Then he was inside her, his hands tugging her down—down, until his hugeness stretched and filled her.

"Love me, sweetheart," he repeated, the words thick on his tongue, his eyes glazed, his face flushed with passion.

The muscles in his neck corded, standing out in stark relief against his bronze skin as he fought to hold himself in control, wanting Devon to set the pace. Grasping her hips, he guided her in the motion he sought, then waited for her to learn the rhythm and take the lead. Sensing his intent, she quickly grasped his lesson and gave him what he desired, her hips moving against his in seductive invitation. Then he released her to find her breasts. She cried out as his hands cupped them.

Diablo groaned and pulled her down so that he could suckle the tender mounds. He nursed them with savage delight, his hands hot and demanding on the silken roundness of her bottom as he ground himself upwards into her. She gave herself up to the fierceness of his passion, responding with a passion of her own. Finally, a hoarse cry left his throat and he clutched her close, trembling beneath her. As he held himself inside her, Devon felt something deep within her break loose and she cried out, swept up in a firestorm of exploding ecstasy.

Afterwards they lay quietly in each other's arms, quivering with exhaustion and sated passion. "You're mine, Devon, I'll never let you go. If you leave me now I'd search the world to find you."

* * *

The weeks passed swiftly, and since Diablo and Devon had come to an understanding of sorts, life became more bearable. Not even Carlotta's constant bickering succeeded in spoiling the time Devon spent with the man she loved. Diablo was her whole life now, and though she knew he still withheld his trust, he did seem to care for her. Maybe not love her as he once did, but it was a beginning. He certainly was possessive of her, and her own love was as unwavering as it had always been.

Devon greatly admired Diablo's stamina in withstanding Carlotta's attempts at seduction, and credited him with good sense as well as strength of character. Perhaps their marriage actually did mean something more to him than a piece of paper. If only she could convince him to give up piracy their prospects for a life together would be greatly enhanced. It was a wish she prayed for nightly.

Lord Harvey was a broken man. He wore his worry and concern etched in the deep lines on his face. It was inconceivable that Devon would leave on the eve of her wedding with a man wanted by every civilized nation in the world. Had Diablo bewitched her? There appeared to be no simple explanation for Devon's behavior. And why would the notorious pirate risk capture and death to come to London for Devon? Was there something Devon had failed to tell him, something about her relationship with the pirate that she was too ashamed to reveal?

The moment Lord Harvey learned of Devon's disappearance he sent immediately for Winston. When the jilted bridegroom bounded into the earl's study, the older man merely handed him Devon's hastily scrawled note.

"The bloody sod! How could this happen?" Winston exploded, showing more spirit than Lord Harvey had given him credit for.

Winston was livid with rage. Not only had his cousin come back from the dead to haunt him, but his bride-to-be had jilted him for the notorious pirate whom he, as well as half of London, believed had ravished her. If he wasn't in desperate straights and in need of Devon's fortune he'd say to hell with the whole mess. Kit's return had shaken Winston badly, for his cousin could do all kinds of damage to him and his father, should he so desire. The thought of facing the many creditors hounding him was just too much, and he flew into a frenzy.

"How could Devon do this to me? I offered her love and protection from the gossips who would make hash out of her reputation. Is this how she repays me?" Winston's face contorted into an ugly mask, shocking Lord Harvey. Few people had seen Winston's violent side. Most thought him a pleasant, even-tempered man somewhat lacking in spirit with mild manners and rather insipid charm.

"I refuse to believe this note is Devon's doing," the earl offered, leaping to his daughter's defense. "It may be her handwriting, but 'tis my theory Diablo forced her to it. 'Tis my belief she intended to go through with this marriage."

Somewhat mollified, Winston whined, "Devon changed after she returned to England. No one really knows the truth about what happened between her and that pirate. Devon spoke little of that time. How do we know Diablo didn't—"

"That's enough, Winston!" thundered Lord Harvey. "I don't care what happened between them. None of it matters, and I supposed you felt the same. If you didn't want to marry Devon, you had only to say so. The stress of being held captive affected her greatly, but Devon never let it destroy her. Lesser women would have buckled under the strain."

Winston had the grace to flush, realizing he must tread carefully if he hoped to remain in the earl's good graces. "No offense meant, Your Grace," he blustered. "I'd marry Devon today if she were here. Or anytime she reappears."

His words seemed to satisfy the earl, for he beamed gratefully. "And so you shall, m'boy. How soon can you leave?"

"Leave, your grace?"

"To get Devon, of course. I know you've already resigned your commission, but I'll buy or hire any ship you want."

"After the shelling of Diablo's hideaway I doubt he can still be found there. By now he's moved his base to another cay," Winston contended.

"Perhaps, but I want my daughter back. I'm prepared to risk all I possess to wrest her from the clutches of that blackguard. She's all I have left in this world. How soon can you find a ship?"

Winston's hesitation brought a curse to Lord Harvey's lips and a generous offer Winston could not afford to turn down. "If you leave within two weeks I'll settle twenty thousand pounds on you the day you marry Devon. That's in addition to her dowry."

"Your Grace, I don't know what to say." Winston was stunned. With so much money he'd be free from financial worry for the rest of his life and able to pursue his dreams. "Of course I'll go. I love Devon."

The words dripped from his lips like warm honey. Though he held a certain fondness for Devon, he wasn't capable of the kind of love expected of him. He was confident he could do his duty and father an heir for the earl's fortune, but it wasn't something he looked forward to.

"I'm aware that Diablo might have changed his base, and there's dozens of islands and cays where he could hide, but I expect you to search diligently. I want that bloody bastard and I want him bad. But most of all I want my daughter."

Two weeks later Winston sailed from London harbor. Lord Harvey's wealth made it possible to hire a shallow draft schooner carrying thirty cannon whose original destination had been China. The *Mary Jane*'s captain happily changed his plans when approached by Winston and offered a fortune for the use of his ship.

Chapter Fifteen

"What are you thinking, sweetheart?" Diablo asked, his voice a husky purr. They had just made love and Devon still lay warm and trembling in his arms. Only much too introspective for Diablo's liking.

"Nothing important, Kit." In their private moments Devon nearly always called him Kit. It didn't seem right to call one's husband "Devil."

Diablo refused to let the matter rest. "Are you so unhappy here on Paradise?"

"Oh, no, it's not that."

"Then what? I know Carlotta is a terrible burden, but she'll soon be gone."

"Carlotta's not the problem," Devon said with a hint of sadness. "You'll leave soon, your men are getting restless, and so many things could happen to you while you're gone."

"Do you care so much?"

"I—I've always cared. I realize you must sail

soon to keep your men happy, but I can't help wondering what will happen to me should you fail to return."

Diablo frowned. He had given that nagging worry much thought of late. "Nothing is going to happen to me, sweetheart."

"You can't be certain, Kit. Will your men choose lots to see who gets me if, God forbid, you're killed or captured? What if there's a child?"

"Are you—"

"No, but it's bound to happen."

"Are you suggesting that I give up piracy?" In truth the idea had been much on his mind of late. So were Devon's thought-provoking questions. Having a wife was so new to him that he hadn't yet become accustomed to considering someone else's feelings besides his own.

"If you truly cared for me you'd give up the dangerous life you lead. Aren't you rich enough?"

"Aye," Diablo admitted grudgingly. "I suppose I am. Enough to keep you and our children in comfort for life with a good bit left over."

"Then give it up, Kit. We can stay here and raise sugar cane, or settle anywhere you say. I know England is out of the question, but what about America?"

"Is preserving my life so important to you? I hardly know what to think, you guard your emotions so close."

Devon hesitated. Though Diablo freely admitted his love for her, she had yet to utter those words. Fear held her back. Fear that the vast differences in their lives and circumstances would one day tear them apart. Yet she loved him more than her own life.

"Your life is—is more precious to me than my

own," Devon admitted slowly. The words did not come easily. She had withheld them so long it was like losing a part of herself. She wanted to say she loved him, but for the time being this must suffice. "I know you still don't trust me, but I can live with that as long as you don't hate me."

"Hate you! God's bones, woman, you're everything to me. I loved you even when I thought I hated you. Does it hurt so much to say the words? Why can't you express your feelings like a normal woman?"

"Fear," Devon whispered. "Stark fear. There are so many things conspiring against us, I don't want to tempt fate. You know as well as I that there can be no real future for us as long as you continue to ply the seas for plunder."

"You want me to give up my wicked ways?" Diablo teased, flashing the dimple Devon loved so much. Since returning to Paradise he had shaved his beard, exposing the devastating dimple in his cheek.

"Can you? Will you?" Devon was so serious that Diablo immediately sobered, maintaining a tense silence that made Devon fear she had angered him.

"Aye," he said finally. "I've given a great deal of thought lately to choosing another profession."

Devon was stunned; she hadn't expected Diablo to capitulate so easily.

"Oh, Kit, you don't know how happy that makes me!" she cried, throwing herself into his arms. "When? How? Where?" She had so many questions they came tumbling from her mouth one after another.

Diablo laughed. "Not so fast, sweetheart. When I return from Nassau I'll share my plans with you.

But at the moment I expect you to be appropriately grateful."

"Kit, not again!" Devon squealed as Diablo lifted her and settled her astride his lean hips.

"Aye, sweetheart, and again and again, until I've had my fill. Though I seriously doubt, considering the way I feel now, 'tis likely to happen any time within the next hundred years."

Two days later the *Devil Dancer* sailed out of the cove. She carried a full complement of men in addition to Carlotta and Marlena. Their destination was Nassau where they would collect Carlotta's ransom. Unwilling to expose Devon again to the rough, rowdy men who congregated in Nassau, Diablo left her behind, this time certain she would be safe.

Winston whooped with joy, his grip tightening on the telescope clapped to his eye. "There she is, Block! I knew if we hid long enough in these blasted islands, that blackhearted bastard would show himself. Mark well her course, Block, for we're going in as soon as she's out of sight."

"What if the devil has the woman with him?" Block asked. Jonah Block was the proud owner and captain of the *Mary Jane*, the ship hired by Lord Harvey to rescue his daughter.

"You heard the gossip. Diablo is expected to arrive soon in Nassau to exchange a Spanish don's daughter for ransom. Seems the devil's been up to his old tricks. I'm willing to bet he's not taking Devon with him into that den of iniquity. We'll find out soon enough. Do you think you can find the way in?"

"If there's a way through the barrier reef, Jonah

Block will find it," the captain bragged. "Fortunately we stopped in Nassau first and learned Diablo had moved his stronghold. It saved us from endless hours of searching."

"Aye," Winston concurred. "Lucky for us that sailor, Patch, held some kind of grudge against Diablo. He didn't mind at all repeating the rumor that Diablo had moved his stronghold to another spot on his island. Since I already knew the exact location of Paradise, the rest was easy, although we lost considerable time and nearly ran aground trying to reach the bloody village by sailing inside the reef."

"Aye, who would have thought there'd be so many bloody sandbars blocking our path?"

Once the *Devil Dancer* slipped into a passage between two cays and was out of sight, Winston ordered the *Mary Jane* out of the hidden inlet of a neighboring cay. When they neared the dangerous reef, Captain Block set a parallel course, guiding his ship with an expertise born of years of experience. When they located the place he'd been looking for, Block turned the wheel and sailed directly into the reef, apparently bound for total destruction. Winston gripped the rail and waited for the crunch and jolt of the hull being ripped apart by the jagged coral. But Block was a skilled seaman who had marked well Diablo's passage earlier. His only concern was that the *Mary Jane*'s six-foot draft might not be shallow enough to scrape clear of the reef. It was—just barely. And to Winston's amazement they were safely inside the reef.

The river was much more difficult to find, but Winston used his previous knowledge of the secrets of Paradise to good advantage. It took nearly the entire day to locate the entrance to the cove. Rather than wait till morning, they sailed in at twilight, anchoring a short distance from shore.

"Shall I order the guns out?" Block asked, eying the peaceful village with misgivings. It was obvious that none of the pirates had remained behind, and Block wasn't the type of man who enjoyed senseless killing.

"Nay," Winston decided. "There's nothing to be gained from it. I intend to go in after Devon and get out as quickly as possible." He recalled Lord Harvey's dismay over the previous shelling and had promised him he'd not take innocent lives unless necessary. "I'll take a landing party ashore immediately."

Devon stretched lazily, enjoying the spectacular sunset descending over the peaceful cay. The sight was so inspiring she hated to go inside. Besides, the house seemed so cold and empty since Diablo had left that morning for Nassau with Carlotta and Marlena. She had no idea when he'd return, certainly not until he had Carlotta's ransom in hand. How pleasant it would be without the disruptive and volatile woman around to whine and complain.

Devon looked forward to Diablo's return for more than one reason. He had promised to seriously consider giving up piracy during his absence and reveal his plans for their future. Had he finally come to realize they had no future together unless he gave up his wild ways and lived within the law?

They'd been so happy these past weeks, Devon thought wistfully. Diablo gave every indication he had come to trust her again. Hopefully they'd learn the truth about the sneak attack upon Paradise one day, and then nothing would interfere with their happiness.

Suddenly Tara came running from the direction of the village, out of breath and frantic with fright. "There's a strange ship in the cove!"

"Are you certain it's not the *Devil Dancer*?"

"Nay, I'd know the *Devil Dancer* anywhere. "'Tis an English ship."

"Navy?" Devon asked fearfully. "How . . ."

"Nay, 'tis no naval vessel. I can't imagine how they found their way here. They were preparing to come ashore when I left, and I ran all the way back. What shall we do?"

Devon bit deeply into her lower lip, her mind working furiously. "I'll go down to meet them. If there's only one ship, perhaps they mean us no harm."

Tara balked, remembering the last time ships had found their way inside the reef. "Nay, don't go. I fear they're up to some mischief. Come with me, I know a perfect hiding place. Diablo would want me to keep you safe."

"Do what you want," Devon shrugged. "I'll go alone if I must."

It hadn't occurred to Devon to hide. Why would the English wish her harm? She considered it a good omen that they hadn't shelled the village and felt it her duty to greet the visitors. Perhaps Diablo had sent them.

She arrived in the village out of breath and panting from her exertion just as two longboats filled with armed men scraped against the shore. Immediately spotting the assortment of weapons the landing crew carried, Devon panicked. What if Tara was right? she asked herself. What if these men meant her harm? As the men leaped from the boat and splashed ashore, Devon came to a sudden decision. Turning on her heel, she fled in the opposite direction, hoping to lose herself in the woods lining the beach.

"There she is! Don't let her get away!" Though the voice was vaguely familiar, Devon did not stop to investigate. Only when she heard someone call out her name did she hesitate. "Devon, don't run! 'Tis Winston."

She skidded to an abrupt halt. "Winston?" She turned slowly and waited for her ex-fiancé to catch up to her. "What are you doing here?"

"Your father sent me. He's worried sick about you."

"How did you find your way inside the reef?"

"That's not important. What does matter is that I found you and you're going home. We'll be married immediately."

"I won't go," Devon refused, backing away. "Didn't you get my note? I came with Diablo willingly. I'm his—his woman."

"Obviously the man has cast some kind of spell over you," Winston said disgustedly. "But don't fret, dear, I'll not hold it against you. Our wedding will take place just as planned. Come along."

"Nay, I won't go," she repeated stubbornly.

Winston's eyes narrowed. He was vividly aware that Diablo had been bedding Devon and probably had from the very first. But that bothered him less than the knowledge that he couldn't afford to lose Devon's fortune.

"I didn't risk my life to come away empty-handed," Winston pronounced with grim determination.

Before Devon realized what he intended, Winston grasped her about the waist and dragged her toward the beach. "Let me go!" she shrieked, aware that no one was likely to come to her aid.

"Stop struggling, Devon, 'twill do you no good."

"I can't leave like this. What will Diablo think?"

"Let him think what he will."

It was like a repetition of a bad dream. Only this time Devon was leaving the island against her will. But Diablo wouldn't know that, he'd think she'd left him, just like the last time. The fragile love that had grown between them these past weeks would wither and die if he was given no explanation. That thought brought a renewal to her struggles.

Winston cursed. "If you don't come quietly, I'll order Captain Block to shell the island. What will your lover think when he returns and finds nothing but rubble?"

Devon's struggles ceased instantly. "Nay, please, Winnie, there are innocent lives to consider. I'll go with you willingly if you promise not to destroy the village."

"Now you're being sensible, dear. I see no reason to attack women and children." He took her arm and propelled her toward the beach.

"You did once," Devon accused. "I know it was your *Larkspur* that attacked Paradise while Diablo was elsewhere, destroying the village and killing dozens of people."

"I don't know where you heard that," Winston denied, refusing to meet her glare. The less Devon knew about that fiasco, the better.

Devon would have delved more deeply into the matter, but they had reached the beach now and Winston lifted her into the longboat while two dozen armed men looked on. As soon as she was settled they all scrambled into the boats and shoved off, rowing at a furious pace to where the *Mary Jane* rode at anchor.

Seething with rage, Tara watched as Devon calmly accompanied the Englishmen to their ship. She had failed to see Devon's struggles earlier, and was aware only of her willingness to leave Paradise. It broke her heart to think this should happen when Devon had finally won Tara's trust. Tara pitied Diablo, for she knew he loved Devon with all his heart. How could Devon abandon Diablo so easily? Did she have no feelings? No conscience?

Hours later, her heart heavy, her cheeks wet with tears, Devon watched sadly as the *Mary Jane* carefully cleared the reef and set a course for England.

A few days later Diablo made a triumphant return to Paradise. Don Esperez had been so anxious to have his daughter back that her ransom arrived on time, delivered in person by Carlotta's elderly fiancé. When he saw the man, Diablo better understood the desperation that drove Carlotta. Don Fernando was probably older than Carlotta's father. His stern, dark visage and proud bearing left little doubt that he'd accept no foolishness from the youthful Carlotta. Still, Diablo thought the fiery senorita would prove more than a handful for her elderly husband.

Carlotta's plight was complicated by Marlena's adamant refusal to accompany her mistress home. When it came time to leave, Marlena clung to Kyle with desperate pleas that she be allowed to stay. Anguish twisted Kyle's handsome features, for he had come to care a great deal for the little maid. In the end he proposed marriage, and Diablo invited Marlena to accompany them back to Paradise. He knew that Devon would welcome another woman on the island, and it would certainly ease Kyle's mind to have Marlena safe on Paradise.

Carlotta was livid, flying into a rage and ordering Marlena to accompany her aboard the Spanish ship that would carry her home. But for once in her life Marlena obstinately refused to obey her mistress, saying she had nothing to look forward to in Spain but a life of servitude. She had chosen to remain with the man she loved, and nothing could change her mind.

Taking over the wheel, Diablo sailed the *Devil Dancer* into the cove, noting with satisfaction that all appeared serene in the little village. Several women could be seen engaged in various chores and children cavorted in the surf. With an expert hand he maneuvered the ship into its berth beside the pier and ordered the gangplank run out. He was the first to leap ashore, leaving Akbar and Kyle to tend to the docking. Anxious to see Devon and discuss his new plans for their future, Diablo raced all the way to the house. During the time he was gone he had decided to give up piracy and devote himself to legal pursuits.

Such was Diablo's preoccupation that he took little notice of the people gathered on the beach to welcome him, or their pitying expressions. Everyone on Paradise was aware of Diablo's obsession with Devon and what her leaving was likely to do to him. They watched in silent commiseration as he walked briskly toward his house.

Tara came out to meet him, her face grim, her

generous mouth tightened into a thin line. Diablo scarcely noticed his housekeeper, looking past her for his first glimpse of Devon. When she failed to appear, he looked questioningly at Tara, her expression sending his heart plummeting.

"Nay, not again!" he cried, refusing to acknowledge what Tara's expressive features revealed. "Tell me it's not true!"

"I can only speak what I know," Tara replied with infinite compassion. She hated to be the one to disillusion Diablo, but there was no help for it. "Your wife is gone."

"How? Why? I know Devon wouldn't leave here willingly. Who carried her off? Were they corsairs?"

"Pirates? Nay, English. An English ship arrived the same day the *Devil Dancer* left the cove. I urged Devon to hide, but she refused. Instead, she walked to the beach to meet the intruders. I hid in the woods and watched Devon speak to one of the Englishmen. Then she left with him aboard his ship."

"You mean she was taken against her will, don't you?" Diablo asked hopefully.

A long, tense silence ensued as Tara carefully considered her reply. "I saw no struggle. Devon simply walked with the man to the beach, and he carried her out to the longboat."

Torn between disbelief and rage, Diablo cried out, "God's bones, she's played me for a fool once too often! Her lying lips drip with honeyed words that hold no meaning."

"What is it, Diablo?"

Diablo whirled to find Kyle and Marlena standing behind him, having walked up from the village at a slower pace.

"Devon's gone, Kyle. The little bitch left aboard an English ship."

"That's impossible," sputtered Kyle, stunned. "How in the hell could a strange ship find its way in here?"

"There's only one way," Diablo said grimly. "They were spying on us when we left the cay. Tara said they arrived the same day we left, so I assume they were hidden somewhere nearby, watching our comings and goings.

"I can't believe the lass would leave without a word," Kyle refuted. "She loves you." Marlena added her own agreement to Kyle's words.

"The woman is incapable of love," Diablo observed with a bitterness born of shattered pride. "Her words, her actions, were lies meant to beguile me until the time came for her to leave. Akbar has the right idea. Women are good for but one purpose, to be used for what God intended them and promptly discarded."

"Had you listened to me you would have been shed of the witch long ago," Akbar said with a scowl, arriving in time to hear nearly all the conversation. "No woman is worth the anguish you're suffering."

"Perhaps you haven't met the right woman, Akbar," Tara injected, her dark eyes hinting that she might be the woman to teach the Turk about love and trust.

The beautiful Indian woman had long admired Akbar, for his cunning, his courage, and his devotion to Diablo. But thus far she hadn't been able to crack the hard shell of mistrust guarding Akbar's heart. Though she had tried many times to prove herself worthy of his trust, Akbar had made it perfectly clear he had no use for her—or any woman. But Tara stubbornly refused to relent, hoping that one day Akbar would notice her many fine qualities and regard her with fondness.

Akbar slanted Tara a sharp glance, then promptly ignored her. Actually, he wasn't as immune to Tara as he let on. Little by little her gentle nature and loving regard were beginning to erode the wall around his heart, but he refused to acknowledge it. He had lived too long with his reputation to change now.

"Aye, you were right, Akbar," Diablo agreed bitterly. "I loved too deeply and unwisely."

"Are you going after the lass?" Kyle asked, ready to risk life and limb to reunite Diablo with his wife.

"Nay!" Diablo thundered, glowering fiercely. "Not this time. I know when I'm defeated. Round up the men, we sail with the tide in search of riches and adventure. The first ship sailing to England from Nassau will carry a letter to Devon telling her I never want to see her again. If she ever steps foot on Paradise or anywhere in this part of the world, she'll find herself in deep trouble for I'll not be charitable a second time."

Diablo sprawled drunkenly in a chair at the Wheel of Fortune Inn, resting his swimming head in his hands, the image of utter dejection. He'd kept the *Devil Dancer* at sea two months, attacking, pillaging, robbing, until his men had had their fill and insisted on putting in at Nassau to replenish their supplies and slake their lust with the many whores plying their trade in the rough port. First he set Kyle and those of his men with women ashore at Paradise, but Diablo did not tarry there himself.

Already too many ghosts were haunting him without spending a night in the house where he and Devon had loved one another all those long, passion-filled nights.

He missed her, missed her with a deep abiding ache that often plunged him into a despair so profound he could not find his way out. More nights than he cared to count he drank himself into a stupor, hoping to lose himself in a drunken mist of forgetfulness. On most nights he succeeded, but when he failed, Devon appeared in his dreams to plague his darkest moments and plunge him into the depths of hell. If he weren't such a brilliant captain, drunk or sober, his crew would have replaced him long ago.

Now, blurry-eyed and disheveled, he paid little heed to the ruckus around him as he concentrated on filling his glass without spilling a drop. He failed miserably.

"What in the hell have you done to yourself?"

Diablo raised his heavy head, squinting as two wavering figures finally merged into one stunning redhead. He grinned crookedly. "God's bones, Scarlett, you're a sight for sore eyes. Sit down, both of you. Join me in a drink."

"Haven't you had enough?"

He flashed a roguish grin, reminiscent of the Diablo of old, his bold black beard enhancing the aura of mystery surrounding him. "Who's to say what's enough?"

"That highborn bitch has done this to you, hasn't she?" Her words were met with a black scowl. "Did you think I wouldn't hear how you're making a fool of yourself over a woman? Word spreads quickly in this part of the world."

"My problems are no one's business. I don't want to talk about D—her."

"First we'll get some food in you and then put you to bed," Scarlett said briskly. She turned to speak to a passing serving wench, then sat down to wait until the food arrived. After watching him eat a meal he scarcely tasted, she engaged a room and helped Diablo up the stairs and into bed. Then she flopped down beside him.

The next morning, Diablo awoke slowly. Dawn had arrived with subtle hints of mauve dusting the dingy room. His head was pounding; he couldn't remember when he'd last awakened without a fuzzy brain and thick tongue. As he stretched and tested his limbs, he became aware of a softness pressed against him, and the word slipped smoothly over his tongue. "Devon."

Scarlett stirred, snuggling closer. "Are you awake?"

"Ummm," Diablo answered dreamily, savoring the delicious softness he'd missed so desperately these past months. "God's bones, I've missed you, sweetheart." In his heart he knew it wasn't Devon teasing his flesh, but he couldn't bear another day of emptiness, so he pretended. The dream was too real, too vibrantly sensual to give up so soon. "Devon."

"You bastard! Your precious Devon is gone," Scarlett lashed out. "Wake up and realize I'm flesh and blood, not some elusive dream."

He was fully awake now, and enough light filtered into the room for Diablo to see a naked and enraged Scarlett bending over him. "What in the hell are you doing here?"

"I slept here last night, remember?"

Diablo frowned, the effort bringing a frustrated groan to his lips as he recalled Scarlett helping him up the stairs. Then he drew a blank, for he had no recollection of what transpired afterwards. He tried to rely on humor to placate Scarlett, but she merely snorted in disgust when he said, "I hope I pleased you."

"Please me! How could you please me when you fell asleep almost immediately?" Suddenly her expression softened and she ran her hand along the hard ridges of his chest. "But now that you're awake it wouldn't take long to put you in the right mood to please me. I know what you like, Diablo." Her hand slid beneath the sheet draped loosely around his middle, boldly brushing against his manhood.

Diablo jerked, but not from desire as Scarlett assumed. In the first place, she wasn't Devon. In the second place, he needed a drink. And lastly, as expert as he knew Scarlett to be, his body might cooperate but his mind rejected the idea of making love with anyone but Devon.

"I'm in no condition to make love, Scarlett," Diablo hedged. "Besides, I need a drink."

"Has the witch stolen your balls?" Scarlett said with a smirk, her disparaging remark not only vulgar but hitting a raw spot.

Had Devon hurt him so terribly that she had robbed him of his manhood? Diablo wondered bleakly. Since Devon had left him he'd bedded no other woman, wanting no one but his wife to lavish his love upon. Abandoning him as she did had turned him into a bitter lush who found solace in a bottle. Suddenly it all became quite clear, though he had rejected Kyle's dire predictions that he was on his way to self-destruction. Hearing Scarlett echo his friend's sentiments just now opened his eyes. He had become a man mired in self-pity, traveling the well-worn path to total ruin. Only Devon had the power to change him, and she had chosen to leave him, Diablo thought despondently.

"Leave me alone, Scarlett," he growled testily. "I didn't ask for your help and I certainly don't need your pity."

"Have you forgotten how Devon left with Le Vautour?" Scarlett baited. "The moment you turned your back she was gone. Is it any wonder she did it again?"

Diablo's eyes narrowed suspiciously. He never did find out how Le Vautour had learned the secret of Paradise Island. "What do you know about it? I never considered that you, one of the brotherhood, would betray me. Did you? Did you tell that bastard Le Vautour how to find Paradise?"

"We've been through too much together, Diablo," Scarlett lied smoothly, afraid of Diablo's reaction should he learn the truth. "I believe Le Vautour chanced upon the entrance by accident. Or he spied on you."

Had Diablo not been so hung over he would have debated the point, but feeling as rotten as he did and unwilling to pursue so painful a subject as Devon, he dropped the issue. "Just get out of here. But if I ever find out differently, you'll wish for an easy death."

Scarlett flounced out of bed, flaunting her voluptuous charms before him. "I don't know why I bother with you, I have lovers aplenty. Call me when you're in better humor."

She began throwing on her clothes, ignoring Diablo's sour look. Scarlett hadn't been in Diablo's

bed since Devon came into his life and it drove her
wild with jealousy. The little witch had ruined him
for any other woman. Someday, she didn't know
when or how, Scarlett vowed to get even with Lady
Devon Chatham.

Chapter Sixteen

Woodes Rogers, a former privateer, had been given permission by King George of England to develop the Bahamas. It was April when his expedition reached New Providence Island. His arrival marked the beginning of the end of the golden era of piracy in the Caribbean. Rogers' first order of business was to wipe out the pirates who made Nassau their home base. He was received royally in the town amidst cheering men and much merrymaking. At the end of the feasting and drunken revelry, Rogers, speaking for the king, offered unconditional amnesty to men who willingly denounced piracy and embraced a new way of life.

Before the week was out, over six hundred pardons had been granted. Among the receivers were Diablo, Scarlett, Kyle, and after much soul-searching, Akbar. Hardened pirates like Blackbeard and Calico Jack departed for other bases. Eventually some of the men who accepted amnesty drifted back into the life, while the smart ones took their treasures and settled elsewhere. A good number went back to their homes to eventually die in poverty. Many ended up in England.

Diablo had debated long and hard before deciding to accept amnesty. He didn't like what he had become or where his life was leading. Kyle was all for changing his way of life, especially since he had Marlena to think about. Piracy was being eradicated the world over, so he was all for accepting amnesty and beginning anew. Akbar wasn't too certain about living a dull, conventional life, but if Diablo decided to live within the bounds of the law, he could do no less than give it a try.

Diablo, one of the wealthiest pirates, sailed boldly into London harbor several weeks later, flying the Union Jack from the *Devil Dancer*'s tallest mast. Despite the harsh words written in a letter to Devon, Diablo knew he was in England only because of the love he bore her—a love that refused to die though he had tried to pound it to death with alcohol and unnecessary danger. One day, when his good name was restored, he would find Devon and try to make her understand that the letter was a result of the terrible pain he was suffering.

Upon hearing that Diablo had accepted amnesty, Scarlett followed him to England a few weeks later, the hold of the *Red Witch* carrying enough wealth to last several lifetimes.

"Come now, m' dear, don't you think Winston deserves better than you've accorded him?"

"I told you before, Father, I can't marry Winston. I don't love him."

Lord Harvey sighed wearily, having gone over the subject time and again. "There's plenty of other swains around, take your pick." Devon chose not to reply. "I know you fancy yourself in love with Diablo, but a young and impressionable girl like you is easily duped into submitting to the base desires of a man with his experience. He obviously has worked some sort of magic on you. How else can you explain your fascination with him? What hold does he have over you?"

"There was no magic involved, Father," Devon replied, sick unto death of being badgered, no matter how kindly. "I love Diablo, and he loves me. Or he did before Winston carried me off. Now he hates me."

"How do you know that?"

Devon sighed dejectedly, unwilling to reveal the extent of Diablo's hatred and how she knew for certain how he felt. "I just know."

"Be reasonable, Devon," the earl cajoled. "There's no future for you with that—that pirate."

Devon deliberately withheld the knowledge that Diablo had made her his wife. What purpose would it serve other than upsetting her father more than he already was?

"I purposely refrained from delving too deeply into the relationship between you and Diablo," the earl said slowly, "and I won't do so now. You're my daughter, and I love you no matter what occurred. But it seems to me if Winston is still eager to marry you despite your—er—adventure, you should at least consider his proposal. You were willing enough once to have him as your husband."

"That was before . . ." Her words faltered and she fell silent, letting her father draw his own conclusion.

"Aye, before that devil got his hooks into you," the earl muttered, tossing his hands up in defeat. "If you want that scoundrel so badly, I'll see that you're taken back to him. That's the least I can do to make you happy."

Devon blanched, recalling the letter delivered to her one day when her father was away. It was a message from Diablo spewing hatred and vile accusations and telling her he never wanted to see her again. He promised swift retribution if she showed up on Paradise again.

"Nay, Father, I can't go back. Diablo doesn't want me. Don't speak of it again."

The poor earl was truly puzzled by Devon and was sorry he'd had her dragged back to England against her will, but if she wouldn't return to the man she professed to love, then why wouldn't she consider Winston? "What do you have against Winston?"

Suddenly Devon recalled the odd things Diablo had said about Winston. "Father, have you heard anything—er—any strange gossip involving Winston?"

"Everyone has his enemies, m'dear. You know I put no store in gossip. Winston risked his life to restore you to me. I personally find no fault with the man. His father died while you were gone, making him a duke."

Truth to tell, Lord Harvey had heard odd snippets of gossip about Winston, but could put no truth to it. Rather than add to Devon's distress he kept it to himself. As far as he was concerned, any misgivings he harbored about Winston's life-style had been laid to rest when he succeeded in wresting Devon from Diablo's lair.

"Viscount, duke, it makes little difference to me," Devon said. "I can't marry Winston."

"Will you at least see him, and give him a chance to court you again?"

"Father, I—"

"For me, Devon, please. It's not doing your reputation any good to remain a recluse. Everyone knows you disappeared on the eve of your wedding, and all our friends are wondering why you deserted Winston at the altar. Fortunately, most believed my explanation that you'd had second thoughts and needed time by yourself to think. I hinted that you went to the country in order to reach a decision. Now that you've returned, I think it wise for you and Winston to be seen in public together."

"All right, Father," Devon agreed reluctantly, worn down by the earl's badgering. "I'll see Winston socially, but nothing will come of it."

Lord Harvey watched his beloved daughter walk from the room, saddened by the change in her. And all because of that devil's spawn, Diablo. It was obvious the girl pined for him. He could kill the man for what he did to her. Not only had he taken her innocence, but he had ruined her for any other man. Devon didn't have to reveal what happened on that island, Lord Harvey was no fool. Devon was young, beautiful, and desirable, no man could resist her. He blamed his daughter for none of the terrible things that had befallen her. She had been taken forcefully and made to bend to Diablo's will. Love, bah! The man didn't know the meaning of the word, and now Devon was suffering for it. Why couldn't Diablo have been hanged that day as the good Lord intended?

Christopher Linley paced back and forth in short, jerky motions across the palace antechamber, waiting for his private audience with the king. He had waited over two weeks for the meeting, and now that the moment had arrived he wondered what the hell he was doing here. Did he really want to reclaim his title after all these years? The answer was simple. Before he could approach Devon, he had to establish himself in society.

He had thought a great deal about Devon these past weeks, and the reason behind her leaving. It was much easier to do with a clear head. Kyle had been right, he had been destroying himself with drink without taking time to sufficiently analyze the situation. What he discovered had shocked him. Deep in his heart he felt Devon loved him, and that her reasons for leaving could be explained if he gave her a chance. He should have given himself time to think before sending off that letter, but his pride had been wounded and his heart broken. At the time he truly felt he never wanted to see her again. He had no idea he would see her night after night in his dreams and spend every waking hour thinking about her.

But first things first. He'd not confront his wife until he was the Duke of Grenville and a social equal. If the king refused to grant his petition, he'd join Blackbeard and men of his ilk in new ventures, and try his damnedest to forget the woman he loved.

The door opened and the king's secretary motioned him inside. Squaring his broad shoulders, Diablo walked into the king's chamber, his steps sure, his composure steady. Kit had no fear over his appearance, for he was impeccably groomed in the latest fashion, clean-shaven, and wearing a huge powdered wig, which he hated. He intended to throw it away the moment he reached home. Christopher Linley bore no resemblance to the fierce pirate feared by mankind. And if the king favored his petition, he'd be free to assume his rightful place in society and claim his wife.

Two hours later Kit left the king's chambers, his step lighter, his tanned face wreathed in a smile that crinkled the corners of his eyes. Without interrupting once, King George had listened to his story, fascinated by the tale of conspiracy, murder, and piracy. He scowled deeply upon learning that Kit's uncle had paid to have him abducted and murdered, but somehow his plan had gone awry. At times the story sounded so improbable that if the king hadn't known Kit's father personally he wouldn't have believed it. But King George recognized the Linley gray eyes and strong chin immediately. Besides, Kit was able to provide intimate details of his family which no one but the true heir could possibly know. The ring with the family crest on it was further evidence of his identity. Diablo had hung on to it throughout the years with a tenacity he could never understand.

Confessing that he was the infamous Diablo had nearly been Kit's undoing, for that feared and hated name brought an immediate reaction from the monarch. If Kit hadn't been determined to begin a new life, he might not have felt compelled to reveal his secret. Thank God he had persuaded King George that the life he led had been the natural result of his uncle's deceit and grew out of those desperate years he had endured more than any young lad ought to.

King George was sympathetic, but what really convinced him to look favorably on Kit's petition to reclaim his estate and title was the fortune in precious gems Kit presented to the monarch. It was a magnificent offering, but one Kit could well afford. As the king pointed out, since amnesty had been offered and duly accepted, he could hardly deny a repentant subject and duke of the realm—a very rich duke—his request to give a present to the king.

When Kit left the palace he had in his possession a document stripping the title from Winston Linley and restoring everything to Christopher, the long-lost heir. Kit had suggested that his other identity not be made public for obvious reasons, and the king had readily agreed. Kit had decided on some vague story involving kidnapping and loss of memory to satisfy the inquisitive. The less said about Diablo, the better.

"My God, Kit, why now? After all these years! Why couldn't you remain dead? You said you didn't care about the title, why did you come back? You realize, of course, that there's little money left. Father went through the bulk of your inheritance before he died."

Eying his imposing cousin malevolently, Winston felt his world come tumbling down around him. His respectability, his prestige, such as it was, everything he took for granted in life was suddenly being wrested away by someone who should have died years ago.

"I don't need money," Kit claimed, thoroughly enjoying seeing his cousin squirm. It was all he could do to keep from tearing the man apart limb from limb for the devastation he had wrought on Paradise. Winston was also probably the one who had carried Devon away from him. But in order to protect his identity, Kit could not confront the

coward with the foul deeds he had perpetrated. Kit
felt no compassion for his cousin, no need to take
care of his future. Though he had no proof, Kit
strongly suspected that Winston had known of his
father's plan to do away with him. Aye, he had every
right in the world to hate Winston.

"I suppose you'll want me out of here," Winston
said tightly.

"I believe that would be best." Kit fought the
urge to tell Winston that he was Diablo and Devon
was his wife. All in good time, he thought, all in
good time. Once he was firmly established and
acknowledged as the Duke of Grenville, he'd find a
way to punish Winston for his misdeeds. First he
needed to see Devon, tell her the letter had been a
mistake, and persuade her father to think of him as
a son-in-law. Linley Hall needed a duchess, and no
one but Devon would do.

"How am I supposed to live?" whined Winston.
"I'm deeply in debt, my creditors are hounding me,
and I've lost my fiancée."

"Are you referring to the heiress you were engaged to?" Kit probed.

Winston scowled. "Something—happened and
the wedding was postponed. She's yet to set a date,
and I doubt she'll have me once she learns I'm not
only penniless but stripped of my title."

"The title was never yours," Kit reminded quietly.

"So you're tossing me out to fend for myself,"
Winston observed bitingly.

"You've had use of my title and money all these
years, be content I'm not demanding restitution.
Get out of my home, Winston, before I change my
mind. Let me know where to send your things."

"You're a bloody devil, Kit," Winston gritted from between clenched teeth, his choice of words bringing a smile to Kit's lips. "What I'd really like to know is where you've been hiding all these years and how you obtained your fortune. Why did you decide to come forth now after all these years? I'll wager that's a tale worth telling. You couldn't have come by your wealth honestly. For now, I've no recourse but to leave, seeing as how the king granted your petition. We may be kin, but one day you'll pay dearly for what you've done to me."

He slammed out of the house, aware that his future depended on his ability to convince Devon to marry him. If not, he'd end up in debtor's prison.

Devon primped before the mirror, unable to muster enthusiasm for tonight's ball. Winston would be here soon, and she fervently wished she hadn't indulged her father by agreeing to accompany Winston to the party. She had disappointed him so often lately that she hadn't been able to resist his pleading in Winston's behalf. She also felt pity for Winston after learning that his long-lost cousin had returned after all these years to claim the dukedom. Devon knew it was a blow to Winston's pride, especially after years of considering himself the sole heir to the Linley estate. Though she wasted no love on Winston, Devon felt sorry for him.

Devon wondered how it could be that a man considered dead for years should suddenly show up alive and possessing great wealth. She had suggested he might be an impostor, but Winston assured her the man was indeed Christopher Linley and had a ring with the family crest he'd held onto all these years to prove it. Idly Devon wondered if she would meet the new duke tonight, for she knew he had been invited to the Smythes' party. For some unexplained reason a tingle of excitement raced up her spine at the prospect.

Winston's predicament wasn't the only problem plaguing Devon. She had finally accepted the fact that she was carrying Diablo's child. She had suspected it for weeks but refused to believe it until she began vomiting each morning upon arising. Tender breasts and having missed two monthly cycles added to her conviction. Somehow she had to find the nerve to tell her father, but as yet hadn't found the right moment. Weeks ago she would have welcomed the pregnancy, but now she wasn't so certain. Not that she wouldn't love Diablo's child, for she would, with her whole heart and soul.

Unable to delay the inevitable, Devon heaved a fretful sigh and left the room to join Winston, where he awaited her at the bottom of the stairs. She was surprised that Winston had been invited to the prestigious affair since he had been demoted to his old title of viscount. Perhaps the fact that the golden-haired Freddie Smythe and Winston were close friends accounted for Winston's invitation. Devon knew it couldn't be easy for Winston to lose everything he held dear as well as face the new duke tonight in public, and she felt a stirring of pity despite the fact that she hadn't forgiven him for carrying her away from Diablo against her will.

Kit arrived at the Smythes' palacious home while the party was in full swing, a gorgeous redhead gracing his arm. They had arrived fashionably late just so Scarlett could make a grand entrance.

Poised in the doorway, Kit bent to whisper in his

companion's ear, "Are you ready, Scarlett? You've been waiting a long time to be presented to society."

"Damn right," Scarlett hissed in reply. Dressed in a gown of vivid purple that should have clashed horribly with her red hair but was actually enhanced by it, Scarlett clung possessively to Kit's arm.

Immensely wealthy from her ill-gotten gains, Scarlett had followed Diablo to London, posing as a rich widow newly arrived from France. Unaware of Diablo's true identity as the Duke of Grenville, she was stunned the day she had encountered him at Lady Davenport's afternoon affair. Since her arrival in London Scarlett had carefully courted the denizens of society, hoping for a smooth entrance into a way of life she had been denied all her life. A quick study, Scarlett had easily mimicked the manners of London's upper crust until she felt quite at home with the rich and titled.

Lady Davenport's affair was the first social function that Kit had attended as Christopher Linley. He had gone primarily to test the waters and gauge his reception by his peers, which proved excellent. He was immensely pleased by what he had accomplished. So pleased, in fact, that he felt confident enough to confront his father-in-law and claim his wife. Encountering Scarlett that afternoon at Lady Davenport's hadn't exactly thrilled Kit.

With the exception of Kyle and Akbar, Kit hoped to avoid all former acquaintances who could identify him as Diablo. When he finally claimed his wife he wanted no stigma attached to her name. So meeting Scarlett had left Kit with an uncomfortable feeling in the pit of his stomach as well as a strange premonition. It didn't help that Scarlett immediately attached herself to him with a tenacity that dismayed him. He held vague misgivings that Scarlett aspired to the title of duchess and sought to stake her claim.

Kit found it difficult to escape Scarlett's persistent badgering and soon became her reluctant escort to the Smythe ball. He couldn't wait to be shed of Scarlett and hoped that one of the many swains vying for the attention of the beautiful, rich "widow" would succeed in luring her from his side.

Chapter Seventeen

It occurred to Kit that he might encounter Devon at one of the affairs he had attended recently, but so far he had met neither his wife nor Winston. During his rounds he heard snippets of gossip about Devon and Winston since they were still believed to be engaged. There seemed to be much speculation whether the twice postponed marriage would ever take place now that Winston had lost the coveted title of duke.

Kit surveyed the room with cool disdain. Though he was officially one of the nobility, he felt little kinship with his own kind, having consorted with pirates and scoundrels most of his adult life. Yet he could not deny his place among them and was prepared to spend the rest of his days living the lawful life he had previously scorned. And all because of the woman he loved more than his own life. When he had found Devon gone from Paradise he tried to despise her, but now all he wanted was to claim her for all time.

"Everyone of importance is here," Scarlett enthused as they approached the intrepid butler whose duty it was to announce the guests.

Her green eyes glowed like emeralds as they swept over the large room congested with opulently dressed women wearing enormous powdered hairdos and satin-clad men sporting wigs. Powdering her hair or wearing a wig was the one current fashion Scarlett decided to forego, preferring her own flaming tresses. Kit bowed to the trend, donning his hated wig as a means of escaping recognition as Diablo.

"Christopher Linley, Duke of Grenville, and Lady DeFoe," intoned the butler loudly, the staccato beat of the long cane against the floor commanding attention.

Dozens of necks craned to observe Kit's slow progress into the room. More than one man envied him his companion, the flamboyant redhead known only as Scarlett DeFoe, a wealthy widow newly arrived in London.

"Bloody hell, I was hoping he wouldn't be here," Winston complained testily.

Devon turned, hoping to catch a glimpse of Winston's mysterious cousin, but she was too late. He and his companion had been swallowed up in a sea of curious people anxious to meet the darkly handsome duke.

Devon had been speaking with an old acquaintance when the duke's name was announced and missed the introduction of his companion.

"Did you know your cousin would be here?" she asked Winston. From what Winston had said, the duke was hardly a paragon of virtue.

"I suspected he might be," Winston allowed sourly, "but hoped he wouldn't. It didn't take him long to find a woman. The redhead on his arm is stunning. Wonder who she is."

The odd premonition that had plagued Devon all evening once again arose on hearing the word "redhead." Then it struck her: Wasn't Kit a shortened version of Christopher?

"Winston, do you call your cousin Kit?" Devon asked, shaking. Her breath came in little puffs of air that left her panting.

"Why, yes, how did you know?"

"Oh God, no! It can't be."

Devon's knees turned to rubber and a shudder passed through her slim form. She clutched her belly as if to protect her child and turned to flee—running straight into Kit's arms. Neither of them could have been more surprised. Unless it was Scarlett. If she thought Diablo no longer cared for Devon, the look on his face instantly disabused her. In all these weeks he had made no effort to see Devon, and Scarlett had assumed he had finally had his fill of her. Scarlett had no idea they were husband and wife, for Diablo's men had been forbidden to speak of the marriage.

Devon's body responded to his immediately as Kit clutched her close. A thrill of remembered bliss shot through her at the brief contact, and she gazed up into a pair of shuttered silver eyes.

"Is this your fiancé, Winston?" Kit drawled with lazy humor. "You've done well for yourself, she's a raving beauty. Aren't you going to introduce us?"

Scarlett's eyebrows shot up in wonder at what kind of game Diablo—she still had trouble thinking of him as Kit—was playing. She decided to go along with it until she learned his purpose and what she might gain by it.

Reluctantly disentangling herself from Kit's arms, Devon stilled her wildly beating heart, waiting for the devil to make his move. Knowing Diablo as she did, she assumed he would claim her immediately as his wife and find perverse pleasure in making her miserable for the rest of her life.

Winston, decidedly uncomfortable, made hasty introductions. Unwilling to stay and exchange small talk with a man he heartily disliked, Winston turned away to lead Devon onto the dance floor, politely excusing himself.

"I was hoping to dance with Lady Devon," Kit said, staying Devon with a firm grip on her arm. "As the head of the family, I should like to become better acquainted with your bride-to-be." Without waiting for Winston's approval, Kit swept Devon onto the dance floor, leaving a fuming Scarlett behind.

Ignoring Scarlett, Winston stomped away, itching to wrest Devon from Kit's grasp but afraid of causing a scandal. From the corner of his eye he caught a glimpse of Freddie Smythe observing him with unfeigned interest. Nodding his blond head toward the stairs, Freddie waited only until Winston signaled that he understood the implied message before drifting off. Winston waited a discreet interval before following, hopeful of salvaging something from this disastrous evening.

As for Scarlett, she was soon surrounded by men anxious for her attention and had little time to waste on Kit and Devon.

"I've missed you," Kit whispered, his eyes drinking in Devon's features like a man long denied the sustenance essential for life.

"That's odd. Your letter swore eternal hatred. Why didn't you tell me who you were?" Devon hissed in reply. She was angry—damn angry. How could Kit keep his identity from her while knowing that Winston was her fiancé? How could he now say he missed her after writing such a hateful letter? "Are you mad coming here like this? What if someone recognizes you?"

"Forget the letter. I have. After you left I was so hurt and stunned I hardly knew what I was doing. But it no longer matters, sweetheart." Kit grinned roguishly. "Haven't you heard? The king granted unconditional amnesty to pirates of the Caribbean. In return we had to agree to leave the Bahamas and give up piracy."

"And you agreed to that?"

"Aye. Over six hundred men have left the brotherhood. I am no longer in danger of losing my life, and the king has heard my tale and seen fit to grant full restitution of my title and estate."

"What tale? This is the first I've heard of amnesty. I've paid little heed to politics of late."

Devon was just beginning to recover from the shock of seeing Kit and learning he was other than what she knew him to be. All these weeks she had assumed he never wanted to see her again and had wallowed in remorse and dejection. Her first reaction had been one of overwhelming joy, which soon gave way to anger. The thought that Kit had neglected to tell her something as important as his real identity rankled. Surely he could have trusted her to keep his secret, couldn't he?

"Why didn't you tell me you were a duke?"

"What purpose would it serve? That sort of life was denied me. I saw no reason to reveal facts that would only confuse you."

"I'm confused now. Winston told me the Linley heir had disappeared when he was a mere lad. How did it happen?"

Kit could see that Devon was becoming more agitated by the minute and that people were beginning to stare at them. By the time the music stopped he had carefully maneuvered them so they stood close to the open French doors. While they were lost in the crush of people streaming from the dance floor, Kit whisked Devon out the door. Their escape did not go unnoticed as Kit had hoped. Scarlett observed their hasty departure, her green eyes narrowed dangerously.

"What are you doing?" Devon cried. "Take me back inside. Winston will wonder where I disappeared to."

"The hell with Winston," Kit returned tersely. Grasping Devon's small hand, he literally dragged her out into the blackness of the night.

"Wait! Where are you taking me? I don't want to go with you. You hate me, remember?" she taunted.

"I don't hate you, I never did. Will you forget that damn letter, it was a mistake. We need to talk. Privately. We were so conspicuous on the dance floor the gossip mongers were having a ball speculating on our relationship."

Despite Devon's protests, Kit's superior strength easily won out as he propelled her down a path leading to an orchard. When nothing of the house was visible but the twinkling of thousands of lights from the windows, he paused beneath the widespread branches of a gnarled apple tree, releasing Devon's hand long enough to pull her into his arms. With a small cry of surrender she melted into his embrace.

"God's bones, sweetheart, I missed you," he

murmured against her lips. "I nearly lost my mind when you left me."

"I didn't leave you, Kit, I was—"

The words died in Devon's throat as Kit's lips slanted over hers, his drugging kiss flooding her mind and body with memories of rapture they once shared. She loved this man, though she had never mouthed the words for fear of tempting fate. Given his profession, it was inevitable they'd be parted one day.

Without breaking the kiss, Kit shrugged off his coat, letting it fall to the ground. Then he sank to his knees, bringing Devon with him.

"Kit, no," Devon pleaded. "You said we needed to talk. I'm ready to listen. Tell me how and why you went from duke to pirate?"

"Later, sweetheart. Can't you see how starved I am for you? I've dreamed of this moment for months. You're the reason I accepted amnesty. You're my wife, Devon, I need you."

"I'm Diablo's wife," Devon denied hotly, "not the wife of Christopher Linley, Duke of Grenville." The hurt of having been deceived sparked her anger. "You're a charlatan, a pirate, a rogue—and worst of all, you lied to me."

"Had you cared to inspect our marriage papers you would have seen my legal name affixed to the document, my love, all legal and aboveboard. And now I'm aching to make love to my wife."

His tongue whispered across her parted lips, then slipped inside to sip the sweet nectar. His hunger for her was enormous, his desire a beast that ruled his body. Then his mouth bent to the high curve of her breast, his breath burning through the thin silk until Devon thought it would burst into flame. She scarcely felt his fingers working on the fastenings at the back of her gown until the cool night air caressed her heated flesh. Kit made no attempt to stifle a groan of frustration as he shoved the delicate material down to her waist. Her shift was the next to go. As if by magic the corset strings parted and moonlight bathed the perfect mounds of her pale alabaster breasts.

The virile scent of arousal teased Devon's highly aroused senses as Kit moved his hips against her, his member instantly erect. Suddenly the ·pulsing between her thighs became a roaring throb.

With great tenderness Kit pressed her to the ground, sliding his coat beneath her slender body. Then he gently tugged her gown and underthings over her hips until she lay like a gilded statue beneath dancing moonbeams. Kit sat back on his haunches, his silver eyes glowing with rapt appreciation.

"I dreamed of you so often like this. I thought I'd forgotten nothing of your beauty, but when I look at you now I find my memory a poor substitute for reality. You're exquisite, sweetheart, lovelier than I remembered. And I love you just as fiercely."

His erotic words turned her body to putty and her mind to mush as Devon reached out to caress his cheek, sliding down his neck to the buttons on his spotless white shirt. With a will of their own her fingers parted the material and pushed the garment over his broad shoulders. Pulling his arms free, Kit removed his trousers, stockings, and shoes while Devon's hands roamed restlessly over the wide expanse of his chest, his back, the lean curve of his hips. They played teasingly over flat male nipples, through dark, curling hair, wanting to explore fur-

ther but suddenly turning shy. It had been so long
since they'd been together like this.

But Kit was not so inhibited. Taking her hand he
moved it to his fully distended member, letting her
feel his great need for her. His breath exploded in
his chest as her fingers curled around him. His
groan echoed through the darkness of the night,
eloquently conveying the exquisite torture filling
every corner of his mind and body.

"God's bones, sweetheart, your touch sets me
afire. Another minute of this torture and I'll leave
you behind." Gasping hoarsely, he gently disen-
gaged her hands. "Lie back and let me love you."

His head dipped down and Devon felt the wet-
ness of his mouth on her breast as he licked then
suckled first one then the other diamond-hard tip.
Her nipples puckered deliciously beneath his tender caresses as he nipped, licked, and pulled them
deeply into his mouth. Then abruptly the pleasure
abated as Kit's mouth slid downward over her
ribcage to sip lovingly at the tiny indent of her
navel, and a new pleasure exploded in her loins.
Moving restlessly beneath his tender assault, Devon
invited deeper caresses by arching upward, and Kit
gladly obliged by pushing her thighs apart to nuzzle
the mound of tight golden curls he found there.

Cupping his hands beneath her, he pressed the
searing heat of his mouth against her, spreading her
legs wide. A delicious weakness set her to trembling
as Kit's mouth came hungering, dipping into her
and exploring her roughly, his tongue bolder and
more urgent. She grew dizzy as the bright flame of
desire swiftly ignited a blazing ecstasy that brought
a low moan of surrender to Devon's lips, and she
called out his name in blind and mindless rapture.
The first penetration of his tongue brought a shriek

to her lips, sending her senses spiraling out of control as tremors of ecstasy jolted through her.

She was half-sobbing when he rose above her at last, and she screamed with incredible pleasure when he plunged deep, deep within her. She screamed again as he stroked her to climax, the sensation so strong and volatile her insides contracted into a hard knot. While Devon writhed and spasmed with exquisite pleasure, Kit had yet to gain his own release, thrusting wildly into her, wanting to reclaim her in the most primitive way. He pierced her deeply, again and again, and then cried out his own rapture.

Embarrassed, she buried herself against the slick dampness of his chest and tried not to think of all the wanton things she had done.

"Don't be embarrassed, sweetheart," Kit said, his soft breath fanning her cheek. "I love your passion. Don't ever change."

Scarlett didn't linger to see Kit and Devon consummate their love. The moment she saw them sink to the ground she hurried back to the house and began searching for Winston. It was much later when she saw him at the top of the stairs with his arm linked through Freddie Smythe's in a manner suggesting more than friendship. Wise in the ways of the world, Scarlett smiled slyly as she watched the couple part and descend the stairs in a more circumspect manner. She waited until Freddie headed off in a different direction before accosting Winston.

"I must talk to you," she whispered, startling Winston with the intensity of her words. "Alone."

"Of course, Lady DeFoe," he replied, his brows angling upward. He had no idea what his cousin's beautiful companion could want with him. "Let me see if I can find Devon first. I wouldn't want her to think I've deserted her."

"You won't find her, she's not in the house," Scarlett said. "Where can we be alone?"

"The library," Winston returned, recognizing her urgency as he led the way to another part of the house.

The library was deserted and he ushered Scarlett inside where a lamp glowed invitingly. Before Winston could mouth his question, Scarlett blurted out, "They're together, you know."

"What! To whom are you referring?"

"I'm speaking of your cousin and your fiancée."

"Impossible!" Winston denied hotly. "They just met. Has Kit been annoying Devon and creating gossip by dancing with her more often than good manners decree? Where are they now? I should have known Kit would try something like this. Isn't it enough that he took my title?"

"Sweet Jesus, you are dense, aren't you?" Winston had the sense to look affronted. "I saw them just minutes ago in the orchard, engaged in more than friendly banter. Had I chosen to remain I'm certain I would have seen them coupling on the ground like animals."

Winston blanched. "Your assumption is absurd! Devon wouldn't do such a thing. Besides, she and Kit just met."

"Winston, you're either very stupid or incredibly dense," Scarlett snorted. "'Tis difficult to believe you know nothing about Kit when he's your own kin."

"Know what? For years I thought him dead until he showed up just recently to claim his title and estate. If you know something that I don't, you'd better tell me."

"You've heard of the pirate Diablo, haven't you?" Scarlett asked.

"Of course, who hasn't? But what's that got to do with—" Suddenly comprehension dawned. "Bloody hell!" Winston exploded. "I should have realized something like this when Kit returned rich beyond belief refusing to reveal the mysterious void he's existed in for the past fifteen years." He paused, his mind working furiously. The thought that suddenly occurred to him left his face drained of all color. "If Kit is Diablo, then he and Devon are—are—lovers! Dammit, I won't allow it! I'm bankrupt. I need her dowry to keep out of debtors' prison. If I was hounded by creditors before I lost my title, you can well imagine what it's like now."

"What are you going to do about it?" Scarlett goaded mercilessly. "Obviously Diablo and Devon have resumed their—illicit relationship."

"Why, I'll—I'll . . ." Winston stammered to a halt. Obviously he was no match for his cousin's superior strength and cunning and could do little to wrest Devon from his grasp if Diablo wanted her. Besides, where did Scarlett fit into all this? How had she become so knowledgeable about the pirate? "I sense your concern is more than mere interest. Why are you telling me this?"

Scarlett fixed Winston with a baleful glare. "I have my heart set on becoming Duchess of Grenville. I want Diablo, or Kit, or whatever you care to call him. I've always wanted him. We were lovers before Devon interfered. The only reason I accepted amnesty was so I could follow Diablo to London."

"You're a pirate?" Winston's mouth hung open in stunned disbelief.

"Aye, but that's all in the past. I'm a lady now, and rich enough to be accepted by society."

"What do you want from me?" Winston asked. "I understand Diablo is a ruthless killer who takes what he wants. And he's proven time and again he wants Devon. Only a fool would think himself capable of taking from Diablo something he considers his property."

"Coward!" hissed Scarlett.

"Unless . . ." mused Winston thoughtfully.

"Unless—?" prompted Scarlett.

"If I went to the king and told him about Kit he'd—"

"—do nothing. You are a fool," sneered Scarlett. "The king knows all about Diablo. Don't you understand? It no longer matters who he was. He's been granted amnesty and can no longer be punished for piracy."

"It might make a difference to some people," sniffed Winston, miffed at being considered a fool. "What would you have me do?"

"Take Devon away. Force her to marry you. Anything to keep Diablo from claiming her."

"You're the fool, Lady DeFoe," Winston retorted. "Devon has refused to marry me countless times during the past weeks. Being penniless hardly helps my cause."

"What about her father? Can't you enlist his help? If he loves his daughter he won't want her involved with a pirate and scoundrel like Diablo, duke or no. He should be grateful to you for wanting to save Devon from Diablo's cluches."

"I can't do it! 'Tis a damn bloody mess! Find some other way to get Kit for yourself."

Scarlett's eyes narrowed into dangerous green slits and her mouth thinned into a stubborn line, which should have given Winston warning of the length she was prepared to go to gain her own end. "You'll do exactly as I say or find yourself ostracized by your peers. Think of Freddie's family. The shame will kill them."

A horrified expression crept over Winston's face. "Wha—what are you talking about?"

"How long have you and Freddie Smythe been lovers?"

Absolute silence reigned as Winston's face turned a sickly shade of green. "I—I—"

Scarlett grinned smugly, Winston's dismay serving to reinforce her theory. "I wasn't born yesterday. Mayhap you can dupe your peers but you can't fool me, I've seen too much of the world. One has but to see you and Freddie together to know you're lovers."

"That's blackmail!" Winston sputtered lamely. He was astute enough to realize that Scarlett would not stop at vile methods to obtain her goal.

"Aye, I'd attempt anything to get Diablo. I may no longer be a pirate, but I've forgotten nothing of my former life."

"What do you want from me? I'm virtually powerless against my cousin."

"Take Devon someplace where Diablo can't find her. Wed and bed her. Better yet, get her with child. You *are* capable, aren't you?" Scarlett mocked.

"Of course," Winston said uncertainly. Though the idea sickened him, he thought he could perform if he had to. "But I told you before, Devon won't have me. I think she fancies herself in love with Diablo."

"Devil take you! Have you no guts? Use your

head, man. If Devon isn't taken to where Diablo can't find her within forty-eight hours, your abnormal sexual preferences will become common knowledge. And Freddie Smythe will be exposed as your lover."

Winston blanched, his mind racing furiously. If Devon refused to marry him, Scarlett's disclosure would make it impossible to pursue another heiress, and he would surely have to flee England or go to prison. His only salvation lay in convincing Lord Harvey that Devon must marry him in order to save her from Diablo. With luck and the earl's cooperation, it could work. The old man loved his daughter and would go to any lengths to save her from a disastrous liaison.

"Well," Scarlett said, tapping her foot impatiently. "Have you come to a decision?"

"Do I have a choice?"

"None that I can see. Where will you take her?"

"If all goes well I'll take Devon to Cornwall. I'm sure Kit has all but forgotten the family hunting lodge near Penzance. We'll be safe enough there until I can arrange a marriage."

"If Devon returns before I'm wed to Diablo, I'll see you ruined," Scarlett warned ominously. "Or perhaps I'll revert to my old ways and slit your gullet. Even if you have to hold her against her will, keep Devon away from London until I send word that I'm Duchess of Grenville."

Winston swallowed the lump of fear rising in his throat. He didn't doubt Scarlett's ability to kill him should she so desire. But instinctively he knew it would take more than his efforts alone to keep Devon confined against her will. First he had to inform Lord Harvey of Kit's identity and impress upon the man the threat that Kit posed to Devon.

Next he had to hire a couple of unsavory characters to help carry out his plans. But first there was the problem of money.

"I'll need cash to accomplish all this—hire a carriage, hire someone to help, feed us while we're in hiding. I have no money. Kit stripped me of everything."

"I'll see to it." Scarlett nodded with smug satisfaction. "Come around in the morning and you'll be taken care of." She turned to leave. "Say nothing of this to anyone if you value your worthless hide."

"You're coming home with me, sweetheart," Kit said, his arms tightening possessively around Devon's slender form. "I'm afraid I'll lose you again if I let you out of my sight. You make a habit of disappearing the moment I turn my back." His voice held a hint of censure, and Devon turned in his arms to peer up at him.

"I didn't want to leave you. Winston threatened to shell the village if I didn't go with him. I couldn't allow that to happen again."

"Bloody bastard!" Kit spat venomously. "I was too easy on the coward. You have no idea the anguish I suffered because of him. The thought that you could leave me so easily nearly broke my spirit, and I became someone I scarcely recognized. I penned the letter to you in a moment of despair so profound it nearly destroyed me. You don't know how often I regretted acting so rashly."

"It didn't take long for you to find solace with another woman," Devon accused, bristling angrily. "How long have you and Scarlett been together?"

"We've never been 'together,'" Kit denied. "Not in the sense you mean. I brought her to the ball tonight for the sole purpose of introducing her to society. Scarlett accepted amnesty and is posing as a rich widow. I've not wanted another woman since the day I saw you. It's always been you—only you I love and want. I've had no other woman since you entered my life."

"Oh, Kit, I love you, too," Devon exclaimed, her mind searching for the words to tell him about the baby. "I was desolate when I thought I'd never see you again. I want to know how and why you disappeared years ago and never returned to claim what was rightfully yours."

"It's a long story, and not a very pretty one."

"Please, Kit, you owe me an explanation."

"My father died when I was a lad, and my uncle, Winston's father, became my guardian," Kit began slowly, all those years of hurt and pain spilling from his memory in a flood of bitterness. "I had no idea my uncle coveted the title and estate for himself and his own son, but, alas, I learned too late the extent of his hatred."

Kit licked his dry lips, recalling the betrayal and disillusionment he suffered as if it happened yesterday. "One day I was abducted from my home by two men hired by my uncle. They were under orders to kill me, but being greedy as well as lawless, they sold me to an unscrupulous sea captain to serve aboard his ship, obtaining his promise never to allow me to go ashore, fearing I'd escape and make my way back to England."

"My God!" Devon gasped, stunned. "Did—did Winston know of this?"

"He says not, but who's to prove or disprove it? His father is dead and there's no one else to question."

"Go on," Devon urged. "How did you become

Diablo, and why didn't you return to England to the life you were born to?"

"I served aboard the ship under deplorable conditions nearly ten years before we were attacked by pirates. I chose to join Black Bart's crew rather than meet an untimely end. I was young and strong, and men looked to me as their leader. Fed up with Black Bart's depraved cruelty, the crew asked me to join them in a mutiny. I agreed. We took over the ship in a bloody battle and I was appointed captain. Black Bart was dead and I assumed the name Diablo, deciding to keep my identity a secret."

"You could have gone back to England," Devon suggested.

"By then the lure of excitement and adventure was too great to leave it. I'd been at sea over ten years. I was twenty-three years old and for the first time in full control of my life. Assuming my rightful place as Duke of Grenville held little appeal to me. If my uncle wanted the title so badly, I decided to let him keep it.

"From that day forward I embarked on a career that made it impossible to return to polite society anywhere in the civilized world. I've been Diablo for five years and not regretted one minute of it. And then I met the woman I came to love more than my own life, more than adventure, riches, and freedom to rule the seas. I fell in love, sweetheart, and my life was never the same afterward.

"There's so much sadness in my heart for that young boy," Devon said wistfully. "But life will be different now. I swear I'll make you happy, my love."

"You already have, sweetheart," Diablo vowed earnestly.

Now, Devon decided, was the time to tell Kit about the baby. "There's something—"

"God's bones, sweetheart, we can talk later, at home. I know we still have much to discuss, but I can't wait to have you all to myself in the privacy of our own home. Get dressed."

Kit's words brought back a sense of reality, making Devon aware that this was neither the time nor the place to bring up the subject of their child. She also realized that she couldn't accompany him back to Linley Hall. "Kit, I can't go home with you, not yet," she said, sighing regretfully. "We both owe Father the courtesy of an explanation. I've disappointed him enough already without disappearing again without a word."

"But you're not disappearing, sweetheart, you'll be with me." He couldn't bear the thought of another separation, no matter how short.

"Please, Kit, try to understand," Devon pleaded as she turned to receive Kit's help with the fastenings at the back of her gown. "Father is not a young man. He tries to hide it from me, but he isn't well. Let me prepare him first. Tomorrow we'll tell him together. Come for lunch."

"Dammit, Devon, you're my wife! I want you with me."

"I know, my love, I haven't forgotten. Please humor me in this. I want to be with you more than anything in the world, but what can one more day hurt?"

Reluctantly, Kit agreed, but not just to please Devon. He'd caused Lord Harvey enough heartache in the past without currying his disfavor yet one more time. Fully dressed now, he pulled Devon into his arms, reluctant to part with her, fearing that something was bound to happen the moment she was out of his sight, as it always did. All kinds of strange premonitions played havoc with his mind. Now that he and Devon were happily reunited, why did he sense danger? What could go wrong? he scoffed. Burying his fear beneath an out-pouring of emotion, he slanted his mouth across hers, a driving desperation turning his doubt in-to fierce possession. His kiss softened when he heard a small whimper of protest float past her lips.

"I'm sorry, sweetheart, 'tis just that the thought of losing you again tears me apart. I didn't mean to hurt you."

"Kit, nothing can separate us now," Devon pledged solemnly.

"All right," Kit sighed, finally convinced but still reluctant. "I'll take you home."

"What about Winston and Scarlett?"

Kit frowned. "What about them?"

"Do you think we should let them know we're leaving?"

"The devil take them. I'm taking no chances now that our lives are on the right track. I don't give a damn what they think, we owe them nothing. Come along, sweetheart, my coach is waiting."

Arm in arm they strolled beneath the lovers' moon toward the line of vehicles parked along the circular drive outside the house. Stopping before the handsome carriage bearing the Linley crest, Kit opened the door and boosted Devon into the dark interior. Her gasp of dismay brought him instantly alert.

"What is it, sweetheart?"

"I suspected you'd try something like this." Scarlett's bright red tresses gleamed darkly in the moonlight as she leaned out the door.

"God's bones, Scarlett, why aren't you inside having a good time?"

"I saw you leave the ball with Devon. I'll not be dumped like so much unwanted baggage. We came together and we'll leave together." So saying she settled herself against the squabs, spreading her skirts about her with regal disdain.

Muttering an oath, Kit hauled himself inside, plopping down beside Devon. He'd be damned if he'd allow Scarlett to spoil a perfect evening. He signaled the driver, and the coach took off with a lurch. Then he relaxed, slanting Devon a secret smile that spoke volumes about his love, and his determination that no one would interfere with their lives.

But Scarlett succeeded in thwarting Kit's intentions, refusing to budge from the coach until Devon was taken home. Roaring mad but unwilling to resort to violence, Kit acquiesced with bad grace. He was forced to make do with the goodnight kiss he and Devon shared in the dark shadows of the doorway. Knowing that Scarlett sat fuming in the coach while he bid Devon goodnight added zest to his passion.

At the touch of his lips, Devon melted into Kit's embrace, molding her body into the contour of his hard-muscled form. Her mouth parted beneath the gentle probing of his tongue and Kit ached to partake again of her sweet warmth. Once would never be enough with his fiery love. He had to forcibly stop himself from stripping the silk material from her perfect breasts and savoring the taste and feel of those hard-tipped mounds.

"God's bones, sweetheart, if I don't stop I'll take you right here on your front steps," Kit breathed raggedly. "I'm stupid for not taking you home with me where you belong."

Blushing, Devon reluctantly pulled away, her own breath dangerously shallow. "Nay, Kit, I've already told you, we owe it to Father to explain how things are between us. Tomorrow, my love. Then I don't care if all of London knows we are husband and wife."

"I'm sorry about Scarlett. I should have kicked her out of the coach on her backside."

"Nay, I no longer fear Scarlett. Nor do I doubt your love. Tomorrow will be the beginning of forever."

Their parting kiss left Devon so unnerved she entirely forgot to tell Kit about the baby.

Tomorrow would be soon enough, she thought, smiling dreamily. Tomorrow they would begin their life with the knowledge that they would soon be a family. Tomorrow.

Chapter Eighteen

Reeling groggily, Lord Harvey staggered to answer the insistent racket at the front door. It was long past midnight and the servants had retired to their quarters on the third floor. Shuffling along in slippers and robe and holding a candle aloft, he mumbled a string of oaths. He knew it couldn't be Devon for he had heard her come in earlier. Hastening his steps, he prayed Devon wouldn't be awakened by his late-night caller, whoever he might be.

"I'm coming, I'm coming," he grumbled crossly as the pounding continued. He flung the door open, surprised to see Winston in the doorway beneath the candle's mellow glow. "What! What!" the stunned earl sputtered. "What the devil are you doing here at this hour?"

"Is Devon home?"

"Devon? Are you mad? She hasn't left since you brought her home."

"I didn't bring her home."

"She came home alone?" Lord Harvey asked, frowning with disapproval. "Did you quarrel?"

"N—nay, not exactly," Winston stammered, chosing his words carefully. "She left with my cousin."

"The Duke of Grenville? I wasn't aware that Devon knew the man."

"There are many things you're not aware of," Winston said cryptically.

"Can't it wait till morning?" the earl asked, yawning hugely. "I don't know what possessed you to stop by so late."

"Nay, Your Grace, it can't wait," Winston persisted, shoving his way past the older man. "This needs to be said now."

Seeing no way out of it, Lord Harvey sighed in weary resignation and led the way to his study. "Come along then, m'boy, just keep it brief."

Lord Harvey barely made it to the comfortable chair behind his desk before Winston blurted out, "That devil's got her again! He's put some kind of spell on Devon."

"What in bloody hell are you ranting about?" the earl asked, puzzling over Winston's words. "I thought you said your cousin brought Devon home."

"That's what I've been trying to tell you! My cousin and Diablo are one and the same. The Duke of Grenville *is* Diablo."

"Diablo? The pirate Diablo? He's in London? By God, that man has nerve!" Lord Harvey thundered. "But you're wrong about Devon, she's upstairs in bed. And what does your cousin have to do with that blackhearted scoundrel?" Still not fully awake, only half of what Winston said registered on the older man's mind.

"Have you heard nothing of what I've said, Your Grace? The mysterious earl is really the pirate Diablo. He was granted amnesty and came back to claim his estate. More than likely 'tis Devon he's after. Evidently she recognized him immediately tonight, for they disappeared shortly after they met and no one saw them after that. I feared he's carried her off again. Lord only knows what went on while they were alone," Winston hinted slyly.

"That bloody bastard! I won't have it!" The earl was painfully aware that Diablo had seduced Devon long ago and she hadn't been the same since. "Are you certain? You could be mistaken. I told you Devon came home hours ago."

"I was never more certain of anything in my life," Winston said with smug assurance. "I've been suspicious of him ever since he showed up after being thought dead all these years. He was kidnapped as a young lad and nothing was heard of him until a few weeks ago when he turned up with enough wealth to convince the king to strip me of all my possessions. It seems utterly beyond belief that a notorious pirate accustomed to adventure should choose to accept amnesty and return to resume the dull, rather colorless life of an English lord and all the restrictions placed on him by society."

"You—you think he came back for Devon?" Suddenly Lord Harvey clutched at his heart as a sharp pain squeezed the breath from him. He couldn't lose Devon again. Not to a man with no morals and a heart as black as his reputation.

"I'm certain of it. The same person who revealed Kit's identity to me intimated that Diablo intended to use Devon to satisfy the animal lust he developed for her. Nothing can save her from ruination once he gets his hands on her."

"She's virtually powerless against him," Winston continued relentlessly. "Diablo's proved time and again he has total control over her senses. Do you want your daughter corrupted by the likes of a man who attained his wealth by preying on others? What will happen to Devon when he tires of her? One day he'll look for a young and innocent wife, and I can assure you it won't be Devon."

Having done what damage he could to Kit's reputation, Winston waited for Lord Harvey's reaction.

The earl's normally ruddy complexion turned white, then went slack with terror. He loved Devon far too much to see her corrupted and humiliated by a pirate who would use and discard her at his convenience. He'd see Diablo dead first.

"Nay," he denied vehemently. "I'll not let that happen. I'll do whatever necessary to keep Devon away from that vile man."

"Let me help you," Winston pleaded eagerly. "I have a plan, but it won't succeed without your cooperation."

The pain in his chest was terrible, but not great enough to interfere with Lord Harvey's keen mind. "Tell me your plan. I'll not lose Devon again."

Casting a wary eye toward the closed door, Winston sidled closer to the earl. "Assist me in taking Devon away where Diablo can't find her. Once we're alone, I'm convinced she'll come to her senses. Why, when we return," he boasted, "she may even be carrying your first grandchild." At Lord Harvey's incredulous look, he hastily added, "Naturally we'll wed first."

"You'd hold Devon against her will?" the earl quizzed sharply. "It won't be easy."

"I can do it with your help. Once Devon is in the coach with me there'd be no turning back. I won't return till we've been properly wed and bedded. I know I could convince Devon to be my wife once she's away from my cousin's influence."

"It didn't work before," came Lord Harvey's skeptical reply.

"Would you hand your daughter over to Diablo without a fight?" Winston goaded. His devious words were meant to strike terror in Lord Harvey's heart in order to force his cooperation. He must not fail. Winston feared Scarlett's retribution almost as much as he feared Kit. If Lord Harvey agreed to help him in his efforts to take Devon to a secret place, it would give Scarlett time to capture Kit's heart. If anyone could do it, Scarlett could.

"By God, that devil won't have her!" the earl reiterated, pounding the desk to reinforce his words. "What must I do?"

Their voices lowered in conspiracy, Winston instructed Lord Harvey to arrange for Devon to be delivered to his coach, which would be waiting outside the front door early the next morning—just a few hours hence. Then he would take her with all haste to the little-used Linley hunting lodge near Penzance in remote Cornwall. Before he left he slipped the earl a vial of brownish liquid given to him once by a doctor for pain when he had broken his leg. There was still a goodly amount of laudanum left in the bottle.

Lord Harvey slumped dejectedly in his chair, burying his gray head in his trembling hands. Must he stoop to betraying his own flesh and blood to keep Devon safe? Was he doing the right thing?

Surely Winston, weak though he was, was a better choice for his beloved daughter than a ruthless pirate like Diablo. Once she was married to Winston, not even Diablo—or the Duke of Grenville—would dare pursue her.

A terrible pain tore upward through his body and Lord Harvey stiffened, his pale face shiny with sweat. Then slowly his breathing eased and the pain subsided enough to allow the tortured earl to seek his bed for what remained of this eventful night.

Despite having retired late, Devon awoke early the next morning, lighthearted and happily expectant. In a few hours Kit would arrive and set things right with her father, and they could settle down to a life she'd always dreamed of with the man she loved. A dreamy look turned her beautiful features soft and wistful as she bathed, dressed, and went downstairs to breakfast.

"Father, you're up early," Devon trilled happily. "I'm glad, there's—" Suddenly she noticed his waxen complexion, his pinched features, and alarm seized her. "Father, you're ill! What is it?"

"Nay, daughter, I'm fine," the earl denied, managing a weak smile. "But I'm glad you're down early. I have an errand to attend to and I'd like you to accompany me."

"Of course, Father," Devon readily agreed, "as long as we return in time for lunch. I've invited a guest and—and I have something to tell you. But it can wait until later."

The earl knew exactly who to expect and was determined that Devon wouldn't be here when Diablo arrived. Refusing to look into Devon's trusting eyes, he nodded. "We'll be back in plenty of time." It was a deliberate lie but one he felt necessary under the circumstances. "Help yourself to breakfast, m'dear, the food is quite tasty."

Ravenous, Devon went to the sideboard and heaped her plate with the tempting array of food prepared by the cook. When she returned to the table, the earl had already poured her tea. Devon smiled her thanks and concentrated on her plate, unaware of her father's warring conscience and plaguing doubts over the terrible thing he must do in order to save his only child from corruption and ruin. When she finished, she sat back, replete, draining the last drop of tea from her cup.

"I'm ready, Father, whenever you are."

"Fetch your cloak, m'dear, and I'll see if the coach is out front. I've ordered it brought round early." Lord Harvey made a half-hearted effort to rise, then sank back quickly in his chair, as if the effort were beyond him.

"Perhaps we should delay this errand for another time," Devon suggested, gravely concerned over her father's obvious weakness.

"Nay, I'm fine, truly. Run along now, I'll be waiting by the door."

Planting a kiss on his forehead, Devon hurried off, determined to summon the doctor the moment they returned.

Rising somewhat unsteadily, Lord Harvey walked to the door, peeked out the side window, and saw Winston's hired coach waiting by the curb. Immediately a stab of guilt pierced his heart and he very nearly couldn't go through with it. But the thought of Devon being used and corrupted by Diablo firmed his resolve. Heaving a troubled sigh, he waited for Devon to reappear.

A frown furrowed Devon's smooth brow as she removed her cloak from the wardrobe and drew it over her shoulders. A strange lassitude turned her legs to rubber as she mounted the stairs, and her weakness increased with each passing minute. Pausing at the top of the stairs, she started down, clinging tightly to the handrail as she tried to think above the buzzing in her head.

Immediately Devon's hand went to her stomach. Was it the baby? The conspicuous absence of pain told her all was well with the child. Perhaps both she and her father were coming down with something. By the time she reached the front door where Lord Harvey waited, her vision was blurred and her knees trembled from the effort it took to remain upright. With keen perception the earl noted Devon's distress, and he took her arm, leading her to the door, his face a study of grave concern. Did he really want to do this?

"Father," Devon demurred, "perhaps I should stay home. All of a sudden I feel—strange."

"Nonsense," the earl blustered. "I'm sure it will pass once you're out in the air."

Thinking perhaps her lethargy was but another manifestation of her pregnancy, Devon reluctantly agreed, leaning against her father as he carefully helped her down the steps to the waiting coach. Suddenly Devon experienced a disturbing premonition that something was amiss. "This isn't your coach, Father. Where is the coat of arms?"

"This is a rented coach, Devon, mine is being repaired," the earl was quick to reply. "In you go, m'dear."

Even as he handed her inside, guilt rode him mercilessly. Was he doing the right thing by his beloved daughter? Would she thank him for protecting her from a liaison that would be disastrous for her reputation and ultimately break her heart?

Or would she despise him for interfering in her life? Just when he would have snatched her back to the safety of his arms, the coach shot forward and Devon fell backwards into Winston's viselike embrace.

"Father! Help!"

"Please forgive me, daughter, I love you!"

Then darkness descended and she fell into a void as black as death.

A bubbling well of happiness burst inside Kit as he approached the front door of Chatham House. At long last he could let the world know that Devon was his wife. Last night was the longest night he had ever endured. He had rehearsed his speech to Devon's father over and over until he had it perfect, well aware that the man had little reason to like him. Hopefully he could convince the earl he had shed the identity of feared and hated pirate and was now a respected member of society. Setting the knocker into motion, Kit vowed that Milford's opinion of him would make little difference, for Devon was his and he meant to claim her with or without her father's approval.

Stating his request to speak with Lady Devon, Kit was stunned to learn from the dour butler that she wasn't at home. A strange prickling commenced at the back of his neck and intuition told him something terrible was wrong. He quickly asked for the earl and was shown into the library by the servant, who batted not an eyelash when given Kit's name and title.

"So, 'tis true, you are Diablo. You're a despicable scoundrel, sir, and a seducer of young virgins. If you are looking for my daughter, she's not here.

With luck she's where your corruptive influence can't touch her."

Kit whirled to find the short, ruddy-faced earl staring at him with undisguised loathing. He leaned heavily against the door frame, his face a grimace of agony.

"I'm sorry you feel that way, Your Grace," Kit replied evenly. "You have every right to hate me, but I hope to change your mind."

"Never!" the earl denied vehemently. "What you did and continue to do to my daughter is unforgivable."

"Might I speak with Devon? I'm certain she'll—"

"I wasn't lying when I said she wasn't here," Lord Harvey repeated.

"I'll wait," Kit replied with staunch resolve.

"She may be gone for months."

"What! Impossible! Devon asked me here today with good reason. We hoped to explain our situation to you and gain your approval. I've been granted amnesty and fully intend to live within the bounds of society. We hoped you'd be as forgiving as our king, who restored to me all I once possessed but lost due to an act of treachery."

"You ask too much. How can I forgive what you did to my daughter?" thundered the earl. "What about all the innocent lives you've taken, the helpless women you've ravished, the shipping disrupted by you and those under your command?"

"No women were raped by me, and I've deliberately refrained from taking lives during my years of command," Kit defended stoutly. "I'll not deny I'm guilty of seizing cargoes and disrupting shipping, but in the beginning piracy was not my choice. It was thrust upon me. While my peers wallowed in luxury I slaved aboard a ship as a common seaman, driven by a cruel master. I grew to manhood hardened by years of servitude and abusive treatment. Devon was the only good thing to happen to me after I was kidnapped from my home by henchmen hired to kill me by my uncle. He was a greedy man who coveted my inheritance for himself and his own son."

Appalled, Lord Harvey sank into a chair, his face a mask of disbelief. "Kidnapped? By Winston's father? Do you expect me to believe that drivel?"

"'Tis true. The king believed me, and Winston admitted knowledge of the deed, though he denied knowing about it until years later. 'Tis also true I love Devon with all my heart and soul."

"If what you say is true, then I've done both you and Devon a grave injustice," the earl said slowly, his breath coming in short, painful gasps. "If Devon's actions these past weeks are any indication, I'd be safe in saying she returns your love."

Kit smiled, a shudder of relief passing through his body. "Devon is my life," Kit admitted. "Without her I'd have no reason to return to a society that rejected me."

"What are your intentions toward Devon?" the earl asked, still not completely convinced. Yet he had a niggling suspicion that he'd been thoroughly duped by Winston. Had he foolishly delivered his beloved daughter into the hands of a man who wanted her only for personal gain? A man capable of assisting in the murder of his younger cousin?

"My intentions," Kit responded with alacrity, "are for Devon to assume her rightful place as my duchess and my wife."

"Your wife! But—" The earl started to rise but fell back, stunned.

"We have been wed for many months. The ceremony was legally performed by a minister in Cornwall and duly recorded. For Devon's sake I have freely renounced my former life and accepted amnesty. Now, Your Grace, if you'd be so good as to tell me where I might find my wife."

Lord Harvey opened his mouth to speak, and though his jaw worked furiously, nothing but choking sounds issued forth. "Your Grace, what is it? Are you ill?" Alarmed, Kit knelt before the older man trying to make sense of his mumblings.

"Winston." It was the only word Kit could understand, but one that brought a chill of foreboding racing down his spine.

"Is Devon with Winston?" A slow nod from the afflicted man brought Kit his answer. "Where? Where has he taken her?"

Suddenly speech was beyond Lord Harvey as he clutched at his heart and slumped over in Kit's arms. Acting instinctively, Kit picked up the older man and darted into the hall and up the stairs in search of a bed. As he dashed past a startled servant, he called over his shoulder, "Summon a doctor, quickly! The earl's life depends on how fast you can run."

"Will he live, doctor?" Kit asked when the doctor joined him in the library hours later. "What ails the earl?"

Never having met Kit before, the doctor was reluctant to confide in him. But Kit seemed so genuinely concerned he decided to trust him.

"The earl suffered a heart seizure," came the

doctor's solemn reply. "I warned him this might happen after his last examination when he complained of pain and shortness of breath. I told him the least little excitement—" He shrugged, looking at Kit helplessly, as if it were now up to a higher authority.

"Will he recover?" Kit asked anxiously.

"I've done all I can, 'tis up to God now. Time will tell." Then he looked at Kit curiously. "Who are you, sir?"

"I am the earl's son-in-law," Kit replied without hesitation. "Christopher Linley, Duke of Grenville."

"You're married to Devon?" the doctor gasped. "But I thought she and Winston—"

"We've been wed some months. We met shortly after she left London on—er—holiday."

"Of course—I didn't realize—I'm sorry, Your Lordship." Once the doctor realized he was dealing with nobility he immediately changed his tone.

"When might I speak with the earl?" Kit asked apprehensively. He despaired of saving Devon from Winston's machinations unless Lord Harvey recovered sufficiently to tell him where she had been taken.

The doctor shook his head sadly. "'Tis doubtful his grace will gain consciousness anytime soon. So severe was his pain I was forced to sedate him and will continue to do so until he is out of danger. It could be weeks."

"Weeks!" Kit blew up. "I can't wait that long! It's imperative I speak with him the moment he opens his eyes."

"I'm afraid it will gain you naught. I suspect the earl will be incoherent and confused long after he awakens. Where is your wife, my lord, she should be with her father at a time like this."

"Devon is—visiting out of the city," Kit improvised. "I'll see that the earl is properly cared for and your orders strictly adhered to. Someone will remain with him night and day."

"Excellent," nodded the doctor. "I've left medicine and instructions with Mrs. Givens, the housekeeper. I'll stop by twice a day, more often if needed."

After he left, Kit was in a state of panic. How would he find Devon if the earl was incapable of speech? What if the earl died and he never learned where Winston had taken her? God's bones! He couldn't bear it. He'd nurse Lord Harvey back to health himself, Kit vowed, if it would help.

Once he composed himself, Kit gathered the staff, introduced himself as Devon's husband, and issued orders for the sick man's care in a crisp, no-nonsense voice that demanded instant obedience. His commanding air of authority left no question in the minds of the servants that the Duke of Grenville was anything other than what he claimed and as such must be obeyed. But when Kit questioned them about Devon's destination that morning, he was met with blank stares. So after looking in on Lord Harvey one last time, Kit returned home to ponder his dilemma. If need be he'd search London from end to end to find the woman he loved. In the meantime, he'd hover over the earl day and night until the man regained his wits. Nothing mattered but finding Devon and keeping her safe for the rest of their days. A love like theirs happened only once in a lifetime and he'd be damned if he'd allow anything or anyone to keep them apart.

Chapter Nineteen

Devon was aware of nothing but the bouncing of the coach over rutted roads and being forced to swallow a loathsome liquid from time to time. Just when her head began to clear, the bitter brew forced between her lips sent her plunging back into a dark void. Once she roused herself long enough to recall being carried into an inn and put to bed by a sympathetic maid who worried over the "poor woman's" illness. After another dose of her "medicine," Devon soon drifted back into a bottomless abyss, too confused to ask for help.

Two more nights slipped past in the same manner before Devon fully awoke to find herself in an unfamiliar bed in a strange room. Devon's hands flew to her stomach, relieved when her fingertips brushed the slight swelling where her child rested. Gingerly she pushed herself to a sitting position, gulping back the rise of bile in her throat and struggling against the dizziness that threatened to plunge her back into darkness.

Surging to her feet, Devon stood with difficulty, but managed to remain upright until her head cleared and her vision returned to normal. The china water pitcher across the room drew her like a magnet to its thirst-quenching promise. Empty! Another urgent need was appeased when she found a chamber pot beneath the bed. Then determination stiffened her wobbly legs and carried her to the door. It opened before her hand found the doorknob.

"You're awake! Good."

"You've done it this time, Winston," Devon flounced with angry indignation. "Why have you drugged me and brought me to this place? Father will have your hide for this!"

"This may come as a surprise, but I have your father's blessing," came Winston's smug reply. "He agrees with me wholeheartedly. We had to get you away from my cousin's corrupt influence. You know Lord Harvey hates Diablo and all he stands for."

"Father knows about Diablo?" gasped Devon with alarm. "How did he find out? I wanted to be the one to tell him about Kit."

"I told him," Winston revealed slyly. "I had your best interests at heart. I know you fancy yourself in love with Diablo, or Kit as he's now called, but the man is a notorious pirate, a defiler of women, and a murderer. I thought your father should know the truth."

"But how did *you* know?" Devon persisted. Then abruptly the answer came to her. "Scarlett! I should have known. The woman hates me. She's always wanted Kit."

"It doesn't matter who told me, only that I

learned the truth in time to save you from being ruined beyond redemption. Your father made it possible to take you away where Kit can't find you. He expects us to return as husband and wife."

"Father drugged me?" Devon gasped, disbelief coloring her words. "I—nay—he wouldn't do such a terrible thing. He loves me."

"That's why he did it. He loves you too much to see you corrupted by an evil man like Diablo. My cousin may be a duke, but his past will never allow him to live a respectable life or fit into society. He'll only use you, then discard you when he tires of you."

"Nay! You're wrong about him! Kit loves me and I love him. He was to call on Father and explain about us, but now you've ruined everything. Why, Winston? Why are you doing this?"

"To save you, of course," Winston lied smoothly. "You're going to marry me, Devon, do you understand? Your father expects us to wed before we return. Until you agree to become my wife you'll remain here. I don't care how long it takes. You'll learn to love me once you banish my cousin from your mind and heart. I'm not such a bad fellow. You were prepared to marry me once."

"I can't marry you, Winston, I told you that weeks ago."

"It doesn't matter that you've bedded Kit, my dear," Winston allowed magnaminously. "All that's in the past. After we're wed we'll travel abroad for a year or two and soon you'll forget that pirate ever existed. Your father would be thrilled should you return with a child in tow."

"Marriage is out of the question for us," Devon tried to explain. "Truth to tell, I can't marry anyone. I'm already—"

"Bloody hell, Devon, I've tried to be patient with you, but you are being exceedingly difficult. We'll see if your disposition improves after a period of isolation. Perhaps if you're allowed sufficient time to ponder your wicked ways you'll come to realize I'm offering a way to save your badly bruised reputation. I've always fancied you, my dear."

"You've always fancied my dowry," Devon corrected contemptuously. "Few men are generous enough or willing to overlook a woman's indiscretions unless money is involved. I know you're penniless, and no heiress would have you now that you've not even a title to offer. Besides, I can't believe Father would agree to this unless you deliberately lied to him."

"Have it your way." Winston shrugged, turning to leave. "Let me know when you change your mind."

"Wait! Don't leave me like this! I'm thirsty and hungry and—and filthy. I want a bath and food."

"I have no intention of starving or mistreating you, my dear," Winston said coolly. "I've hired a woman from the village to see to your needs. She's a deaf mute and has been told in sign language that you are slightly demented following the loss of a child. You'll be adequately cared for but not allowed to leave this room until you agree to our marriage." Then he was gone.

"Where am I, Winston? At least tell me that much!"

Her plea fell on deaf ears as the door was slammed in her face and securely locked from the other side.

"Damn you, Winston!" Devon sobbed, pounding on the door to relieve her frustration. "I'm already married!" The sound of absolute silence told her it was too late for confessions, Winston had removed himself to another part of the house.

A short time later the woman hired by Winston unlocked the door and sidled inside carrying a pitcher of fresh water and towels. She was middle-aged, tall and stout with the sturdy build of one accustomed to a lifetime of hard work. Her graying hair, pulled back in a severe bun, provided a perfect frame for her stern features. Yet Devon saw nothing in her dark eyes to indicate cruelty in her character. The woman eyed Devon warily but went efficiently about her work. Though Winston had said the servant was mute, Devon felt she had to try to communicate in some way.

"Please help me," she begged as the woman turned to leave. "Winston lied to you, he's holding me against my will."

Nothing registered in the servant's expression but a brief flash of compassion that swiftly faded when she recalled her instructions. She was being well paid to care for the poor demented soul. She left quickly to prepare a meal for her charge.

The next two weeks passed in a blur of suffocating boredom and intense anger on Devon's part. Her attempts to communicate with the mute servant failed miserably, as did her efforts to speak with Winston. She was confident that once he learned she was already married he'd lose all interest in her and release her.

As the days slid by Devon knew in her heart that Kit was turning London upside down looking for her. She wondered what had happened between Kit and her father when Kit appeared at her door and found her missing. It seemed inconceivable that her father hadn't told Kit where to find her once Kit explained everything to his satisfaction. Perhaps her father didn't know where to find her, Devon reasoned, searching for a plausible excuse for her father's failure to reveal her hiding place. She knew her father to be a stubborn man but not when his daughter's welfare was concerned. Just what had Winston told him?

Throughout her ordeal Devon's primary concern was her baby and keeping it from harm. Though Winston had never resorted to violence with her, she guarded the child in her womb jealously, fearing Winston might turn abusive once he learned her secret. She recalled how he had shelled Paradise at the cost of innocent lives without a smidgeon of remorse.

To Devon's chagrin, Winston ignored her for another week. All her efforts to escape were handily foiled by the stout servant who watched her like a hawk. When Winston finally did show himself, Devon was appalled at his appearance. Signs of dissipation clearly visible on his handsome features led her to believe he had been spending his lonely hours drinking far more than was his custom. His face was puffy, his eyes bloodshot.

"I hope you've come to your senses," he said sourly. "By now you must be thoroughly sick of your own company. Once you agree to become my bride you'll please not only me but your father. And you'll find your circumstances greatly improved. After we're wed we'll go on a grand tour; you can buy a new wardrobe and dine on the finest food the continent has to offer. What say you, my dear?"

Devon's answer astounded Winston as well as brought his world crashing down around his ears. "You simply must listen to me, Winston," she began with deceptive calm despite the wild tattoo of her heart. "I tried to tell you before why marriage is out of the question for us. I'm already married. Kit and I were legally wed months ago."

A blaze of anger turned Winston's features into an ugly mask. Blindly he struck out, catching Devon in the shoulder when she ducked, sending her sprawling across the bed.

"You wanton whore! You opened your legs for my cousin like a bitch in heat, caring little that he was a pirate and you were my intended bride. You women are all alike. You sicken me with your rounded thighs and jutting breasts, your sweating bodies and clinging ways. The thought of having to bed you makes me want to vomit, but I would have swallowed my revulsion and done my duty to get you with child and remain in your father's good graces. I'd have done anything for your inheritance, even though it made me physically ill."

Horrified, Devon watched helplessly as Winston continued to rant and rave. She hardly recognized him as the same man whose gentle wooing and flowery words had charmed her into an engagement months ago. And the terrible things he was saying! He sounded as if he hated women. She knew now that Kit had been right about Winston all along but she had been too stupid to see it. How had he managed to hide his true nature from her and most of their peers all these years?

Winston's angry tirade came to an end as abruptly as it began, leaving him sullen and withdrawn. Normally not a violent man, he turned away from Devon in obvious disgust. Her bombshell had left him more shaken than he cared to admit. His first thought was to wonder how Scarlett would react when she learned that Kit and Devon were already man and wife. Throw a fit, he reckoned, and was grateful he'd be nowhere around when she was told the news. She must be notified immediately. Locking the door behind him, he hastened to find one of his hirelings to send posthaste to London with a message for Scarlett and await further instructions.

"Scarlett, what in the deuce are you doing here?" Kit asked as he greeted the ex-pirate in his drawing room where she'd been cooling her heels.

"Where have you been keeping yourself, Diablo?" Scarlett asked archly. "I've seen little of you these past weeks. Have you no time for old friends?"

"I was under the assumption you were swamped with admirers these days." Kit's mouth slanted in a mocking smile. "You no longer have need of me, Scarlett."

"I'll always need you, Diablo," Scarlett said, her voice a husky whisper. "No other man can compare with you. Call yourself Kit, Diablo, or anything you want, I'll always find you fascinating. These dull creatures fawning over me and my money are poor excuses for men with their fancy duds and pompous airs. Give me a lusty buccaneer any day. This amnesty isn't all it's cracked up to be."

Scarlett put her arms around his neck and pressed her lush body to his. How many nights had she imagined stroking his hard-muscled shoulders, savoring the texture of his smooth, golden body, so lean and virile in comparison with her own softness? How many nights had she yearned to experience the sweet stimulation of his magic touch? Too many—far too many.

"You still want me, Diablo, I see it in your eyes," Scarlett murmured, her voice made ragged with desire. "And I want you. Touch me! Oh, please touch me, darling." In his anguished state he was vulnerable, as Scarlett shrewdly guessed. Her offer of a moment's oblivion her body could provide him was a temptation most men couldn't resist.

Taking his hand that rested at his side, she deliberately placed it on her breast, holding it there while she struggled to control the lust racing through her body. "Feel my heart, Diablo? It flutters like the wings of a hummingbird. All for you—only for you." She lifted her face. Her breath came thick and shallow as the tip of her tongue danced out to moisten her dry lips in eager anticipation of his kiss.

Her lips were red, inviting, slightly parted, her breath sweet. Had Kit not had a woman like Devon in his life he would have accepted Scarlett's generous offer instantly and responded with all the vigor his young, virile body afforded. Now it was out of the question. What he and Devon had together far surpassed the mere satisfaction of lust that Scarlett offered. Never would he defile the hallowed love that he and Devon shared by falling into Scarlett's silken web. No longer was he the notorious Diablo who loved and fought indiscriminately. He was Christopher Linley, Duke of Grenville, and Devon, wherever she might be, was his beloved duchess.

"If you're trying to seduce me, Scarlett, you've failed miserably," Kit said with cool disdain, his hand falling away from the soft mound of her breast. "I want no other woman but Devon. From the moment we met I knew she was the only woman I could ever love."

"Love! Bah!" blazed Scarlett contemptuously. "People like us don't need love to complicate our lives. Men are ruled by what's between their legs. Use your head for once in your life. If Devon loved you she'd be with you now instead of off somewhere with Winston. They're still engaged, aren't they?" she hinted slyly.

Kit's eyes narrowed dangerously. "Who told you Devon was with Winston?" Outwardly he was calm but inside he boiled like a witch's cauldron. Did Scarlett know something he didn't?

Unmindful of the anger bubbling below the surface of Kit's cool words, Scarlett continued blithely, "Why, Freddie Smythe told me he heard Devon and Winston had eloped and gone off on an extended honeymoon."

"The devil you say!" roared Kit. "Devon wouldn't do such a thing. She'd never marry Winston when—" Abruptly his words slid to a halt, aware that he was about to divulge information that did not concern Scarlett.

Scarlett watched Kit's face with avid delight. It had been part of her plan for Winston to casually mention to a few of his friends that he and Devon were eloping. And of course Freddie had been the first to hear it. The young man had been angry enough at losing his lover to spread the gossip throughout London. Eventually Kit had heard the rumor but knew better than to believe such rot. Kyle and Akbar, who helped him in his fruitless quest, had also reported hearing gossip to that effect, but in light of what Lord Harvey had revealed before suffering a stroke, Kit knew that Devon had been an unwilling participant in the supposed elopement.

"If Devon isn't with Winston, then where is she?" Scarlett asked sweetly. "Have you hidden her away somewhere?"

"Get the hell out of here, Scarlett, I've had all I

can take of you," Kit gritted from between clenched teeth. "You've got nothing I want. If your heart is set on becoming a duchess you'll have to look elsewhere. Please excuse me, I have an appointment. You know the way out." Turning on his heel, he stomped from the room, leaving Scarlett shaking in impotent rage.

"Bastard!"

"Is the earl improving, doctor?" Kit asked as he paced anxiously outside Lord Harvey's sickroom. Every day for the past three weeks he'd kept a vigil outside the earl's door, hoping for improvement in the man's condition. His brief visits to the sickroom only added to his frustration, for the stricken earl had yet to utter a lucid word.

"'Tis my belief a full recovery is entirely possible." the doctor beamed. "Lord Harvey is a strong man, and he seems determined to recover. I'd like to credit my medicine, but in truth 'tis the earl's strong will that's keeping him alive."

"How long before he can communicate?"

"I have every reason to be optimistic, but I can't predict a time. 'Tis in God's hands."

"May I attempt to speak with my father-in-law?" Kit asked.

"Of course, just see that you don't tire him," the doctor advised. "I'll be back tomorrow."

Kit entered the sickroom and nodded to the housekeeper, who quietly left the room at Kit's signal.

"Lord Harvey," Kit prodded with an urgency that belied his calm exterior. "Can you hear me?"

At first the earl remained absolutely motionless, then slowly, oh so slowly, one eye cranked open, then the other.

"Can you hear me, Your Grace?" Kit repeated with an excitement he hadn't felt in weeks.

An awareness that had been absent since the earl's seizure flickered in the watery depths of his eyes, and Kit's spirits soared. The old man's pale lips opened, but try as he might, nothing but garbled words issued forth. Words without meaning or clarity. Then the light faded, replaced by a familiar blankness that pierced Kit's heart. Please God, he prayed fervently, let him find his love before Winston forced her into something beyond her control.

"Rest, Your Grace," he said kindly. "I'll return tomorrow. Perhaps by then you'll feel more like talking."

"You have a visitor, m'lady," the dignified butler announced when Scarlett returned to the sumptuously appointed house she'd purchased with her ill-gotten gains. "A rather—er—disreputable-looking fellow who says he has an urgent message that requires an immediate answer. He's waiting in the drawing room, which I'm certain the house-keeper will want to fumigate after he leaves."

"Thank you, Jeevers," Scarlett said, smothering a smile. She'd dealt too many times with unsavory characters during her adventurous life to be offended by one more of their ilk. She wondered if the proper butler would look down his long nose at her if he knew he was employed by a notorious pirate captain. "I'll take care of it."

His disapproval evident, Jeevers replied, "As you will, m'lady. I'll be nearby if you have need of me."

Nodding her dismissal, Scarlett entered the drawing room to find a tall, gaunt man carefully examining a priceless sculpture that was part of her pirate's loot. His filthy, ill-fitting clothes gave him the appearance of a scarecrow. His obsequious smile revealed sparse yellowed teeth, and his offensive odor hinted at an aversion to bathing.

"Be careful with that, my man, 'tis worth a fortune," Scarlett snapped. Her commanding tone brought the man sharply to attention, and he released his hold on the sculpture immediately.

"The name is Tibbs, m'lady," the man said, pulling off his cap and bobbing his head.

"I understand you have a message for me, Tibbs." Scarlett wasted no time on formalities.

"Aye, m'lady, traveled night and day, I did, to bring it 'ere."

"Well," Scarlett said impatiently, "where is it?"

Hastily Tibbs extracted a much creased and begrimed slip of paper from a pocket and handed it to Scarlett. Wasting no time, Scarlett devoured the words, her frown deepening as she reached the end of the brief message. Then she flung the offending paper to the floor and flew into a rage.

"The bleedin' bastard married the slut!" she cried out viciously. "Why didn't he tell me?" Cursing and pacing, Scarlett had nearly forgotten Tibbs until she saw him cowering before her. "Have you read this?"

"N—nay, I 'aven't 'ad much schoolin'."

Satisfied, Scarlett said, "You'll have the answer before you leave. Go around to the kitchen, cook will fix you something to eat. You can sleep in the stable and start out at first light tomorrow. A servant will bring my message to you along with your breakfast. Be off with you, man!"

"Aye, m'lady," Tibbs obeyed, anxious to have a hot meal under his belt. Because his employer had stressed speed he'd wasted little time on amenities, camping out most of the time and eating cold food that had been packed for him.

Scarlett spent most of the evening forming her reply to Winston's startling revelation. If the perverted coward thought the news would alter her plans, he was badly mistaken. Scarlett was still determined to have Kit no matter what drastic measures it took. As a pirate she had made life-and-death decisions every day, so what did one more matter? Her message to Winston was concise. "Kill Devon."

Three days later Winston read Scarlett's terse note, blanching with horror at the words. A bolt of terror coursed through him at Scarlett's order. What would that vicious pirate do to him if he failed to follow instructions? he wondered bleakly. Kill him? Probably. Spread vicious gossip about him and Freddie, leaving their reputations in shambles? That too was a distinct possibility. But could he kill Devon? Nay. If Scarlett wanted Kit badly enough to kill, she'd have to do it herself. A second message was prepared and sent posthaste, once again carried by a disgruntled Tibbs. Winston's words were, "If you want Devon dead, do it yourself."

Tibbs cringed beneath a barrage of curses as Scarlett flung Winston's note in his face. "That lily-livered coward! How dare he defy me. I'll see him rot in hell for betraying my trust. He took my money in good faith, yet refuses to do my bidding. I can see this is something I have to do myself if I want it done right. Remain in London until I'm ready to leave for Cornwall, you can drive the coach for me. But there are things I must do first. You can sleep in the stable and eat in the kitchen."

Somehow Tibbs found the courage to protest. "Nay, m'lady, I've 'ad all of the country I can take. I don't like bein' away from me digs so long. Me mates will be wonderin' what 'appened to me. I'll not be returnin' to Cornwall. Ye can drive yer bleedin' coach yerself, I ain't goin'. This situation is gettin' too deep fer me."

So saying he turned and fled, leaving Scarlett staring open-mouthed at his departing back. Nothing had gone right since she'd left the rolling deck of the *Red Witch* and men she understood and who understood her, she reflected with an angry toss of her flaming tresses. Obviously she could depend on no one but herself in this world of fools and fancy-dressed idiots.

Her eyes narrowed into catlike slits, Scarlett set about planning revenge on Winston Linley. First things first, she thought, and smiled deviously. Before she departed for Cornwall she'd make damn certain all of London was rocked to its core by the news of the perverted love life shared by Winston and Freddie Smythe. Neither of them would be able to show their face in town again without being openly ridiculed.

Within hours Scarlett had planted the seeds of malicious gossip throughout the city. But if things went her way, Winston wouldn't be alive to hear any of it. Three days after receiving Winston's note, Scarlett left London, well pleased with her scurrilous deeds. With that out of the way, she could concentrate on ridding herself of Diablo's wife. Once Devon's death was reported, she'd give Diablo sufficient time to recover, then press her suit while he was still suffering and vulnerable. Aye, Scarlett reflected gleefully, she knew men and was confident of her ability to lure Diablo to the altar once Devon was disposed of.

Chapter Twenty

Devon languished in her bedroom prison while a vindictive Scarlett was planning her short future. Since Winston learned of her marriage Devon had seen nothing of him. She was adequately provided for and her needs attended to by the dour servant whose name she had yet to learn. She was allowed to bathe regularly, given a change of clothes, and fed nourishing but plain fare. And consequently her child thrived, evidenced by her increasing waistline, which was disguised by the ill fit of the clothing provided her.

For exercise Devon paced the room, back and forth, back and forth, until the mute servant took pity on her and accompanied her outside for brief strolls twice a day. During those outings Devon surreptitiously studied her surroundings, but they told her nothing about where she was being imprisoned. And the hawk-eyed servant remained staunchly by her side the entire time. Devon felt in her bones that something was amiss, the very atmosphere crackled with tension. Call it intuition, but Devon existed in a high state of expectancy, waiting with bated breath for something to happen.

It seemed inconceivable that her father hadn't relented and told Kit where she was being held. Assuming he knew, of course. And of late she began to wonder about many things, including exactly what Winston had told her father about Kit, and whether he was aware of Winston's sexual preferences. Devon couldn't imagine her father falling in with Winston's plans if he knew the kind of man he was dealing with.

The dilemma facing Winston was nearly more than he could cope with. If he remained at the hunting lodge he could expect Scarlett to show up and demand her pound of flesh. Winston never bargained for murder when he agreed to Scarlett's harebrained scheme. Marrying Devon was one thing, murdering her was another. Except for her bullheadedness in refusing to marry him, Winston didn't hate Devon. Yet he realized that if he defied Scarlett he'd end up as dead as Devon was likely to be. Of course he could release Devon to find her way to London and safety, then quietly disappear himself and hope Scarlett wouldn't stalk him. It would be difficult without money, but there seemed to be little alternative. Those were his options, none of them attractive, when he decided to hie himself to the nearest tavern and drown his problems in a bottle using the last of the coins given him by Scarlett.

Leaving the mute servant in charge, Winston rode his hired mount to the village where the

Hound and Hare stood at the end of a busy street. He had visited it on several occasions these past weeks and was greeted with familiarity by the innkeeper.

The tavern was crowded, it being the time of day when workers gathered for companionship and revelry. He found an empty table and ordered a bottle from the slovenly waitress, settling himself for a lengthy stay. He was well into the bottle when a voice he'd never expected to hear again interrupted his solitude.

"By God, Winnie, I never thought to find you so easily!"

"Freddie!" Winston exclaimed, ogling his handsome lover with astonishment. "How in bloody hell did you find me?"

"Pure luck, old son, pure luck."

"Sit down, Freddie, and tell me what brings you out here to this wilderness."

"You've had no word from London? Heard no gossip?" Freddie quizzed sharply.

"Nothing of importance," Winston shrugged, discounting Scarlett's brief missives. "Why, has something happened?"

"You may as well know," Freddie sighed bleakly, "seeing as how you're involved. It seems, old son, that our secret is out. Our—er—past intimacies are being bandied about London and spreading like wildfire. My parents are livid. They've kicked me out of the house and disinherited me. I've made them the laughing stock of London Town and they'll never forgive me."

"My God, Freddie, I'm sorry! I never thought the bitch would actually do it. I know what it means to lose one's birthright."

"The money is no problem, Winnie, I've a private fortune of my own, left to me by my doting grandmother. But what did you mean? You spoke as if you knew who blew the whistle on us. Was it Devon?"

"Nay, not Devon," Winston said bitterly. "Scarlett DeFoe."

"Lady DeFoe? But why would she . . ."

"It's a long story, Freddie. Join me in a drink and I'll explain."

When Winston had finished his story, Freddie shook his head in wonder.

"You can't imagine, old son, how hurt I was when it leaked out that you and Devon had eloped. I knew you two were engaged and your marriage inevitable, but after all those postponements I had hopes that you'd finally come to your senses. Grenville had his men out scouring London for Devon. That wild Turk was especially fierce. I assumed that Milford knew where you and Devon had disappeared to but withheld the information for reasons unknown to anyone but himself. And then I heard the old boy had a seizure and was hanging onto life by a thread."

"I'm sorry to hear about the earl, Freddie," Winston said. "I hope he makes it."

"Did Devon finally consent to marry you? The way Grenville has been acting of late, you'd think Devon was his fiancé instead of yours. It's all so confusing. I can't believe Lady DeFoe threatened to take your life if you didn't fall in with her plans. What are you going to do?"

"As it turns out, Devon isn't free to marry me. She's already married to my cousin."

"Grenville? But how? I didn't even know they were acquainted until just recently." Suddenly he snapped his fingers, comprehension dawning. "By

jove, I remember now. Wasn't she kidnapped by
Diablo the day he escaped from the gallows? I recall
that escapade set London on its ears. Didn't she
return and disappear again on the eve of your
wedding? Seems like the earl said something about
her going to the country to make up her mind."

"You've got the right of it, Freddie. One day I'll
tell you the whole story, if I live so long. Including
what drove Kit to take up piracy. But at the present
time I'm enmeshed in a devious plot I've no
stomach for. But before I get into it, tell me how
you found me."

"After being booted from my happy home,"
Freddie began earnestly, "I made the rounds of all
my friends. They treated me like an outcast, refusing to receive me or acknowledge my presence.
Then I began hanging around the waterfront dives,
hoping to book passage to France and start life
anew. I've enough money to do as I please with my
life. While drowning my sorrows one night, feeling
particularly bereft after hearing that you and
Devon had eloped, I met a disreputable character
by the name of Tibbs."

"Tibbs! He was my hireling who failed to return
on his last trip to London at my behest."

"The same," Freddie concurred. "He was well
into his cups and began spouting off about being
stuck in Cornwall these past weeks, hired by a man
to abduct a beautiful woman who refused to marry
him. According to Tibbs, he got tired of being
messenger boy and just stayed in London during his
last trip carrying messages back and forth to a
madwoman. After listening to your tale, I assume
the madwoman is Lady DeFoe.

"I asked Tibbs to describe the lady being held in
Cornwall against her will and he gladly obliged. The

description matched Devon perfectly. Then I put two and two together but still couldn't come up with four. Abduction didn't sound like you no matter how desperate you might be. So I decided to hie myself to Cornwall to see for myself. There was nothing to keep me in London. Discrete questioning provided me with the directions to Penzance, but by then Tibbs was too drunk to be of further use. I left immediately and stopped at the first inn I came to in Penzance, intending to seek knowledge of you. Imagine my astonishment when I saw you sitting here."

"I'm glad you've come, Freddie, but it still doesn't solve my problem."

"What problem? Devon is already married. What choice do you have but to release her and allow her to return to her husband?"

"Scarlett wants Devon dead."

Freddie blanched. He hadn't a violent bone in his body, and what Winston told him shocked him badly. "Jesus, Winnie, you're no bloody killer."

"I know, that's why I told Scarlett I couldn't do it. She's a devil, Freddie, disguised as a beautiful woman. She's proved herself capable of evil by spreading gossip about our relationship and ruining our reputation. She's promised to kill me if I failed her, and she's vindictive enough to do it. She also wants Kit badly enough to do away with Devon. Hell, Freddie, I don't know what to do!" Winston's anguished plea tore at Freddie's soft heart.

"Calm down," Freddie advised, his mind working furiously. "First of all, killing Devon is out of the question, we both agree to that. Second, you've got to get back to wherever you're keeping Devon and release her immediately. And last, the sooner you place yourself out of Scarlett's reach, the better.

The same goes for Grenville. Though I scarcely know him, he doesn't strike me as a man who forgives easily. Kidnapping his wife was a despicable deed."

"The first two can be accomplished easily enough, but the third is more difficult. It takes money to travel abroad."

"I've got plenty of money, Winnie. Come to France with me. I hear the French are more tolerant of our kind than the English. There are bound to be several ships in Penzance or Land's End bound for France. I'll inquire and book passage for the two of us. Later we can travel to Italy, or wherever you want."

Suddenly Winston's prospects didn't appear so bleak anymore. Freddie's providential arrival had been a godsend. His cool head and clear thinking— not to mention his money—had painted an entirely different outcome to his agonizing dilemma.

"You'd do that for me?"

"Of course, Winnie, all we've got left is each other. I've alienated my family, they never want to see me again. And my friends shun me like poison."

"Then we'd best leave now. Scarlett could show up at any time."

His shoulders slumped in dejection, Kit slowly opened the door to Lord Harvey's bedroom, fully prepared to encounter the same suffocating disappointment he'd experienced each time he visited the earl's sickroom. It seemed as if fate were conspiring against him and he'd never find Devon. She seemed to have disappeared from the face of the earth. Though he'd hired a veritable army, no one had turned up a single clue about Devon's whereabouts. That bastard Winston had chosen his hiding place well.

Shortly after Winston and Devon disappeared, gossip mongers had themselves a field day hinting at their probable elopement. Jealousy nearly killed Kit, but the knowledge that Devon harbored no feelings for Winston and was being held against her will saved him. Recalling how, when he was a young lad, he had surprised the eighteen-year-old Winston in a disgusting act with an older man, Kit felt confident Winston had little use for Devon as a woman. It shocked him that Winston had tried this crazy stunt, for his cousin was neither very imaginative nor excessively brave.

Yet Kit knew of no one else who would aid Winston in a scheme that could hardly succeed. Surely Devon had told Winston that she was a married woman, Kit reflected, more puzzled than ever by his cousin's devious thinking. Why hadn't Devon been released once Winston found marriage to her out of the question? Why hadn't Kyle or Akbar turned up a clue to Winston's destination? Someone in this city had to know. If Winston harmed Devon in any way, he'd make the man wish he'd never been born.

Then, just yesterday Kit had been privy to a rumor that Winston and Freddie Smythe had been carrying on a homosexual relationship. The rumor spread like wildfire, and Freddie's parents had banished their son from their home and disinherited him. Thinking, hoping, that Freddie might offer a clue to where Winston had taken Devon, Kit attempted to locate the young man, once more meeting with disappointment. Hounded by ridicule, Freddie had apparently hied himself from the scene of his embarrassment. Another dead end.

The first thing Kit noticed as he entered Lord Harvey's room was that the windows had been thrown open and the drapes drawn to allow fresh air and sunshine to circulate. Previously the room had remained darkened and suffocatingly close. Then he saw the earl sitting up in bed, clear-eyed but obviously highly agitated.

"Thank—God—you've come," Lord Harvey gasped, finding difficulty in forming the words. "I—asked the doctor to send for you—hours ago."

"I haven't been home, Your Grace," Kit confided, elated to find the earl awake and lucid. "This past month has been pure hell for me. I've prayed day and night for your full recovery, while searching relentlessly for my wife."

"Your wife," repeated the earl slowly. "So I didn't dream it. You and Devon are wed. Does she love you?"

"I have every reason to believe she does." The earl nodded, satisfied. "And I love her more than my own life," Kit revealed. "Please, sir, if you know where Winston has taken Devon, I beg you to tell me."

"Aye, Grenville, I'll tell you, but first tell me all that's transpired since I've been disabled."

"Not much, Your Grace, and please call me Kit. I'm worried that Winston hasn't released Devon once he learned we were married. It leads me to believe that something terrible has happened to her. It's been four weeks and I've turned London upside down to find her."

"Four weeks! Good Lord, that long? Winston's a bloody fool. He's taken her to Cornwall. Where exactly, I don't know."

"Cornwall! God's bones, why didn't I think of it before? I'd completely forgotten about the family hunting lodge near Penzance. 'Tis remote enough to provide strict privacy yet easily accessible. I'll leave immediately."

"Grenville—Kit, wait!" Kit turned, chafing impatiently to be off. "I want you to know that for my daughter's sake I'm willing to forget all that's transpired in the past. Devon must have seen some redeeming qualities in you or she wouldn't have chosen you. Bring her back, Kit, and as long as you make her happy I'll not interfere in your lives."

"My finding Devon doesn't depend on your forgiveness, Your Grace. I'd do it regardless. Devon is everything to me. Even when she betrayed the secret of my stronghold I loved her. I was angry enough to slay her but too consumed by love to wish her harm."

"What?" the earl gasped, stunned. "You blamed Devon for that? Nay, lad, 'twas Le Vautour who betrayed your secret. Devon refused to speak a word against you. I deliberately kept the knowledge of Winston's raid from her, fearing she'd hate us both for so cowardly an act. Though I take full responsibility for sending Winston to Paradise, I didn't order or condone his taking of innocent lives."

It was as if a great load had been taken off Kit's broad shoulders. "I believe you, Your Grace," Kit allowed, "and thank you for telling me." Then, seeing how quickly the man was tiring, he added, "Rest and get well. Fear not, I'll bring your daughter home safely. And if Winston has harmed her, you'll have his head on a platter."

The sound of voices somewhere in the house brought Devon instantly alert. At least two male voices drifted to her beyond the door. One be-

longed to Winston and the other sounded vaguely
familiar. She hadn't seen the mute servant since
early in the day, and that seemed strange also, for
no one had brought her dinner. Suddenly the
doorknob turned and Devon rushed forward, ready
to assault Winston with harsh recriminations. How
dare he keep her prisoner? If he didn't fear Kit's
retribution he was a bigger fool than she thought.
Kit would find her soon, she adamantly believed,
stifling a smidgeon of doubt.

It worried Devon that Winston hadn't already
released her. It was almost as if he feared letting her
go. Was there someone or something he feared
more than Kit?

Her pregnancy was another reason for Devon to
fret. The past month had wrought a great change in
her appearance. Previously her pregnancy had remained largely undetected. Now into her fourth
month, she seemed to have blossomed in more ways
than one. Her breasts sorely tested the fabric of her
bodice and her stomach curved outward into a
small, hard bulge.

The door opened, and Winston stepped somewhat hesitantly into the room.

"You look well, Devon," he said. His words,
meant to appease, only spurred her anger.

"No thanks to you!" Devon returned. Her eyes
blazed with angry fire and a reddish tint crept up
her neck. "Have you finally come to your senses
and decided to let me go?"

Winston cleared his throat nervously. "Ahem,
why—er—aye, you're free to leave. I've already
dismissed your servant."

Stunned, Devon stared uncomprehendingly at
the man she might have married had she not been
tempted by the devil and learned to love him.

"You—you mean it? My God, Winston, why did you wait so long? Why didn't you let me go immediately when I told you I was already married? You've earned nothing for your despicable act except Kit's hatred."

"Winston acted on my orders," a feminine voice from behind Winston said. "He kept you away from Diablo. And I'm here to see that the separation is made permanent."

A loud groan escaped Winston's lips. He had hoped to be gone long before Scarlett arrived to complicate matters. But Scarlett's untimely appearance answered many of the questions that had plagued Devon since Winston had spirited her from her home. Though Winston had proven himself capable of dastardly deeds, she had been mystified by his refusal to release her. It did not surprise Devon to learn that Scarlett was behind her ordeal. Somehow she didn't feel her life threatened by Winston, though she had to admit he acted with incredible stupidity. But Scarlett was another matter entirely, for Devon suspected Scarlett fully capable of committing murder.

"It seems I arrived not a moment too soon," Scarlett said coolly, her green eyes glittering maliciously. "I knew Winston was a spineless pervert but didn't think him witless as well. What did you think to gain by letting Devon go?"

Winston swallowed the lump of fear choking him. "I'm through with your crazy scheme, Scarlett. Murder isn't my way. I would have married Devon, but that's impossible now."

"Murder!" gasped Devon, looking from Winston to Scarlett. Apparently Scarlett wanted her out of Kit's life badly enough to kill her. "This isn't the Caribbean where piracy and murder flourish,

Scarlett. You accepted amnesty in good faith and promised to live within the law. You'll be punished, you know."

"I'll take my chances," Scarlett replied, shoving Winston aside as she took a menacing step toward Devon.

"Don't let her do this, Winston!" Devon cried, flinging out her hand in mute appeal.

The tip of Winston's tongue flicked out to moisten his dry lips. Where was Freddie? he wondered anxiously. He'd left the house to ready their horses for a hasty departure and by now would be wondering what was keeping him. If there was some way he could stall Scarlett . . .

Realizing she couldn't depend on Winston, Devon turned to confront Scarlett, fear for her child making her desperate. "Kit is lost to you, Scarlett. Do you seriously think he'd turn in love to the woman who killed his wife?"

"Wife! Bah! *I* was meant to be Kit's duchess, not you. Who will tell him? There will be no witnesses left to tell the tale."

Winston's loud gasp brought a wicked smile to Scarlett's beautiful features. "You can't involve me in murder, Scarlett. I'm leaving," he blustered with false bravado.

"You're not going anywhere, Linley," Scarlett warned, whipping forth a cutlass she had concealed beneath her voluminous cloak. Only then did Devon realize that Scarlett was garbed as she'd first seen her, in tight trousers, white silk shirt, and high black boots. Not only was there a sword in her hand but a small arsenal strapped around her slim waist. "Stand here where I can see you." She motioned to a place beside Devon.

Sidling around Scarlett, Winston stood hesitantly

beside Devon, facing the notorious pirate while Scarlett stood with her back to the open door. She brandished the cutlass in their faces, enjoying their terror. It was just like old times when people quailed before her and the power of life and death lay as near as her cutlass. She savored the heady feeling to the fullest.

"Once you two are disposed of, no one need know what happened. Your murders will remain a mystery. I came to Penzance by ship, my own *Red Witch,* and rented a horse in town. My face was muffled and I spoke not a dozen words. I could have been anyone."

"Penzance!" exclaimed Devon. "I'm in Cornwall! Damn you, Winston, for bringing me here. If Scarlett doesn't kill you, I will."

"Enough!" Scarlett snarled, possessed by the need for vengeance and consumed by jealousy. Devon stood between her and all she desired. "You first, Linley. I'm going to enjoy this. Society will thank me for ridding it of a man of your perverted tastes."

The cutlass in Scarlett's hand pressed ominously into the soft flesh of Winston's neck. He whimpered in terror as a drop of blood trickled down his throat.

Devon stared in horror, powerless to stop Scarlett. Once Winston lay dead she knew it would only be a matter of seconds before she joined him. And her baby would die with her.

Just then the figure of a man loomed in the doorway behind Scarlett, his hand raised menacingly. Before Devon had time to blink, the heavy candlestick held in their rescuer's hand came crashing down upon Scarlett's head. The cutlass clattered from Scarlett's hand, and she began a slow spiral to the floor. Devon's gaze shifted from the pirate's prone form to the man bending over Winston, cooing and fussing with grave concern.

"Did the witch hurt you, Winnie?" Freddie asked, dabbing his handkerchief at the thin line of blood oozing from the tiny puncture in Winston's neck. "When you failed to meet me outside I came to see what was keeping you. And lucky I did. Scarlett must have entered through the rear entrance, for I swear I didn't see her."

"I'm so grateful, Freddie," Winston croaked. His face was white, his voice quivering with fright. Never had he been so close to death.

"Freddie Smythe, what are you doing here?" Devon challenged. "Are you involved in all this?"

"Nay, Devon, Freddie is innocent," Winston quickly defended. "'Tis a long story and one I have no time to divulge. Suffice it to say that Scarlett's vicious tongue made it impossible for Freddie to remain in London so he came looking for me."

"Vicious tongue? I don't—" Then suddenly comprehension dawned. Everything Kit had said about Winston was true. Obviously Winston could never have been a husband to her, as she had begun to realize weeks ago. It rankled to think that he only wanted her for her money. From the very beginning it had been her money, not herself—never herself.

"You're—you're vile, Winston Linley!" she cried, shocked by what she'd discovered. "And you, too, Freddie. I'd never dreamed you two could be—that you—" Her tirade trailed off as she was unable to understand the perverted acts the two men engaged in.

"We've got to get out of here," Freddie urged, ignoring Devon as he cast a wary eye on Scarlett.

She hadn't moved a muscle since being clubbed, and he wanted to keep it that way. "No telling when that bitch will stir."

"Is—is she alive?" Devon asked.

Dropping to one knee, Freddie felt for Scarlett's pulse. "Aye, she's alive. Too bloody tough to die. Let's go, Winnie, before she regains her senses. I don't fancy being skewered at the end of her sword." He turned to leave, Winston hard on his heels.

"Wait! What about me?" Devon was incensed to think they could leave without a thought for her safety.

Freddie frowned, as if suddenly remembering her. "You'd best leave too, Devon," he urged "From what little I heard, Scarlett wants your life. Winston and I are off to Land's End. I heard a ship is sailing for France on the morning's tide. If we're fortunate our past won't follow us there. You're welcome to accompany us if you want."

"Nay," Devon demurred. "I must get back to London. To Father—and Kit."

"Then you'll have to find your own way," Winston said impatiently. "I value my skin too much to remain in England. If Scarlett doesn't do me in, Kit will. Please believe that I never intended to hurt you. Aye, I needed your money, but once I learned you were married to my cousin I was willing to go on to greener pastures. But Scarlett made it all but impossible. She learned about me and Freddie and threatened us with exposure if I didn't comply with her wishes. I couldn't let her ruin Freddie, so I gave in. But I never would have killed you."

"Here," Freddie said, handing Devon several

gold coins. "You'll probably find Scarlett's mount tethered at the rear of the house. Take it and make your way to London. Good luck."

Good riddance, Devon thought as the sound of pounding hooves faded into the distance. Depositing the coins in her pocket, she grabbed her cloak, stepped gingerly around the unconscious Scarlett, and made her way to the back door with a haste born of fear.

At least she now knew she was in Cornwall and could make her way home easily enough. Devon didn't relish riding horseback the long distance to London in her delicate condition and thought it best to go first to Penzance and hire a coach and driver.

She found Scarlett's mount tethered to a tree, contentedly munching grass. Leading him to a rock, she hoisted herself on his broad back, and with the last rays of the sun to guide her, headed in the direction she assumed Penzance to be. Actually, it was a wild guess, for she had no idea where the hunting lodge was situated. Darkness descended on the wild moors not thirty minutes later, and she became hopelessly lost.

Riding was out of the question in the darkness, for Devon couldn't risk falling and harming her child. Sliding from the saddle, she gripped the reins in her hand and led the frisky animal over the rough terrain, tripping over roots and stones until she called a halt for safety's sake. Not a glimmer of moonlight lit her way. Nor were there stars to lend her comfort. To add to her misery, a cold drizzle pelted her, and she pulled her cloak tightly about her to ward off the penetrating chill.

A loud clap of thunder rumbled across the heavens and a streak of lightning hurtled to earth, frightening the horse so badly it reared high on its haunches, pulling the reins from Devon's nerveless fingers. With its ears plastered to its head it bolted off into the darkness.

"Damnation!" Devon spewed helplessly as she watched the frightened animal crash through the night. What was she to do now?

Chapter Twenty-One

Inky darkness flirted with the empty corners of the room as Scarlett struggled through the suffocating layers of unconsciousness. Her head was splitting and her hand came away with blood when she touched the swelling that throbbed so painfully. Intuitively Scarlett knew she was alone in the house, and a stream of unladylike curses spewed from her mouth. What had hit her? Who had hit her? God, her head hurt. When she found Winston and Devon, they'd pay dearly for the pain she was suffering.

Struggling to her feet, Scarlett slowly made her way from room to room, lighting a candle to guide her way. Nothing but gloom and darkness lingered in the lodge, and her first instinct was to leave immediately. But the roar of thunder and rush of rain changed her mind. Aware that rain would hamper her efforts to track her prey, she settled in a comfortable chair to await the coming of dawn. No one could travel far on a night like this, she reasoned as she drifted off to sleep.

Kit approached the lodge on silent feet. Chilled, hungry, and drenched to the skin, he had ridden till he was ready to fall out of the saddle, and he prayed it wasn't too late. Devon had been missing so long, all kinds of terrible things could have happened to her by now. If Winston had harmed her he wouldn't live long enough to regret it.

The house was dark save for one feeble light flickering from the front window. Circling around to the rear, Kit found the door open and entered, moving with the grace and stealth of a stalking cat. The winking candle drew him like a fluttering moth to the chair where Scarlett lay slumped in slumber. At first glimpse Kit assumed that the sleeping figure was Winston, but something about the long slender legs stretched out in repose soon disabused him of that notion.

As he sidled closer, Kit's keen eyes encountered the curving sweep of a feminine hip, the high arch of a breast. The fiery gleam of long red tresses caught and reflected the candle's dim glow. "Scarlett!" Kit hissed from between clenched teeth. He should have guessed she was mixed up in this, that Winston was neither bright enough nor brave enough to attempt something so foolhardy on his own.

Drawing his sword, Kit pricked Scarlett's shapely thigh, his gray eyes cold as cement as he watched her awake with a start. "Diablo! What—how did you get here?"

Kit was dressed all in black, reminiscent of all those years he'd lived as Diablo the pirate. His flowing white shirt was tucked into black trousers that hugged his muscular thighs like second skin. A bright red kerchief covered his jet hair, and the the beginnings of a blue-black beard darkened his cheeks and chin. Shiny boots fashioned of the softest leather clung to his calves, widening at the knees. A gold loop swung from one ear. He looked every bit as dangerous as he had when balancing on the windswept deck of the *Devil Dancer*.

"By horseback, all the way from London," Kit snarled, answering her question. "Where is Devon?"

"Your *wife* is gone," Scarlett replied with bitter emphasis.

"Where? What have you and Winston done with her? If you've harmed one hair of her head . . ." His words trailed off, but his implied threat hung in the tense stillness.

"As far as I know, no harm has come to her. She left with Winston after I was attacked." Scarlett's pouting lips and narrowed green eyes warned Kit that Devon wouldn't have escaped so easily had she been left to Scarlett's tender mercies.

"Are you the brains behind Winston's rotten act?" Kit asked disgustedly. "No one knows better than I just how capable you are of dastardly deeds, including murder. What did you hope to gain from Devon's disappearance? Would you actually have done away with her?"

"My original plan was for Winston to marry Devon, and if she refused, to keep her under lock and key until she complied. But it didn't work out that way. We learned too late that you and Devon were already man and wife. You cur! *I* deserve to be your duchess, not Devon," Scarlett spat. "Marriage

was never important in the world we lived in, but
amnesty brought many changes in my life. Now I
want the respectability of marriage. I want to be
your duchess, Diablo," she said with a sudden
seductive smile. "You know me better than anyone."

"Aye, I know you," Kit concurred, a sneer hanging on the corner of his mouth. "I was a fool not to
suspect you were involved. I realize now you were
the one who told Le Vautour how to get to Paradise.
I doubt that Winston has the guts to commit
murder, but you do. Was jealousy your motive? Or
is viciousness so ingrained in your soul you know
no other way of life?"

"Damn you, Diablo! I've never loved any man
but you! I accepted amnesty on your account,
despite the fact I'd rather spend my days with my
feet on a rolling deck and spindrift blowing in my
face. I followed you to England hoping you'd return
my love, but instead you ran into Devon's arms."

"I've given you no indication I cared for you,"
Kit said coolly, unmoved by Scarlett's passionate
words. "And I've already wasted too much time
listening to your nonsense. I want to know, and I
want to know now, where Winston has taken
Devon."

"I'm telling you I don't know! They were both
here when I arrived several hours ago, but . . ."

"Go on." Kit's sword wavered menacingly before
Scarlett's nose.

"When I was—er—talking to them, someone
came up behind me and struck me on the head.
When I came to hours later, the house was empty.
Then it started to rain and I decided to wait till
morning before—" Her mouth snapped shut, un-

willing to divulge her true purpose in coming to Cornwall. But Kit knew exactly what Scarlett had intended to say.

"How did you find out Devon and I were married?" Silence. "Did Winston tell you?" More silence. "You might as well confess, for I'll find out soon enough." The point of his sword pricked the tender skin of her upper arm ever so gently.

"You bloody bastard! Aye, Winston told me and I ordered him to kill the little witch. But the cowardly pervert refused. So I came to do the job myself. But first I made damn certain Winston and his loverboy were exposed and their perversions made public knowledge."

Panting with repressed rage, Scarlett paused to catch her breath. "But your whore escaped me, and so did Winston. I'm only sorry I didn't find them before you arrived."

Kit's eyes were as cold as stone, his face implacable. "Devon is my wife; don't you dare call her names. Get up. You're coming with me."

"I hoped when I told Le Vautour how to reach Paradise that was the last I'd see of the witch," Scarlett complained bitterly.

"Hold your tongue and move," Diablo ordered tersely.

Glancing out the window, Scarlett noted that mauve streaks dusted the eastern sky and rays of early morning sun had chased nearly all the clouds away. Traces of moisture still clung to the branches and leaves and sparkled like giant teardrops amid damp blades of grass. Unwinding her long legs, she rose from the chair.

"Now what?" she asked.

"I'm taking you to a friend for safekeeping while I find Devon. Later, I'll decide what's to be done with you. Had you harmed Devon I'd have killed you without a qualm. And I still might. But I have no time for you now. Cormac is man enough to handle you until I return."

Prodding Scarlett with the point of his sword, Kit pushed her out the door to where his mount was tethered. After disarming her of the arsenal of weapons attached to her body, he hoisted her in the saddle, lashing her hands to the pummel. Then in one agile leap he sprang up behind her.

"Diablo, my devilish friend, what brings you to my remote castle?" Cormac's laughing blue eyes settled on Scarlett's shapely form and flaming head, and his shaggy brows rose to meet the bushy lock of ebony hair trailing down his forehead. "Who might the lady be?"

"I need your help, Cormac," Kit said, his expression grim as he pulled Scarlett from the saddle.

"You have it," boomed Cormac. "Join me for breakfast while you tell me what you want of me. The tale should prove quite interesting." While he spoke, his appreciative gaze lingered longingly on the exquisite redhead who appeared not the least bit cowed by Kit's rough handling. Never had he seen so magnificent a specimen of womanhood.

"Scarlett, meet Cormac, Duke of Pembroke and master of this crumbling castle and all the land as far as the eye can see. He's also the best damn smuggler in Cornwall. Cormac, this is Scarlett, pirate extraordinaire, and deceitful bitch who tried to rid me of my wife."

"Ah, the plot thickens." Cormac nodded sagely. His perceptive eyes roamed greedily over Scarlett's shapely form and lovely features. He liked everything about the glorious redhead, except what she'd tried to do to Devon. But women were made to be tamed, he reflected, and taming Scarlett was a task he would relish.

Over a plain but hardy breakfast Kit related all that had transpired during the past months, including accepting amnesty, reclaiming his title, and Scarlett's attempt to get rid of Devon. Scarlett had been consigned to a cell-like room, enabling the men to speak openly without her interference or knowledge.

"What would you have me do, Diablo? I draw the line at killing women. Besides, Scarlett is too toothsome a creature to suffer an early death."

"I ask only that you keep Scarlett for me while I find Devon. What I do with her depends on Devon's condition when I find her. Presently I'm very close to strangling the red-haired bitch. Can I depend on you, my friend?"

"I won't let that gorgeous creature out of my sight," Cormac promised, his blue eyes glowing with wicked delight. "I'm just the man to make Scarlett repent her evil ways. She may be a handful but I'm up to the task."

Cormac's grin was infectious and Kit joined him in laughter despite his bone-weary fatigue and worry. "If you think to tame Scarlett, I wish you luck. But don't complain to me if her sting proves more potent than a scorpion's, for she'll not submit to taming without a fight. She's a taker, not a giver, and more deadly than a black widow spider."

"I'll take my chances," Cormac boomed, eagerly anticipating an encounter with the fiery pirate. "Never knew a woman I couldn't handle."

"You've never known a woman like Scarlett," Kit returned.

After he had eaten his fill Kit stuffed a sack with food, changed his tired mount for a fresh one from Cormac's stable, and left in search of his beloved.

A short time later Cormac carried a tray of food to his beautiful prisoner. A current of keen anticipation charged through his huge body at the thought of what awaited him on the other side of the door. He'd waited many years for a woman of fire and courage to come into his life, and from all indications Scarlett was just such a woman. According to Diablo she had a soul as black as his own, but he didn't hold that against her. Like a fractious mare, all she needed was a firm hand to guide her and a real man in the saddle.

"What in the hell do you want, you grinning toad?" Scarlett snarled when Cormac stepped into the room.

"Is that any way to greet a man offering food and friendship?"

"Friendship, my arse!" Scarlett flung back. Her vulgar language was meant to shock, but Cormac appeared unfazed as he carefully set the tray on the table.

"Now, lass, you'll find I don't shock easily. See what I've brought you? There's scones and jam and oatmeal and hot tea. Be a good girl and eat."

His cajoling tone served only to goad Scarlett into a towering rage. No one spoke to her in such a condescending manner and lived to tell of it. Didn't this bear of a man know she was the master of her own ship and feared by friend and foe alike? Casually she sauntered over to the table where Cormac had placed the tray, eying it with cool disdain. Then, before the huge man realized her intent, she grabbed it up and hurled it at his head.

Fortunately he was alert enough to duck, receiving only splatters of food as the tray whizzed harmlessly by to crash against the wall behind him.

"That's what I think of your food and your friendship!" Scarlett sneered. "We both know what Diablo intends to do with me. If you really wanted to be my friend you'd let me go."

"Ah, lass, you know I can't do that. Then neither of our lives would be worth a damn. Right or wrong, I'll not cross Diablo."

"Then we have nothing more to discuss," Scarlett proclaimed, her chin raised at a stubborn angle. "Get out of here!"

From the corner of her eye Scarlett studied the powerful giant, thinking him every bit as imposing as Diablo. A bit more rough around the edges perhaps, but every solid ounce of his magnificent frame exuded male sexuality at its most powerful best. Not an ounce of flab resided on his thickly muscled and blatantly virile torso and legs. Not handsome in a conventional way, Cormac's features possessed a rough-hewn beauty that Scarlett found more sensual, more compellingly attractive than men with classical good looks. Of course she wasn't about to let him know how deeply he affected her.

Taking full measure of Scarlett's tall, lithe body, Cormac had no intention of allowing the lady pirate to outwit him. "You're a feisty wench, Scarlett, but you've finally met your match. I'm no puny coward afraid to challenge your authority. Clean up this mess," he ordered, pointing to the upended tray and spilled food dripping down the wall onto the floor.

"Go to hell!" Scarlett defied. "I'm no man's drudge. Clean it up yourself."

Her flaming hair flying in wild disarray around her head, Scarlett stood her ground as Cormac took a menacing step in her direction. She had never backed down before any man and she damned well wasn't about to do so now. "Come ahead, you hairy ape," she taunted boldly. "You'll find I'm no easy target."

A low rumble of laughter tumbled from Cormac's mouth. Scarlett excited him as no woman ever had before. His nostrils flared as he breathed in the musky scent of her, sending the blood pumping through his veins at a furious rate. He felt alive and vital, and he wanted Scarlett. Wanted her with a compelling need that transcended every other need that had ever plagued him.

Scarlett's green eyes narrowed dangerously. She recognized Cormac's lust and reacted to it as only a woman of her fiery nature could, preparing to do battle. Lord knows she was no innocent. She knew exactly the moment the smuggler wanted her the way a man wants a woman. She could smell his excitement, reach out and touch that vibrant part of him that yearned to possess her. They stood facing each other like combatants on a battlefield, legs spread, arms akimbo, challenging one another in the age-old battle of the sexes.

Suddenly the thin line separating lust and hate shattered. Like animals in heat they fell upon one another, tearing at each other's clothes, clutching, grasping, falling to the floor to continue the fight for sexual supremacy. They coupled energetically and swiftly with little tenderness, carried away by a heady lust that surpassed anything either of them had ever felt before. Rolling around on the floor like two healthy animals, each trying to impose their will upon the other, they speedily reached an explosive, noisy release that drained and bewildered them. Neither had the slightest inkling of the monster they had unleashed between them.

"My God," Scarlett gasped reverently, "I've traded one devil for another!"

Thoroughly drenched, her hair plastered to her head in wet strands, Devon trembled with cold as she pulled her sodden cloak tightly around her. She had stumbled along in the soaking rain for hours and hadn't encountered a solitary soul crazy enough to be out on a night like this. It seemed incredible that she hadn't passed a single cottage or crofter's hut or found the village. Since there were no stars to use as a guide, she had been literally stumbling around blindly for hours. Weary beyond belief, Devon could at least be grateful that Scarlett was unlikely to find her trail in such dismal weather. Since nothing remotely resembling shelter had presented itself, Devon forced herself to continue moving, sheer guts and determination keeping her on her feet.

The last of her stamina had nearly deserted her when a large shape loomed before her, rising ghostlike through the darkness and mist. A house! Thank God, she prayed fervently, help was at hand. Her flimsy shoes squishing with mud, Devon experienced a strange feeling as she approached the cottage. It appeared dark and deserted and far too familiar for her liking. Oh, Lord! A groan of despair passed through her chilled lips.

The hunting lodge! She'd been traveling in circles for hours. At the end of her endurance, she dropped wearily to her knees, tears coursing down her smooth cheeks, ready to admit defeat. Then suddenly something stirred in her and she clutched her stomach. The baby! For the first time the child she carried made its presence known. Kit's child. Spurred by a growing sense of responsibility and love for her unborn baby, Devon struggled to her feet and approached the lodge, determined to survive.

It suddenly occurred to Devon that Scarlett might be gone, or asleep if she had remained, and thus might be easily overpowered. The door opened noiselessly beneath her hand and she paused on the threshold until her eyes adjusted to the violet shadows inside. Outside, dawn was breaking through the lowering bank of dripping clouds.

Stepping into the room, Devon felt the emptiness surround her and shivered. Intuition told her the lodge hadn't been vacated long, and the candle burnt down to the wick proved her correct. It was just light enough to see her way as she moved stealthily from room to room. Empty. No sign of Scarlett remained except for the heavy candlestick on the floor where Devon had last seen her lying unconscious.

Returning to the room that had once been her prison, Devon laid a fire in the grate, eager to dispel the chill from her bones. Once the fire burst into flames she hastily shed her clothes and wrapped herself in a thick quilt. The thought that Scarlett might return gave her a moment's pause, but she quickly discarded that fear, certain this would be the last place Scarlett would expect to find her.

Padding to the kitchen, Devon found cheese, bread, apples, and a portion of cold rabbit still left in the larder. Preparing herself a veritable feast, she carried it into the warmth of her cozy room, sat before the fire, and devoured every morsel. By now every bone in her body ached from weariness and long hours of abuse pushing herself through mud and pouring rain; she felt as if she could sleep for a week. Curling up on the bed, she fell asleep just as watery rays of morning sun broke through the mauve and silver clouds. Evening descended long hours later, and Devon slept on.

Slumped in the saddle, feeling as if the whole world rode on his shoulders, Kit reined in before the hunting lodge. His search had taken him so close to the lodge, he decided to spend the night in one of the bedrooms instead of returning to Cormac's ancient castle and starting out again in the morning. Weariness had rendered him nearly incapable of coherent thought, but every instinct told him to stop at the place where Devon had been kept so many weeks. He hadn't had a decent night's sleep since he left London days ago, snatching only brief naps in the saddle. Deep lines etched furrows across his brow, and his mouth drew taut with anguish. Hours spent scouring the countryside had failed to yield any sign of Devon. He should have found her by now, he reasoned, unless Winston had managed somehow to spirit her out of England.

Suddenly Kit straightened in the saddle, a frisson of sensation prickling his spine. It was almost as if something within the silent house was beckoning to him with an invisible finger. Compelled by a force stronger than his bone-wrenching weariness, Kit slid from the saddle and stared at the lodge through the encroaching darkness.

Tethering his drooping horse where it could easily feed on tender blades of grass, Kit approached the lodge like a sleepwalker moving through a dream. The fact that the house appeared deserted barely registered on his numb brain as he strode unerringly toward one of the bedrooms, drawn by some mysterious voice inside him.

Warm embers glowed dimly in the grate, providing just enough light to see the slender figure slumbering peacefully on the bed. Stifling a cry of incredible joy, Kit stood above Devon, gazing at her like a man whose sight had just been restored. Unwilling to startle her from so deep a sleep, Kit turned and walked back through the house and out the door to where his horse was tethered. After unsaddling and rubbing down the poor animal, he carried his saddlebags inside and prepared a simple meal for himself and Devon from the remnants of food provided by Cormac's larder. By the time he bathed and shaved, the need for his wife was like a burning brand inside him. He crawled in naked beside her.

Devon stretched with catlike grace beneath the quilt, a delicious languor painting her cheeks a delicate pink. Still sleeping, she could almost feel Kit's tender regard, experience his gentle hands exploring the hidden secrets of her body. It had been so long—too damn long—since she'd tasted the magic of his loving, savored the unique essence of his being. God, she loved him. Would they never be reunited and free from Scarlett's machinations? she wondered even in her sleep.

Reaching out to grasp the elusive object of her dream before he evaporated into pure fantasy, Devon imagined she could actually feel Kit beside her in bed. "I want you—I want you so," she whispered throatily. Just as she had so many times in the past, she ran her tongue over his skin, recalling how he had done the same to her on countless occasions.

How salty he was to her taste! How rough and smooth his magnificent body felt to her lips! If only he were real. The texture of his skin alternated from the velvet of his shoulders to the pleasant hairiness of his chest and the smooth hardness of his belly, and then the toughness and power of his muscled thighs.

"I want you, too, sweetheart," Kit's voice answered, startling Devon from the last vestiges of sleep. "But if you keep that up I'll not be able to love you properly."

Devon's heart catapulted to her throat. "Kit! Am I dreaming or is it really you? Thank God," she sobbed. "What took you so long to find me?"

"Your father just told me where Winston had taken you. I've had men scouring the countryside for you all these weeks. I left London the moment I knew. I'm no fantasy, sweetheart, as your lips and hands discovered."

"It's been so long I despaired of ever seeing you again," Devon said, choking back the lump in her throat.

"I'd have found you even if I had to search the world over."

"Not if Scarlett had her way." Suddenly Devon froze. "Kit, Scarlett! She wants to kill me. What if she returns to the lodge?"

"Don't fret, Scarlett won't bother us. I found her here in the lodge when I arrived earlier and took her to Cormac for safekeeping. You've nothing to fear where Scarlett's concerned. She's confessed everything. She admitted it was her idea to abduct you and that she blackmailed Winston into doing her bidding. Where is that bloody coward? If I know Winston, he's probably hiding someplace hoping I won't find him."

"By now Freddie and Winston are on their way to France," Devon revealed.

"Good riddance," Kit said with bitter emphasis. "But how in the hell is Freddie Smythe involved in all this? I would never have expected it of him."

"He's not involved, really. At first he thought Winston and I had eloped. Then Scarlett spread gossip about Freddie and Winston. I should have believed you when you told me Winston was—was —odd, but it seemed so far-fetched at the time. Somehow Freddie found Winston, and since he'd been turned out of his home he offered to take Winston along with him to France."

"It's beyond me how Freddie learned where Winston was when the men I paid to find him turned up no clues," said Kit. "If Winston sets foot in London again, I'll strangle him with my bare hands. Not only did he persuade your father to help him in this crazy stunt, but he caused me weeks of unbearable anguish."

"I don't understand why Father didn't tell you immediately where Winston had taken me. Didn't you tell him we were married? It's not like Father to hold a grudge. I know he doesn't like you, but he's not a vindictive man and I felt certain he'd capitulate once he learned we loved each other."

Kit scooped Devon into his arms, settling her comfortably against his chest as he searched for words to tell her about the earl. "He would have, sweetheart, but your father suffered a seizure the same day you left. I was with him at the time. I had just told him that we loved each other and were man and wife when he collapsed. He did manage to say that he would never have consented to Winston's wild scheme had he been told the truth about us."

"Oh Kit, no! Is—is Father—"

"Nay, love, your father was recovering when I left London. He temporarily lost the ability to speak, and it was touch and go for awhile, but he's a strong man and the doctor predicts a full recovery. The moment he was able to communicate he told me where to find you. He's sorry for what he did and hopes you'll forgive him."

"I don't blame Father. Winston has a glib tongue and probably convinced him you meant me harm. Evidently you changed Father's mind. The important thing is that we're together again."

"You talk too much, sweetheart," Kit rebuked teasingly. "Didn't you just admit you wanted me? I can wait no longer to demonstrate how badly I want and need you."

Her reply was lost as his lips claimed hers, his hands cupping her face in a firm yet gentle grasp as he kissed her sweet mouth, her chin, her nose, while whispering her name over and over again in a delirious frenzy of wild longing. Then Devon cried out in blissful agony as his dark head lowered and his open mouth closed over the taut peak of her breast while his hands roamed the length of her spine, the small of her back, her firm buttocks, down the silky measure of her thighs.

"You've gained weight, sweetheart," Kit murmured, testing the weight of the soft mounds of her breasts in his hands. "But I don't mind," he assured her, leering wolfishly, "they fit my hands better."

As if to prove his point, he cupped those tender white doves, passing his thumbs back and forth over the sensitive buds till they puckered and stood erect. Then he captured them again with his lips, lashing them with the moist tip of his tongue before drawing them deeply into his mouth and suckling with gentle insistence.

A shudder of intense pleasure wracked Devon's body. Oh Lord, she wanted it, wanted him, wanted all he had to offer.

Raising his head, Kit sighed blissfully. "Ah, sweetheart, you'd tempt the devil, how do you expect a mere mortal to resist you?"

"Mere mortal? Nay, Kit. You're Diablo, the devil who wove a seductive web around my heart. I love you so."

His breathing was thickened and unsteady as his hands danced over her curves, sliding downward to cup the taut mounds of her buttocks. He stroked and caressed them, tugging her hard against his hips, letting her feel his eagerness, know how compelling was his need of her.

The intimacy was unbearable, destroying what little restraint Devon had left. Drawing a quick breath, she turned wanton in his arms, boldly touching and caressing and stroking his hard male body with her hands, mouth, and tongue, arousing him to a breathless need that bordered on madness. His tenuous grip on reality vanished when her tongue traced a hot, wet path across the flat muscles of his belly. Flipping her on her back, Kit nudged her legs apart with his knee and lodged his entire length in the tight, hot sheath of her body. A groan of pure ecstasy tore from his lips, spurring Devon's need to an aching throb. Then their bodies forged into one, hands searching, exploring, lips hungry and eager as Kit began to rock back and forth.

Although he had meant to be slow and sweet, the strength of his desire compelled him to strike a far more rapid pace as he plunged ever deeper into the soft sweet center of her being. He pushed harder, deeper, swifter into her, her murmurs spurring him to bring them both to tempestuous release as quickly as possible.

Locking her legs around his buttocks, Devon urged him deeply and snugly within her, turning him wilder, crazier. The explosion erupting within her turned her insides to liquid fire, but her legs remained firmly locked in place, unwilling to release him until he reached his own climax, until the last shudder left his body, the final sigh trembled from his lips.

"God's bones, sweetheart, I expected to find this kind of ecstasy only in heaven. Now I know what I suspected all along. You *are* my heaven."

In the aftermath of love he began caressing her, her breasts, her thighs, her stomach—where his hand froze on the undisguisable bulge just below her waistline. Devon drew in a ragged breath, realizing belatedly that Kit still knew nothing about their child. Now it seemed as if he had discovered it for himself.

"Kit . . ."

"God's bones, you're growing a babe! Why didn't you tell me I was going to be a father? Or had you decided to wait until you placed the babe in my arms? You should have told me at the Smythes' ball," he reproved, annoyed by her omission of something so important. "Had I known I would have been more gentle."

"You didn't harm me, my love," Devon replied, her blue eyes glowing with love, "or our child. He's fine. Here," she said, placing his hand against the hard little bulge, "feel him move within me. He's strong, just like his father."

A look of awe replaced the frown darkening Kit's brow when he felt the tiny thump against his hand. "Why didn't you tell me sooner?" he repeated. "How long have you known? My God, Winston could have harmed our child! If Scarlett had succeeded in her plan, I could have lost you both." A look of horror turned his features into a mask of repressed rage.

"I began to suspect about a month after I returned to England. I was going to tell you at the ball, but Scarlett interfered. Then the next day, Winston carried me off. In a little over five months you'll have a son, Kit. Are—are you happy?" Devon asked, her lips curved into a tentative smile.

"Ecstatic, sweetheart, but I thought a daughter would be nice first. A blue-eyed angel as beguiling as her mother."

"Nay, a son first, Kit, to carry on your name, then as many daughters as you wish."

"Not too many," Kit teased. "I've no wish to wear you out with constant childbearing, nor endanger your life each time I fill your belly."

"I want your children," Devon assured him. "I'm strong and healthy, nothing will happen to me."

"And you'll have them, sweetheart, but just enough to satisfy my male ego and feed your mother's instinct. I want you to always have time for me."

"There'll always be time for you, my love, beginning with right now. Love me again, Kit. Love me for all those lonely nights I've cried myself to sleep for need of you."

"I will, sweetheart, but first, the supper I fixed for us is waiting and I'm famished. I've been in the saddle for days and haven't eaten since I left Cormac this morning. If I'm to love you properly I need sustenance of another kind."

Blushing, Devon acquiesced, using the time Kit was in the kitchen preparing their tray to wash and freshen up. Then she wrapped up in the quilt and fed the fire, having a nice blaze going by the time he returned. Sitting side by side on the bed, they devoured every last bite of the cold repast. Licking her fingers, Devon lay back, replete.

"Ummm, good. I was hungrier than I thought. I slept for hours with little thought for food or drink."

"Are you still tired, sweetheart?" Kit asked, his silver gaze hungrily devouring her face before dropping to her full breasts, exposed where the quilt had slipped under her armpits.

"Sleep isn't what I crave right now," she hinted brazenly.

"Then 'tis more food you want." His teasing tone set her heart racing in her chest.

"Nay, not food." Her soft, throaty voice flowed over him like a caress, surrounding him in a warm cocoon of desire, and his weariness dropped away.

His kiss was unhurried, moving slow and sweetly over her mouth as his right hand gently stripped the quilt from her body. His fingers slid over the smooth swell of her breasts, circling the pale pink tips until they were firm peaks; then he slid his hand over her hip to draw her closer. His mood was so relaxed now that he felt no urgency, simply wanting to give her more pleasure than she had ever known. His hand slipped between her legs, parting tender flesh to slide a finger inside the warm crevice. His intimate caress yielded a moist response from her body that made Devon shift uncomfortably.

"This won't hurt you or the babe, will it?" Kit asked anxiously as his fingers explored with maddening effect.

"Nay," Devon gasped, rotating her hips in rhythm with his probing and spreading her thighs to allow him greater access.

Kit's thumb located the tiny hidden bud and stroked it to pebble hardness. He scooted downward between her legs, and the tip of his tongue replaced his thumb to send a jolt ripping through her body, arcing her upward.

"Kit! My God!"

"Relax, sweetheart. I want to love you in every way. Don't be afraid to show your joy. I want to give you as much pleasure as you bring me."

"Kit, please—don't—don't stop!"

"Never, my wonderful love, never."

Then abruptly her whole world shattered and she went spiraling out of control into a kaleidoscope of brilliant colors and shooting stars. Waiting until her body was completely still, Kit shifted upwards, impaling her with the swollen length of his manhood. Desire thundered through him, for he had teased and aroused himself by deliberately delaying his own pleasure while enjoying hers.

He moved within her, driven by a need more potent than the headiest wine, thrusting, withdrawing, rekindling the banked fires Devon thought had been thoroughly doused just moments ago.

"Aye, sweetheart, that's it. Come for me again.

Let me feel those delicious tremors inside your sweet body. Hurry, love—ah, you're so tight, so warm—"

His highly erotic words had the desired effect as Devon caught fire and blazed out of control. This time they flew away together, reaching the highest level of pleasure God granted to a man and woman.

"Are you all right, sweetheart?"

"Ummm, wonderful," Devon sighed dreamily. "I never thought it possible to be so happy."

"Nor I," Kit concurred. "Had I chosen to remain a pirate I could have been captured and hanged at any time, and lose you forever. I never dreamed I'd be a respectable citizen again with a beautiful wife and a child on the way. It frightens me to think that Winston and Scarlett nearly succeeded in taking you from me."

"What will happen to Scarlett?" Devon asked.

"I'd like to wring her beautiful neck," Kit muttered darkly. "But I've decided to turn her over to the authorities. She'll be charged with attempted murder and violating amnesty. She'll be punished for her crime according to the dictates of the law. I'm through taking the law into my own hands."

Feeling little sympathy for the woman who had resented her from the moment of their first meeting, Devon did not question Kit's judgment.

They lingered at the lodge three more days, resting, talking, and loving, sleeping late each morning and making love again in the bed still rumpled from the previous night's exertions. Sometimes they whiled away the afternoon making love yet another time, sharing a rapture that had long been denied them. Fortunately, enough food remained in the larder to keep them from starving, supplemented with small game that Kit caught.

Devon proved a fair cook despite her woeful lack of experience, and Kit never tired of watching her at her domestic chores.

"We'll leave in the morning," Kit said as they prepared for bed one night. "Cormac will be sending out a search party if I don't return soon. Besides, Scarlett is probably driving him mad and he'll be anxious to get her off his hands."

"It's been so lovely here I almost hate to leave," Devon sighed wistfully.

"You'll be happy at Linley Hall, sweetheart," Kit promised. "And as soon as we're certain your father is recovering we'll sail to Paradise Island for a proper honeymoon. I left Tara in charge and need to make plans for the disposition of the island."

"I'd love to go to Paradise, Kit, providing we'll be back in time for the birth of our child." Devon recalled with pleasure the warm, sunny days and balmy, moon-drenched nights on the tropical isle. "Do you still have the *Devil Dancer?*"

"Aye. She's been engaged in commerce these past weeks. But I left orders before coming to Cornwall that she's to meet us in a cove close to Cormac's castle for the return trip to London. She's probably there waiting now. But enough talk, the night grows short and I want to love you."

"Will you always want to love me?" Devon teased. "What about when I'm old and gray and no longer beautiful?"

"In my eyes you'll never grow old, sweetheart. You'll always be as lovely and desirable as you are at this moment. Each time I make love to you, be it once or a thousand times, will be like the first. But if you keep asking silly questions we may never get around to that thousandth time."

Giggling happily, Devon held out her arms, inviting him into the warmth of her embrace, offering her lips and her body as a fitting sacrifice to their love.

Chapter Twenty-Two

"Damn you, Cormac, you're not a man, you're a sorcerer," Scarlett accused, gasping for breath.

They had lain together each night since their explosive coming together three days ago, engaging in the most satisfying sex Scarlett had ever experienced. Cormac was a huge bear of a man, rough yet incredibly tender, completely lacking in finesse but compensating for it with erotic expertise. In the three short days she'd known him she'd not thought of Diablo once. Even more astounding was the fact that Cormac appeared as fascinated with her as she was with him.

It seemed to Scarlett as if she had waited all her life for a man strong enough to match her in strength of will and wits. She thought she'd found him in Diablo and would have been satisfied with her first choice if he hadn't fallen hopelessly in love with Devon.

"And you're a red-haired witch, Scarlett,"

Cormac laughed delightedly. "I've been looking forever for a woman like you. We're a matched pair, my long-legged wanton, and that's for sure. 'Tis doubtful which one of us will prevail, but I'm willing to bet we'll both enjoy the combat. Taming you might take a lifetime, but life would never be dull."

"Are you man enough to tame me?" Scarlett challenged. Her voice was a throaty purr, daring him to try.

"Aye. Are you woman enough to enjoy it?" Cormac growled in response, rolling to capture her tall frame beneath his huge body.

What followed next was a night of wild and unrestrained sex that lasted until pink streaks made bright patterns across the eastern sky. Exhausted, they fell asleep in each other's arms, neither stirring until the door to the bedroom crashed open to reveal the nude couple, limbs entwined, sleeping peacefully amid the rumpled disorder of the big bed they shared.

"What the hell!"

Kit and Devon had returned to Cormac's castle just moments before, finding no one about except stammering servants. Though the staff knew full well where their master had spent the last three nights, loyalty prevented them from speaking. Vexed, Kit made immediately for Scarlett's room, Devon close on his heels. Contrary to Kit's orders, the door was unlocked, and he flung it open. Empty! Turning abruptly, he raced to Cormac's chamber, thinking Scarlett had somehow managed to do away with the burly giant and escape. He would put nothing past the witch. Not bothering to knock, Kit propelled himself into the room, skidding to a halt just inside the door.

Cormac reared up, scrambling for the sheet wadded up at the foot of the bed. Sated after her night of sexual rapture, Scarlett was slower to react, stretching languidly before opening her eyes. When she saw Kit and Devon staring at her she made no attempt to cover herself, merely smiling like a well-satisfied kitten.

Kit's eyes rolled heavenward, highly amused but also much relieved to find that Scarlett hadn't flown the coop. "So, my friend, I'm pleased you found the onerous chore of keeping my captive to your liking. Scarlett can be a handful but quite entertaining when the mood strikes her. I trust you've enjoyed yourself?"

Cormac had the grace to blush, but wasn't inclined to explain or excuse his actions. Instead, he adroitly changed the subject. Now modestly covered by the sheet, he turned to Devon. "'Tis happy I am to see you, my lady, though I'd much prefer to greet you under—er—different circumstances. I'm hardly at my best dressed in a bedsheet. But I truly am glad Diablo found you unharmed."

Devon stifled a giggle. Never had she seen anything so hairy as Cormac's massive chest except on a four-footed creature. "Thank you, Cormac," she replied, swallowing the laughter bubbling in her throat. It did her heart good to see Scarlett looking so subdued lying beside her huge lover. "If you'll excuse me, I'll leave you to your privacy. I—we didn't mean to barge in." She turned to leave, and when Kit failed to follow, she tugged determinedly on his sleeve.

Reluctantly Kit gave in to Devon's prodding. "I'll wait for you downstairs, Cormac. I'm sure there's much we have to discuss," he threw over his shoulder.

"He's angry enough with me to slit my throat," Scarlett said when she and Cormac were alone.

"Nay, lass," Cormac denied. "No real harm has come to Devon, though I won't say you aren't deserving of his contempt. What you did was despicable." His stern visage sent Scarlett's heart plummeting. It sounded as if Cormac had no intention of allowing the past three nights of un-equaled bliss to interfere with Kit's plans for her.

"I'd like a bath," she said testily, unwilling to grovel at Cormac's feet. She'd been caretaker of her own destiny far too long to relinquish her pride by begging for her life.

"Aye," Cormac agreed, his lips twitching suspiciously. "I'll see to it. Meanwhile I'll go down and face the devil. I strongly suspect he'll have some choice words about finding us like this."

"Did you seduce Scarlett or did she seduce you?" Kit asked.

"A little of both, I suspect," Cormac said with the barest hint of humor. "It just happened. I couldn't wait to get my hands on the witch, and she couldn't keep her hands off me. I always thought men were masters of their own fate, but now I'm not so sure."

A look of stunned disbelief passed over Kit's face. "Are you saying you have feelings for Scarlett, knowing what she is and what she's done? She would have killed Devon without hesitation if given the opportunity. The woman is capable of murder. She's the one who betrayed me by giving Le Vautour directions to Paradise. Scarlett masterminded Devon's abduction. If she had harmed Devon or our child, I would have retaliated swiftly, with the same kind of mercy she showed my wife."

"Your child! Is Devon—"

"Aye, in five months she'll give birth to our babe."

"Thank God you found her," Cormac said sincerely. "What's to become of Scarlett?"

"I'm turning her over to the authorities, charging her with attempted murder and breaking the terms of amnesty. I doubt she'll escape the hangman, but if she does she'll rot in jail for the remainder of her days."

"Nay, I'll not allow it!"

"What? You want me to be lenient with a woman capable of murder and deceit? You want me to extend mercy to one who doesn't deserve it?"

"Aye, I want Scarlett," the huge smuggler admitted somewhat sheepishly. "At first I took Scarlett to prove my mastery over so vibrant a woman. I had no idea she would affect me so deeply. Now I find I want far more from her. I want to marry her and keep her with me forever. I promise as long as I live she'll not harm another soul."

"God's bones, you're mad!" Kit cried. "The treacherous witch will reward you with a knife in your ribs the first time you turn your back."

"I'm willing to take that chance," Cormac argued stubbornly.

Kit regarded Cormac with piercing scrutiny. He couldn't believe what he was hearing. Normally Cormac was a sensible man with good instincts. What had Scarlett done to him? The only explanation seemed to be that Scarlett had bewitched him. Yet Cormac seemed in full control of his senses. It also occurred to Kit that Cormac had never failed to come to his aid. Along with Kyle and Akbar, Cormac had been an integral part of his life.

But somehow Kit couldn't mouth the words that would free Scarlett and give her to his friend. Her underhanded dealings had fouled up his life too often in the past. He belatedly realized that Scarlett had been part of Le Vautour's scheme to lead him on a wild chase after Spanish galleons while Le Vautour took Devon from Paradise and wounded Kyle while making good their escape. Scarlett was a constant irritant, always trying to tempt and tease, though he told her long ago their affair was over.

Kit's mouth twisted in a wry smile as he was suddenly struck with a solution. "Since my wife is the one who's been affected the most by Scarlett's dirty dealings, I'll place her fate entirely in Devon's hands."

At first Cormac was stunned, but then he realized Kit's intentions. He also knew that Devon's heart was too soft and forgiving to condemn a woman to death. "Aye, 'tis no more than right," he agreed.

Minutes later Scarlett stood before Kit, her green eyes wary, body tense. Devon was also present, having been summoned by Kit.

"Kill me now," Scarlett said defiantly. "I'd prefer it to rotting in jail." She had expected Cormac to leap to her defense, but his features were deliberately blank.

"I've decided to place your fate in Devon's hands," Kit said evenly.

Devon started violently, gasping in horror. What in the world was Kit thinking?

"Since it's Devon's life and that of our unborn child you endangered, 'tis no more than right she should make the decision. I'll abide by her wishes."

"Child!" choked out Scarlett, aware that she was already as good as dead. In all her long illustrious days of pirating she'd never deliberately harmed a child or allowed her crew to do so. "I—I had no idea."

"Might I speak before you decide?" Cormac injected.

"Aye," Devon said with a nod. "Please do."

"I've told your husband of my desire to marry Scarlett. Once she's my wife I swear she'll not cause you further grief. I intend to make her a full partner in my smuggling operation. I believe she'll find sufficient excitement to keep her happy and content, so she'll have no need to return to London Town. I'd stake my life 'twill be enough adventure to satisfy any craving Scarlett might harbor in that exquisite body of hers."

Scarlett could do little more than stare at Cormac, flabbergasted by his suggestion. Would Kit allow it? Would Devon agree?

"You want Scarlett for your wife?" Devon repeated, as stunned as Scarlett.

"Aye."

"What does Kit think?"

"Ask him."

She cocked an inquiring eye in Kit's direction. "Well, my love?"

"The decision is yours, sweetheart. Keep in mind Scarlett is a conniving bitch who would have felt no remorse over murdering you."

"Is Scarlett willing?" Devon addressed the question to Cormac.

"I've good reason to think so. You have no idea how fantastic we are together, how we seem to explode the moment we come together. I want her, damn it! If Scarlett agrees, I'll marry her tomorrow. She'll become my duchess and full partner in a lucrative smuggling operation. But if she even thinks of returning to London I'll wring her neck—after I beat the daylights out of her."

Devon felt the weight of decision pressing down upon her narrow shoulders. Scarlett deserved everything she had coming to her for wanting to harm her, yet no human was without redemption. Perhaps all the woman needed was a forceful man like Cormac to take control of her life. Besides, Devon knew she could not order another person's death, and Scarlett would surely die confined in prison for any length of time.

Scarlett's hopes soared, despite the fact she'd never thought of herself married to anyone but Diablo. But Cormac was offering her a second chance at life in a most intriguing manner, one she couldn't refuse. Each time Cormac set his hands on her tingling flesh it was a unique and thoroughly rewarding experience. She knew if she lived as his wife she'd have neither the inclination nor the energy to return to London, not for any reason. The antics of the rich and titled were beginning to bore her anyway. Besides, if she married Cormac she could still be a duchess as she'd always dreamed.

"Do you agree to Cormac's terms?" Devon asked, finally turning to Scarlett.

A long, tense silence ensued before Scarlett spoke. "Aye. If Cormac wants me, I'm his, though he's getting no bargain." She turned to Cormac. "You'll find me difficult to tame, but I promise you exciting days and nights for your trouble. If you still want me, then you have my consent. I'll be your wife and partner."

"What say you, sweetheart?" Kit asked, awaiting Devon's final judgment.

"Let Cormac have her," Devon decreed, "and I wish him luck. He'll need it."

Whooping with joy, Cormac scooped Scarlett up in his arms and bore her out of the room and up the stairs where he began his domination by making wild, passionate love to her.

The next day Devon and Kit witnessed the couple's wedding, performed that evening by the same minister who had officiated at their own nuptials. On short notice the staff had prepared a magnificent feast, and when the bride and groom retired to their wedding bed, Devon and Kit sought their own privacy.

"Do you think we've done right by not turning Scarlett over to the authorities?" Devon asked as she undressed for bed. One small part of her hated to see Scarlett go unpunished for her evil ways.

Kit had already disrobed and slid beneath the covers. "I think we can trust Cormac to keep that hellcat out of our lives," Kit murmured, too enthralled by Devon emerging from her clothes to give Scarlett more than a passing thought. "Come to bed, sweetheart, I want to make love to you." Thrilled by his hungry impatience, Devon complied, slipping eagerly into his waiting arms.

The next hours were spent making tender, leisurely love, oblivious to everything but their obsessive need for one another. Devon's craving was so devastating that her entire body quivered uncontrollably as she was drawn toward an all-consuming flame. With lips and hands Kit brought her carefully to the brink of ecstasy, and when she could stand no more of his sweet torture, he invaded the last of her body's defenses, bringing them both to explosive climax.

In another room in the vast crumbling castle, Cormac and Scarlett created their own fireworks, his potent seed finding fertile ground in Scarlett's receptive body.

The following morning only Cormac was on hand as Kit and Devon prepared to leave, excusing his bride with a sly wink that said more than mere words. When they had gathered their meager belongings, Cormac drove them in the coach to the deserted stretch of beach where they were to meet the *Devil Dancer*. It was a comforting sight to see her riding at anchor in the secluded bay. A signal was sent out, and they waited on the beach while a longboat was dispatched to pick them up. Their last sight of Cormac was of the bearlike smuggler grinning from ear to ear and waving goodbye, obviously quite pleased with himself.

Four days later they reached London. A hired coach took them to Chatham House, where Devon was ecstatic to find her father sitting up in a chair engaged in a game of chess with the butler. When Devon and Kit burst into the room, the servant sent them a grateful smile and scooted from the room, happy to be relieved of the onerous task of entertaining the cantankerous earl.

"Devon, thank God!" the earl cried, opening his arms to welcome his beloved daughter.

"Oh, Father, I've been so worried about you! Kit told me what happened. How are you feeling?"

"Well enough, now that you're back," replied Lord Harvey in a voice made gruff with emotion. "More importantly, how are you? Has Winston been turned over to the authorities? I fully intend to press charges. The man is utterly devoid of scruples. He deliberately lied to me. Can you ever forgive me, daughter?"

"Winston hoodwinked you, Father," Devon soothed, concerned by the earl's significant weight loss and haggard appearance. "He fooled us both. Winston wasn't what he seemed, he was—"

"Devon," Kit cautioned, "don't tax your father with useless information. Suffice it to say Winston has fled England and no longer poses a threat to us."

Taking Kit's hint, Devon continued cautiously. "It's over with, Father. I'm here with you and my—my husband, and we have something to tell you. Something wonderful."

Intrigued, Lord Harvey shifted his gaze from Devon to Kit, a man he'd been prepared to hate until Devon chose him for a husband. "Well, daughter, what is this wonderful news you're so anxious to convey?"

A foolish grin hung on one corner of Kit's mouth and his chest puffed out proudly. "Let me, sweetheart. Your Grace, your daughter will soon present me with an heir."

"Bloody hell! I just recently learned my daughter was wed, and now you're telling me she's to be a mother," Lord Harvey grumbled, feigning annoyance. "You've cheated me out of hundreds of pounds in trading goods over the years, but that wasn't enough, you had to steal my daughter. If I wasn't absolutely convinced Devon loved you I'd send you packing."

"'Tis too late, Your Grace," Kit argued happily. "I fully intend to raise my children and become the husband Devon deserves. I've been offered another opportunity to live my life as it was meant to be lived. Few men are allowed a second chance to make things right. So with or without your blessing, Devon will remain my duchess."

"Do you think I'd turn down the opportunity of knowing my grandchildren?" Lord Harvey asked incredulously. "I'll take my daughter's word that she's tamed the devil and Diablo no longer exists. I welcome the Duke of Grenville into our family and wish the two of you every happiness."

He extended his hand, a truce eagerly accepted by Kit.

"You'll not regret it, Your Grace. I'll make Devon so damn happy she'll find her heaven on earth."

"I think Father took it well," Devon giggled, resting her head on Kit's broad shoulder. They lay in bed gloriously naked, arms and legs entwined. They were home now, at Linley Hall, where Devon once expected to reside as Winston's bride. It was a house she knew well and had always loved. It seemed so right that she should be its mistress and Kit's wife.

"Well enough," agreed Kit, recalling the earl's eagerness to become a grandfather before he breathed his last.

A long, painful sigh escaped his lips. Once they reached London he promised himself he'd allow Devon several nights' rest without subjecting her to his lovemaking, but was having a difficult time keeping his word. After Devon's ordeal and their journey home, Kit decided that for his child's sake his wife deserved a period of uninterrupted rest.

"Did you mean what you told Father, my love?" Devon purred in a seductive whisper.

"That depends. I told him many things."

"You said you intended to make me so happy I'd think I was living in heaven."

"True enough," concurred Kit, perplexed.

"Then do it."

"Do what?"

"Make me happy."

"I thought you'd appreciate the rest tonight."

"The first night in my own home and you want me to rest?" argued Devon, jolting upright and glaring at Kit indignantly. Her action gave him an unrestricted view of her full breasts bouncing enticingly. "Perhaps you're the one who needs rest. I *have* been rather demanding lately."

"Are you questioning my virility, wife?" Kit roared in mock anger. "Have I given you reason to doubt my ability to perform?"

Grinning with wicked delight, Devon taunted cheekily, "Nay, but if you are tired I could make love to you for a change, so as not to tax your strength, of course. Why should men do all the work?"

"Devon, making love to you is no chore, but I don't think—"

"Then don't think, just relax and let me . . ." Her words trailed off as her lips slashed across his. With a groan of delight, he surrendered himself into her tender care.

Putting her mouth, hands, and tongue into good use, Devon taunted and teased unmercifully, filling her senses with the salty taste of him, his musky odor. Her moist lips hovered on each male nipple and her roaming hands sought out each sensitive point on his body, leaving a trail of white-hot flames. Unable to resist, Kit reached for her, wanting to crush her to him, but she glided out of his

reach. When she began anew with her tender torture, Kit forced himself to lie back and endure the
delicious agony of her loving.

Kit nearly flew off the bed when she brought her
hand over his hip, resting it there for an eternity
before attempting a caress of a far more intimate
nature. Then her hand found him, tracking the
incredible length of him with long, teasing strokes.

"God's bones, sweetheart, you're killing me!"

"Turnabout is fair play," Devon taunted, giggling
delightedly. Then her lips replaced her hands and
Kit howled as if in pain. Only then did she relent,
straddling his hips and taking his massive staff into
her body and sheathing it lovingly in her moist
warmth.

"Oh no you don't, you little temptress!" Kit
groaned, adroitly reversing their position. "'Tis
your turn now."

Though it cost him untold anguish, he withdrew
from her, covering her body with tiny nipping
kisses, deliberately ignoring the pouting tips of her
breasts. He paid loving homage to the indentation
of her navel, the soft mound of her stomach, the
inside of satiny thighs, before finally returning to
those ripe buds that begged for his attention. Drawing each nipple deeply into his mouth, he suckled
them gently one at a time until Devon moaned and
arched beneath him, a burning beginning in that
place she yearned for him the most.

"Had enough?" Kit teased, a roguish grin bringing his dimple into play.

"Aye, please," Devon panted raggedly.

"Nay, I think not."

And then, before her shattered senses could an-
ticipate his next move, he slid downward to the
thickly thatched crest of her womanhood. When his

lips invaded the tender, hidden slit, he thrilled to the liquid heat of her passion. Hungrily he parted her with his hard thrusting tongue, greedily exploring deep inside.

Crying out, Devon writhed beneath his tender probing, begging for mercy just as Kit had begged moments ago. Finally taking pity on her, he shifted upwards, lunging forward with a groan of pure ecstasy. Employing extreme patience, he moved carefully against her, ever thoughtful of their babe. His hand slid beneath her hips, lifting her to him, his need a throbbing ache now. Devon was suspended in a whirlwind of sensations that touched every nerve and sinew in her body. Now she was moving in gentle rhythm to his coaxing, consumed by such heat she could never again claim to being an identity unto herself. From now into eternity they would be forever one.

As Kit soared to lofty heights, he became Devon's possession, a living, breathing part of her never again to be separated.

Several weeks later the *Devil Dancer*, with Kit at the wheel, safely sailed through the jagged reef guarding Paradise Island. A surprising number of people, including reformed pirates and their families who had chosen to remain on the cay, came out to greet them. There was one other ship anchored in the snug bay; it belonged to members of Kit's old crew. Before he left, Kit had shown them how to navigate the reef so they might come and go as they wished. He was pleased to note that the village appeared to be thriving and that another pier had been built to accommodate increased traffic.

Kyle and Marlena had accompanied Kit and Devon aboard the *Devil Dancer*, as had Akbar, who seemed to have mellowed somewhat in his opinion of Devon after he learned she was carrying Kit's child. With infinite care Kit guided Devon down the gangplank. She was well into her pregnancy and absolutely blooming. By the time they all stood on the dock, Tara was running down the path from the house.

"Diablo! I knew you'd come back!" she squealed breathlessly, throwing herself into his arms.

Kyle received an equally joyous welcome, as did Marlena. Akbar was greeted last, but no less exuberantly. Devon was granted a sour smile but little else, for Tara still held Devon responsible for deserting Diablo as well as all the bad things that had happened on Paradise. Kit sensed Tara's animosity, and as they all walked to the house he carefully explained much of what had happened since leaving the Caribbean, including the news that Devon was expecting his child. Instantly Tara's disposition toward Devon changed and she offered a tentative smile, begging forgiveness. Devon freely gave it.

They spent a blissful month on Paradise before Kit decided it was time to take Devon home to England where expert care was available for the birth of their child. Besides, he'd promised Lord Harvey they would return in plenty of time for the big event. Kyle and Marlena, already an essential part of their lives, would also be returning to England. Kyle had money enough to go into business for himself and at Kit's urging decided to launch a shipping venture. His voice bursting with pride, Kyle informed everyone that Marlena was expecting a child.

That left only Akbar at loose ends. He had yet to indicate his intentions. It became increasingly evident that he missed piracy and was almost of a mind to return to the profession. London definitely had not been to his liking.

Several nights before they were to leave, Tara took matters into her own hands, seeking Akbar out in the small hut he occupied while on Paradise. "What are you doing here, Tara?" he growled, eying the lovely, dusky woman warily. In the moonlight her hair gleamed like thousands of black diamonds, and Akbar had a difficult time concentrating.

"Don't you know?" Tara asked softly. Beneath her sarong her heart beat a wild tattoo. Her pride suffered coming here like this, but if it won her her heart's desire it was well worth it.

"You're no whore!" he snorted. "You know I've little use for women except for an occasional lusty encounter. Do you want to share my bed on those terms? Is that why you've come?"

"Would you turn me away if I said yes?"

"By Allah's beard! Do you think me stupid? I've been desired by women before, and betrayed by one whose jealousy ate at her like a canker. Would you bed me knowing I despise all women, that I use them for only one purpose?"

"I think you've hidden behind your hate too long. 'Tis time to forget and forgive. Let me help you."

"Why?"

"I wish I knew. All I know is that when I look at you I tremble inside, and not from fear. Oh, you try hard to maintain that fierce exterior, but I sense a softness in you no one else has discovered."

"A softness!" Akbar roared, scowling furiously. "There is nothing soft about me." Roughly he pulled her inside. "Don't you know I devour women like you?" His lips slashed across hers with a violence that would have frightened lesser women. "Don't you fear me? You should."

"Nay, what I feel is not fear. What I do fear is never seeing you again."

Akbar could not believe his ears. Even when he paid women for their favors they still feared him. "Would it really bother you not to see me again?"

"It would make me very sad. You're—you're magnificent, Akbar."

Akbar regarded Tara from beneath shaggy brows, finding it difficult to believe that Tara found any redeeming qualities in his character. Didn't she know he distrusted all women? Only when Tara stepped up to him, slipped her slim arms around his huge neck, and lifted her lips did he respond to her gentleness. Suddenly all his years of enforced loneliness and bitter hatred, of distrust and unfounded discrimination, dropped away. Then his massive arms crushed her to him and his lips seized hers with a hunger he'd never known or allowed himself to dream about.

During all these years he'd told no one of his attraction for the luscious Tara, fearing to reveal too much of his soul. The knowledge that the ravishing creature in his arms returned those feelings melted the hard knot of denial he'd harbored in his heart since he'd caught the eye of the sultan's fickle favorite and earned her jealous friend's betrayal. Chained to an oar provides an adequate setting to nurture one's hate. Now Tara had set him free—free to express an emotion so foreign to him as to be nonexistent. Lifting Tara off her tiny feet, he bore her to his bed, closing the door to the outside world and opening his heart to love.

When the *Devil Dancer* sailed a few days later, Akbar remained behind with Tara. Kit never would have guessed that anything remotely resembling love existed in Akbar's huge body. Only Devon remained strangely complacent upon hearing the news. She knew that the power of love could work miracles, for hadn't she experienced it herself?

Actually, the arrangement was much to Kit's liking. Akbar agreed to act as overseer on Paradise and continue the production of sugar cane and rum. Kit arranged for the *Devil Dancer* to return to transporting rum to markets around the world. It was also decided that Kit, Devon, and their children would return to Paradise whenever time allowed.

Standing at the rail, Devon watched the jewel-like islands disappear over the horizon. His arms wrapped around her ample waist, Kit hugged her close, thinking he held all his hopes and dreams of the future in his arms. As she snuggled into the curve of his body, the baby made its presence known in a most abrupt manner.

"Am I holding you too tightly, sweetheart? The babe's protesting." Kit laughed, his palm settling lovingly on the quivering mound of her belly.

"Nay, 'tis more like he's anxious to make his appearance."

"Not too soon, I hope," Kit said, eying her worriedly.

"You fret too much, my love. The babe is well and so am I. Join me in our cabin and I'll demonstrate just how wonderful I feel."

"Don't you think 'tis time you gave up that kind of strenuous activity?"

"Not for a few weeks yet, unless the sight of my inflated body disgusts you."

"Never! That's my child you carry inside you. You're as beautiful to me as the first time I saw you."

"I'll never forget the first time I laid eyes on you,"

Devon mused. "A ferocious black beard concealed much of your face and I thought you quite fierce, though not unhandsome."

"Did you now? I didn't notice you swooning in fear at Diablo's feet."

"Not even the devil is threatening standing on a gallows with a rope around his neck," Devon returned saucily.

"But he was dangerous enough to seize the woman of his dreams and take her to Paradise. And now you're suffering the consequences of his love."

"Consequences? Nay, my blackhearted rogue. You stole my heart and replaced it with your love."

"And the fruit of that love is precious to me. But as long as you insist it won't hurt him to love you, I'm more than willing to do my part."

Inside the cozy privacy of the moon-drenched cabin, time stood still while the star-crossed lovers rededicated themselves to love. For without the magic of love and the power of passion their story could not have been told. It would have ended where it all began—on the gallows.

ICE & Rapture

CONNIE MASON

**Winner of the *Romantic Times*
Storyteller of the Year Award!**

Cool as a cucumber, and totally dedicated to her career as a
newspaper woman, Maggie Afton is just the kind of
challenge brash Chase McGarrett enjoys. But he is exactly
the kind of man she despises. Cold and hot, reserved and
brazen, Maggie and Chase are a study in opposites. But
when they join forces during the Klondike gold rush, the
fiery sparks of their searing desire burn brighter than the
northern lights.

___4193-6 $5.99 US/$6.99 CAN

Dorchester Publishing Co., Inc.
P.O. Box 6640
Wayne, PA 19087-8640

Please add $2.50 for shipping and handling for the first book and
$.75 for each book thereafter. NY, NYC, and PA residents,
please add appropriate sales tax. No cash, stamps, or C.O.D.s. All
orders shipped within 6 weeks via postal service book rate.
Canadian orders require $2.00 extra postage and must be paid in
U.S. dollars through a U.S. banking facility.

Name_____

Address_____

City_____State_____Zip_____

I have enclosed $_____ in payment for the checked book(s).

Payment <u>must</u> accompany all orders. ☐ Please send a free catalog.

SHADOW WALKER
CONNIE MASON

Bestselling Author of *Flame*!

"Why did you do that?"

"Kiss you?" Cole shrugged. "Because you wanted me to, I suppose. Why else would a man kiss a woman?"

But Dawn knows lots of other reasons, especially if the woman is nothing but half-breed whose father has sold her to the first interested male. Defenseless and exquisitely lovely, Dawn is overjoyed when Cole Webster kills the ruthless outlaw who is her husband in name only. But now she has a very different sort of man to contend with. A man of unquestionable virility, a man who prizes justice and honors the Native American traditions that have been lost to her. Most intriguing of all, he is obviously a man who knows exactly how to bring a woman to soaring heights of pleasure. And yes, she does want his kiss...and maybe a whole lot more.

_4260-6 $6.99 US/$8.99 CAN

Gypsy Lover
CONNIE MASON

To the astonishment of the *ton*, the late marquis had disinherited the petulant Lord Lonsdale, leaving his vast estate to a darkly handsome Romany horse trader. Fabulous wealth was his for the taking, provided Dante would also take the bride his grandfather had specified.

The arrogant gypsy had swept Lady Esme Harcourt into his arms, awakening both her desire and her disdain. Though her hand might be promised to the new Marquis of Alston, she swore never to wed a man whose birth put him so far beneath her. But no matter how she protested against Dante as her husband, her heart had already accepted him as her wild... *Gypsy Lover*.

Dorchester Publishing Co., Inc.
P.O. Box 6640 _____5462-0
Wayne, PA 19087-8640 $6.99 US/$8.99 CAN

Please add $2.50 for shipping and handling for the first book and $.75 for each additional book. NY and PA residents, add appropriate sales tax. No cash, stamps, or CODs. Canadian orders require an extra $2.00 shipping and handling and must be paid in U.S. dollars. Prices and availability subject to change. **Payment must accompany all orders.**

Name: _____

Address: _____

City: _____ State: _____ Zip: _____

E-mail: _____

I have enclosed $_____ in payment for the checked book(s).

For more information on these books, check out our website at www.dorchesterpub.com.
_____ *Please send me a free catalog.*

CONNIE MASON

The Last Rogue

All London is stunned by Lucas, Viscount Westmore's vow to give up the fair sex and exile himself to St. Ives. The infamous rake is known for his love of luxury and his way with the ladies, just as the rugged Cornish coast is known for its savagery, its fearsome gales and its smugglers.

But Luc is determined to turn away from the seduction of white thighs and perfumed flesh that had once ended in tragedy. He never guessed the stormy nights of Cornwall would bring unlooked-for danger, the thrill of the chase, and a long-legged beauty who tempts him like no other. As illicit cargo changes hands, as her flashing green eyes challenge his very masculinity, he longs for nothing so much as to lose himself in . . . *Bliss*.

The Pirate Prince

CONNIE MASON

She is a jewel among women, brighter than the moon and stars. Her lips are lush and pink, made for kissing . . . and more erotic purposes. She's a pirate's prize, yet he cannot so much as touch her.

Destined for the harem of a Turkish potentate, Willow wonders whether she should rejoice or despair when her ship is beset by a sinfully handsome pirate. She is a helpless pawn in a power play between two brothers. She certainly had no intention of becoming the sex slave of a sultan; and no matter how much he tempts her, she will teach her captor a thing or two before she gives her heart to . . . *The Pirate Prince*.